WHEN A WOUNDED KOREAN WAR VET ARRIVED IN A SLEEPY ANDEAN PUEBLO AND MET A NUBILE MORENA...

A ROMANTIC COMEDY

BY

AUGUST QUESADA

ISBN 978-0-7414-6032-5 Paperback
ISBN 978-0-7414-7258-8 eBook

Printed in the United States of America

Published January 2013

Book Cover Design by:
CREATIVE PUBLISHING
1328 Harrison Avenue
Panama City, FL 32401
www.getcreativepc.com

INFINITY PUBLISHING
1094 New DeHaven Street, Suite 100
West Conshohocken, PA 19428-2713
Toll-free (877) BUY BOOK
Local Phone (610) 941-9999
Fax (610) 941-9959
Info@buybooksontheweb.com
www.buybooksontheweb.com

I dedicate "Gabby" to:

My father, who is my role model for diligence, professional leadership, intellectual pursuit, and insatiable love for books;

My paternal grandfather, whom I admire for his frugality, community leadership, and piousness; and

My maternal grandfather, whom I never met in my lifetime but pieced together from others who he was. I revere his altruism, love for adventure, and penchant for risk-taking activities.

CHAPTER I

"**Voy a saltar**!" Scottie heard a young woman cry from the belfry to the jeering crowd below where he was. Still nursing his hangover from a long flight which started in Houston, he was forced to shift away from the details and updates of the highway construction Clyde was explaining minutes before. They left their coffee and **huevos rancheros** at an outdoor cafe′ to focus their attention at this woman who was about to kill herself. Still holding on mindlessly to his empty cup whose contents Scottie spilled on his boots, he cranked up his jaded brains to size up the situation inflicted on the crowd and himself. That young woman reminded him of his sister, Carrie -- and how he failed to save her. That tragedy from the past suddenly seared his memory compelling him that he must save this woman in order to redeem himself.

Oh my God! Is this a nightmare or for real? Scottie doubted himself having arrived in the lush green Cuyapo′ valley only yesterday from Bogota′ where his new bosses briefed him on the highway project he was taking over from Clyde. *I got to save this woman. I got to.*

Locked in by the crowd, Scottie and his companions, Clyde and Juancho, pushed forward for a closer look at the young woman, who wore a yellow dress with her auburn brunette hair braided in two dangling tresses. She stood perilously on the ledge while her hands braced the pillars of the belfry. *A **morena***! Scottie discovered.

"**Voy a saltar**! I am going to jump!" she shouted again to the tense crowd gathered on the cobblestone plaza.

"**Porque′?" Diganos**. Why? Tell us," Clyde yelled to her at the top of his voice with the few Spanish words he knew.

"My **novio** left me...," she cried, tears rolling down her cheeks confirming a private tragedy. Scottie fully understood her agony. His own adolescent's bitter memories left their deep scars.

The woman moved placing her feet closer together for what appeared to be a last-minute stance before her final plunge. The iffy situation infected the native crowd, emoting their peculiar groans and whimpers, gripped by helplessness to foil this suicide. With their ancient faces swathed in seedy **ruanas**, these **indios** were shifting inanely while jostling the few **campesinos,** the two irrelevant gringos, and Juancho, the waiter, in their midst. That predicament became intolerable to guilt-ridden Scottie as well who, by then, was very frustrated.

"Keep shouting to distract her," Scottie told Clyde. Elbowing his way through the crowd towards the church, he entered a side door leading to the vestry. The possibility of failure to rescue this woman caused the blood vessels to throb at his temples. Closing the door, he became aware of the tranquility inside God's sanctuary away from the blasphemous crowd, some drunk and many high from chewing coca leaves. For a moment he sought tranquility within himself and summoned an inner strength to allay his doubts. Then behind the altar, he located the stairway to the belfry. Sitting down on the first step, he pulled off his cowboy boots.

Leaving his socks on, he ran up noiselessly on the spiral stone stairway and stopped just below the belfry floor. Resting to catch his breath, he calmed himself down. Looking up, he saw the enormous bell yawning like the toothless mouth of some mythological monster. Peering cautiously above the stone floor, he viewed the back of a frail, slender **morena** silhouetted against the bright sky.

Then, his attention was distracted by the noisy crowd-filled plaza below and the sleepy town's monotonous rows of adobe houses beyond stretching to the arching backbones of the sierras which held the narrow valley of Cuyapo´ in a tight earthy embrace.

"**Vayan, por favor**," she cried. "Give me space or I shall fall on you. Move away, please." Her words were ignored by the unruly crowd, now noisier and rowdier, shoving each other which appeared to Scott like several undulating accordion bellows. Tempers were short as fisticuffs erupted among them. Clyde and Juancho were tightly surrounded and were bracing for their lives. The tumult attracted more natives increasing the crowd and spilling beyond the plaza into the side streets. Only during the feast day of Santiago Apostol, the town's patron saint, did the size of the multitude exceed this gathered rabble.

The rickety bus from Barranquilla, arriving half an hour late, stopped by the plaza behind the bus from Santa Marta which was unloading its passengers. Alighting from the buses, the passengers were unwittingly drawn to the noisy plaza. They joined the crowd swelling their numbers further. The rest of the town's police force, eight of them, arrived on the scene to help their two beleaguered fellow officers on the beat. But these officers, unaccustomed to the mob they were faced with, stood baffled and paralyzed, benumbed by the massed humanity as far as they could see.

"You are too young and pretty to die." Scottie heard Juancho's low-pitch voice shout in Spanish from below. A waiter at Cafe´ El Porvenir on the eastern edge of the plaza, Juancho joined his gringo customers for a closer look at the unexpected spectacle.

"No! I am not!" she protested in her thin voice. "I am nothing! That's why my **novio** left me. I am already dead...."

Please keep it up, Juancho, Scottie pleaded silently, *while I decide what I must do.* Rattled and nervous, he tried hard to think straight. Then, he took hold of himself: *Steady, fellow. Steady!* A bit calmer, he rehearsed thoughtfully the moves he must do to grab this woman without both of them crashing down into the plaza. Taking a few catlike steps, he crouched behind the stairway post, a mere three meters behind her. A casual backward glance by her, he surmised, could trigger her to jump. He breathed very slowly, afraid to make the faintest noise which might betray his presence.

"Señorita, **no saltes por la gracia de Dios**!" Scottie heard some-one else plead. *Probably an old man judging from his trembling voice,* he figured. The simple words of this old man caught the imagination of the crowd as they repeated again and again: "Señorita,...do not jump...by the grace of God." Each time louder than before.

Still crouched behind the post, Scottie was reminded of that incident in Laredo, when attracted to an election poster at a street corner, he neglected Carrie who began to run. *No! I can't think about that now. I must concentrate on saving this woman*! But the vision of that past tragedy returned to punish him: Too late! Carrie continued running across the street beyond his grasp. Surprised, he hesitated, and felt condemned for failure to save his sister.

The woman leaned forward alarming Scottie that she might jump any second now. A fast car ran over Carrie and he condemned himself forever. Very upset with his failure to save Carrie, he was distracted from the immediate emergency.

"No! no!" The woman disagreed with the crowd still chanting to stop her from jumping. "I must jump. Life is over for me...." When Scottie heard her say *jump*, he realized time was running out again for him too. Something clicked inside him which triggered his decision.

Got to...now! flashed through his mind as he sprung from behind the post with a flying tackle wrapping his arms around her legs. Caught by surprise, the woman screamed as she was nudged out and keeled over the ledge with outstretched arms suspended in mid-air. The momentum also pushed Scottie perilously outward while he dug hard with his feet. The crowd yelled their alarm as the couple hung momentarily motionless over the ledge. Their bent bodies moved downward but Scottie's feet held firm inside the ledge.

"**Quitate de mi!** Get away from me!" she screamed while attempt-ing to kick her legs loose. But he held on to her. Using his strong arms he pulled her slowly, carefully inside; then, down to the floor. Enraged by his interdiction, the **morena** slapped his face.

Only his father had slapped Scottie's face many times when he was a child willy-nilly. He hated his dad for what he considered frivolous punishment. Scottie's demons were turned loose by her unexpected slap.

Becoming furious, he retaliated by slapping her face mercilessly until her freckled skin burst with red blotches. His furious reaction sobered her into a submissive disposition. She did not resist him anymore as anger dissipated from his face.

The **morena** was looking at the stranger who surprised and subdued her. Staring at her innocent face, Scottie felt awful for losing his temper and realized how rough he was with such young woman.

"**Lo siento**. Very sorry. I didn't mean to hurt you," he said contritely. Becoming aware of her features close up, he was shocked. "Oh no! no! It couldn't be." *She can't return back to life. Carrie is dead!*

*"***Algo mal***?* Something wrong?" she asked noting the surprised look on his face.

"No, nothing," he answered not desiring to reveal his private distress. Her turquoise eyes were looking squarely at him. *Carrie's eyes were hazel but this woman's face and auburn hair are a dead ringer to Carrie's. Is reincarnation possible?* His thoughts raced for more clues. He disliked most women but not Carrie, his sister, whom he loved and doted on.

The young woman just kept her eyes on him while he re-examined her face over with guarded doubts. *Same freckles crowding on her tiny upturned nose. Oh my gorse! Fantastic! This is a miracle! Carrie has come back!* Scottie was compelled to believe.

With his hands embracing her thighs, lying side by side, the encounter could have been a romantic interlude for a loving couple atop a barren sierra. Becoming self-conscious, he released his grip withdrawing his arms as she smoothed down her dress. They sat up side-by-side on the floor against the wall becoming aware of an undefined mutual fascination.

"**Como te llamas?** What is your name?" he asked.

"Gabriela," she answered in a subdued voice, then, asked shyly, "**Y tu**?"

"Scottie...."

"Oh! You must be a foreigner. I never saw you before," she said in rapid Spanish. Their friendly chat, ensuing right after a near tragedy, followed by a fist fight, seemed rather bizarre to him.

"Yes, I just arrived yesterday from Bogota´. I'm American. I shall be working on a new highway project to Barranquilla. It's not really new and has already started. I'm replacing somebody."

Talking about highway construction was beyond her world and did not mean much to her. Then, she remembered her decision to end her life. "Why do you want to save me? **Porque´**?" she asked bitterly.

"Do I have to tell you why? I can't stand to see you jump to die." He could not reveal that in saving her he was also redeeming himself before God to atone for his fatal neglect of his sister. "You're so young.

Your life is still ahead of you." Nobody spoke so caring for her before.

A new dimension was bridged between them. Their mutual combativeness melted away. They have identified each other and silently knew there was a reciprocal attraction between them. Her eyes blinked and their turquoise tint reminded him of those several pieces of precious stones which he had bought from that Isfahan bazaar. Still, he was baffled why such a lovely woman would want to kill herself.

"**Porque´** ? Why do you want to kill yourself?"

"My **novio** left me...." She lowered her eyes becoming ashamed. Then, looking up at him, she wondered how he would react.

His mind had already moved to another level as to whether he should help this beautiful but hapless woman. All his life he helped people along the way. There was that orphanage for Iranian boys he organized with his boss, Hubert, near Isfahan. "Orphanage for girls? That's charitable work for women. Not for me," he told the visiting wives of diplomats from Tehran. But this time, he was leaning towards a unique decision but with some misgivings -- whether he would grant an exception for this young woman who mysteriously resembled Carrie.

He remained silent in thoughtful introspection which Gabriela misinterpreted as an unspoken censure compelling her to justify her suicidal intention. "I have nothing to live for..," she confessed.

"Don't say that!" he interrupted her. Her anguish struck a sensitive nerve in him bringing back those youthful feelings of loneliness and desperation after he was raped by those bribed whores in Nuevo Laredo. Just like her, he himself had contemplated suicide after that incident. "You haven't begun to live yet." Tears were about to betray him. "And forget about that **novio**, will you?"

For the first time, someone else cared to talk about her feelings and even gave her advice like Uncle Berto. "You talk just like my uncle," she said comparing Scottie's imposition of authority on her. "Tio Berto was a very strong man and took care of me. Unfortunately, the Liberales killed him." Talking about her amiable late uncle caused her to sniffle.

"I'm sorry to hear that...." Scottie was cultivating a growing compassion for her; and it was becoming impossible to turn her away and open another opportunity to kill herself -- as much as he loathed any nearness to women. Her resemblance to Carrie had strongly influenced him and finally tipped the balance to a commitment from him. "I shall take care of you just like Tio Berto," he volunteered without hesitation. "Perhaps even better." His words came out easily as if the young woman were Carrie herself.

"I believe you will," she answered with unflinching trust. An oral compact between them was sealed and followed by a fermenting silence of bonding.

Suddenly, they became aware of the impatient crowd's roar below.

"Listen," he said after a while, "we better go down." She nodded. Getting up himself, he pulled her up from the floor. Touching her hands made him uneasy -- but it was done and over with.

After coming down to the vestry, the reality of the situation came back to her. She hesitated to come out and show herself to the unruly crowd waiting on the plaza. "**No puedo**.... I cannot...," she protested, adjusting her hair instinctively in front of an imaginary mirror. "**Simplemente no puedo**...." Scottie realized her appearance was unsightly and anticipated some harsh **indios** might jeer her for failing to carry out her threat to jump.

"Don't worry. I shall take care of you," he repeated, reiterating his promise.

Cheers and **vivas** greeted them, surprising Scottie as they sneaked out through the vestry's side door. The ebullient, joyous crowd chased after them. There was no escaping for them as the **indios** and **campesinos** squeezed their arms and slapped their backs. Gabriela appeared dejected, subdued but grateful that her ordeal was over.

"**Felicidades,"** offered a gray-haired man with soulful eyes as he clasped Scottie's hand. "Good work, señor." He looked back at the stooped man ambling away as the crowd persisted to surround them.

"Who is he?" Scottie wondered as the old man vanished behind the horde pursuing them.

"**El alcalde**, Don Jose´ Luis Calderon," Gabriela replied.

"Hey! Remember me?" Clyde shouted at the besieged pair while he struggled to approach them. An embarrassed Scottie smiled at Clyde and knew exactly what was uppermost in his mind. "Follow me," Clyde told them as they closed ranks. Using his hulking frame, he broke a path through the shifting crowd intimidating and bluffing while trailed closely by the two escapees. Juancho was left behind to fend for himself. Clyde's gaunt size and defiant gaze discouraged the now thinned-out mob from harassing them near the **ayuntamiento** building at the west end of the plaza. They boarded the company pick-up truck.

"Damn! I forgot my boots!" Scottie just remembered he left his boots at the foot of the belfry stairway. But he didn't have the nerve to wade through that mob again.

"Where to?" Clyde asked after starting the engine.

"To the airport. Where else? Do you want to miss that flight to Bogota´?" Clyde did not ask any more questions while they drove to the airport. He stole glances at Gabriela like she was about to bite him.

They arrived at the airport with ample time to spare before the flight's departure to the Big City. Astride on a narrow ridge, the airport was Spartan in appointments with corrugated metal sheets for its shell and the control tower which was typical in these frontier towns. Two window-type air conditioners jutted out on the control tower's backside dripping with condensed moisture. As soon as Clyde parked the truck, he handed the keys to Scottie and hinted he wanted to talk with him in private before boarding the plane. "I left a set of construction drawings, the certified approved ones, in the compartment behind the truck's seat," Clyde reminded him. "Oh, also the field log book and the metric triangular scale." **Indios**, in black skirts, sat by themselves in the lobby's entrance and stared at them as the two men got off the truck.

"Please wait inside, Gabirela -- oops!" She cracked a smile as Scottie, embarrassed, fractured her name. "Sorry, I mean Gah ... bri...eh...lah. I got it right this time. Anyway, please wait while I help Clyde with his bags. **Maletas**." He tried to demonstrate with his hands like he was holding those bags. "I shall leave the engine and the aircon running so you stay comfy, okey-dokey? **Comprendes**?"

Gabriela smiled thinly and nodded that she understood although the Spanish of these gringos, mixed with their strange words, was intimidating to her. She didn't mind waiting alone inside the truck for she was still recovering from her ordeal and not eager to be seen by her people.

While the airline agent was checking his bags, Clyde wasted no time to speak his mind. "Hey buddy, I do hope you're fully aware what you're getting yourself into with that broad. Look what happened to me." He leaned closer to Scottie with his piercing hazel eyes. "You got yourself a hot cargo. I would advise you to get rid of her. The quicker the better. Before you get burned like me. There are enough headaches with the project as it is."

"I'm surprised at you, Clyde. You sweet-talked her while she was in distress, and now you're telling me to abandon her."

"Ah ha! I didn't want her to jump. I didn't want her dead. But neither you nor I should get involved with these local girls. You also saved her from killing herself. Fine! That's as far as you should go. There are local organizations that can help her. Don't get involved."

"I promised to help her and I shall keep my word." Scottie was adamant, annoyed at the gratuitous advice from one whom he considered a blundering hypocrite.

"Holy Moses! Did I hear you right?" Clyde was puzzled. Incredulous at his replacement who, in his perception, would be snared into the same trap he himself got into. Scottie, half smiling, nodded. "I don't believe you!"

"You heard me. I'm going to help her. Period."

Clyde was shocked, frozen into a dead stop, apprehensive his own downfall would be repeated by his successor. The agent, noting the other waiting passengers behind them, called Clyde's attention, asked for his ticket, and issued him a boarding pass. They headed for the gate.

"Holy Moses, Scottie. I hate to say this but I'm afraid you're cracking up and this is just your second day in here." He shook his head. "It must be something in the air here that affect us Americans. And the people and their culture, perhaps. Glad to be outta here, buddy."

Scottie laughed inside, thinking of the more severe situations he and his fellow Americans faced with the Moslems in Iran. *This Clyde is a chauvinist and female predator. He would never understand me and my motive,* Scottie thought, after chuckling at this fellow's far-fetched diagnosis of him.

Arriving at the gate, Clyde felt duty bound to save a gullible fellow American from an impending personal disaster. "You need a good rest and just don't realize you're undergoing a cultural shock as some would say. It's the air and the people in these highlands. Too late now. You should have stayed longer for your R-and-R in Texas."

"I know what I'm doing," Scottie insisted, unyielding.

"Sooner or later, her relatives will force you to marry her. And then, like poor people on dole, they will live off you and you won't have any peace from then 'til eternity." Scottie, tiring of Clyde's persistent advice, forced himself to grin. "Hey, there are enough loose floosies in Barrio Luciente you can rent for the night if you get lonesome."

"I hear what you have been preaching all this time. Don't worry about me. You better check into the plane before the relatives of your ex-girlfriend get wind of your departure and seize you." Clyde's eyes widened looking apprehensive. "Have a nice long vacation . Ha! ha! In Texas. Or wherever."

Scottie felt relieved as Clyde finally disappeared into the plane. Heading back to the parking lot, he was convinced that Clyde and himself came from different molds and could never agree on humanitarian issues. Uneasy while he argued with Clyde inside the airport, he had envisioned an empty truck with Gabriela gone. Seeing her pretty face inside the cabin, he felt reassured.

"Hello again." He greeted her climbing back into the driver's seat. Handling the stick shift, he felt awkward driving another company truck again after getting accustomed to that rental car with the automatic shift in Houston. Driving back to town, they stopped near Peñalosa's outskirts while a boy guided his slow herd of cattle across the road. He noted the white-washed **ranchos,** some painted in blue, green or yellow with rusty corrugated roofs, strung out unevenly on both sides of the dusty road. This panorama caught his attention reminding him he was in the Colombian highlands and far away from the arid Persian desert. The lush greenery around them with its myriad furry and feathered wild tenants bobbing in and out of their hidden sanctuaries along the road amused him.

"I'm not familiar with the streets yet. You have to guide me.

Where do you want me to take you?" He started moving again.

"I cannot ...I cannot go back to my uncle. He ruined my life... and my relation with my **novio**."

"I thought you said your uncle was good to you."

"That was Tio Berto. May he rest in peace and the angels bless his soul!" She made the sign of the cross. "No, this bad uncle is Tio Manolo. I do not want to go back to his house. **Nunca**! Never! I would rather die."

At that moment, Scottie was reminded of Clyde's warning about these local women and their scheming relatives. *Am I getting myself into something? Can I trust Gabriela? Her relatives?* Throwing side glances at her, he was shocked to confirm once more her likeness to Carrie. *This is incredible!* he thought. Despite his reservations, his heart was warming up to this young one, a dead ringer for Carrie: He was determined to help her, make her happy.

The boy thwacked the last cow crossing the road with his over-sized staff. Scottie started to move the truck -- but where to -- he did not have the faintest clue. *Gabriela has to make up her mind where she should live. Does she have any friends? She said no. Any other relatives other than Tio Manolo?* "No," again from her.

Noticing her hesitation and her soiled dress, a practical notion popped in his head. "Look, Ga-bri-ela." He was careful pronouncing her name. "While you decide where you want to stay, let us go to the **centro** and get you some nice clothes, okey-dokey? I always feel good when I put on new clothes, don't you?"

Gabriela's face drew a blank, not sure if she understood him. "What do you mean -- 'nice clothes' ?" This time, he explained slowly in Spanish he was going to buy her many beautiful clothes so she would look nice and feel better inside.

"**Pero porque´**? But why?" She was puzzled. "Why are you good to me? You do not even know me."

"I shall tell you one more time: I want to help you. So you'll be happy. **Comprendes**?" He could not tell her he was making up to her where he failed miserably with his own baby sister. *Such confession, such explanation, would only confuse her,* he was convinced, *perhaps some day, not now.*

"Still I do not understand. Others wanted me dead. You appeared from nowhere to save me. Now… you even want me to get new clothes and you pay for them? **Que caramba**!" She scrutinized him closer, still intrigued by his protectiveness, wondering if Scottie and the whole situation was a fantasy of her confused mind. Then, she reached out and stroke his arm. *He is real, **de por si**! Indeed!*

"Hey! What are you doing?" Not expecting her caressing touch, he was distracted.

"I want to make sure you are real. **Autentico**."

"Don't tell me!" He laughed shaking his head. "I'm alive all right. But not for long if you distract me from watching the road."

"I am not sure of anything lately," she confessed. "Maybe... you are...**mi angel de la guarda**."

"Oh no! Me? Your guardian angel? You're too much for me! I'm just a country boy from Laredo." Despite his usual disdain for close familiarity with the opposite sex, he was beginning to feel at ease with her. Beyond his empathy for her declarations of sufferings and miserable circumstances, her mysterious likeness to his long-dead sister cast a powerful spell on him.

"Laredo?" She asked. "Where is Laredo? Mexico?"

"Nuevo Laredo is in Mexico. The sister city across the river. My Laredo is in the State of Texas, **Estados Unidos**."

"You mean **America del Norte**?"

"Yes, ma'am. Every bit of it."

After parking the truck a block off the main drag, he helped her get off. *He is* ***muy simpatico,*** she thought, *treating me like a lady. Nobody ever cared for me before, not since Tio Berto passed away*. Her spirits took an upswing.

"How about some **cafe´** before we tackle the stores, okey-dokey?" He asked, ready to relax a bit.

This man has to be an angel sent from heaven! she reaffirmed, stunned somewhat by the sudden change of her fate.

They entered a **cantina** where they were gawked at by the waiters as they always did when the local señoritas were escorted by foreigners. Scottie hid his self-consciousness while Gabriela frowned at them. A waiter brought their coffee cups and a flan for her. Her manner of pouring two teaspoons of sugar into her cup grabbed his attention.

My God! Is reincarnation possible, really possible? The way she moves her hand...left hand too!...is exactly like Carrie's with her hot chocolate, he observed. Feeling spooky, he was afraid what to think of next considering the violent incident which took Carrie away forever. *But why should I be haunted by the past? Oh God! I can't do anything about it.*

*"**Oye***, why are you staring at me?" she asked becoming aware of his rather unabashed stare.

"Oh, I'm sorry," he said, withdrawing his gaze. "I didn't mean to." He was immersed in this unexplained transposition of Carrie into this woman. *Why would the Lord do this to me?* he pondered.

"**Lo siento**, sorry but I forgot your name," she said, "I was too confused this morning to remember anything."

"Car.... I mean Scottie." Being reminded of Carrie spooked him.

"Scootee.... Scootee," she repeated, pursing her mouth. He laughed at how she latinized his name.

"Well, that's close enough." He checked his watch and noted there was still enough time to linger a bit but the open-mouthed ogling waiters got him peevish. "Drink up. Let's spend more time at the stores before they close down for the siesta."

Two blocks down the main drag, they entered a store emblazoned with a huge sign: Paquita's Boutique. Señora Paquita introduced herself while Scottie noticed she was as ample as her trade sign. With gleaming eyes and inspired like she just won the lottery, an excitable Gabriela began sorting out, examining the dresses on the racks. Instantly, Scottie became aware he was in no-man's-land surrounded by womenfolk. Some were adjusting the dresses as they came out of the dressing stalls. He felt cornered and was becoming embarrassed.

"I must be dreaming!" Gabriela exclaimed as she modeled a green bolero dress with a frilled skirt before a mirror. She already tried a pink chiffon dress before. In near frenzy, her bolero dress was slipping off her. Señora Paquita came to the rescue and zipped her up.

"Go ahead, try some more and whatever accessories," Scottie encouraged her. "Señora Paquita, get whatever she needs. I'm going next door for **cafe**. Send somebody to let me know when the señorita is through." The uneasy bachelor was in full retreat.

Shoe boxes, dresses in plastic bags, lingerie, and bric-a-bracs in big paper bags were on a table next to the cash register by the time Scottie returned, fetched by the señora's maid. "Gabriela's **monton**," her pile, as pointed out by the store owner, worried Scottie. The peso bills in his pocket were not enough to pay for Gabriela's shopping binge. When Señora Paquita started showing him pieces of intimate apparel out of the bags for him to admire the quality, he was embarrassed and told her to put them away. Divining from the señora's face, he surmised that she already took Gabriela as his young mistress.

Looking at her **monton**, Gabriela became remorseful for buying so many items. "I have been greedy. I shall return some of them." She confessed. "Are you sure you want to buy me all these nice things? **Si**?" She went over the items and started separating them into two **montones.** Scottie intervened and told her to take everything back when the señora agreed to accept payment with traveler's checks.

It was past the siesta but the señora did not mind and sent her maid to help them carry the boxes and bags to the truck. Looking at her "loot" at the back of the truck, Gabriela was close to tears and openly thanked "the Virgin Mary for the bonanza thrown at my feet." Scottie felt odd not accustomed to such spontaneous religious ejaculations.

Once inside the cabin, she kept her eyes peeled to the boxes behind them. "**Pero porque**′? But why?" She asked, her sparkling pools of turquoise were looking at him, still in disbelief. "Why are you doing this for me? You expect me to become your mistress?"

"Oh no! Far from it!" Scottie, getting hit once more on this mistress issue, started the truck moving. *Young lady, if you only knew how I dislike women! I just made an exception for you because of Carrie.* He would not betray his thoughts loudly to her. "I'm past that age. Well past," he reassured her. "You have been through a lot. I simply want you to be happy. **Confíes conmigo**. Trust me." Still she could not fully understand his motives. He drove slowly taking his time while waiting for the young woman to make up her mind.

"I can't go back to Tio Manolo's house." She pulled her skirt up exposing the bruises on her thighs. He took a quick glance and turned quickly away shame-faced. "He drinks too much at the **bodegones** and when he comes home, he beats me up. I am treated worse than a slave."

"Looks like we have to plan something else for you, huh?"

"**Lo siento**, Scootee. I am very confused right now. You see, Tio Manolo is my only relative left in Peñalosa. The rest of my relatives live in Cartagena."

"So, why don't you go back to Cartagena?"

"I cannot face my relatives and friends after what happened to my engagement. My **novio** married my cousin in Cartagena."

"Now, I'm beginning to get a better picture of your situation," he answered, not sure if she was making up a story. Nevertheless, he was determined to find a solution even a temporary one, before nightfall. "You got a problem and we must find a solution. Maybe a couple of solutions until one of them can solve your problem for good. Let's see...a room at a **pension** perhaps, while you decide where you want to live... and what you want to do with your life, okey-dokey?"

Gabriela seemed to take in what he just said but kept silent long enough to get him concerned. All of a sudden, she said, "I want to stay with you!" Her instinct told her it was safest to stay with this kind man.

"Oh no! That won't work!" He got visibly nervous. Just the idea of a woman living in the same quarters was unsettling to him. "You're a young woman and I'm a single man, an old bachelor at that. You can't stay in the apartment. No, we got to find you another place." His thoughts reached back to Clyde as he speculated whether that tomcat got his local girlfriend pregnant in the apartment.

How he wished he knew some upper-class people in town or even middle-class ones who would be willing to accept her as a boarder on a temporary basis. It was wishful thinking for he just arrived less than forty-eight hours before. Clyde had caused a scandal with his indiscretion but Scottie suspected Clyde was framed up by the girl's conniving relatives. With Clyde's soiled reputation and he as his replacement, Scottie anticipated that the power brokers of Peñalosa would be chary of him until he could prove to them he was more prudent. *Perhaps I won some brownie points with the landed gentry by rescuing this woman.*

However, I can't afford a scandal with her living in my apartment. No sir, I can't take that risk.

The siesta and the rest of the afternoon passed by rapidly as they went checking into one **pension** after another. Scottie found something objectionable in all of them: too dirty, oversized "closet" with an outside door, rough-looking boarders, loitering tarts, a dumping place for senile people. Until that afternoon, he did not realize how hard it was to find a decent place. The search depressed him and he appreciated more his assigned housing which at first displeased him due to the debris and junk left by Clyde. Nonetheless, he was grateful to be spared the task of hunting himself for a place. As the evening closed in, he was tired, disgusted at himself for failure to solve Gabriela's housing problem.

An ice-cream vendor with a pushcart came by the street corner where the tired couple stood for a breather. Bushed and thirsty, Scottie ordered cones for her and himself. Soon they were surrounded by smelly street urchins. Hated being stared at while licking their cones, he ordered cones for these ragtag onlookers and in his best Tex-Mex slang, he told them to get the dickens out of their sight. Not very long, they climbed back into the truck.

"Please, Scootee, let me stay with you...just for a short while...." Again those pools of turquoise caught his attention and her face reminded him of dear Carrie. "**Solamente una visita cortita**, okey-dokey?"

"Where in the world did you pick up this 'okey-dokey' ?" He asked wondering, suspicious she had associated with Americans before.

"From you, **patron**. You have been saying 'okey-dokey' since you captured me this morning."

"Hey! I wasn't aware of that!" Raising his eyebrows in amazement and remembered another thing. "You better use a better English word than "capture." I didn't capture you. I rescued you."

"Scootee, I shall be good to you. I shall keep house for you. I shall cook tasty **comidas colombianas**. Okey-dokey?"

He had to smile at her funny articulation of "okey-dokey". But he didn't answer her. He found it inconceivable for her or any woman for that matter, to just move in with him not even taking into account of a possible scandal.

Reality set in and once more he was at a loss how to find a place for her even for one night. He was wondering if his foremen and clerks would be willing to help out -- but he just met them and didn't know how they would react if asked. The long shadows at dusk began merging with the dark shady spots around them while they sat idle inside the truck. Music and coarse laughter wafted out from a nearby **bodegon**. Clyde's warning to him about getting mixed up with the local women kept surfacing in his mind. Then, she asked him again if she could stay with him until she could find another place -- he was increasingly uncomfortable. Another hour or so passed as the darkness prevailed and brought on the light beams from the lamp posts to commingle with the subdued lights from the store fronts.

"Scootee, **por favor**, it is late. **No tienes hambre?** Aren't you hungry?" She added, "Let us go home...."

He was shocked to his roots with that "Let us go home..." feeling she had already presumed to stay with him. Recovering, he was reminded that he was hungry too. *This poor woman is hungry and I didn't even gave that a thought.*

Gabriela picked another **cantina** a couple of blocks away from the town's **centro**. Scottie did not like anything on the menu. Although hungry, he ordered **café con leche**. She ate ravenously a plateful of cheese arepas, a glass of local milk and ice cream with sliced pieces of coconut meat. By the time they left the **cantina**, his heart had softened.

"You can stay at my **apartamento** until we can find a suitable place for you." He gave in, for the time being as he promised himself.

Her face lighted up, mouth ajar, not expecting his change of heart. "Oh, Scootee, I am so happy!" She hugged a surprised Scottie and kissed him several times. Excited with her good fortune, she talked in rapid-fire Spanish to which he could not catch up.

"Please, Car...Ga...bri...ela.... You mustn't do this to me, ever," he protested pulling her away. She was too excited to even notice his reluctance for closeness.

"The Holy Virgin must have sent you from heaven. **Soy muy feliz!** I am very happy! You must be my guardian angel!" She could not stop bubbling over him. "**Te quiero, mi angel**!" Despite his dispassion, she was overflowing with affection.

"Stop, woman! Don't do this to me. **Calmete**. Calm down," he nearly shouted for he was very annoyed. She got the abrupt message. Street urchins became curious flocking around the truck and soon were taunting them. "What are they saying¨?"

"**No importa**. Do not listen to them." She said something nasty to the street urchins.

"Let us go to the apartment, then," he said, turning the ignition while pushing the gas pedal down against the board with the gear shift in neutral caused sudden, loud back-firings, like rapid shots scaring the urchins away. An instant trick Clyde taught him on the truck. Once on the move, he chastised her for excessive show of affection. "I'm not used to be hugged or kissed. I get upset. If we are to get along, you must refrain from doing any of that."

"**Si, patron**," she replied obediently, feeling sort of crest-fallen.

He didn't expected to be addressed as **patron** and wondered if she is distancing herself now.

She was not through yet. "But we have our customs **aqui**. We hug and kiss people we love and care for. I cannot suppress my feelings for you. **Si lo no hago, me muero**."

When Scottie heard her say, "**Me muero**, I die," he decided to turn her attention to something else. "Last night when I unloaded my bags at the apartment, I discovered that the place was a mess. **Mucha basura**. So, I'm warning you -- don't get shocked with what you see. It's gonna be a big job to clean the place."

"**No se preocupe**. Do not worry, I clean the total house for you," she volunteered eagerly. "I swear before the **Virgen Santissima**."

"Please do not invoke the name of the Virgin Mary all the time. I'm not used to that."

Still unfamiliar with the town, Scottie used the tall belfry as a landmark to bring him back to the town's old quarters where his apartment was located on a narrow winding cobbled street which like every street led to the plaza dominated by the lichen-covered church and the surviving colonial buildings including the **ayuntamiento**. The second-floor apartment, which he had inherited from Clyde, was three blocks east of the plaza, an elongated stone house with red-tiled roof and consisted of twenty or so original rooms. The interior was knocked out and renovated into apartments with open balconies.

Having seen the apartment rather quickly last night before checking into the Hotel Nacional, he was even more shocked at the extent of the trash left by Clyde as they walked through the rooms. Empty cartons littered the floors. The kitchen sink was greasy and its faucet was dripping. A dirty sock was hanging over the shower curtain. He was afraid to look into the tub. The living-room furniture was covered with a thick layer of dust. She pointed to the greasy spots on the carpet. The sight of the place betrayed Clyde's slovenly nature. He could not hold back his vehemence any longer.

"Damn! This place is a pig sty!" He could not reconcile how an engineer, like Clyde, who must be precise in his job, was untidy, like an irresponsible teenager, with his house.

"What do you mean peeg stay?"

"Just look what you see around here. I never thought Clyde was a ...." He stopped short. *The guy probably ate out most of the time, tomcatted all night long, and went home just to sleep.* "Anyway, this place needs to be turned inside out. Perhaps this weekend. Are you sure, you still want to live here?"

"**Si, si,** Scootee, I am staying with you. I will clean good."

"That's my girl talking!" Praising her attitude, grateful that she was willing to do the dirty housework for him. Anticipating a busy work schedule and long hours at the job, he was not eager to do these house chores.

"Am I your girl now?" She asked a bit astonished by his offhand remark.

"It's just a manner of speaking."

"I do not understand. You said I am your girl now."

"In America, when you praise somebody, you call him or her 'my boy or my girl'. I believe you are thinking of a boyfriend or girlfriend. Nothing like that." *Whew!* he thought, *I better be careful with what I say.*

Walking along the hall from the kitchen to the only bedroom, which Clyde told him he had the owner enlarged from two rooms, Scottie realized for the first time how small the place was. With only one bathroom at the other end of the hall and one bedroom, he was baffled how to preserve each other's privacy even on a temporary basis.

He was thinking back of his former comfortable trailer house inside the company camp near Isfahan. *Another disaster area!* he said to himself as they surveyed the bedroom. *A thief could do a better job ransacking it. Maybe Clyde went to bed without turning the light on!* Opening an **aparador,** he saw a life-size nude of Marilyn Monroe on its backside door. He closed the door hurriedly.

"**Hace mucho frio**. It is very cold here," Gabriela complained. "Do you Americans like it this cold?"

"We are used to cooling with the aircon. Besides you can't hear the street noises when the machine is running."

"I am cold, very cold," she said, hugging herself and began to shiver. "I need a sweater."

"I'll fish one out of my suitcases. Oh, by George! We forgot your clothes at the back of the truck."

"**Ay! Dios mio! Las ropas!** I forgot!" With her mouth ajar, she was stunned. Running down the stairs into the street with him following not far behind, the boxes and bags were safe and still in the truck. They carried them upstairs and piled them neatly on the living room's floor.

Gabriela wanted to take a shower but Scottie protested that he was hungry and that her bath could wait. After wet-towel washing herself quickly in the bathroom, she came back to the living/dining room where he was waiting, very hungry to wolf down anything Clyde left in the refrigerator. But he didn't trust the food left by him. He opted to go to a restaurant after he refused to eat at a **cantina** again.

"**Mis ropas**! My beautiful, beautiful clothes." Her face lighted up with this first opportunity to put on another new dress. Opening a box, she pulled out a sundress with bright printed flowers. A childlike joy radiated on her ruddy face as she slipped off the green culotte, revealing her nubile breasts, and started to put the sundress over her head.

"Ga-bi-rela! You shouldn't undress in my presence!" Startled, he became nervous with her childlike behavior. Again, he was doubting the wisdom of letting this free spirit live with him.

"My name is not Gabirela," she giggled. "It is Gabriela. You are my **patron** and I am your, **niña**, your girl, remember?"

"You're not a little girl anymore." It was past Scottie's supper time and he was getting annoyed. "Please, let's not argue. I'm tired and hungry, Gabi...." She laughed aloud as he was about to jumble her name again. Her twinkling laughter put him at ease again. "I think we should shorten your name to Gabby. So I won't twist my tongue again. Gabby...Gabby…Gabby…," he tried it out. "Hey, it sounds good to me. Do you like it?"

"As you wish, Scootee**. Ahora mi nombre es** Gabby. Gabby, h-m-m-m. **Me gusta tambien**! I like it too." She turned her back to him. "Now, if you can zeep my back, I shall be ready." Feeling uncomfortable, he nevertheless zipped up her dress. Something he had never done before but oddly enough, he didn't mind at all. *This gal, this woman intrigues me.*

"Now, what else needs to be done before you're ready?"

"I will wear my beautiful red shoes!"

The red shoes are really overdressed for just going for a quick bite, he thought, but he was too hungry to argue. Draping his blue cardigan sweater over her shoulder, finally, they were heading out. Even though it was not cool in the streets, he insisted that she wear the sweater so that -- to his perception -- she would not attract too much attention with her bare top.

They picked the restaurant, La Esmeralda, on the main drag toward the airport and more to his liking after they were greeted by polite waiters who did not gawk at them like at the **cantina**.

Gabby was slurping her soup noisily which she said was called **ajiaco** and made from yucca. Scottie was not interested to try that soup and being famished, he settled for a large plate of grilled steak and a bottle of **vino casero**, a non-descript local red wine. After the soup, Gabby ordered a steak in tomato sauce with black beans, rice and fried bananas.

This poor girl is very hungry indeed, he observed trying not to be obvious. *I wonder when she had her last decent meal. Probably never before.* He glossed over her terrible table manners: cutting the fried bananas with the fork; biting a big piece off the steak and having a hard time chewing it. *She needs to be taught some table manners,* he concluded, *without hurting her feelings. Also, more elegance with her handling of the silverware. I got to find someone who can coach her. But meanwhile, I must suffer!*

"I can cook all of these," she said proudly pointing to each plate with her knife, "and you can save money." This asserted ability surprised him but he was weary to think about cooking at home in order to save money.

Returning to the apartment, Scottie was astonished to discover some clean sheets and pillow cases in the linen closet. *I take back those nasty things I accused you, Clyde,* he said silently in jest. They worked together replacing the old sheets of the only double-bed in the apartment. Smiles broke out as they became aware of their unusual domestic partnership. After the bed was made, she blushed to her ears wondering what might happen next.

"You sleep here on this bed and I on the couch in the living room," he told her feeling bushed and desirous to resolve their awkward sleeping arrangement right away. Gabby was relieved that he did not ask her to sleep with him. Yet she did not feel right taking over his bedroom.

"No, no. **Duermo en el lecho de la sala**, I sleep in the **cooch** in the living room. You must sleep on your bed. **Necesita su descanso, patron**. You need your rest."

"I'm so tired, Gabby. Please just jump into this bed and go to sleep, okey, dokey?"

"If that is what you want, **patron**," she said while wiggling out of her sundress.

"Well, I better get some sleep," he said with haste and picked up his coat from the chair when confronted again with her penchant for impromptu undressing. "You better take your shower now. I'll take mine later. Good night" *I hope there's enough butane in the bottle for tonight's hot water.*

Throwing her dress down, she ran after her retreating benefactor and hugged him with all her might. "**Gracias**, thah...ank you, **patron**. I love you so much." Kisses landed on his cheeks.

"Don't, Gabby! You don't have a thing on," he protested. Buffeted with unbridled affection, he got flustered feeling a tremor inside.

"But you are my **papi, mi patron**!"

"See you tomorrow," he said breaking gently from her naked embrace retreating hastily to the living room.

Smoking a cigarette to calm his nerves while earnestly opening and closing the kitchen cabinets, he found a nearly empty whiskey bottle left by Clyde. Pouring its contents into a glass, he threw in a couple of ice cubes. Leaning on the couch's three pillows, he began to relax and finally had time to catch up with his thoughts. *I wonder if I'm so stupid to put up with this young woman when I swore off dealing with the entire womanhood a long time ago. I must not confuse her with Carrie. And yet, she's so natural being a free spirit. Maybe I'm a puritan and too uptight considering what happened in my youth. No, I got to find her another place. She can't live with me. I have a job to do.* Sipping the whiskey on the rocks mellowed him somewhat as he turned away his thoughts from this woman sleeping in his very own bedroom to Isfahan, his last assignment. Then, after four uneventful days in San Francisco, he left for this Colombian assignment. Originally, he had planned to take a few days off on reaching Houston after that long flight from London, his sleepover point after a night in Tehran. Pangs of nostalgia affected him about his native Laredo with memories of his youth. He wanted to return. Since his mother's funeral, he had not been back.

An unforeseen incident during the Houston weekend threw cold water on his desire to see Laredo again. A state trooper stopped him while he was driving on the Gulf Freeway with a rented car. Just routine and thank you, sir, the trooper said returning his driver's license. This trooper reminded him, by a stretch, of that deputy sheriff whom he suspected connived with his father to disgrace him away from his religious avocation by taking him to that whorehouse in Nuevo Laredo. That shameful treachery still rankled him, even though that incident happened a long time ago when he was barely fifteen, then a highly impressionable teenager.

After that encounter with the trooper, Scottie continued on to Galveston beach. Watching the relentless pounding of the shoreline by the waves while the seagulls dove into sea for their evening meal, had a calming deliverance on him. Despite his yearning to see Reverend Dan in Laredo, he decided to postpone that return to memory lane once more.

Becoming aware of the water running in the bathroom, he realized that Gabby was still showering. Then, he remembered that naked picture of Marilyn Monroe. He tiptoed into the bedroom, pulled the picture from the closet door, tore it to tiny bits, and threw them into the kitchen garbage pail. Retreating again to the couch in the living room, he fell asleep.

A distinct but persistent sobbing woke him from a deep slumber. Walking to the bedroom, he saw Gabby rolled up on her right side, partly covered with the blanket, with knees bent and pressed against her breast in a fetal position.

"Gabby! Gabby! Wake up!" He shook her shoulder until she appeared to be awake. Eyes closed, she grabbed his forearm as if she was about to fall off. Moments later she opened her eyes, becoming aware of his presence.

"O-h-h! O-h-h-h!" she gasped, holding on tighter to his forearm.

"Everything's under control," he reassured her. "You were having a nightmare. **Una pesadilla**. Try to breathe normally. I mean… regularly. You'll be all right."

"I'm scared," she confessed. A wild look possessed her eyes. "They are after me!"

"Who are 'they' ?"

"Those ugly people with hairy skin, tattoos on their faces...."

"It's just a bad dream. It's over now. Relax...."

"Scootee, I'm afraid," she cried, pulling him and causing him to fall on the bed next to her. "So afraid." Latching onto him with both hands, he sensed her trembling body.

"Gabby, I can't lie with you...."

"Please, Scootee, stay for a while. I am scared...."

Gently, he extricated himself from her grip and got up. "I will sit there," he said pointing to the recliner by the window. "Don't be afraid. I'll be right here." Tired as he was, he fell asleep on the recliner with arms hanging limp on the sides.

Early next morning, Scottie woke up stiff as the native hardtack while getting up clumsily from the recliner. Gabby was still asleep curled up in a ball like a kitten. With a taut back, he limped across the bedroom quietly with his shoes in tow. Inside the bathroom, he was rudely awakened by the new reality -- for the first time in his life, he was sharing his home with a strange woman. Pieces of lingerie were draped on the bathtub curtain bar, the wash bowl, and towel bar to dry. *How's this possible?* he was puzzled. *I didn't see these unmentionables last night. I bet she woke up and did her wash when I was already fast asleep.* Removing some soaked panties in the wash bowl gave him the willies. He had no choice since he must shave, wash his face and upper torso. Last night he fell asleep without showering. That morning, there was no time for such leisurely amenity.

"Damn and damn it!" He cursed, his patience was becoming frayed. Looking at his watch, he knew he would be late. Opening his suitcases in the living room couch, he hurriedly fished out the clothes for this morning. Breakfast, he reckoned, was out of the question. *Mauro has to bring me some coffee and* ***tostados*** *from the Cafe. I got to go.* Driving the car out to the street and waiting to warm up the engine, he had misgivings leaving this disturbed woman alone in the house. Also, that she washed her undies last night without waking him up, got him worried.

"Scootee! Scootee! Don't leave me!" Gabby burst out into the street screaming dressed in a flimsy nightie with its price tag still attached. She opened the door and entered the truck's cabin.

"What's the meaning of this?" he demanded, now irritated.

"Please don't leave me, Scootee."

"I'm not leaving town. I have to work now." Her nightie slipped off her right shoulder. "Gosh almighty! What's the idea of running out into the street almost naked?"

"But I did not have time to dress," she pleaded holding on to his arms. "I heard you start the engine. You did not wake me up. You did not say goodbye...."

"I'm sorry, Gabby. I woke up late for the office." He loosened her grip gently but firmly. Close contact annoyed him. "Gabby, I'm already late." Becoming irritated with the silly situation, he was ready to shout at her. Her face reminded him again of Carrie tempering his ire. "I left some pesos on the dresser top in case you need to buy something or go out for lunch, okey-dokey?"

"No, no! I do not want to be **solita**, alone." She let out a torrent of Spanish expressing her objections. As her nightie slipped farther a perky nipple peeked above its lavender lace.

"You better go back to the house before the neighbors see you in your nightie." She did not budge while adjusting her nightie. "Come on! Come on!" He tried to raise her rump and gently push her out the door.

"I want you...to carry me upstairs," she demanded in a sudden fit of caprice, her face in an impish grin.

"What...! You must be crazy!"

"**Una vez**, Scootee? Just once? Pleese?"

"Listen. I have lots of work to do. Must I spank you?"

"Go ahead, **papi**, spank me." She raised her derriere toward him and closed her eyes in gluttonous anticipation.

Scottie knew he could not spank her concerned what the neighbors might think. *Damn! The foremen are probably gathered already in the office waiting for me,* he anticipated and became more provoked.

He relented but was very chagrined. *Oh God, what did I get myself into! Clyde might be right after all,* he thought. After covering her with his coat, she jumped into his arms like a puppy as he stood outside the pickup truck. Struggling up the steep stairs with his playful fragile load, he told her to hold on to the banister in case they fall back.

"I love you, **papi,**" she burst out and kissed him on the check.

"I told you not to kiss me!" He was getting mad feeling foolish about the situation.

"I love you, **papi,**" she repeated.

"Now, you fancy I'm your papa, huh?" He remarked, depositing her on the living room floor. Breathing a sigh of relief, as he retrieved his coat from her.

"It feels good to be carried in your arms. **Que precioso!** Some day, will you let me sleep in your arms?" He was stunned. Young Carrie spoke the same words years ago in the back porch that night their grandmother died. Recovering his composure, he decided to keep that strange coincidence to himself. His annoyance with Gabby's childish behavior evaporated and his preoccupation with this reincarnation enigma suddenly forged a palpable yet mysterious relationship between them.

"Gabby, you're not a little girl any more. Don't do anything I won't be proud of while I'm at the office. I shall call you at noon time.

Remember that. Here's my telephone number at the office. Do you know how to dial the telephone? Remember, you have to dial eight first and then these numbers."

"**De por si**, I know how to dial a telephone."

"But don't call me unless it is an emergency. Remember that too. **Emergencia**."

"Okey-dokey, **patron**." Gabby was effervescent not realizing her benefactor was baffled and becoming obsessed with her mysterious preemption of Carrie's self by reincarnation.

Just as Scottie had anticipated, all the foremen were waiting in the office when he arrived. They all stopped their animated chit-chat when he entered. *This is not a good impression,* he admitted, feeling embarrassed to be late on his first day. Aside from being late, he noticed his clothes were crumpled, and worst of all, his socks did not match!

"**Cafe,** señor?" Mauro, the office clerk, knew just what Scottie needed. Noting that everybody was drinking their tea or coffee, he nodded.

"Yes, Mauro**. Cafe negro**. Plenty of it. Get me a big cup."

"**Si, si**. I have a big pot in the backroom."

"I didn't notice a coffee pot yesterday when I came over with Señor Clyde." All the foremen were assiduously watching their new boss, his every word, his every movement. They were amazed their new boss spoke fluent Spanish.

"Señor Cleedeh did not like **cafe colombiano**. He drank only imported instant cafe." Mauro sneered. "So I keep the pot hidden in the back room. But I swear by the good Lord, **cafe colombiano** is the best in the world. Expensive in America del Norte."

"Yes, I know. A wise man told me so." Scottie became mischievous.

"A wise man?" Mauro was not sure what his new boss meant.

"Juan Valdes! Who else?"

Mauro, puzzled by the Latino name, did not understand the intended joke but beamed anyway at their new boss.

Black coffee kept Scottie alert while he was briefed by his foremen, Rafael, Diego, and Fermin, each one taking his turn to speak in a sort of round-robin on the progress in his assigned sector and any problems he was faced with. Scottie commented and gave his opinion on how to solve each problem and at the same time, he asked his foremen if they had better solutions than his. They were surprised that he would ask for their opinions since Señor Cleede never did and only gave orders. Later, the foremen told him that Melquiades, the most senior foreman, was at the blasting site at Monte Perdido.

After the meeting and the foremen left, Scottie browsed through the morning report prepared by Mauro and made some minor changes before it was telexed to the Bogota′ office. The details of the blasting operation at Monte Perdido were not included since Melquiades had been on location since Saturday and had not been heard from. The land agent from Bogota′ office was also reported to be at the blast site assisting Melquiades with the evacuation of the villagers in the anticipated rock slide areas. Scottie decided to check out that blast site.

There was a weak knock on Scottie's door. Before Mauro could scoot from behind his desk, the door opened and a striking blonde appeared. Recognizing Scottie, she wiggled straight toward him and dropped a plastic bag with a thud on his desk. With her short golden locks, a low-cut red velvet dress accentuating a shapely figure and a fairly pretty face with a pout, she exerted an overpowering presence. Chit-chat among the office workers ceased to unusual silence, and along with Mauro, they stared at the two-legged knockout.

"Come in," Scottie called. The stunning visitor enthralled him. *Gosh almighty, she must be a movie star on location. I didn't know they are doing a movie.*

"Padre Casals asked me to bring your **botas** which you left at the church," she said in a sultry voice, a tad above a whisper, as the tops of the crocodile-skin boots were exposed above the drooping plastic bag.

"Yes...uh...yes, Miss..." Scottie got tongue-tied.

"Heidi Helmer Salas...."

"Please to meet you...."

"**Ay! Con mucho gusto tambien**...."

"My name is..."

"Scootee Reeter!!" She interjected with a loud voice. "You see, you are famous already in our town."

"Oh?" He did not expect that compliment having arrived in town the only night before. *Rescuing Gabby must be the reason,* he speculated. "I forgot them," he confessed after recovering from that unexpected sudden crescendo of his visitor's voice. "I was planning to come to church after work and meet the padre. Thank you...er...thank you," he stammered, still confused by this stunning blonde with that pout. Comely but aggressive females somehow threatened him. *No, she can't be a movie star,* he reasoned. *What was she doing inside the church?* Hinting with body language she was leaving, forced Scottie to expose his curiosity about this visitor. "You must be one of the catechism teachers."

"In a manner of speaking, **ja**," Heidi laughed at her presumed vocation. Hearing this affirmation, Mauro darted his tongue out like a gecko. "I have to go now. **Auf Wiedersehen**." Scottie could only managed a weak fingers-waving goodbye as she closed the door behind her. Her jaunty wiggles accented with Betty-Grable-like legs below that red velvet dress danced before his eyes. Unaware, a suppressed desire churned up inside him in the wake of the woman's lingering perfume.

"Gosh almighty! I've never seen a catechism **maestra** as glamorous as Señorita Helmer Salas." Scottie's vocal opinion was interrupted by Mauro's cracking laughter.

"If she is a **maestra**, then I am Tiro Fijo, founder of the Republica de Marquetalia," Mauro answered with biting satire as he pulled out an imaginary pistol and shot at invisible adversaries with appropriate sound effects.

"What are you trying to tell me, Mauro?"

"She is no **maestra,"** Mauro snorted wrinkling his nose in disapproval. "She is the padre's **querida.** You say...sweethorse… in **Estados Unidos?"**

"Now, Mauro, you shouldn't say such things."

"**Es la verdad**, señor, the truth," he said while making the sign of the cross. "So help me. Everybody knows." Then, he turned to face the other workers in the room and told them in rapid Spanish what their new boss thought Señorita Helmer Salas was. They howled gleefully.

"Mauro, you missed your vocation. You should be on stage instead of working in an office," Scottie remarked, compelled by his clerk's satirical levity.

"As a matter of fact, I tried the stage, señor." Mauro replied, astounding Scottie, "but I nearly starved to death. There's no money for actors in the valley. This is a steady job. Next time there's a **zarzuela** and I am involved, I shall get you a free ticket. That is a promise, señor."

Scottie realized that talking about the presumed girlfriend of the padre was counterproductive and hinted to everybody in the room it was time to go back to work.

The first day of work was over before Scottie realized it. Worried about Gabby alone, he decided to go home and packed his attache case with the unfinished paperwork. At the parking lot, he could not locate the car key in his pockets nor in the attache case. He was about to return to the building, when Mauro appeared

"Having some problem, Señor Scootee?" Mauro asked.

Scottie explained he could not find his car keys. Mauro fished from his pocket what he called his "ever ready **chisme,"** his gizmo. He easily opened the car's door, got inside, placed a copper coin behind the dashboard, and started the engine.

After thanking his versatile clerk, Scottie added, "You can do anything, any time, anywhere, Mauro. I'm impressed."

"That is what everybody tells me, Mauro answered conceitedly. "I shall go back to the office, look for your keys, and bring them to your house. You can drive the car without the key. **Hasta pronto**, señor."

CHAPTER II

Some weeks later, a semblance of order was shaping up Scottie's offbeat domestic life. Gabby's distracting intrusion on his life was compensated for with a big surprise: She began demonstrating her homey resourcefulness. The trash and empty cartons disappeared from the apartment. Suddenly, the tidy place seemed bigger to his perception. He could walk in straight lines instead of zigzagging around the scattered furniture and unwanted trash. Gabby had completely rearranged the furniture and added new native decor to the walls. Vases were all over the place with fresh-cut flowers every day. Drapes and lacy curtain graced the windows. He noticed the walls and windows had been scrubbed and washed. The grease spots on the living room carpet were gone. The yellowed kitchen sink was sparkling white. Entering the bathroom, he noted that the stains on the tiles had vanished. Somehow the apartment was transformed into a pleasant cozy atmosphere. Scottie wondered where Gabby learned such neatness and artistic display of the furniture and furnishings.

"Nice work, Gabby," he complimented her. "You transformed this house into a real home. Very relaxing. I like it. Where did you learn such flair? I mean **domesticos**, housework? Understand?"

" **Solamente aqui y alla**´. Here an' there." She was pleased.

****

A few days later, on a Sunday, Gabby was dismayed to discover that Scottie hired Carmen, a corpulent cook from Medellin, who was recommended by Juancho. That very Sunday, Carmen demonstrated her culinary prowess by whipping up a sumptuous dinner. The following day, they were treated to a gourmet lunch. Gabby became unhappy to have Carmen around. She had planned to do the cooking herself for her **patron** as well as maintaining the apartment. To her perception, the new cook became a threat to her scheme of making herself absolutely indispensable to her **patron.** She did not say anything to him about Carmen for the time being.

Gabby inveigled Scottie to buy a secondhand convertible sofa/ bed for herself in the veranda instead of sleeping in the bedroom. After much argument, she had convinced him that he must sleep in the bedroom. She told him the bedroom was a mess in the morning because she slept there and where he kept his clothes also. *Where did this woman acquire her common sense?* Scottie wondered. Actually, he was glad to be able to sleep again in the bedroom which he had planned as "his office-away-from-the-office" at night and he would not mind her sleeping in the living room. He agreed to buy her a sofa/bed, but a new one, and let her sleep with it in the veranda for more privacy after jalousies and wire-mesh screens were installed. When she asked why all these changes, he said, "to keep the thieves and mosquitoes away." What he did not tell her was his concern about her suicidal tendency. In any case, she would be happy to sleep in the veranda outside the cold air-conditioned apartment especially the bedroom.

Scottie could rightfully believe he was now at full speed with his job. For the first time his fluency with Tex-Mex Spanish, and picking up some variations due to local Indian patois, came in handy in dealing with the Colombians who appreciated a boss speaking more or less their own tongue and to their perception understood their customs. Sincerely interested in people and unassuming in dealing with them, he was becoming an "invisible gringo" among the natives in these backwater highlands. And there was Mauro, the versatile bilingual clerk, whom he consulted for advice on local customs or asked for help with unusual and sometimes clandestine chores which needed to be taken care of.

"You have to explain what's the difference between the **campesinos** and the **indios.** Most of them look alike. Those called **campesinos** appear to dress better than the **indios.** Is that it, Mauro?" Those well-heeled dagos and bureaucrats, he had been meeting in Bogota′ during business trips, offhandedly classified most of the inhabitants in Cuyapo′ valley as such -- better dressed **campesinos** and threadbare-dressed **indios.** Scottie was visiting Mauro's **ranchito** outside Peñalosa where this versatile clerk showed off his marksmanship by shooting tin cans on top of the adobe wall surrounding his backyard.

"Here in the jungle, people are not classified by race like you do in America del Norte and perhaps by our upper class, the **hacendados** or landholders, who live most of the time in Bogota′. Money and education determine one's social status in Cuyapo′." Mauro explained. "A poor illiterate native, especially if he wears a **ruana,** the **alfargatas,** and folksy native clothes, is called an **indio.** However, another native who has some schooling, has some land and income, and can afford gringo clothes, is called a **campesino**. Does my explanation satisfy you, señor?"

"**Si**, Mauro. **Muchas gracias**." Noting the bitter tone in his voice, Scottie decided not to press further on this sensitive topic of the native haves and have-nots in their internecine tapestry of a still feudal society in this post World War II Colombia.

Next day at the office, Mauro handed Scottie a brown hand-made envelope not of the standard size sold in the stores. “This strange-looking envelope came with the mail today,” he said with a funny, contemptuous face, “postmarked at Barranquilla.”

Mauro, curious, stayed on to watch. Scottie shook and then smelled and twisted the thin envelope. Opening the envelope carefully, he found a message composed of cut-out letters, of varying sizes, from newspapers pasted hodgepodge on a cheap newsprint paper. It read:

YOU LEAVE PEÑALOSA 72 HOURS IF YOU VALUE LIFE

Horrified at the violent message, Scottie was dumbfounded as who might be threatening him. After all, he had just arrived and had not encountered anyone who might have taken offense from him. *Who could this guy be?* he wondered, perplexed. At Mauro’s suggestion, he turned over the paper to Colonel Perez Alvarez, the chief of police.

The chief recalled that Clyde mentioned a similar threat but he was soon in serious trouble with a pregnant local girl and never followed up on the threat. “I then suspected the threatening letter came from a disgruntled landowner on whose **estancia** the new highway will be running through.” And the police chief added, “But we are not sure who.” The letter and its envelope were sent to the forensic laboratory in Barranquilla for fingerprints detection and other tests. His lieutenants, he told Scottie, will contact their paid informers to keep their eyes and ears on leads for hearsays in the marketplace and Barrio Chino, the town’s shanty district. “Someone was paid handsomely for this dirty work and might brag about it at some **botequin** and that is where we can catch this fellow and find out who paid him for the dirty job.”

After recovering from the shock, Scottie decided nothing would spoil that sunny morning. Besides, he rationalized the threat letter was a big bluff since Clyde also received a similar one and nothing happened. He told Mauro he was leaving for Section G-57 with Rafael who will guide him to that section. They drove their own trucks.

While driving on the unfinished highway and maintaining a distance behind Rafael to avoid the billowing dust stirred up by his foreman’s truck, he nursed an ambivalent feeling toward Gabby about their tenuous relationship. Her immature behavior by running out into the street dressed in a nightie was an incident he did not want to be repeated. *Downright preposterous,* he thought, *and I, getting involved in such silly high jinks*. While helping all sorts of people in the past wherever he might be and volunteering in charitable organizations as well, he never shared the very roof of his home nor his private life with them. His home, his retreat, was very personal to him, and he would never allow anyone to transgress his privacy after he endured dorm living in college. With a silly Gabby ensconced in his apartment, he got annoyed the more he thought about it. Moreover, he knew himself well enough to be extra careful with Gabby or any woman for that matter. Becoming a "softie" dealing with her due to her suicide attempt, he scolded himself to be firmed with her, move her to another place and simply hire a middle-age woman to clean the house.

Moreover, the real reason why each time he closed the door of his "home" wherever that might be in the world -- that threshold beyond his front door -- was to guard his well-kept secret from curious, nosy people whose exposure, he feared, would bring humiliation of calamitous proportions to himself. Despite his constant fascination of that Carrie-turned-into-Gabby mystery, the cautious rationale ticking in his brain, he reminded himself: *that this woman, this girlish woman must move out of his apartment lest she discovers, wittingly or unwittingly, my secret.*

Sipping hot coffee from a thermos bottle, thoughtfully provided by Mauro, kept him attentive on the dusty road while glancing at the set of soiled construction drawings spread out on the other front seat.

Coming to Sector G-57, he gave Rafael a thumb's-up and waved him away. There were chunks of rocks lying on the road which were still to be hauled away leading him to speculate that demolitions had been going on. Farther up, the grade became steeper and he shifted to first gear. However, he did not notice any tell-tale sign of fine dust hanging in the air which was indicative of just-finished blasts. Melquiades and his crew were nowhere to be seen. A road sign confirmed he was indeed at Sector G-57. The site was unusually quiet broken only by the intermittent snorting of an unseen bulldozer's exhaust. Minutes later while driving farther, he saw a group of workers sitting under an acacia tree. He speculated which one was Melquiades and why they were idle. When they recognized Clyde's truck, now Scottie's, they all promptly stood up. Jose Romero, the land agent, was among them whom Scottie had already met at the Bogota′ office.

"Who is Señor Melquiades?" he asked Romero as soon as he was within earshot.

"Mel had to hurry home when he got word his wife was having labor pains," Romero told him.

Why in tarnation didn't he inform the office by radio? Scottie asked himself annoyed by the foreman's dereliction since all foremen's trucks had radio transmitters while the other company vehicles did not.

"What has been done today, so far?" he queried them in Spanish. Nobody volunteered. So Romero spoke again and informed him a tent camp had been set up about three kilometers away for the people from two villages below the mountain. The probable area for landslide had been roped off and warning signs were posted. Security guards had been deployed in the area.

"Aren't we exposing the guards to the danger of falling rocks? The plan shows where they are and from my experience, they are too close to the landslide area." Scottie expressed concern.

Romero explained that sandbagged barriers were built around the watch posts where the guards were given orders to take cover during the demolitions as well as to keep unwitting or curious villagers from these landslide areas.

The crew, surprised to hear their new boss speaking their tongue, were eager to talk to him. They explained the explosives were already in place according to the demolition procedure sheets -- that the connecting cables were attached to the detonator at a centralized sandbagged shelter .Mel, being the foreman, had to inspect and approve the set-up prior to triggering the detonator.

"I shall do the inspection myself," Scottie told them. After the inspection, he authorized them to begin the demolition. Hiding inside one of the shelters together with some of the crew, he watched with a pair of binoculars as the explosives went off in four series of detonation. Even with protective earmuffs, the blasts were deafening and caused the ground to shake each time. Like thundering rolls, the explosive noise echoed back and forth against the surrounding sierras. Chunks of broken rocks and loose boulders anticipated by Clyde to roll down, started their ominous rumble down the slopes threatening the abandoned villages below. Trees, in the paths of the rolling, tumbling rocks and boulders, were knocked down like oversized match sticks. Scottie worried about the security guards closest to the slide areas despite those sandbagged barriers laid out to slow down and divert the rocks away from their sandbagged shelters. A stray boulder leaped over a barrier like a high jumper and struck a bulldozer flipping it to its side. Luckily, no one was close to the incident. Otherwise, the operation went smoothly with no further mishap. By radio contacts, the guards reported they were unharmed much to Scottie's relief.

As the dust settled to a tolerable level, the shovel tractors, bulldozers and dump trucks began the removal of the debris. Checking the blasted mountainside, Scottie was dismayed to note a narrow chunk of the sheer cliff remained untouched by the explosions. To climb up again over that untouched portion, set up the charges, and string the cables to the detonator below, Scottie concluded, would present a tricky and hazardous chore for his crew. Romero added that in a similar situation in Peru's Andean region, artillery guns loaned out from the military were utilized to knock down the untouched side of the mountain. Scottie promised to consider that rather unusual measure. Otherwise, a special team of mountain climbers with explosive experience, he considered, should be hired to do that job. Meantime, he ordered the crew to move to Section 48 and help the crew there already grading the road.

Given the directions to Mel's house, he drove back close to town determined to reprimand the sloppy foreman at least. Firing the fellow was foremost in his mind but he hated to start his tour by dismissing the most senior foreman. *Maybe the fellow was too confused and excited about his pregnant wife,* he thought, mitigating his foreman's negligent behavior.

There was no mistake identifying the cozy-looking adobe house with its bright splashes of red and yellow colors as described to him by the crew. A pickup truck with the unmistakable company emblem was parked on the gravel driveway; he noted the truck's antenna. Under the raised hood, a fellow was bent down apparently working on the engine. The crunching of the gravel by Scottie's approaching vehicle alerted the fellow who then raised his head to see who was coming. *That must be Mel all right,* Scottie concluded, fitting the description given by Romero noting the handle-bar moustache was as sweat-soaked as his red undershirt. Gesturing with his greasy hands, Mel explained he could not shake his hand. Scottie noticed his unusually tiny head in proportion to the rest of his body.

"Engine trouble," Mel told him after their introduction amidst a woman's screaming inside the house. Sensing Scottie's apprehension, Mel explained his young wife, Paula, was having birth pains. With a dead engine, he said he was unable to drive his wife to the clinic. Scottie knew then it was not the right time to chew him out. *But why didn't he radio a message to the office? I need to bring this problem up during the next foremen meeting without embarrassing Mel.*

A nervous girl ran out of the house. "The baby is coming! coming!" she shouted at them excitedly. At that moment, the wife screamed louder as if to confirm the girl's cry. Mel's face turned distant, impassive. But suddenly he dropped a wrench. Both ran inside the house. Scottie got his first glimpse of the young wife, writhing and screaming as she lay on a low bed. *She looks like a teenager,* he thought. The improbable circumstance he was abruptly confronted, froze his mind with another cultural shock. A wishful thought invaded his mind: It would be nice to be back in Iran where my job became routine and those Moslems kept their families and personal problems hidden from me. *These* ***latinos*** *are just the opposite. They want their boss to get involved with their problems!*

"Niña," Mel, now looking very stressed, called the girl, "Run to the midwife's house...." She started running along a trail behind the house before Mel could finish his sentence.

As the wife's screams became more frequent and shrill, Scottie was not sure if it was too late for the midwife's services. He shuddered to think that Mel and himself might have to deliver the baby. Without much of a word between them, Scottie and Mel began gathering soap, towels, linens and wash basins. Pots and kettles were filled with water from a cistern and these were set on the kerosene stove to boil.

Mel was washing his hands once more. Scottie asked him if he had ever delivered a baby before. Mel said no but mentioned he had witnessed several deliveries and told him not to worry since the midwife was coming soon. Not assured, Scottie developed a headache.

The labor pains kept coming at closer intervals. Each time the wife screamed, Scottie got closer to becoming unhinged. Dealing with babies, even without the mother's screaming, was not his strong suit. Those screams reminded him of that captured film he saw of POWs being tortured by those communists in the Korean War.

The water bag broke and the woman screamed the baby was coming out. Mel jumped on the bed and was quickly astride between the wife's spread legs with his hands under the duster dress. He told Scottie to hold on to the wife's shoulders. Her intense screams affected Scottie's ear drums while he tried to distanced his mind from an inescapable situation by pondering how an object as big as a nine-month old baby could come out of a narrow vagina.

Much to Scottie's relief, the midwife finally appeared with the girl both catching their breath. Mel replaced Scottie while the midwife squatted on the bed like a baseball catcher, then busied herself demanding whatever she needed from Mel. Stunned by the on-going delivery, Scottie just stood frozen by his own inexperience of an ungracious rustic chore. Recovering, he went outside and swore he would never get involved delivering babies again.

Mel came out and told him proudly the baby was a boy. His babies with his first wife were both girls, he said. His right hand grasped a Tolima rum bottle and he was ready to celebrate. Scottie was too shaken up and forgot about the reprimand. Mel began describing to Scottie what transpired in the bedroom after he went outside, unaware his new boss was still in shock. After a token sip from the rum bottle, Scottie headed back to town.

****

To Scottie's satisfaction, his live-in ward had become more sedate, eager to learn table manners and social graces from Doña Luisa, the mayor's wife, whom he had asked to help on this endeavor. Gabby, overawed by such a refined lady as Doña Luisa, was eager to adapt "**el chic de los ricos**" as she told Scottie about the smart super rich of Peñalosa. In a few weeks, she became more ladylike, less frivolous in demeanor, more conscious of her make-up, dressing more demurely mimicking Doña Luisa and her lady friends from "rather insufferable provincialism of the **campesinos**" according to the mayor.

One Sunday morning, Scottie could not resist his persistent

obsession any longer -- "his what if" - possibility of a make-over of Gabby's face to what he remembered of Carrie. He knew it would not be fair to Gabby to tell her what he intended to do. But he could not stand the impasse any longer but to take that step forward to make-over Gabby into a dead ringer of his sister down to the last details he could remember. With advanced arrangement, he brought her to a by-appointment-only **salon de belleza** where a beautician changed Gabby's coiffure and used cosmetics to remake Carrie's likeness from a picture and coaching the beautician while hiding behind curtains.

"Oh, my God! How exquisite! How beautiful you have become!" Scottie was excited, a bit scared with his Carrie-look-alike experiment and even more confused about his feelings toward this young woman.

"**Pero porque**′? Why you doing this change to me?" She was puzzled but wondered why he was eager to alter her hair-do to 1950s-style and put cosmetics to lighten her **morena** face puzzling to her -- Scottie was imagining how a grown-up Carrie might have looked. But he refused to tell her why. Nonetheless, she allowed him this makeover to please him.

"Just to see how you would look differently," he told her. But she was not impressed and the following day quietly returned to the make-up routine she was accustomed to. Scottie didn't dare object.

The rough edges of their peculiar living arrangement were smoothed out more and more by every day contact and inevitable compromises, spoken and unspoken. Scottie became inexplicably accustomed to having her around by then; and in many respects, he had already taken her presence for granted and began to fantasize that Carrie had reincarnated into Gabby and somehow their lives from the distant past had crossed again. That simplistic changeover which he defined to himself as an "exquisite experiment" of changing Gabby to Carrie's image was a big step of a fantasy towards his very own Nirvana -- after sequestering an unhappy youth -- his belief of a sister's reincarnation whom he had doted on and shall be living with him again. His obsession made him insensitive how Gabby would feel should she discover the truth behind that "exquisite experiment." Gabby, unaware of her **patron's** peculiar obsession about her, was happy with her new easier life. When he was down to earth and not fantasizing, he perceived her as a well-adjusted young lady whom he would like to think never tried to take her life and had gone beyond that perilous episode for good. Lately, her spooks and sleep-walking malady did not bother her.

Yet there were incidents in their daily life together which he could never get used to but which he had to tolerate. Mornings, Gabby ran around in her diaphanous nightie or next-to-nothing brief while Scottie was still in bed or getting dressed in a hurry to be in time for the morning meeting with his foremen. They were sharing the same **armario** or wardrobe for his underwear, socks, undershirts and dress shirts with her blouses, skirts, stockings, and lingerie in the only bedroom. She would burst into their only bathroom while he was brushing his teeth or shaving, looking for her cream or cosmetics. At first, he used to reprimand her for their shared but free-spirit intimacy. She ignored his scolding with the excuse that she was in a hurry too like him to start early talking up a torrent with repeated "**esta´ bien**" because he was her **patron** and sharing the space was "**no es gran cosa**" or "like you say **patron**, 'no beeg deel.'"

Several times, he reined in himself when he was about to chastise her vocally about their intermingling privacies: *even though you're probably my sister* -- uttered silently. This Carrie-turned-into-Gabby mystery would not go away and kept spooking him.

****

Three months passed. Scottie was very busy with his work. Often times he came home late for supper. His schedule had become unpredictable to Gabby's chagrin. Yet she was always there waiting for him with the dinner dishes inside the oven to keep them hot. When he finally arrived home, they would sit in the veranda with drinks and talked about trifles -- which relaxed him and in turn pleased her to have her **hombre** all to herself. When he was not in the mood to chat, she would play the flute with the music of the Andean highlands soothing him from the stress of the job. Their daily after-work routine became the quality-time highlight of the day which in jest, he dubbed "return-to-paradise hour" and their dinner was consumed later and later into the evening.

At the end of each day, he looked forward to that bewitching interlude like his reward after a hard-earned day. Then, before the wee hours of the morning caught up with him, he had to read the pile of correspondence and draft his replies. The following morning those drafts were ready for Mauro to either type letters or telex them to the Bogota´ office. Now and then, he would reflect back and wonder how he ever got used having Gabby, a woman, around when he renounced any close contact with women since his youth. *Gabby*, he tried to rationalize, *when taken in small doses and accumulated for months later, becomes an affirmation of their symbiotic relationship. It was sent from heaven above to compensate my loss of Carrie. Besides she's an exception.* A mystique was crystallized from that affirmation enveloping two unlikely human beings living together under unlikely circumstances with unconventional unwritten terms.

****

Don Jose′ Luis Calderon, the mayor, whom Scottie met briefly for the first time at the church plaza after Gabby's rescue, became a familiar habitue′ at Scottie's office, sort of invited himself. Scottie didn't mind since this bored but honest politician gave timely advice for the bureaucratic paperwork required at various government offices in Bogota′ and Barranquilla. Their special collaboration got started when Scottie asked the mayor's opinion on how best to draft a complicated letter to the provincial governor petitioning a design variance for a bridge in the highway project to which objections were raised by some bureaucrats. Eventually, the mayor was spending more hours doing Scottie's administrative chores and had become his unofficial "chief of staff" directing Mauro and the other office clerks. In consequence, Scottie provided him with his own furnished room. Well respected by all the town folks, the clerks felt honored working for the mayor and did not resent his meddling and the coming and going of the mayor's own clerks.

The gratis assistance cheerfully given by the mayor was not without ulterior motives. Don Jose′ Luis, as he was addressed by everybody including Scottie, made certain that Scottie was aware he was a power broker in his political bailiwick to be reckoned with. So when the mayor decided the backyard of his country retreat should be cleared of scrubs, leveled, and gravel spread to cover his driveway, it was a cinch to guess which company and whose machineries would spare a day or so from the highway construction to comply with any request of this power broker. When the mayor needed an item or two from Bogota′, the packaged article found its way to Peñalosa, courtesy of the company plane. This you-scratch-my-back-and-I-scratch-yours was socially acceptable in Cuyapo′ valley.

Before long, it was also inevitable that Scottie would meet the spiritual leader or more forthrightly the rather spirited somewhat wayward shepherd of the region's flock and top gourmet connoisseur west of the Andes none other than Padre Jose Maria Casals Antonijuan or simply "Padre Joe" as Scottie began to address him for short. Scottie's unexpected meeting with the voluptuous Heidi (whose relationship with the padre was the worst-kept secret in the parish) became the harbinger of Scottie's friendship with this power broker of the cloth, and more importantly, of the much appreciated town fiestas. Old timers told Scottie once the padre had made up his mind and a justifiable excuse for a fiesta had been conjured, then on with the fiesta **con mucho gusto** and full speed ahead! Although their backgrounds and personalities were opposites, Padre Casals and Scottie hit it off well. Their relationship blossomed into a warm camaraderie. Soon they were having supper together at Cafe El Porvenir on Sunday evenings and at least one night during the week, usually Fridays, to Gabby's dismay. She wanted Scottie all to herself each evening after he came home from the job, and Sundays too. Don Jose´ Luis began attending that "supper-meeting" until Maria Luisa, his wife, put her foot down.

One evening after supper, Padre Casals and Scottie sat at the Cafe sipping their favorite drinks, swapping news and watching the people promenading on the plaza with Juancho, the waiter, listening in rapt attention. The padre recalled that Sunday evening last year when "Tiro Fijo" appeared on the plaza to recruit more followers for his outlaw band. The guerrilla leader sat on the terrace, where they were sitting, and tried to convince the waiters to join. Juancho, unwilling to join but afraid to offend the famous outlaw, acted like he was mentally retarded with a speech impediment. The leader laughed hard at the antics of the "idiotic" waiter and left soon after. Since that unique incident happened, army soldiers arrived two days later and began combing the region for "Tiro Fijo." He was not found. Nothing that exciting had happened in town since "Tiro Fijo's" debut. There and then, the padre made up his mind once more that the boring town was ripe for another attention-getting fiesta. "**Y tambien mas sorpresas**, more surprises," the padre added without elaborating.

"I think you should accept Melquiades' request that you become his baby's godfather, Scootee. After all, you helped bring that pretty bambino into the world." The padre had been attempting to steer their conversation to this topic since they took the first drink that evening but unfortunately his friend did not take the hint and was engrossed discussing the merits of Argentine wines having ordered three cases of his favorite "Felipe Riesling" last week from Bogota´. As Scottie named the best years of "Felipe Riesling," the padre, impatient and becoming impolite, suddenly interrupted him in a loud voice practically ramming the godfather notion down into his unsuspecting companion's throat.

With his thoughts jarred, Scottie was aghast with the padre's tactics and he, being a Protestant, was not interested in becoming a godfather for a Catholic baptism. But he recognized it would be impolitic to reject the padre's demand without giving a plausible excuse.

"Padre Joe, I came to this job barely four months ago and might stay another nine months to finish this road project. My next assignment might be in another place like Tierra del Fuego and far away from Peñalosa. How can I fulfill my duties as a godfather to this baby after I am gone? Besides, I'm an Episcopalian. Not a Catholic." Recalling some bitter incidents from his youth, he added a private revelation: "Besides, I have lost my religious avocation a long time ago. My father and his cronies took care of that."

"**Tu padre**? You mean your father?" The padre's curiosity was piqued and could not imagine that the gentle Scottie would be resentful of anybody, especially his own father.

"It's a long painful story. I would rather not talk about it."

Since Scottie arrived, he learned quickly that any revealed tidbits from one's private life zipped faster than lightning through the local grapevine. Listening to Mauro and the other clerks, he knew the spicy tattles going around town before they hit the gossip columns, hardly sanitized, of the local newspapers. Convinced that his friend would not elaborate on his confession, the padre returned to his current obsession.

"About your becoming a **padrino**. **Caramba**! You are taking your godfather duty too seriously. This godfather business is largely ceremonial like, **como digo yo,** being a beauty queen. You know what I mean. What these **campesinos** need is some excitement so they can forget their personal problems and be happy for two nights, perhaps three. Get what I mean, amigo? They need a fiesta after that baptism. And if we shall go to the trouble of organizing a fiesta, why not make it a **feria! Si, una feria!** Let us plan **a feria! Eso es! Una feria!** Amigo, it will be a great honor for you to become the **padrino** and everybody can enjoy **a feria!** The padre winked at him and gave the thumbs-up signal hinting strongly his idea of a **feria "**was a very good one" right now.

"You're telling me, Padre Joe, my answer has to be ... yes?"

"Oh, Scootee!" The padre jumped up and nearly choked him with a fervent **abrazo.** He never expected such an overwhelming embrace. "I'm so happy for you. So happy for me!" The padre's eyes were aglow with anticipation, imagining the **feria** preparations were already underway. "Just think, this very plaza will be filled with bright lights, plenty of good food, **cumbia** music, plenty of wine, and **aguardiente** to drink, pretty girls in pretty dresses...." He punched Scottie's tummy playfully. "And all those happy, smiling **campesinos** and bewildered **indios**... those pretty girls wanting to dance with the popular Scootee, eh?" This time the padre nudged his tummy with an elbow.

"Padre Joe! You, of all people, are the one to promote these worldly pleasures. You surprise me."

"Well, **porque´ no**! Why not! You live only once. So why not enjoy the food, music, pretty girls..." The padre stood up and raised a glass of Santa Helena as if he was offering a toast of his life style to Scottie and others in an imaginary testimonial banquet. His happy face turned serious as he noted the worried look on Scottie.

"You do not look happy, eh? What is it, amigo?"

"Padre Joe, how could I organize a fair? Every day, I'm busy with my work. Sunrise to sunset. And sometimes at night. Besides, I never organized a fair before. I don't know that many people here."

"**Santa Maria**! Do not worry about those details. I shall appoint a committee among our good people. Relax, my friend. I just want a prestigious fellow like you to be the honorary chairman. Everything will be taken care of. **Ya veras**. You will see."

"Honorary chairman?" Scottie was becoming foggy about the

whole idea. "I thought I was going to be the **padrino** for the baptism. Now you want me to be the honorary chairman? I don't understand."

"You will be the **padrino** for the baptism of Melquiades' baby. And since we agreed the fiesta, after the baptism, is now a **feria,** you might as well be the honorary chairman too." Scottie did not react. "You will get plenty of help. I promise you." With the padre's reassuring words, he felt much better even though still dubious.

"We didn't have these Latin fairs in Laredo except across the border in Mexi..."

"Padre! Padre!" A middle-aged woman, materialized from nowhere, interrupted them. She stood holding on to a vacant chair looking scared and was catching her breath as if a raunchy bull had been chasing her. Scottie noticed her complexion of intermingled bluish and reddish hues. A wide-brimmed hat fell from her grip.

"Pablo beat me up again. Look at this arm which I held up to protect my face. And my legs! They are dark with bruises. This time he beat me with a leather belt. Help me, padre. You must talk to him. He is drunk up to his ears, padre. One of these days, he will kill me. **Dios sera´ mi testigo.** God is my witness."

"I will, Señora Lebrun…in due time," the padre replied reluctantly, having witnessed with God this recurring marital dog-fight since the first week he set foot in Peñalosa some eight years ago. "As you can see, I'm in the middle of an important discussion with Señor Scootie. **Ademas**, you must fight back. **Que barbaridad!"**

"Oh, I am sorry," she said, covering her mouth and directing her apology to Scottie who was in the midst of standing up to shake her hand. After a limp handshake, she turned again to the padre with her cry-baby look. "If I go home now, Pablo will beat me up again. My weak heart cannot take it anymore. He has been drinking **guarapo** since this morning."

"See Colonel Perez Alvarez. That is his job as the chief of police, maintaining law and order," the padre advised her.

"But...but padre, he just left for Bogota´ this morning. I saw Anita in the market."

"Well then, there is his deputy, **Capitan**..."he hesitated experiencing a temporary loss of memory, his deputy...."

"You mean **Capitan** Jose´ Figueras Soto," she helped out.

"**Si! si!** That is his name. Go tell him your pesky problem with Pablo."

"In reality, Jose´ is afraid of Pablo. My husband has been bullying Jose´ ever since they were classmates in grade school. They are cousins which complicate matters."

"**Por Dios por santo!** Now I have to be **capitan interino de policia** besides parish priest. **Mierdas**! Sh_t!" The padre got up in a fit, walked a few steps toward the plaza, stopped and returned to finish his sherry. He motioned her to take a seat. "Now, Señora Lebrun, stay with Señor Scootee while I have a man-to-man talk with Pablo. **Hasta luego**."

Like the sudden downfall of a felled tree, she sat down on the padre's chair while holding down her hat. Juancho was instantly behind her adjusting the chair while she redistributed her ample derriere.

"**Lo mismo**," she said, without even a glance at Juancho who understood what she wanted and promptly disappeared to fetch her drink.

"I'm sorry, ma'am," Scottie addressed her, "but I didn't catch your name."

"Maria Aurora Lebrun Cabrera."

"Mine is Scott Ritter. I'm called Scottie for short." Juancho came back and placed down her drink of Tolima rum mixed with Coke.

"Tee-hee-hee," she giggled in a peculiar fashion which made Scottie uncomfortable. "Your nickname is longer than your real name." Scottie smiled but inside his mind, he could not easily attribute her easy laughter with her obvious bruised arms and face. There was something about this woman that bothered him. Most women made him uneasy anyway, and Aurora was no exception. Notwithstanding their imposed togetherness, he wanted to be polite.

"I know you Americans are informal people," she went on relishing Scottie's captive attention. "I used to live in Bogota´ and got acquainted with the then American consul, Willie Wainwright and his family. You must know them. They are from Peoria, Illinois."

To Scottie's ears, her words sounded more like "Peor Rio, Alley noise" amusing him how **latinos** unwittingly fracture American names and places.

"I'm afraid not. We, Americans, are just too many...multiplying and breeding everywhere in the world like rabbits."

"**Que bruto**! How uncouth! I like that joke." Aurora, while tippling her favorite drink, seemed altered by magic into another persona. Her intimidating husband with his lethal belt had disappeared conveniently into the dark recesses of the evening. After several more slugs of rum/Coke, her frivolous disposition turned serious. "Padre told me to organize a **feria** after the baptism of Melquiades' baby with you as the **padrino.**"

"Wha...t! Why, the padre just told me...." Scottie flustered, then realized the padre did a preempted hop ahead of him.

"Something wrong, Señor Scootee?"

"No, never mind. I was thinking of something personal."

"I organized an arrangement committee with ten people, and of course, I'm the chairwoman." She was proud to tell this foreigner. Wanting to impress Scottie further, she decided to recite her credentials. "**Desde cuando tenia** 25 years old, I have managed all the fiestas and

verbenas or saints' days of the parish. Even before Padre Casals arrived here. They were all successful and made **mucha plata,** money for the church. Some people do not like my style, but señor, I get the job done. **Dios sera´ mi testigo.** Tomorrow we shall start collecting donations for the **gran feria.** In as much as you are the **padrino principal**," she paused again, "**seiscientos mil** pesos from you would be appreciated." Hearing the amount she requested caused a minor jolt inside Scottie. Then, his mind got busy converting those six-hundred grand into dollars. "It's really a modest sum when converted into your money," she said, reading his mind.

"I guess I'm in for it, huh?" he said, wondering in jest if he could justify this donation on the company's expense account. Cornered by whom he considered a crafty woman, he reluctantly pulled out his wallet, checked his money, then peeled off the peso bills to her.

Suddenly, Gabby materialized behind Scottie and whispered to his ear: "What are you doing giving all that money to her?"

"I'll tell you later," he whispered back not wishing to be distracted when dispensing and counting his money. Then, becoming aware that the ladies were eyeing each other icily, he introduced them to each other. "In a small town like Peñalosa, you two should know each other." The ladies, still watching each other warily, nodded but kept mum.

"I have been waiting for you. Supper is ready," Gabby said loud enough for Señora Lebrun to hear while hinting strongly to him for immediate compliance. Scottie was well aware he could not simply walk away leaving Señora Lebrun by herself despite Gabby's silent wish for him to leave right away, reading her thoughts: *Never mind the old tart.*

Propitiously for Scottie, the padre reappeared marching across the plaza towards them wearing the resolute look of a matador after piercing a perfect "**cruz**" on an imaginary bull's aorta with his sword.

"Buenas noches otra vez," the padre trumpeted, reverberating with an echo. Juancho was already there holding another chair for the padre and placed another glass of Santa Helena on the table. Sitting down, he turned his face immediately to the señora. "Everything is taken care of," he said succinctly. Then, looking furtively at Gabby, he continued, "Next time Pablo becomes violent, he goes to jail. **Sin duda.** Without doubt."

Soon, Scottie mumbled an apologetic excuse and left with an impatient Gabby leaving the padre and the battered woman to their private talks and to savor the cool evening with their drinks.

****

"I like this **quinta**. It has class. Look at the view down below, Gabby. Isn't it beautiful?" From the balcony, Scottie and Gabby were admiring the fountain in the courtyard which had been turned on by the caretaker for their benefit. What influenced him to lease this new place was that fountain with its relaxing cascading waters gurgling over the moss-covered stones, the manicured leafy hedges separating the patio from the rose garden, and best of all, in his perspective, the **quinta's** countryside ambience convinced him to lease the place. Stepping down to the patio and looking back at the house, he was shocked to note that the outside appeared discolored and slightly rundown. Determined to move in anyway, he envisioned how the place would look like with a new paint job, some repairs and additional lighting to brighten the patio for parties. "What a spectacle the patio would create in the evening with several spotlights converging on that fountain."

"What ***spootlaits***?" she asked, puzzled, her eyes wandered.

"My imagination is running away from me, Gabby. The spotlights are lamps which can focus their lights on something like the waters of the fountain. Those lamps can be of different colors. Just wait and see after they are installed. I'm gonna change this place like magic. I like this place! Really." He signaled to the caretaker to turn off the water. He was satisfied with the demonstration.

"After a good paint job and some improvements, especially some gutter and plumbing repairs, this colonial-style **quinta** will be a dream place to live. I can hardly wait to move in." He was thinking out loud justifying to himself that he had enough reasons for leasing the place.

"This house is too ***beeg***." Gabby spoke her mind having lived in tiny overcrowded dwellings all her life. "Very hard to ***cleen***. Five bedrooms, very large **sala**, large **comedor,** ***beeg keetchen,*** everything *beeg, beeg."* What do you need five bedrooms for? The apartment you said ...is cozy." She walked to the south end of the balcony adjacent to the kitchen.

"The bosses in Bogota′ said I have to start entertaining because the business is expanding. The other bedrooms will be used by other employees coming to town. The apartment is too small. We need the space. Besides, I'm tired of listening to the church bells ringing every half hour. They keep me awake. It's nice to be out in the country. Lots of trees and fresh air. **Nada de ruido**. No noise."

From the balcony, Gabby kept quiet. The slant of the late afternoon sun cast long shadows on the courtyard. Her attention was drawn into the interplay of slow-moving shades and shadows against the fading sunlight -- mesmerizing her until she was gripped in their mysterious spell. Immobilized, she heard a wailing sound coming closer and closer.

Scottie was still talking aloud about the improvements for the house assuming she was quietly listening. But she could not hear his rambling voice. Out of the dark recesses of her mind, emerged those perceived tattooed tormenters again, closing in on her, threatening her once more. Staring at those mangy hairy spooks, she froze, paralyzed, unable to move a muscle.

Still engrossed with the upgrading of the to-be leased **quinta,** Scottie didn't notice her spellbound taut body was twisting silently over the railing unable to flee from her tormentors. "With the electrical conduits running along the outside walls below the eaves, several spotlights could be installed. That water tank is too small and leaking. The hot water in the bathroom will probably run out while soap suds are still in my hair. A tank about five times the size of the present one should do the trick. We need ten aircons, two or even three refrigerators, you know, **neveras,** and an adequate power juice for them. That means a hefty generator. Maybe ten 25,000 kilowatts generators...."

The tattooed menacing horde below the courtyard were shouting insults while jumping high almost touching her with their knotted hairy reptilian hands and daring her once more to jump. *These ugly people want me dead,* her sick mind told her. *Nobody cares for me. Nobody....*

"That downspout drain is loose. Metal straps at the top and bottom should secure it." He jotted down that repair job on a pad. "Those patio tiles by the kitchen entrance are shabby and should be replaced. Might as well replace those bathroom tiles too."

"You...all of you...want me dead...." She moaned weakly, feeling defeated. "**Soy muerto ya**." Tears rolled down her cheeks as her head gravitated toward the patio below. "**Mu...er...to...ya....**"

"See that window there, the second one to your right? That will be your bedroom window. You can watch the roses bloom and smell their fragrance. The pigeons will come and bathe in the fountain. You'll love that, Gabby."

"**Voy a saltar**!" she shouted straining her throat. This time her desperate words, familiar to Scottie from the past, zinged his ears. Bent over the railing, she was about to slide and fall onto the patio. Dropping pen and pad, he ran up to the balcony grabbing her waist with stretched-out arms and pulling her away from the railing gently and down on the floor. Cradled in his arms, her body was tense, her eyes glassy.

Damn! It has begun again, he was forced to recall what happened at the church belfry. He was frightened. "Wake up! Gabby, wake up!" he shouted repeatedly while slapping her cheeks. Finally, she blinked her eyes and recognized his presence much to his relief.

"Am I still alive?" she asked shivering. "I jumped into those ugly people. Where are they now?"

"Gabby, I grabbed you just as you were about to fall off into the patio. There's nobody here except the caretaker and ourselves. You scare the wits out of me."

"What...what do you...mean...scare the wits?"

"That means, you were behaving strangely.. Not normal. I'm

taking you to a doctor... right away."

"No, no," she protested, "**Estoy bien**. I'll be all right. I don't wanna see no doctor. Nothin' wrong with me. **Estoy bien**." Her last visit to a doctor was traumatic. She overheard that doctor telling Scottie she might have to be committed to an asylum. Regaining her composure, she was adamant to see any doctor afraid what that doctor might tell her **patron.**

"But...Gabby you acted like someone put a spell on you. You were in a trance. You know, **estas hechizada**. I don't like how you looked." He placed his hand on her forehead. Her skin was hot. "Geez! You have a fever too! I'll take you to Doctor Viola."

"No! no! Pleeze. No Doctor Viola." She began to cry.

"We're not taking any more chances., Gabby. Let's see another doctor and get another opinion." From his determined look, she knew there was no point to argue any more.

After spending more than two hours at Doctor Aristeguieta, they returned to the apartment for a **merienda** or late lunch. This time, Carmen prepared hot roast beef sandwiches. Soon the rain fell in torrents cooling what otherwise would have been another warm humid evening. While already working on his third beer, Scottie was unusually slow munching his sandwich. Gabby noticed.

"You look worried, Scootee. What did the doctor tell you?" She was gamely eating the roast beef sandwich she did not like. But the sandwich was his favorite and she was eating it to please her **patron.**

"Doctor Aristeguieta just mentioned the same things over and over again. I think he was practicing his English with me prior to attending a medical convention in Miami next month." He lied to her. *Why worry her about her sickness*, he thought. The doctor knew Gabby's family background and told him her relatives had abused her from childhood, especially Tio Manolo, eventually causing hallucinations in her. The doctor said it might take a long time for Gabby to heal and must be watched closely for the next two weeks. He emphasized to Scottie the importance of taking the prescribed pills. "If the symptoms reappear, she must be brought to a neurologist in Bogota´." Doctor Aristeguieta wrote the specialist's name and address on his calling card, which Scottie hid carefully inside his wallet.

****

After signing the lease for the **quinta,** Scottie moved in right away even though the interior needed some carpentry work and a paint job. He wanted Carmen could live in and keep a close watch on Gabby while he was at work. Renovating and painting the interiors would now take longer and bothersome since the furniture would have to be moved around and protected with drop cloths from wood dust and paint. Making this decision to move hurriedly due to Gabby's illness was more than he could have imagined when he decided to help her.

Living at close quarters, their relationship had the predictable ups and downs. The first three months were the hardest for him being set in his ways since he had been living alone from college days except for bunking with his army buddies during the Korean War. Mixed feelings living with her brought moments when he longed for his privacy and he was ready to march her off to a convent under the sisters' care in Barranquilla. Then, there were those periods when he really enjoyed her silliness providing some comic relief from the problems at work. Paradoxical to his intense dislike for over-familiarity with women, he developed a feeling of protectiveness for this young woman who mysteriously resembled his dead sister. Resigned to share his life and private space for the time being as weeks went by slowly, he was becoming used to have her around, more tolerable of her zany spirit and outbursts of affection. Oddly enough, he would even miss her whenever he arrived early from work and she was still in town, usually with Heidi. By then, he was anticipating to relax with drinks during their "happy hour" at the courtyard, soothed by the cascading fountain.

During another early evening while waiting for Gabby, he remembered his long talks with Reverend Dan on predestination and reprobation back in his youthful days in Laredo. "The fact that God knows the future for everyone of us doesn't mean we don't have the free will to do either what is wrong or what is right...." Reverend Dan's words stuck in his mind. He recalled many more talks with Reverend Dan which came back so easy and clear that evening.

But Scottie was not sure any more about eternal glory in heaven or perpetual damnation in hell. With less than a decade to go before attaining his mid-century mark, he was not certain if God had abandoned him with the rest of mankind to the pervasive evil men who gloated from one shameful triumph to another over him -- their victim: his own father, the depraved deputy sheriff, the bribed Mexican prostitutes, the destruction of his war buddies. And now, another threat letter showed up in his mail which he suspected was from one of the amoral caciques of this Latin backwater. His intuition told him these local bullies were determined to scare him off. In a sense he was almost commiserating with Gabby and her tattooed tormentors, except his own spooks were for real.

While thinking back on Reverend Dan's condemnation of predestination and reprobates, he tended to believe his chance encounter with Gabby at the belfry was preordained in heaven. *Perhaps to compensate for Carrie's abrupt departure from my life. A sort of bartered exchange, a second chance for me to erase the stigma of my negligence for her untimely death.* His morbid yearning to relive that past with Carrie when she was so dependent on him -- her big brother -- persisted to haunt him. His thoughts burdened him with the Carrie/Gabby mystique -- an intermittent consuming fascination that Gabby might be Carrie's reincarnation: a strong motivation for him to retain this sick, free-spirited, beguiling young woman to observe covertly for now.

Before Gabby showed up that evening, he thought of his deepening involvement with her. Despite his obsession of that mysterious superposition of Gabby over Carrie, the harsh truth remained that the highway project should be completed in another five months. Cold logic dictated to his technically disciplined mind that he must extricate himself from their unconventional relationship before leaving Peñalosa. Yet there were captious moments when he wished time and again that decision would be delayed, even indefinitely. Meanwhile he concluded never to let his guard down that might increase the chance for her to discover his well-kept secret. He decided to do everything in his power to transform Gabby into an independent salary-earning woman. Furthermore, he would take Don Calderon into confidence and leave a savings account in a local bank which would serve as a financial safety net for her after he was gone. Lastly, he hoped to God that his departure would not trigger her relapse into that mental torment. To calm down his agonizing decision to leave her, he promised himself he would return and claim her as his very own blood relative if later events would convince him that Gabby were truly the reincarnation of Carrie.

Another decision he made was to accelerate the renovation of the **quinta** and start entertaining the public officials as planned by his bosses in Bogota´. These business-related parties, he anticipated, would enliven his job and would not be a repeat of the boring stint in Islamic Persia. Yet he was determined to confine the guests and other visitors solely to these parties and to be careful these acquaintances do not become too familiar and spill into his after-hours daily life.

One evening when Scottie and Gabby were strolling in town, the church bell tolled the Angelus. The cobbled streets, still wet from a late afternoon downpour, gave a reflected sheen from the street lamps. Few people were walking about. He was thinking of hiring temporary help and jump start the parties which his bosses had already been insistent lately.

"Gabby, I told you about those parties, fiestas for my business promotions. I have to hire more temporary help, you know, **mas personas,** and start those parties going."

"Why hire more? I can cook. I clean the house." She did not like the idea that her means to please him would be usurped by a retinue of what she perceived as more servants.

"You don't understand. When we first visited the house you said it was too big for you to handle. Besides we might have close to hundred guests. You cannot cook for that many guests."

"I can clean one room each day. Even two rooms. I can do it," she insisted. "Are you tiring of my cooking? I shall change the menus."

The more she thought of servants invading her domain the more she felt insecure.

I think she's upset and cannot take in what I'm telling her. "I love your cooking. You have a variety of menus now and they are different from what I used to eat. I'm talking about big parties, lots of food to cook and many guests, people coming." Aside from parties, he really wanted to wean her away from the house chores and have her tutored to become a competent secretary with passable ability to speak English. *Oh! oh! I hope to God she does not get a relapse.* "Just cooking and cleaning won't advance you towards becoming an independent woman." Having made up his mind, he consulted the mayor on the selection of tutors for her. He hired them and scheduled the lessons to start next Monday. This evening he finally decided to tell her.

"Independent? What do you mean independent woman. I am independent**. Que va**!"

"By being independent, I mean learning a trade. Like being a secretary and working in an office. You told me last week you wanted to read and write better English." He said better English since her English was limited to a few expressions she picked up from him.

"You mean I shall study again like **un estudiante**?"

"No, señorita, You're going to learn a lot. Quite a lot."

"Scootee, you are so, so kind. I still believe **la Virgen Maria** sent you as my guardian angel. **Si**?" Scottie had to smile**.** She looked concerned. It dawned on her that becoming a student would make her totally useless to him. "I still want to cook. I'm very happy when I am cooking. Very happy." Scottie noticed that tell-tale anxiety in her.

"Don't worry. You cook any time you want to. When Carmen was off, you cooked. Remember?" Her face began to lighten up.

"Moreover, I want you to supervise - **dirigir, entiendes?** - the parties we are going to start soon. **Muy pronto."** *I should have mentioned this from way back when, you dummy!*

"Oh, Scootee! You make me feel so happy! I can not believe it! My dreams have come true." Any talk of organizing parties made her ebullient. By supervising these parties, she was certain of being useful to her **patron.** Her self-confidence returned and showed on her face.

On entering the plaza, suddenly, she shouted: "Oh no! oh no!"

"Hey! Are you all right?" With the belfry looming in front of them, he feared it reminded her of that suicide attempt.

"**La escuela**! I do not like going back to school with those children. **Ay de mi!** I would feel ridiculous to sit in class with those little people. I want you to teach me good English."

Thank God, It's not the belfry! he said to himself. "I don't have the time to teach you. As you very well know my work never seem to end. But, now and then, I shall find the time to help you with your homework. And no, you're not going to school. No! no! no! I have hired two tutors who will teach you at home. **Preceptores**. Okey-dokey?" Her puzzled, worried look disappeared from her face.

"After I learn good English and learn how to type on a **maquinilla**...how do you say that in English?"

"Typewriter..."

"Okay, type...writer...do you really want me to work in an office?" she asked, still unsure of his plan.

"Well, you have to earn a living somehow. Or...you can become a policewoman and work for Colonel Perez Alvarez."

She looked dubious, then laughed, revealing her unguarded self. "Oh, you are teasing me! A policewoman. **Que barbaridad!** There are no policewomen in Cuyapo´ Valley." He would continue to kid her about becoming the first policewoman but that "Oh, you are teasing me!" struck a familiar ring together with the manner she creased her mouth. Another reminder of Carrie. Recovering, he was wondering once more how he would cope with this unsolved Gabby-into-Carrie mystery when he was leaving in less than five months. *If Gabby is really the reincarnation of my sister, what am I supposed to do?* he thought, tantalized again by an enigma chipping away on his plan to leave. *Girl! Young lady! If you're really Carrie, I shall keep you forever!*

On arriving back home, Scottie retired to the living room after dinner to catch up with the office paperwork. Gabby finished cleaning up the kitchen and was now showering in the bathroom. Unfailingly, she sent Carmen home so they would be alone for dinner.

The church bells dutifully pealed eleven times to mark that late hour. Being farther away in the countryside, the pealing while faintly audible was not noticed by Scottie who was immersed in his paperwork. Shortly thereafter, someone knocked on the main door. Deep in his thoughts, he did not react. When he finally did, he went downstairs to check the main door at the porte cochere.

"Why, it's you, Señora Lebrun," he greeted her speculating why she would be visiting at such late hour and noted the sequined gown under her coat as if she just stepped out of an opera house. "Come in, please," he said, waving her in. "I'm sorry it took so long. I was buried in my homework and didn't hear you right away."

"Gra...ci...as...." Being on the plump side, the señora took a while to climb up to the second floor puffing heavily with Scottie slowly following her. With gorgeous make-up and hair-do, her appearance now, as observed by Scottie, was a far cry from that evening when Pablo beat her up to a sickly bluish hue. They sat in the living room and she rested before she could talk. "I'm sorry for visiting so late," she apologized. Quickly, he picked up some work papers on the coffee table. "I came by this afternoon but apparently nobody was home," she said looking about curiously with such obvious scrutiny that made him uncomfortable. For reasons only known to her, she was attracted to the silk carpet hanging on display on the room's north wall and proceeded to walk slowly to the carpet and then caressed it with her fingers.

"I purchased that carpet in Iran. Weaved in a town called Qom. I was working in Iran before I came here. I have another one in the bedroom, a Naim. Are you familiar with oriental carpets?" She shook her head. "Please have a seat again. May I fix you something?"

"Fix me something?" she looked puzzled.

"I mean a drink, **una bebida**?" He suppressed his chuckles with this comedy of cross-cultural communications. "I keep on forgetting that my American slang may not be understood here."

"I would like Tolima rum **con** Coca Cola, if you have them."

"I think I do. I hope the bottle is not empty...." As soon as he disappeared into the kitchen, she got up quickly and ran her white hanky across the top shelf of the bookcase. While still checking her hankie for dust, Scottie returned and the hankie disappeared quickly into her bosom. They sat down again.

"Now," he said, sitting across from her on the easy sofa chair after handing her drink, a margarita for himself. "What can I do for you, Señora Lebrun?"

"Please call me Aurora. May I call you Scootee?"

"Yes, of course, Aurora...." He chuckled hiding his dismay with another **latina** twisting his name.

"I came here to tell you about the **feria**. The committee is working very hard especially me," she told him proudly beating her bosom. "It is just two weeks away. Efren Artiaga volunteered to design and handle the fireworks. Three years ago, he was in charge of fireworks during the Independence Day celebration in Cartagena. Next week I go to Barranquilla and hire two brass bands. Has the padre shown you the layout of the **feria**?

"Yes, the padre did. I should have contacted you right away. Sorry, I was busy out in the field with the road construction. Anyway, I would suggest the relocation of the food concessionaires' booths and the general dining tents to the sideshow area away from the VIP dining tent which is planned close to the Ferris Wheel. All the hungry people shouldn't be congregating in one area. Some food stalls should be by the entrance."

"That's a good idea! **Muy bien**. We shall then reassign **mayoridad** of the concessionaires near the entrance." She pulled a ledger from her canvas carrying bag. "So far we have collected seventy-five thousand pesos," she said, leafing through the pages. "More contributions are coming in. You know -- I tell somebody -- 'Here we have a gringo who just arrived and gave **seiscientos mil.** You have lived here for twenty or more years. How much will you give?' It always works!"

Reading the ledger, she recited the names of the donors and how much each contributed. The mayor, not to be outdone, gave five thousand pesos. Turning a page, she unleashed her sharp tongue on rich parishioners who donated niggardly sums calling out their names, one by one, like tarnished souls sentenced to stretches in purgatory. For the first time, Scottie became aware of Aurora's nasty side forewarning him to be careful in dealing with her.

"Before I forget I want you to organize an orphanage for girls," she demanded from him out of the blue sky.

"For girls?" He was hesitant having avoided a similar project when he was working in Iran. "I have to do some thinking about that and let you know in a couple of weeks. "

Immediately after Aurora left, Gabby, who kept out of sight, appeared at the top of the stairs dressed in her new pink lounging gown. Without revealing any clue, she ran down the stairs making a beeline to the living room.

"I heard everything that old witch said," Gabby told him. Apparently, she was eavesdropping all the time. "I would never trust her with money. Do you know why Pablo beats her up?" He whispered no. "Every time she has money, she goes to Bogota´ and bets on horses. When her husband's gold tooth fell out of his mouth, she promptly sold it. When she can not fly to Bogota´, she gambled in the town's **palenque de gallos**. How you say that in English?"

"Cockpit."

"Now, she told you about that trip to Barranquilla next week. The Lord save the **feria**!" Raising her hands above her head, she turned them around the wrists, emphasizing to him the precarious risk of the **feria** funds "in the hands of **aquella bruja,** that witch!"

At that late hour, Scottie was irritable, too tired to worry about the funds for the **feria**. "If there isn't enough money for the **feria,** so be it. It's as simple as that. Padre Joe appointed her as the fund raiser. There's nothing we can do."

Gabby's eyes widened afraid to think of the **feria's** possible cancellation. From those pools of turquoise, he realized his words did not help one bit.

"I shall talk to Padre Joe tomorrow and find out where the collection for the **feria** is being deposited. The town has celebrated so many fiestas and **ferias** for so many years. Don't worry. The **feria** will go on as planned."

"I know you will make sure the **feria** will happen. I believe in you." Again, he reassured her everything will be okay. Although dead tired by the long day, he decided that he better stay up until the rest of the paperwork was done. "Gabby, I'm sorry to break up our talk but I have more work to do before I turn in. Two more draft reports." She did not say a word as she slipped onto the divan attempting to read a local magazine, feeling isolated. In short order, he spread out his papers again over the coffee table and proceeded to write on a clipboard.

Despite Scottie's assurance, Gabby was worried about the fate of the **feria** with her **patron** very busy with his job and she distrustful of "**aquella** Lebrun, **la perra,**" the bitch who disappeared for long periods in the past. *Only God knows, she could disappear with all that money,* she thought while imagining Pablo was beating up his wife with a horse whip from his collection. With her distracted mind, she was flipping the pages thoughtlessly. Then, quietly, like a mouse, she left the living room.

Much later, he felt her arms slipping around his neck from behind turning into a locked embrace. Interrupted, his concentration dissolved as he felt a gentle kiss on the cheek. Annoyed again with the intrusion, Carrie's hugs from the misty past flashed back in his mind neutralizing his irritation. Calming down, he wondered what brought on this show of affection.

"What's this all about?"

"You have been working every night since Tuesday. This is Saturday night and it is almost gone. **Finito."** Her voice betrayed a suffused chord of loneliness.

"Got no choice, Gabby. Mauro will be in the office tomorrow even though it's Sunday morning. I have to finish working on these reports tonight because that's what he will type tomorrow. Then, by three in the afternoon, they'll be delivered to the company plane which will fly to Bogota´ shortly. The bosses will be asking for these reports first thing Monday morning. So, this work rates **prontito** and after that, what do you have in mind?"

She felt intimidated after he explained the urgency of what he was doing that night. Yet she could not stand sitting alone with her thoughts, unable to talk to him, night after night, especially on week-ends.

"Just want to talk to you. All this month, there were people around you all the time. You missed some suppers too. I ate alone. I never get a chance to talk to you with these people around the house. **Que fastidio**! How annoying! **Para mi**!"

"I'm sorry, Gabby. Let me see," he said, after realizing he had been neglecting her lately. Looking at his watch, he suggested: "I can take a coffee break now for ten minutes and we can talk. Okay?"

Appeased somewhat, she poured some coffee for both of them which she had brewed after supper. He was ready to listen. "I wish we could go out to Piscina Tamayo like other people on Saturday nights. You are **ocupado**, busy, **muy ocupado** all the time." She knew already the reason he was busy but still she wanted her frustrations out of the bag and felt much better spilling them out.

Piscina Tamayo, he heard was a recreational park famous for its swimming pool by the river. Saturday nights, however, were popular for dancing at its pavilion with a live string band. Visualizing him dancing with young Gabby while the local folks stared at them, he considered, would be ludicrous.

"Gabby, you are young and beautiful," he began. "You must know lots of young people in this town. Why don't you go out with them and enjoy life? Like dancing at the pavilion."

"Ah, those young ones, they are too young for me," she disagreed with him. He was dubious of her attitude that she was too mature for her generation. "All they talk about are those silly things about their friends, quarrels with their parents. **Que va!** I am very bored. **Muy aburrida**. I rather be with you." Hearing that remark cautioned him that he was not making much progress with loosening the emotional bond between them. Nevertheless, he believed he should be more forthright with her.

"Gabby, you must realize by now that I'm an old bachelor with no plans to settle down. Sooner or later, the company will transfer me to another place...like China…or India…. **Quien sabe....**

"No! no! I do not like to hear that!" she cried, covering her ears imagining he never spoke those dreadful words. All of a sudden, the blissful tie which bound them together was unraveling, and she felt rolling down fast from their cozy Shangrila to the bleak world outside. She was frightened, nervous.

"If you leave me, I shall die, for sure. I shall die...."

"No, you won't die. I shall help you become independent, have a good job, and be a happy woman. On Monday, you will start your lessons with the tutors. You will learn better English, typing, arithmetic, and a lot about office work." He anticipated her reaction and was ready.

Gabby fell silent, immobile, just stared at him and looked displeased. Her deadpan face got him concerned, not sure if her mind closed its curtains from reality and was lapsing into another destructive fantasy.

"I wonder who will take care of you when you are very, very old," she spoke again with those pools of turquoise peering at him.

Scottie began to laugh, amused at the turn of their conversation. "Don't you worry about me. They will put me in a nursing home when the time comes."

"Nursing home? **Que es eso?** What is that?"

"That's a house where they place old folks who can't take care of themselves. They feed them, bathe them, and tuck them in bed at night."

"You mean the old people live alone away from their families?"

"Yep. Everybody lives where they can find work or other opportunities which might be hundreds of miles away from their relatives, young or old." She frowned. "But don't worry. The families come to visit each other whenever they can."

"**Que barbaridad!** Terrible! That will never happen here. **Nunca**! The families are always together." Thinking about her own dysfunctional family, she added, "**para la mayor de familias**."

Looking at his watch, the coffee break was over and he must continue his work. "I got to work again…." It was already past midnight.

"Scootee...." She cooed unheeding of his hint. It was her familiar opening when an important issue was foremost in her mind.

"Yes?" he responded, not wishing to shut her off completely for a few more seconds while keeping his eyes glued on the figures he was copying from the calculator.

"Did you ever love a woman, married her, and had children?" The unexpected question provoked him zapping his thinking process.

"Now, Gabby," he replied in a scolding voice, "Remember what I told you before -- no questions about my family or my past. Besides, I told you already I'm an old bachelor."

"In this country, there are many bachelors, old and young, who have **hijos naturales**," she reflected. Again, what she just said arrested his concentration and wondered if Gabby suspected that he fathered some illegitimate children. He decided not to comment and let her statement blow by. "But Scootee...I want to know more about you...because...because I care for you...."

This time his mind blew up. He saw this interruption as her attempt to keep his attention. "Gabby!" he burst in an angry blast. "Please leave me alone, will you? I have all these damn papers to finish." She jerked back, eyebrows raised, never expecting such outburst from him. He saw that fear on her face which worried him. Only then, did he realize he lost his cool. "I'm sorry, Gabby. I'm very tired. I need some quiet so I can finish this work. Okey-dokey?"

"**No entiendo.** I do not understand!" She sailed out of the room very frustrated knowing she loved him larger than her own life. To her perception, an invisible wall isolated her from him which she could not penetrate. Now, without Scottie always by her side, frightened her. That night she could not sleep and was tossing about on her bed in the veranda, wondering, worrying. Hopelessly in love with this man - - so kind, so caring. Several times that night she tiptoed into the living room just to look at her "guardian angel" just to make sure that he was still there and had not left her -- asleep on the couch in the living room, snoring among the scattered papers, too tired to be awakened by her presence. Going back to bed, she consoled herself with the coming excitement of the **feria** and how lovely she would look in her new green bolero dress and coiffured hair, imagine her arm locked with her **hombre** and walk majestically about the gaily decorated plaza for the people to see them. Relishing this pleasant scene, she was determined to keep her **hombre** forever. She fell asleep.

CHAPTER III

The rains came pouring down on the much-awaited Friday, the first day of the **feria**, but mercifully stopped at noon. The wet plaza was already decked with the national flags and garlands of shiny tinsels. Delayed by the rain, staccato hammerings and scratchy sawing strokes at the stalls could be heard from afar. Excitement and loud banter persisted among the workmen who were ordered by Aurora Lebrun to finish their tasks by five that afternoon. Colored bulbs were strung overhead in endless matrices reinforcing the desired illusion of a magical village surrounding the church plaza. The two bands, contracted by Aurora, had been rehearsing -- marching and playing popular tunes on the streets since dawn -- whetting the festive appetites of the town folks and the early visitors for the **feria** in spite of matinal trickle of raindrops.

As with past festivities, Aurora was always in the midst where the action was -- barking orders to the workmen and other committee members like a female sergeant. Almost single-handedly, she coordinated the **feria** activities and threw her weight around when things slowed down. She made a few more enemies. A personal wish she was not able to fulfill until this time was to convince the Hermanos Steinberg to bring their Ferris Wheel and other unusual fun machines from Bogota′. Gypsies arrived with their caravans from nowhere soon after the rains stopped. They pitched their tents outside the **feria** on the vacant lot next to the cemetery grounds. This ragtag group lost no time in hawking their gimcracks, fortune-telling, and games of chance.

The illuminated **feria**, whose taller structures were reddened by the setting sun, became an irresistible lodestone attracting groves of **campesinos** and **indios** from hundreds of kilometers around. They came on foot, **carreteras,** on burros, and autobuses swelling the town's population for the Friday night opening.

With her major tasks done, Aurora walked regally, arm in arm, with the **alcalde** or mayor surveying the **feria** while acknowledging greetings from well-wishers. Even people who did not know her could not escape but notice her: a buxom body draped in Greek-style white silk chiton with gold trimmings which made her stand out from the crowd. The red flaming tresses wound around her head made her a couple more centimeters taller. Those who did not know her asked whether she was the governor's **doña**.

Unaccustomed to the Latin-flavored spectacle, Scottie arrived from the office, wandered around and was overpowered by the carnival sights and sounds. He listened to the unfamiliar babble of mostly thrill-starved **campesinos**. Walking along a row of sideshow stalls, the rubbernecking gringo almost bumped into a prestigious couple.

"O-o-ops! I'm sorry.... Hey! I mean...how are you'all?"

"Bien, Señor Reeter. **Bueno**, what do you think?" Don Jose´ Luis swung his baton like a magic wand at the enchanting **feria.**

"What do I think! By George, I'm lost for words. It's...it's **fantastico**! Marvelous! I don't recognize the plaza. I have crossed the Mexican border many times for their fiestas but nothing can compare to this...this **feria.** I'm very impressed."

"Listen, Scootee. When I do something, it is always **primera clase.** No compromise on quality. Only the best in Colombia! Eh, Señor Alcalde?" The mayor was distracted by a bunch of passing young beauties. "Señor Alcalde!" She nudged him in the ribcage.

"Ah...**si, si**." The mayor, surprised, turned to face his bemused friends. "Aurora, you are **magnifica**! Peñalosa will never be the same after this...this...." The mayor could not find the words. "Look at those happy faces. **Maravilloso,** eh? They will be talking about this **feria** for months. Perhaps until the next one."

Aurora walked even taller after being praised, satisfied with herself. The awed **campesinos,** who knew her, whispered her name to others. Heidi suddenly appeared, slinking along in a tight-fitting gold sequined jumpsuit, upstaging Aurora's regal triumphant stroll and attracting the guttersnipes in the crowd. They pelted the padre's **querida** with **groceros** or off-color attributes which she ignored. Aurora's benign smile disappeared when her eyes met Heidi's. Her plump body tensed up. Last week at the Casa del Calzado, the just-arrived Heidi was served first by the bedazzled shoe salesman even though Aurora was already waiting.

"**Perra**! Bitch!" Aurora hurled at her nemesis when they were at spitting distance.

"**Hipocrita**!" Heidi shouted back.

Before the mayor realized what was happening, the two felines were locked in combat and were screaming as they tackled each other. Aurora's neat henna-dyed tresses were becoming unwound. But she was no match for the younger stronger Heidi who got her pinned down. Finally, two **campesinos** came to the rescue of the mayor who was helplessly attempting to pull Heidi away from her supine opponent. Scottie, totally astounded by the impromptu wrestling match, looked on disgusted with the ribald spectacle which reminded him of those Mexican whores in Nuevo Laredo. When the scuffling women were separated by several more **campesinos**, Aurora brushed off the dirt off her chiton and rearranged her long tresses back into a chignon. With menacing looks from the workmen, Heidi hurriedly left.

"That bitch is the **querida** of our poor padre. **Consentida**. I mean spoiled. Unfortunately, he is under her thumb. Do you know her?" Aurora asked. By then, Scottie figured the **campesinos**, hostile to Heidi, were hired by Aurora.

"U-uh, y-yes," Scottie swallowed hard, embarrassed to admit any connection with Heidi. "She came by my office."

"Came by your office!" Her vehement voice sounded as though he had contracted the clap from the "maligned bitch."

"She just came to deliver my boots." Compelled to explain further, he was becoming uneasy.

"Deliver your boots!" Her accusing eyes were glowering in amazement as if he left his boots in a hurry after sleeping overnight with Heidi. Baffled by implicating himself with his own words, he was dumbfounded, paralyzed to defend his innocence.

"Aurora, do not spoil your entire evening just because of your long feud with that **muchacha**." Don Jose Luis intervened, afraid that Aurora was working herself into a frenzy. "Actually, she is a harmless **muchacha."**

"A harmless **muchacha!"** she repeated, her voice rising into several octaves.

"Go easy, Aurora," Don Jose´ Luis reproached her sharp tongue, "**suavecita**," attempting to calm her down before she became uncontrollably hysterical. They went to a kiosk and had soft drinks. Aurora, somewhat calmed down, was distracted by the motley noisy roaming crowd. "The padre and Heidi need each other although their motives for their relationship are not the same," the mayor explained softly, privately to Scottie while looking reproachfully at Aurora to keep her mouth shut. "The way life is in Peñalosa, every man needs a woman and our dear old padre is no exception. As for Heidi, she enjoys playing her present role. Before the padre rescued her from Barrio Chino, she knew what it was to be a poor hungry bastard and..."

"...**es una perra**! A bitch!" Aurora, interrupted, could not contain herself any longer, still smarting from that incident at the shoe store where the willowy Heidi looked down insolently at her.

"Aurora! **Basta ya**! Enough!" Don Jose´ Luis was getting annoyed, bored with her ravings and again turned his attention to Scottie who remained quiet all that time. "By the way, where is your Gabriela?"

"My...er...my Gabiri...ela?" His mouth ajar, Scottie stammered, shocked with the mayor's presumption that he was keeping the young woman like his mistress. Recovering somewhat, he answered, "You don't have to believe me but Gabby and I aren't sleeping together as you probably concluded. The poor, confused young woman has to stay in my apartment...until she is back to normal and can get back on her feet.

Then, she'll be... on her own... and out of my apartment...."

Aurora started laughing and shaking her body like she was going out of control. Then, she choked making uncanny sounds. With a hand grasping her throat, her eyes glazed. Quickly, the mayor started slapping her back. Scottie joined in slapping her. Recovering, she became aware of her odd behavior and loudly apologized to them. "Forget it, **mujer**." The mayor, by then, was more interested in Scottie's confession of platonic relationship with the young maiden. Frowning and incredulous, he chided him. "Do not be a fool, Scootee. Gabriela is such a lovely creature wrapped in fertile innocence and ripe for plucking." His friend's sublimated avowal of platonic relationship threatened his own concept of Latin machismo. "Everybody needs a mate in this romantic fertile valley. A woman for every man, and a man for every woman. That is the way it is **y gracias a Dios**!." The drift of their conversation made Scottie uncomfortable for he considered his rather peculiar arrangement with Gabby a personal choice and private matter.

Nonetheless, the mayor, smitten with dewy-eyed romanticism brought on by the **feria's** magic, unaware of Scottie's discomfort, continued his dreamy monologue. "There's not much to do in this valley at night except to flirt with the maidens or make love to a special one under the stars. Ah-h-h, we should have more **ferias**, **mucha alegria,** make merry like tonight before we die...."

"As you are witnessing, Scootee, there is a frustrated poet imprisoned in Don Jose′ Luis," Aurora remarked, crinkles sprouting on her face, with her animosity against Heidi fading away. "And you know, I see a lot of you but not much of Gabriela. Sometimes, I wonder if she is deliberately avoiding me." Scottie knew Gabby did not like Aurora and thought best to kept mum. "But it does not matter. **No importa**."

"Gabby goes to bed early," Scottie tried to placate her. Aurora looked unconvinced. "If you come after six to the **quinta,** she will be there." He had no desire to worsen any bad feelings between these women. *Why does she have to always bring up an unpleasant situation, real or imagined? No wonder, people loathe her.*

"Come, come," the mayor interrupted, tumbling out of the clouds. "Let us not waste any more time. We have to inspect the rest of the **feria** grounds before dinner. And I want to make sure that fees are collected from those gypsies who put up their tents outside the plaza without permits. **Cabrone**s! What a bunch of sneaky thieves!"

At the end of the inspection tour by the Ferris Wheel, a cook came running to Aurora and whispered to her.

"**Muy bien**! Very good!" she reacted, her face lighting up with delight. "**Caballeros**," she demanded attention from her companions, "Dinner is about to be served. I shall lead the way. Don Jose′ Luis..., Scootee...." She hooked her arms into theirs as she strutted between her escorts like an imperial Queen of France. “I want you to note, **caballeros**, that Señor Ortiz Allende, the chef for the **feria**, was with the Alcazar Restaurant in Medellin until he retired. The best chef to hire for special events in Peñalosa.” She prided herself with her choice of people working for the **feria**.

It was getting dark and Scottie thought of Gabby’s whereabouts, not having seen her since five when they went their separate ways at the **feria’s** entrance. Wondering where she might be and what she was doing, he missed her company. With the mayor’s hinted allegation of their concupiscence, he kept these thoughts to himself.

“The enchanted village” -- was the consensus expressed by many revelers on the transformed plaza. The **feria** was throbbing noisily below the multi-colored lights and enveloped in competing musical sounds dominated by the roving brass bands. The mayor, increasingly afflicted by the “carnival fever,” kept repeating, “I never have seen so many happy faces in a long time. **Si,** a long, long time....” Arriving at the circus-size VIP dining tent, the leisurely walk of the trio came to a halt. The canopied entrance was choked with **campesinos** who were arguing with the security guards. Seven other dining tents were set up for these **campesinos** near the sideshows and the **feria’s** entrance. Some hungry, docile-looking **indios** were waiting on the outcome of the argument by the more assertive **campesinos.**

“There must be a lot of hungry people,” Scottie remarked in jest as some **campesinos** attempted to force themselves inside. Aurora recognized the invited dignitaries patiently standing at a safe distance from the entrance. Despite her stare, the **campesinos** kept jostling which triggered her dignified bearing into nasty belligerence.

“Ruffians! **Sinverguenzas!”** Aurora shouted aloud in her coarse commanding voice. “Make way for our distinguished guests! Now!” The crowd froze and obediently parted sideways from the entrance opening a gap. “Jose´! Andres!! Take these people to their dining tents. **Vayan**! Go! Go!” The subdued **campesinos**, quietly left and followed the two security guards. The gate to the VIP dining tent was opened by the waiters. The trio walked inside and inspected the place. Padre Casals appeared and joined them. Aurora expressed satisfaction and snapped her fingers at the waiters, who hurried to her side and were given further instructions. Under her watchful eyes, the guests were announced by name and escorted dutifully by the waiters to the serving tables where the tempting odors of the barbecued meats grilled on the **pachamacas** sharpened their appetites. Mounds of food, such as **empanadas, hallacas, lechones, arepas, sobrebarrigas, papas chorreadas,** seemingly over-abundant, were piled high on serving tables. Clusters of indigenous fruits arrested the guests’ eyes with their rainbow colors. Sliced pineapples and cantaloupe halves competed for attention with ripe papayas, red watermelon chunks, yellow slender bananas, and halved green avocados.

The original trio, together with Padre Casals, were joined at the elaborately decorated dining tables, clustered in polygonal configurations, by the high and mighty of Cuyapo´ valley. Among them were mayors, police chiefs, judges, military commanders, and provincial bureaucrats of the federal government hierarchy. Two ex-governors and a bishop, who spent their childhood in the region, were also there to grace the occasion. For a while, the guests indulged in people-watching, Latin-**abrazo** rituals, and whispered political gossips. Conspicuously absent were the landlords and self-appointed caciques, mostly descended from the region's Spanish pioneer settlers and their **mestizo** progenies.

Someone tagged Scottie's shoulder from behind. It was Gabby. "I have been waiting for you by the calliope," she whispered weakly scolding him. Chatting in full view of the dignitaries, Scottie became embarrassed. But he was glad to see her for he worried about her mental condition and what could happen to her.

"I'm sorry I misunderstood you," he told her in a soft voice and decided to end their highly visible tryst conformably to his discreet perception.. "Have you found a seat somewhere?" he hinted.

"Si," she answered and mentioned that Heidi was sitting next to her. A sudden desire to be with her possessed him as she glided away looking radiantly beautiful in her green bolero dress.

Soon a local combo came strolling by with guitars, **tiples,** and a **raspa** serenading the guests with a jumpy version of "La Saporita" and followed by other popular **cumbias.** Enjoying the good food and fine wines while listening to the music infected the invited guests too with the already endemic "**feria** fever" among the **campesinos** and **indios.** The tedious burdens of daily life in Cuyapo´ valley with its predictable monotony were temporarily forgotten. The waiters came around with the food trays enticing the guests to take more and kept pouring wine into their glasses.

Enjoying his favorite **aguardiente** and relishing the table conversations, Don Jose´ Luis, being the host, felt compelled to reassert his role as the top power broker. Tapping his drinking glass with a knife's edge to get the guests' attention, he stood up behind the directorship table, a bit unsteady with the **aguardiente** rising to his head. He raised his glass slowly and asked everyone to join him in a toast of welcome and brotherly friendship. He requested Señora Lebrun and her committee members to stand too and be recognized by the applauding guests. Scottie, uneasy, hoped he would not be called since he did nothing for the **feria** except to contribute the biggest donation. The mayor asked Aurora to remain standing while the others sat down.

"Señoras y **caballeros**, I am sorry that I do not have a medal of service to award our dear Señora Lebrun which she richly deserves for more than twenty-four years of service to our beloved community," Don Jose´ Luis addressed the guests. "For now I can only give her this bouquet of red roses." He handed the bouquet to a smiling, pleased Aurora kissing her on both cheeks amidst the loud applause and shouts of **bravo!** reverberating inside the tent.

Not to be outdone, Aurora, holding the bouquet like a scepter. approached the microphone facing the distinguished guests. Scottie noted a blooming confidence on her face.

"The task which made this **feria** a success was easy since every committee member helped unselfishly," she said modestly. The guests liked what she said and clapped their approval. Even committee members who hated her for riding herd on them, awash by the tide of applause, felt obligated to clap too. "We could hold a **feria** every weekend," she paused for her improbable hyperbole to sink into the captive audience, "if we could collect the needed money." Roars of laughter ensued punctuated with guffaws and chuckles. Some guests began to stand up to show approval, soon more stood up in groves, and finally a unanimous standing ovation for Aurora -- who bowed graciously several times and waved a handkerchief. The mayor whispered to Scottie that he was next for recognition. Scottie protested he did not do anything worthwhile.

The applause for Aurora hardly died down when shrieks were heard coming from outside the tent. Jose´ and Andres, the security guards, were heard shouting to some gatecrashers not to enter.

A silver-haired man with a dark goatee appeared on horseback at the tent's entrance. The guests stopped talking and stared at the intruder who, after some hesitation, rode through a narrow gap between the dining tables and stopped at the center facing the directorship table. Six others, on horseback, followed the silver-haired man, and lined up behind him ostentatiously displaying their submachine guns and ammo bandoliers. Angry murmurs arose from the guests who recognized the uninvited leader of the intruders.

Suddenly, obscenities flew in all directions like verbal mud cakes. The musicians, from the farmlands around Villapuente, sensing trouble, stopped playing, and fled quietly from the tent.

"Who is Señor Reeter?" The silver-haired man demanded as he kept reining in his nervous stallion whose tendency was to jump up and surge forward.

Nobody was more surprised than Scottie to be singled out by that stranger on horseback. Quickly, he concluded this fellow must be one of the disgruntled landowners affected by the highway project. Sensing a swelling support of those who surrounded him, he rose slowly. "I'm Scott Ritter," he answered simply and remained standing.

The mayor jumped up wading into the confrontation: "Don

Pedrazas! You have dishonored this **feria** like a **sinverguenza**, you scoundrel! What do you want from Señor Reeter?"

One of the horses, apparently unnerved by the strange surroundings and noisy bickering, jumped up unseating its rider. This rider's submachine gun discharged a burst of bullets hitting the ground. Some guests ducked under the tables while others screamed. A woman fainted. Unnoticed, twelve policemen entered the dining tent with drawn pistols and automatic rifles encircling the horse riders. The balance of naked power passed to the mayor and his police chief.

Outnumbered Don Pedrazas and his riders, who had the butt ends of their submachine guns resting on their hips, were silently persuaded to sheathe their weapons by the saddles. Nonetheless, these riders stayed put, still looking defiant.

"My land, the land of my fathers, is being violated and destroyed by a foreign company," Don Pedrazas spoke again in a less bellicose voice. "Señor Reeter is directing this wanton destruction of my lands...I shall not tolerate this aggression much longer."

This outburst by a landowner was no surprise to Scottie. Aside from receiving anonymous threatening letters, his workers had been informing him about harassments by the landowners' henchmen and who, occasionally, engaged them in brawls outside **cantinas** and **bodegones**. However, he had not expected this confrontation to happen during the town's **feria**. The mayor whispered advice into Scottie's ear.

"My company has been authorized by your **gobierno federal** in Bogota´ to construct this highway," Scottie replied in a calm voice. "We have a legal contract. If you have a complaint, go to your federal government. Not to me or my company."

"**El gobierno federal sirve para na-a-da-ah!** Those bureaucrats in Bogota´ have their heads between their legs." Don Pedrazas spat, rose above his saddle, and raised his crotch to emphasize his contempt. Obscenities flew around Don Pedrazas for flaunting the code of social propriety and worst, there were ladies present. "My family has been in this region for more than three hundred years," he shouted above the din of heated exchanges, "and we, the landowners, shall do as we please with our ancestral **estancias**." Looking straight at Scottie, he warned, "You better stay off my **estancia** if you value your life."

Pressure was building up inside Don Jose´ Luis with this intrusion of Don Pedrazas. As the mayor, the guests and townsmen looked up to him to impose their age-old tradition that no armed confrontations nor melees can take place in cemeteries or churches' plazas. Don Jose Luis viewed this bare-faced threat to Scottie as an indirect challenge to his own authority. "Scoundrel! **Sinverguenza**! I give you ten seconds to clear this place or you get arrested. If you resist, I now give orders to my officers to shoot at will." Hearing those words, some men groaned, others cleared their throats nervously.

"You are all excommunicated for desecrating the church grounds. You cannot receive the sacraments or be given Christian burials until you repent and do penance." The padre glared at Don Pedrazas while holding up his chained crucifix toward the intruders with persuasive hokum.

Feeling the duress, Don Pedrazas replied, "**Caballeros**, I'm moving out. **Vamonos**." Turning his nervous stallion around, he was followed by the other riders out of the dining tent. Discovering the horses' droppings, Aurora let out a yell and ordered the reluctant waiters to remove the mess immediately.

The stunned guests were standing, silent, paralyzed by the ugly incident. Don Jose′ Luis, calmed down from his anger, realized their happy **feria** was at a standstill -- he told everyone to sit down again and enjoy the rich food and wine. Snapping his fingers to get their attention, he called in the musicians who had ran outside and told them to begin playing the **cumbias**. The music soothed the shaky guests who began to drink again and took timid bites of the food before them. However, they were still inhibited by the ugly incident. Scottie's festive spirit was dampened. His thoughts wistfully wandered back to the Persian desert where the Shahinshah's word was absolute and no Iranian subject dared to interfere with his waterworks project. Despite the desert's hostile environment, he longed again to go back.

"Come, **patron,** let's go dancing. Chop! chop!" Gabby showed up behind Scottie's chair mimicking his own expression. He whispered to her to go ahead and wait for him at the pavilion. Sneaking out of the dinner tent alone after excusing himself to the mayor and nearby guests, he reunited with Gabby at the pavilion's entrance. Thousands of people were dancing inside under the subdued lights. The pleasant scene in Scottie's perspective was a classless gathering from the social cross section of Cuyapo′ valley. The only requirement to enter and enjoy dancing was to afford a ticket.

Nobody is going to recognize us, Scottie thought as they entered the pavilion. This time he had the urge to get lost among the crowd and forget the ugly incident.

"Come on, Let us dance. **A bailar!** They are playing a **cumbia.** Okey-dokey?" She pulled a disinclined, protesting Scottie to the dance floor who insisted he simply wanted to watch the others dance.

"I got two left feet," he protested. Besides, he did not relish being close to a woman. Even with Gabby.

"You have one left foot and the other, your right foot, **si**?" She replied unaware what he was really implying. "You said you do not know **cumbia**? **Bueno,** I teach you. Come on, **patron**. I teach. You learn **cumbia**."

Maybe it's okay. I can see others dancing cumbia and it doesn't require close contact, he was rationalizing. *Moreover, I consider Gabby, my substitute kid sister. I should please her.*

The padre appeared on the dance floor sans his Franciscan habit wearing a sports shirt and plaid slacks, holding a wine glass. "As soon as I finish my Santa Helena, I shall look for my **mujer** and join you dancing. Do not go away. Promise?" Scottie concluded they were not incognito after all.

Scottie was clumsy, unintentionally comical at times, on the dance floor and obviously he had never danced the **cumbia** before. But he persevered, braving the gyrations with her. Watching others, he imitated them and improved his awkward style. After a couple more numbers, he was enjoying himself dancing, for the first time, to the infectious **cumbia** beat.

Then he was following the steps of cha-cha-cha with Gabby leading, which required him to hold her hand and waist -- something which he loathe to do with any woman before. Strangely enough, he did not mind it at all with Gabby. *She's just Gabby*, he justified to himself. *Just Gabby...or maybe Sister Carrie reincarnated....*

"Señor Scootee!" Mel, surprised to see his boss dancing, greeted them while swirling around with a young girl. Mel's thundering voice uncovered his presumed anonymity making some dancing couple turn their heads. "I have been looking for you. Paula stayed home with the baby. This is my niece, Luz Maria." Mel and his niece drifted away from them. After a few beats, they were dancing close to them again.

"I heard what happened at the big tent, **patron**," Mel whispered to Scottie. "Watch out for that Don Pedrazas. He is very vicious. You better carry a pistol." Then, they danced out of earshot once more.

Gabby overheard the conversation. "Your amigo is right, Scootee. You need protection. Carry a gun and hire bodyguards."

"I'm not afraid of that loudmouth." He scoffed at Don Pedrazas, a local cacique, he considered, with an inflated ego, blowing off steam.

"What you mean...loodmoot?"

"**Un griton**...."

"**Ah si, bueno**." Gabby told him as she made a fast swirl while leading her unsure partner in a **merengue**. "You are new here. There are many things I must tell you about my people. For one thing, Don Pedrazas is a **guambiano**. They are ruthless and will do anything to get their way."

After a few more **cumbias**, Scottie's legs gave up. Although tired, he admitted to himself that he really enjoyed dancing and noted Gabby was bursting with youthful energy. Leaving the pavilion, they walked by the amusement concessions. Glancing by chance at Gabby's profile, back-lighted by the multicolored bulbs from a "haunted house" tent, he became convinced her facial profile matched that of Carrie's even with some allowance of what he remembered from her childhood. "Oh my God! She's really Carrie!" He shuddered.

"You called me by another name?" Gabby overheard.

"No, why should I?"

"You were saying something like Cah-ree. You know, like Caridad. That was my mother's name, Maria Caridad."

Holy Moses! Am I thinking aloud? I better watch out.

They tried games of chance at several amusement booths. Throwing balls at stacks of tin cans, shooting at ducks. Gabby squealed with delight winning a rag doll at one booth, a souvenir plate at another.

Scottie, clumsy with these games of chance, did not win a single prize. Mortified, he walked forlornly still engrossed with the Gabby-Carrie mystery while his young companion was ready to try another game expecting to win again. Her girlish squeals and youthful exuberance only reminded him that Gabby should start socializing with people of her age group. Wishfully, he got the urge to join his more mature friends.

They wandered off to the gypsies' encampment outside the boundaries of the **feria** next to the church cemetery. Someone grabbed his shirt sleeve stopping him dead in his leisurely stride.

"I want to tell your future," an old woman said impudently, holding on to him.

"Let me go my arm! You...you...!" he barked at the beady-eyed woman beaming an impish grin. Reluctantly, she released her grip. Looking up, he noted a faded and weathered sign board hanging above the tent's entrance: Madame Savari, Fortune Teller and Advisor. *She probably stole or bought the sign from someone in another part of the world. Perhaps from Lagunilla, that flea market in Mexico City,* he speculated. *But her face doesn't match the name.*

Gabby, still afflicted with the **feria** fever, was ready for more fun. "Oh Scootee, let us have our fortunes told," she begged. Scottie shook his head. "Pleeze?" On hearing her plea, the old woman smiled enigmatically revealing a nearly toothless mouth and entered her tent as if she already knew for sure they were coming in.

"Na-a-ah, It's nonsense," he told her. "I don't believe in fortune telling." Moreover, this old woman's brashness had turned him off.

"Neither do I," she answered "Just for fun, pleeze, Scootee?" Those doe-eyed pools of turquoise looked at him in supplication -- they were hard to resist.

"Okay, if you insist. But remember, it's only for you, not me."

With him still skeptical, they entered the fortune-teller's tent while Gabby, jaunty, was excited with anticipation. The tent's interior was neat with expensive oriental rugs hanging on the slanted canvas walls. Scottie was amazed, impressed. Two of the rugs he identified as Bakhtiari pieces having purchased one himself from the nomads in the bazaar of Shiraz. *How did she acquire these tribal rugs? Is she really a gypsy despite her looks?*

"**Sientense**," she motioned them to sit on sturdy oak chairs with lambskin cushions placed around an oval-shaped table painted with the zodiac signs surrounding an old Middle Ages painting of the solar system under a plate glass. Hanging from the ceiling, two Coleman-like kerosene lamps provided the interior lighting. Brilliantly colored silk scarves hung down from a macrame network frame above them. An ivory-white carpet with Chinese calligraphic flourishes covered the ground. The old woman grinned widely, revealing only three front teeth, disappeared behind a canvas partition.

"She is a gypsy," Gabby whispered to him. He disagreed but did not say a word in dissent and concluded the old woman must be an Aymara Indian from Lake Titicaca who wore the same black derby hat.

The old woman reappeared carrying a candelabra with crimson candles and set it at the center of the oval-shaped table. Lighting the candles with matches, the candelabra betrayed layers of encrusted wax drippings. Straining herself to reach the lamps, she dimmed the kerosene lights and the tent became infected with a dark ghoulish ambience. Once more, she disappeared behind the canvas partition. The flickering lights from the candelabra cast long dancing shadows on the canvas walls. With his hyperactive imagination, Scottie fancied they were trapped inside a witches' cavern.

Uncomfortable, he was ready to bolt from the tent that instant were it not for Gabby. A peculiar odor permeated them -- a mixture of burning incense and rotten eggs -- in his perception -- creating a sinister illusion for him. With candlelight shining on Gabby, her appearance dramatically altered. The scarves above them were seemingly transformed into ephemeral sharp-pointed helices suspended in mid-air.

Soon the old woman rejoined them and placed tea cups and saucers on the oval table from a serving tray. She poured hot tea and sat down with them. Drinking tea and becoming more relaxed, Scottie was satisfied the woman did not perform any pagan incantations he had anticipated.

"I was in Ciudad de Panama," she related in her crackly voice while they sipped tea, "when the newspapers printed my prediction about a swarthy full-bearded man who planned to assassinate **El Supremo**. Apparently, **El Supremo** resented my prediction and ordered me deported on the first available boat to Colombia. I landed at Buenaventura. His enemies, including a swarthy full-bearded man, ambushed **El Supremo** as he came out of a hotel. And now, señor with the sad eyes," the woman turned her beady eyes to Scottie, "you have come a long way to our country."

"I want to remind you again, señora, that I don't want my fortune told." He spoke slowly in Spanish to make sure she understood him.

"Señor, with the sad eyes, why are you afraid to know the future?" The woman, for her own reason, persisted. "You have found your long-gone sister. Do you not want to know what will happen between her and you?"

He held his breath momentarily, his mind boggled by this fortune teller with her cheeky banter. *Is she implying Carrie reincarnated into Gabby? How did she know their resemblance?* These thoughts rumbled through his mind like flash floods tearing his shaky doubt against reincarnation. His curiosity, now whetted by the provocative intimation, he was tempted to draw her out, eager to find out what more she knew about his past. Then, he realized his well-kept secret might be exposed by her. "No!" He replied with vehemence, now considering her as his nemesis. "**Claro que no**!!"

Discouraged, the woman turned her attention back to Gabby. "**Buenos pues**, may I look into your hand, señorita?" She grabbed her right hand and began squeezing and releasing it while examining the palm, as the lines deepened and intersected. "You have small hands and sensitive long fingers." Although suspicious of this woman's motives, Scottie remained silent.

"**Gracias**, señora!" Gabby was smiling, pleased with the compliments and nodded to him signaling that she made the right decision to go inside. "I inherited my mother's hands," she said proudly.

"Now let me see what more we can learn from your hands," the old woman continued as she held Gabby's left hand bringing the open palm closer to her face as if there were items to scrutinize. "Hm-m-m," she drone in a monotone. After a few more minutes, she cleared her throat. "See this line?" She was holding her right palm again after comparing it with her left. "It is deep and runs down to the plain of Mars. You shall live a long life if you so desire. And see this other line? It goes around here and is called the ring of Venus. Ah-h-h, It reveals your interest in music, especially from the **antiplano**, the highlands, and yes, your love can be very passionate...."

While the old woman examined both hands alternately and together, she picked out some items from Gabby's past to which the latter nodded in agreement. Scottie was getting antsy sitting in the malodorous semi-darkness, bored with the details she was telling Gabby.

"I am through with your hands. Let me look into the tea leaves at the bottom of your cup." She lifted the cup close to her eyes, turning it around slowly, examining the residue as a skeptical Scottie watched. "Ah-h-h!" The old woman's face was drawn into wrinkles after she found apparently something significant. "Ah-h-h! **Tu abuelo!** Your grandpa arrived on this continent on a sailing ship across a big expanse of water."

"**Si,** I was told he was an **alferez** with the Spanish army and was born in Vigo, **España**. He decided to seek his fortune in the New World," Gabby elaborated.

The old woman looked puzzled, stared at Gabby. "**Alferez**? But this man was wearing a brown habit with a white cord belt and sandals. Hm-m-m, he looks like a Franciscan ."

"You mean my **abuelo** was a friar? Not a soldier?" she repeated, trembling, realizing her mother lied to her.

"He settled in a small town near a great body of fresh water...hm-m-m...look like a lake, a big lake...." Her eyes were still transfixed inside the cup.

"**Si**, it is Lago de Maracaibo," Gabby confirmed.

"He was sent back across the ocean by the bishop for his indiscretion with a woman. Months later, this woman was harassed by the townspeople when she became heavy with his child. Nearing child birth, she was forced to flee across the border to Colombia where the baby was born in the sierras...."

"**Si,** my mother was born in Cucuta´. She grew up to be a beautiful woman, married an older man, my father, a sugar broker from Cartagena. But señora," Gabby interrupted, becoming fretful, "you are talking about the past which I already know. What about the future?" Amazed by these revelations, Scottie kept his silence.

"Be patient, señorita. The water flows from one stream to another, the past into the present, the present weaves into the future..."

The woman fell silent, closed her eyes, and began rubbing the teacup against her cheek while muttering unintelligible words. Then, she continued, "My vision is turning to the present.... You desire to get away from your uncle's house for he treats you worse than a servant. By chance, you meet a musician from Tampico at a barrio fiesta. This man put a special charm on you with his ability to play many instruments and even taught you to play the flute. Being lonesome, you soon fell under the spell of this clever musician...even becoming engaged to him...while unknown to you he was also after your cousin, Rosita, whom he..."

"**Basta**! I heard enough! I don't want to be reminded of that man," Gabby interrupted. "Tell me about the future! Pleese!"

"Be patient, señorita. Be patient… The waters of the future are muddy and your meddling makes it worse. I must not be disturbed -- so the eyes of my spirit can penetrate these muddy waters. Let us see...hm-m-m...your love will be reciprocated in a fashion which you might not fully appreciate. A mirror image is interposed on his sister while you were conceived in your mother's womb.... You will mature in the coming year when you shall have the wisdom to understand what that...."

"**No comprendo**! I do not understand what you are talking about!

Un enigma! A riddle!" Gabby, angry, restless, interrupted. "You have talked mostly about the past and the present. What will happen in the future? **Digame**! Tell me!"

The woman, unsmiling, glowered at her. "**Tu, tranquilate**! Calm down!." she said in an irritated voice, "the future is most difficult to see and much less to understand.. Reflect back on what I told you. Go over it many, many times. Meanwhile, you must be brave and hold on to your stout heart...."

"Gabby, the señora has told you everything she knows. It's time to go and take our leave. **Vamonos**." Scottie was just waiting for this chance to leave, not desiring to stay a minute longer inside what he considered a creepy smelly tent. Standing up, he dispensed some peso bills to the old woman who eagerly accepted them.

"**El señor del Norte esta´ muy apurado**. Too much hurry," the old woman said as she hid the bills inside her blouse.

As an impatient Scottie hustled Gabby out of the tent into the street, he chanced to glance back. The old woman had lifted his teacup from the table and was scrutinizing the residue. That sight vexed him for he felt helpless and betrayed, suspecting the woman had discovered his secret.

The far reach of the sounds of gaiety and music went beyond the cemetery grounds where Scottie parked his truck. Once inside the truck, he was already mulling over the paperwork waiting for him to finish in the house before morning. Gabby's thoughts have not left the tent and was brooding over the revelations given by the old woman.

"The gypsy mentioned a connection to my birth with your long-lost sister. What does she mean?"

"That old woman, gypsy or not, is full of garbage. **Basura**!" he dismissed the question eager to hide his own confusion about the Carrie/Gabby mix-up. "You know my kid sister died a long time ago. How could I possibly meet her again?" By then, he was alarmed the old woman knew more about him. *Did that old hag read my mind and uncovered my secret?* He was loathed to speculate.

"No, I do not mean that!" she disagreed. "That gypsy woman was telling something about your sister who is involved with both of us. You intimidated her and she began to speak in riddles. I want to go back and ask her to explain better."

"The hell we will! I'm not going back inside that stinky firetrap of a tent again with that weirdo." Just recalling the old woman's beady eyes caused him to utter, "Ugh!" Then, he felt compelled to warn her. "Don't waste your time on those riddles. It's all garbage. **Basura!** Just meaningless garbage. If I were you, forget the whole damn thing."

Soon they were driving along the dirt road towards their **quinta** away from the fading noises and the bustle of the **feria**. Unknown to him, she was still ruminating about the old woman's revelations.

"That gypsy was talking about real incidents in my past and the present. She was trying to tell me about my future." Gabby's intuition sensed that Scottie bullied the woman into silence about their future. "Are you hiding something from me?" Her pools of turquoise focused on him.

"See what I told you about getting serious with fortune-telling? All that garbage?" he scolded her, determined to coax her away from the old woman's revelations. "Once you believe in all that **basura**, your life becomes complicated. You're old enough to realize that only God knows the future."

That night Gabby could not sleep for a long time with her head buzzing with the excitement of the **feria**. Despite Scottie's discouragement, she was silently determined to ferret out the mystery enveloping the **patron**, his sister, and herself.

In the early hours of the morning, Scottie was awakened by strange rasping noises as if the furniture pieces were pushed around on the tiled floor. Seizing the baseball bat, which he kept under his bed, he walked stealthily bare-footed on the living room. In the darkness, he discerned Gabby's silhouette, with outstretched arms, bumping into furniture, stumbling towards the balcony. Dropping the bat, he rushed and grabbed her before she could reach the balcony. Ensconced in his arms on the floor, he slapped her cheeks until she woke up from her trance. Even though he was rather sleepy, she took her prescription pills in the kitchen. With her back in bed, he lay down on her bedroom floor with a pillow and blanket determined to keep her from sleep-walking at least for now.

A unfamiliar clinking sound woke up a startled Scottie causing him to jumped up. Gabby tapped a tumbler's side with a knife's edge to wake him up. She laughed at his alarmed reaction.

"Why sleep on the floor, papa?" she said in a musical voice with no inkling of her sleepwalking incident. She had prepared a breakfast of scrambled eggs, bacon, pieces of toasts, coffee, and a glass of orange juice on a tray.

"For Pete's sake! Don't call me, papa." He was stretching his arms and bending forward to undo his stiffness after sleeping on the hard floor. The smell of coffee made him ravenous. "You were sleepwalking." He decided to change the subject. "Why did you prepare breakfast so early this morning?"

"I woke with the roosters and decided to make you breakfast. **Solo un capricho**. Just a whim. A neat idea, **si**?"

"Neat idea! You're talking more and more like an American. Does Maestro Molina teach you those expressions?"

"Not Maestro Molina. It is from you! I always imitate what you say. **Soy tu papagayo**. I am your parrot."

"Huh! So it's me again," he said sipping his coffee. Gabby also poured herself a cup in the kitchen and sat cross-legged on the floor leaning against the bed. Complimenting her for the nice "breakfast-by-the-bed" treat, she felt good and rewarded. Now relaxed, he thought of having a small party, sort of a trial run before a big one suggested strongly by the bosses in Bogota'. *Perhaps a birthday party for her?* He did not know her birth date.

"You have been working hard cleaning the **quinta** ship shape," he spoke again. "I was thinking we should throw a party. What about a birthday party for you? Wouldn't that be a neat idea?" This time he was facetious repeating the 'neat idea.' "When is your birthday, by the way?"

"Twenty-first of January," she told him. I will be twenty-nine."

He froze. Her birthday coincided with Carrie's death. Mulling over the coincidence further, he figured Carrie died twenty-nine years ago. *Gabby's age!* Devastated, he did not know what to think. His frozen stance scared her.

"Scootee! Scootee! **Estas bien**? Are you all right?" She noted the sudden dead paleness of his face.

Scottie was mentally distant beyond her reach and did not hear her. Immersed in a dilemma -- he must accept or reject Carrie's reincarnation into Gabby. That Gabby might be the reincarnation of her own sister overwhelmed him.

"No! no! It can't be! can't be!" Crushed by the idea, he broke down and cried. She sat beside him placing her arm around his shoulders.

"What is the matter, Scootee? Why are you sad? Did I do something wrong?"

"No. I just remember my sister's death anniversary...." *Please God, don't allow Gabby to connect her birthday to Carrie's day of passing….*

"Sorry...so sorry, Scootee...."

"I'll be okay..." Her supportive words, her loyalty, triggered an ambiguous desire in him to keep her forever while feeling lonesome for her sister, miserable for causing her death. Although doubtful about her reincarnation, he was searching for a rationale to dote on this sister substitute which he considered rather absurd and yet compelling.

Shaking off his introspection, he recalled what he wanted to find out. "Why are you up so early? On Saturday morning. Tell me." His mood now shifted to being mischievous, trying to be cheerful for her.

"Oh, **nada**. Nothing," she said coyly.

Despite his dilemma over Gabby's unworldly mix-up with Carrie, he was glad to see her bubbly freshness with no sign of last night's sleepwalking. Determined to squeeze the truth from her, he decided a ruse.

"Nothing? I bet you want me to do something this morning," he said and did not wait for her to answer. “You want me...to check your English homework!”

“My homework can wait **mañana**,” she replied, rather alarmed at the turn of their conversation as something else was brewing in her mind.

“Well then, since there’s nothing to do this morning after this nice breakfast, I’ll take a snooze in your bed and be comfortable.” Removing the throw pillows, he extended the sofa into its bed length, and fluffed the long pillow.

“**Espera!** Wait!” She stopped him from lifting the blanket as he was about to slip under.

“What is it you want to do then? Tell me...before I fall asleep again.” He feigned a yawn and acted like he could not keep his eyes open.

“You have been busy for two weeks. You come home, take your snack and go directly to bed....”

“Yes, go on.”

“It would be nice if..., her face was sparkling with anticipation, “we could go on a picnic today...at Piscina Tamayo, for example....”

“So that’s the reason!” Jumping up, he threw the blanket aside and grinned at her.

“Oh! You pretended to be sleepy! Why? **Sinverguenza**! Shame on you!” She began slapping him while he braced his arm up in defense.

“Okay, that’s enough. We’ll go to the Piscina.” She stopped slapping. “But under one condition.”

“**Una condicion de que**?”

“I want you to finish your English homework when we come back from the Piscina, okey-dokey?”

“Tomorrow I will do it before Maestro Molina arrives. I promise.”

“Tomorrow many things could happen and you won’t be able to finish your homework on time. Do it now.”

“**Bueno, patron**. I will do it after we return from the Piscina, okey-dokey? I am your obedient slave.” He gave her a quick slap on her rump. She shrieked. Their silly play alleviated his memory of Carrie’s death anniversary.

Scottie felt he needed a change of scenery and some relaxation too. The past two weeks were pure hell for him. The power machines kept breaking down and the spare parts ordered from Bogota´ were delayed. A trunnion for a bulldozer had to be air-shipped from San Francisco. Rafael came down with measles. Yesterday another threat letter kept him restless last night.

“It will do you good to get out of this house too,” he told her. “Let’s get our food stuff and other things together before the morning is over.” Last Friday she found an excuse to send Carmen to her village before he arrived from the office.

“**Ay**! **Que rico**! **Gracias, patron**!” She gave him an unexpected hug, a quick peck, and took off for the kitchen. Coming back from the storage room with the ice chest and thermos bottles, he heard her humming a Latin song amidst the culinary noises, which to his ears, was indicative of feverish preparations. His taste buds moistened just thinking of his favorite roast beef sandwich she was preparing.

“Don’t forget to use the mustard for my sandwiches,” he hollered from upstairs where he was getting dressed, “and also horseradish…”

“Horseradish? **Que es eso**? **Caballo algo or** horse somethin’ …

“ **Es rabano.** A jar with blue and yellow label. **Caballo!** Ha, ha.”

Minutes later, they sped off on a dirt road, a shortcut to Piscina Tamayo located on the west bank of Rio Chiribichi. He rolled up the windows to keep out the dust being stirred up by another truck ahead of them. Despite the inconvenience of being cooped up inside the humid cabin (she disliked air-conditioning), he was eager to get out of the house that Saturday, a bright and sunny day.

I need time off from my homework as much as Gabby does, he thought as if to assure himself he was doing the right thing. She had high expectations of enjoying this outing and was already scheming to stay until sundown. Looking back through the rear-view mirror, he was appalled. “You practically brought **la cocina entera**, the whole kitchen…on the platform,” he chided her. The badly eroded road caused the food containers to shift and bump each other noisily prompting him to stop and tie down the containers with ropes.

“I want you to eat as if **tu estas en tu casa propia,** like you are at home,” she answered justifying her decision to bring so much. Then, she remembered a bothersome item she wanted to bring up. “I wish you would let me handle Carmen and tell her what meals to prepare.”

“We both can tell her what to cook for us. I really want you to spend most of your time on your studies. Concentrate on them like a good **estudiante.”** This time he imagined himself performing as a surrogate for her departed good Tio Berto.

More than just studying was on her mind. She wanted to make all the decisions with regards to Carmen like sending her home when she wanted privacy or when she wanted to do the cooking herself without Carmen getting in her way. To be indispensable to her **patron** was her abiding goal. “You are spending a lot of money for my **educacion** and in return, I want to do things for you. I cook better than Carmen. I can do more than cleaning the house. Right now, I feel **inutil,** useless.”

“You don’t have to do anything more for me. You’re keeping the house in good order and you’re supervising the **jardinero** to do the garden and backyard. Right now, you’ll make me happier if you concentrate hard on your studies.” “**Me siento mas alegre**,” he added.

While driving through the featureless dirt road flanked by savannah dotted by occasional mud huts in the distance, he was thinking that Gabby's tutored courses should prepare her for an office job in about five months or less. A steady job, he concluded, would mean financial independence for her. Strangely enough, he was feeling sad about her eventual departure from his life. *There would be a void in my life when we part* -- this honest concession of his feelings for her haunted him that morning. Beyond the Gabby-Carrie riddle, her silly naive behavior made her into his very own court jester to humor him and make him forget his problems. But today his bleak outlook of what would happen into their future, was depressing him, making him moody.

"You are not saying much this morning, Scootee. **Demasiado tranquilo.** Is everything okey-dokey with the job?" she asked. He did not answer. They hardly talked since they left the **quinta. "Oye, Scootee,"** she persisted, "talk to me, **por favor**!"

"I have my share of problems at work, but today, I don't want to talk about them." His further somber thoughts of her underlining the inevitable end of their peculiar relationship, brought his spirits even farther down.

"**Entonces**, talk to me about something else. About something funny like your office clerk, Mauro. You said he is a funny gooy?"

From behind, a fast-moving car overtook them at a dangerous bend on the decrepit **carretera,** on the last few kilometers before reaching their resort destination by a river.

"**Tonto!** That's the second reckless fool who passed us."

"I am getting worried about you," she commented, afraid he was heading toward a nervous breakdown. "You must tell me some funny **chistes**, jokes…."

"Maybe I ran out of **chistes**," he retorted glumly. She did not like him stewing in a bad mood today when she had him all for herself. He remained poker-faced, intent on watching other vehicles while his anger swelled inside. Suddenly, her fingers were tickling his rib cage.

"Hey! Don't! Ha! ha! ha! Gabby! Please don't!" Involuntarily covering himself with an arm, he caused the truck to swerve off to the shoulder. Recovering control of the truck, he eased back into the road.

"I wanted to make you laugh and I won!" She said with relish, pleased with her surprise. Distracted from his troubles, he was smiling for the first time. His bad mood evaporated. On reaching the Piscina, he parked the truck inside the premises as a guard looked on. The sight of the resort's swimming pool and its frolicking noises got Scottie into a playful mood.

"Let's take off our clothes and see who can jump first into the water," he dared her.

To his shame, she quickly took off her blouse and shorts revealing her two-piece swimwear while he was still fiddling with his shoes.

Throwing away his slacks, then his shirt, as he ran close behind her but she dived first into the swimming pool. A pool which was claimed from the river, roped off, and held in place with submerged wood pilings at its corners.

They romped and swam in the water like two uninhibited youngsters and slapped water at each other faces. Some locals watched them warily not pleased with a young girl of their own cavorting with a gringo. They ignored their stares and decided to play "catch-me-if-you-can." Gabby was more nimble than the slow-moving Scottie. Her ploy was to allow him to come close within arm's reach and then, with catlike timing, she would kick her legs vigorously to escape from him. After several attempts to thwart her trick, he was getting frustrated.

"You're a tease," he declared, not a bit discouraged, still determined to defeat her bait-and-flee ploy. He was not aware that other swimmers were obviously annoyed with their horseplay in the pool. Changing his strategy, he jumped to his full height above the pool, flying towards her with arms and legs eagle-spread attempting to surprise and panic her into inaction. Gabby, laughing, made a swift turn like a fish as he splashed down into the swirling water just exited by her. At his next try, she shifted sideways colliding unintentionally with a floating fat woman who screamed some foul words at her. Flustered, Gabby darted away from the woman and ended up in a corner. Seeing his rare chance, he jumped forward kamikaze-like, screaming, blocking her escape. Unwilling to be caught, she flipped backwards to evade him and accidentally fell into the turbulent, racing river.

"Help! **Socorro**! Scootee!" she shouted as the river swiftly claimed her. Scottie, standing inside the pool, shocked, watched helplessly, baffled by the unexpected situation while the river carried her off toward a huge rock pile in its midstream.

"Watch out for those rocks!" he shouted to her.

Gabby heard him and began churning her arms deep into the stream towards the opposite bank away from the rock pile. While she avoided the rock pile, the current took her farther downstream closer to the opposite bank. Looking up, she saw some low-hanging tree branches above her. Jumping up high with outstretched arms, she caught a branch, then another, and held on tenaciously while swinging above the water with her legs still submerged and swayed by the current's force. Buoyed by what Scottie saw, he shouted excitedly to her and encouraged her to hold on.

A lifeguard appeared and offered two rolls of rope and a life jacket to Scottie. Putting the jacket on and keeping an eye on Gabby, he asked the lifeguard to tie the ropes together and secure one end around his waist and hold the other end himself.

"**Que haga ahorita,** señor? What to do now?" Scottie explained to him and another fellow, who just joined them, that he would swim toward her if they could hold the other end of the rope together.

Cautiously descending into the volatile river, he swam obliquely towards the opposite bank giving allowance for the current's drifting effect so that he should end up close to where she was hanging. Having succeeded to end just above her, he grabbed her legs and told her to let go her grip from the branches. Dropping down, she nervously held his head covering his eyes. Complaining to her that he could not see, she slipped down and held on to the rope around his waist. Immediately, he gripped one arm around her shoulders and waved with the other signaling to the two men back at the pool to start pulling them.

By that time, all the picnickers were watching the rescue effort. Several other men and a robust woman joined in pulling the pair back as they were drifting towards the rock pile. Scottie shouted at them to pull harder before they were to slam against those rocks. More men joined and the pair were pulled successfully away from the rocks and toward the pool. Arriving safely, the crowd cheered and patted the pair as they got out of the water.

"**Mi salvador**! My savior! You saved my life again." Unashamedly, she planted a big smacking kiss on a shy Scottie and hugged him. "**Te adoro**! I love you!!" The crowd applauded in approval and with overwhelming enthusiasm. Scottie smiled and wondered what happened to those who were annoyed by their horseplay at the pool. This time, he did not feel repulsed with her spontaneous display of affection. The near tragic incident triggered his own repressed emotions to spill over. Sentimentally vulnerable, he was falling in love with this young woman.

Walking back to the picnic grounds close to where their truck was parked, they picked a shady spot under a tree to spread a table cloth and placed their food and drinks. This time they were quiet, subdued, silently collecting their senses while eating their sandwiches.

Minutes later, they became aware of curious people who sat a few meters away from them eyeing their every movement unaccustomed to gringos who seldom showed up at the Piscina. Becoming ill at ease for being watched so avidly, they loaded their picnic items back to the truck's rear and left.

"You saved my life," she told him again in the privacy of the truck as they sped back to town. Leaning her head on his shoulder, she demonstrated how dependent she was on him for affection and moral support -- unaware that he had not yet recovered from the trauma of her rescue. His pent-up emotions, stoked by his self-imposed loneliness which begun from his past, were surging inside him. Surrendering to the emotional breakout, he put his arm around her shoulder in an unspoken act of bonding despite his lingering doubt of their relationship. Inevitably, they stole glances at each other from time to time in the secluded cabin unsure about this undefined affinity, this magical but murky attraction between them while riding through the dusky afternoon.

"**Te quiero**, Scootee," she said, casting those adoring pools of turquoise at him.

"I love you too," he confessed impulsively as tears rolled out.

"Scootee! You are crying? **Porque′**? Why?"

"I can't explain it, Gabby. Sorry, if I broke down. Sorry...." As he wiped his tears with a tissue. *How can I*? he asked himself. *I have a tender feeling for you. Yet you might be my very own sister. And if you're not my sister, how could I love you totally if I'm not capable of making love?* At that instant, he hesitated whether to tell her everything hinting his secret, bit by bit and then *expose, bare my soul, my past.* But his emotional tide turned in the opposite direction. "I'm sorry, I can't. I can't tell you…."

"I understand, Scootee. I understand...."

"You do?" he wondered.

"Yes, I do. I understand."

Does she really understand my dilemma? Does she? He was puzzled by her simplistic answer, perplexed with their heightened relationship.

Chapter IV

From the time that Scottie took over the reins of the highway project from Clyde, he performed expeditiously pleasing his bosses in Bogota´ who were only too glad he was a different persona from the trouble-prone Clyde. The animosity about the alleged rape of a local girl by Clyde shimmered down and became overshadowed by Scottie's sincere concern and rapport with the natives. Adapting his Tex-Mex Spanish to their peculiar lingo laced with Indian words and phrases, he had gradually become "invisible" among them. Only the landlords, whom he suspected of masterminding those threat letters, hated him with venomous passion. When he queried the postal employees about those letters they swore that they did not know who were the culprits. Scottie realized they were too intimidated by these powerful caciques. Nonetheless, those threat letters did not deter him nor slow him down with the construction scheduled target dates. Even when preemptive legal actions were filed at court by Don Pedrazas before the company's legal department in Bogota´ and the government lawyers could file all the necessary permits for the rights-of-way on Don Pedrazas' estancia. However, after two weeks of hearing, the court granted the rights-of-way to the company. The construction time lost by these delaying tactics was regained forthwith by Scottie using two eight-hour shifts.

A month later, another worrisome snag threatened once more the construction schedule. This time, Don Mendieta, another landowner, and a tough **guambiano,** more educated and wilier than Don Pedrazas, hired topnotch lawyers from Medellin to halt the highway construction by claiming there were archeological sites in his estancia protected by sections of the national laws. Moreover, Don Mendieta was under suspicion of sabotaging several road-building machineries using dynamites. These machineries were out of commission until the damaged parts could be flown from Bogota´ and stateside sources.

Two **campesinos** were caught by the town's policemen in the act of strapping dynamite sticks on two bulldozers at night. Thrown into the clink, they refused to speak and seemed content to remain behind the bars indefinitely. Mauro confided to Scottie that Don Mendieta provided food and money to the imprisoned men's families. Despite the obvious duplicity by Don Mendieta with these men, he could not be charged for "humanitarian donations." Then, it was necessary to hire a professor of archeology from Bogota′ to check the authenticity of those alleged sites. These further delays made Scottie a very frustrated man.

His unflappable poise began to unhinge. Short-tempered, he would rage at his men at the least provocation on minor mistakes. Afraid of him, his employees would only visit his office when it was absolutely necessary. Only Gabby escaped his wrath. With her penchant of picking some debris from her **patron's** work frustrations and refashioned them impudently into mocking foibles, she became his emotional relief valve.

As a matter of personal pride, Scottie would not complain to the bosses of his mounting problems with the landowners nor about those threat letters. Complaining to others about his problems, he concluded early in life, was a sign of character weakness and always remembered Reverend Dan's words: "Never complain, never explain." But his bosses from Bogota′ noticed that he was edgy and could not sit still during the meetings. Scottie had to stand up every so often and pace the conference room, puffing a cigar.

"Don't tell me that you're now smoking cigars!" W. Corry, the operations manager, remarked. From their days back at the San Francisco headquarters, he remembered that Scottie abhorred tobacco smoke. W. Corry dismissed Scottie's nervousness and cigar smoking as a belated reaction to his cultural shock -- caused by the drastic change of surroundings and the challenge of a new job. "Be aware of these changes in surroundings, Scottie, and soon you shall outgrow this affliction." Scottie, smiled though stressed, but kept mum.

Cultural shock might be a catch-all diagnosis of Scottie's personal crisis. Alone and back at his Peñalosa job, he controlled his temper better but was still irritable and nit-picking with the office help and the field men. Coming home late, he preferred to sit by the fountain in the patio and unwind while drinking his margarita. There was always a smiling, prankish Gabby ready to pour him another margarita and humor him with jokes, even mimicked Padre Joe and Señora Lebrun, exaggerating their mannerisms. Those turquoise eyes glistened against the fading afternoon sun making him forget his work-related problems. He would credit her for surviving another day. His living with Gabby at close quarters had become a temporary nightly escape from the hostile landlords dogging the highway project.

As if fate did not punish him enough, his war wounds which he would rather forget, came back to haunt him again in nightmares gradually eroding his emotive declaration of love to Gabby after that river accident. Gabby, surprised and then mystified by his sudden manifestation of love, simply believed it was his sincere promise to marry her. Deterred once more by his war wounds, he attempted to sublimate his love for her as if she were his own star-crossed sister.

Alarmed by Gabby's recent attitude toward him and their dialogue which from the import of her tone sounded more and more like wedding bells. He spent many sleepless nights wondering if he could navigate their relationship into a purely platonic friendship. Yet, he realized that would be a difficult turnabout to do since she was a young woman who was still developing her carnal instincts and had already made up her mind to marry him. He worried his idea was not realistic, and sooner than later, end their idyllic modus vivendi. But if he were to do nothing and let her take the lead, he feared that she would become bold and announce their commitment to the world. Then, exposed to honor his word to marry her but incompetent to make love, he would be publicly humiliated. *I got to do something, find a solution.*

****

"Ha, ha, ha," Scottie was forced to laugh and throw up the newspaper he was reading. "Don't, Gabby, don't!" But she persisted to tickle his sides compelling him to jump up from the sofa. Touching his ribs once before, she discovered his **talon de Aquiles** - he was extremely ticklish. Distracted from his reading, he got up and stood in a playful defensive stance. With clenched fists and raised forearms shielding his rib cage, he moved about her in a tight circle like a boxer. Each time she struck her hand towards his ribcage, he blocked the thrust with his forearms. "Now, what brought this on?" He asked laughing and on hair-trigger alert.

"You are moody again tonight," she said, dripping wet from a shower and wrapped in a large bath towel. "I want you to laugh again, **patron**." Still persistent, she attempted to poke his ribcage again. "**Animo**! Come on, **patron.** Laugh some more."

"Gabby, please! I just want to relax and read the papers."

"No, señor! I want you to laugh hard. Right now. **Este momento."** She attempted a quick jab which he blunted.

"G-r-r-r...." Egged by her persistence, he decided to take the offensive. Baring his teeth and spreading his fingers like claws, he menaced her. "G-r-r-r! I'm gonna bite you!"

Happy to see him clown around, she went along with his gag pretending to be scared. "Oh! oh! Señor **Tigre,** do not eat me up...."

As he swung down his spread-out fingers like paws, she would jump back avoiding his lunges. He became more aggressive. Suddenly, her towel unraveled exposing her pink nipples and pubic triangle. to a startled Scottie.

That Sunday night, he could not sleep. The unraveling of her towel and peek of her nubile body kept recurring in his mind. Sleepless for hours, another episode intruded. After a recent sleepwalking incident, he helped Gabby take her pills with a glass of water in the kitchen. He saw her tempting body veiled in a diaphanous nightgown. Tormented that he might weaken during such occasion and make a pass at her, she would expect him to follow through. *My war wounds*, he reminded himself again, *have destroyed that indulgence.* These incidents kept him wide awake and disturbed until dawn broke.

****

Monday morning came and as customary, Scottie started with an open meeting with his foremen. Something was brewing inside him and he decided to make it brief and adjourn early. Then, he closeted with each foreman who needed further instructions on work details which he also cut short and reserved Melquiades, the senior foreman, for last.

Scottie instructed Mel to bypass the Mendieta estancia for now and move to the next section which was a public parcel. Once more, he told Mel to forbid his crew from patronizing those **bodegones** which the Mendieta henchmen frequented. Satisfied that they had threshed out all the work details for that next section, their conversation drifted to more mundane matters. Mel said his baby son was gaining weight and sleeping longer. A week ago, he continued, the midnight feeding was passed over. While Mel chatted about his baby son, Scottie was trying to make up his mind whether to confide his private dilemma to Mel obliquely and hopefully obtain some down-to-earth advice from a male native. Mel, he reasoned, was a simple uncomplicated person who should have the insight on the male/female relationship in the local scene while Mauro was too smart and might see beyond his smoke screen.

"I got a recent letter from a close friend in California," Scottie began. "He wrote me about a personal problem and is asking me for advice. I would like to share his story with you. You're more experienced in these man/woman matters than me. You're married and I'm an old bachelor." Mel guffawed, flattered to be consulted by the boss.

"**A su orden,** señor," Mel replied and was all ears.

"You have probably concluded already that my friend is really in love with this woman. And this woman loves him too, expecting him to propose marriage soon...."

"Well, what is your friend waiting for?" Mel interjected. "On with the wedding, the matrimonial bed, and deflower the bride. **Que va!** Go for it!"

"Whoa, Mel. As yet I haven't told you his problem."

"Pro-oh-blem? **Que problema**?" Mel was puzzled.

"Let me finish the story, will you?" Scottie was getting irritated. "This fellow was in the Korean War. During a battle, he was wounded in the groin."

"What do you mean 'wounded in the groin'? **No entiendo**."

"I mean his sex organ was damaged. **Sus cojones**. **Probablemente,** he won't be able to consummate the marriage."

"**Ay! Muy malo**, señor!" Mel was shaking his head. "He is no more a man after damaging his **cojones**. There is no solution for his problem if he cannot perform. He is finished. **Finito.** Now, how will you answer him, señor?"

"Why, eh...why...I don't really know...." Scottie was nervous, hesitant. "That's why I asked for your advice." On hearing Mel's words, Scottie's whole being felt like a falling crystal vase hitting the ground and shattering into thousand pieces. Holding his private turmoil inside, he decided to wrap up their talk. "Mel, I have to write that telex for Bogota′ now. You have all the plats and survey maps for that section. Any more questions?"

"Nothing more, señor. By the way, what is the name of your friend?"

"Mel, his identity is confidential."

After Mel left, Scottie closed the door quickly. Sitting down, he tried to stem his grief but could not contain his tears. He burst out crying which he muffled with a hankie, not wishing Mauro and the other office help to hear him crying. Later and more calm, he stood up and with his great sorrow, he pressed his hands down on the desk until his tenseness subsided. Summoning an inner strength, he reluctantly told himself to accept his fate -- to continue his celibate life without a woman and acquiescing to the loneliness of his dreary unmarried status since returning home from war. Eventually, he struggled back to his daily routine, wrote letters, and sent that daily telex report to Bogota′.

Chatting casually with Mauro somewhat lightened his sadness. Still the bitter truth expressed by Mel stuck in his mind: He is no more a man after damaging his manhood. *I might as well accept my fate. And when this highway project is finished, I must move far away from this country and...Gabby too.... My doting love for this woman should fade away with the years. My present dilemma was caused by our intimate living together. I must follow the dictates of my brain. Not my heart. It will hurt for a while...for her as well...but I must do it...as I have no choice.... I certainly hope she can take it.* Alone in his office, his thoughts depressed him.

Mauro, talking through the intercom, told him that Gabby wanted to see him. *What does she want?* he wondered. He had told her many times not to call nor see him in the office unless it was an emergency. Opening the door, Gabby came bursting in, heaving with a frightened look on her face.

"I ran out...I ran out of the **quinta**...." she said catching her breath. Aware of the distance between the **quinta** from the town's center, he was amazed as he closed the door behind her.

"What happened?" he asked, handing her a paper cup of water from the cooler.

"Maestro Molina...he...he made...advances to me.... He caressed my breasts...."

"Why, the bastard!" Scottie reacted with furor. He never suspected the mild-mannered bespectacled maestro with the trim moustache to be utterly dissolute. "Let's go to the **quinta** right now!."

Arriving, he searched the **quinta** while his anger escalated to homicidal proportions. The maestro had fled the scene. Running to his study room, he checked for the maestro's address from a notebook. "You stay in," he advised her, picking up a baseball bat from the hall closet. "I'll go to his apartment and beat his brains out."

"Ay, Scootee, **por favor**! No moorder, pleeze!" she pleaded as he jumped into the truck and took off in a hurry. But the intended victim had already cleaned out his rented bachelor pad and presumably left town. Returning to the **quinta**, he was silent, just nodded to her as he came in. Gabby surmised from his angry face that he did not catch the culprit and felt relieved. Then, he stood by the terrace, a frustrated man, gripping the iron railing and brooding the incident. The appealing view of the fountain's cascading waters slowly unwound his sense of failure. *Might as well,* he concluded*, I could beat that cad to a pulp and I would be in jail. Never mind! I shall see the Commandante and let him take care of that cad.*

Ironically, he had made up his mind that morning already that he must ease Gabby into an apartment of her own after that private talk with Mel. But now, that decision was clouded by that unsavory incident with the maestro. In good conscience, he could not turn her loose for he considered her to be vulnerable to unscrupulous persons. He went inside and joined her in the living room.

Sitting down next to her on the white velvet sofa, he was quiet, introspective. She touched his left hand, held it with both hands on her lap. Scottie was deep in thoughts about what to do with Gabby, still on hold about putting her in an apartment and telling her that she must start living on her own. Then, he realized she was rubbing his palm against her right breast.

Taken by surprise, he jerked his hand loose. "What! What are you trying to do!"

"I want to erase the finger marks of the maestro," she explained, "from my breast."

"But...but...that's never done," he stammered. Blushing, embarrassed, he could not speak further.

"I have to erase...." she insisted.

"No! You mustn't do that again."

"You're my **patron.** I have to erase his finger marks...." Baffled and confused about her logic, he refused to comply. After moments of silence, she spoke again, “Pleeze, Scootee, I want to hold your hand. Just hold it, okey-dokey?” She reached out for his hand again and he reluctantly let her while she leaned on his shoulder intuitively depending on him to protect her.

“Sometimes you astonish me,” he confessed, surging with love for the woman so emotionally dependent on him. The setback on his plan to make her independent was weighing heavily in his thoughts. He was in no mood to search for another maestro.

“You can teach me how to read and write at night.” She read his thoughts. He did not respond. “I will study hard, **muy fuerte**, during the day. And Heidi promised to help too.” She was throwing all sorts of ideas. “Could you help me, pleeze?”

“Wha-a-at?” he was back from his profound thinking plateau. “I’m sorry, Gabby. I wasn’t listening.” She repeated patiently what she said before.

“Let’s see what can be done. As you’re aware, I’m very busy in the office and in the field. After work, I’m too tired to do anything. It’s hard to focus as you can see right now. Let’s wait until the weekend when I am rested and have more time to think about your tutoring, okey-dokey?”

The nasty incident with Maestro Molina sharpened Gabby’s perception of her **hombre’s** attributes: generous, kind, patient, protective. There was nobody in her whole life who could match her **hombre**, her **patron’s** concern for her, strengthening her belief that he was heaven-sent. All her sentiments were overflowing and nothing could hold her emotions back.

“Scootee....” She began in a purring voice wanting to confess how much she loved him more than anybody else in the whole world. But the object of her overflowing sentiments was engrossed in his own deep thoughts, so mentally far away. ***Mi amor*** *has so many things in his mind to worry about including little me,* ***la pequeñita****. I am just a little uneducated* ***campesina*** *from the* ***altiplano.*** *My* ***patron*** *will think I am so silly to express my deepest love for him.* ***Dejalo****! Forget it!*

“What is it?” Finally, he was aware she called his name and was not sure he heard the rest of what she mumbled.

“**No importa**. Never mind.”

“Tell me. I want to know. What is it?”

“I shall prepare some lunch.” She took off hurriedly to the kitchen.

Looking back, he noticed somebody was missing. “Where’s Carmen?” He got up and headed for the kitchen.

“She said her baby is sick, took an early bus to her village to see an **herbolario**.”

“Who’s that? **Una bruja**? A witch doctor?”

"Do not make me laugh. That is her native doctor."

"Damn! I told her she can't leave the house without calling me first," he said in a rising voice. *The incident with that damn maestro would not have happened if Carmen were around.* In case of a mental relapse, he was reminded again: *Gabby must not be alone*. "Nothing seems to work right these days," he worried. "If Carmen doesn't show up tomorrow, I shall hire another housekeeper. I mean **otra ama de casa**."

"No! **No mas hooskipper.** I do the house work. I save you money, money…." Nervous about his idea, she was determined to become more useful and indispensable to him.

"Gabby, we can't go into that discussion again. You have your studies and homework to do." Another item had been hanging fire over him. *She must get trained in certain skills which would land her a real job.* Leery of male tutors, he added, "I'm thinking of hiring two lady tutors for you. Your studies and homework, I consider, are serious business. **Son asuntos muy serios**." He paused to gauge her reaction.

"But I like Señor Fajardo. I am learning about bookkeeping and office procedures. Keep him, pleeze, **patron**?"

"Is he to be trusted?"

"Si, si, **patron**. Señor Fajardo is a religious man. He belongs to the **Caballeros de la Orden de Colon**."

"Well then, if you insist, we shall retain him. You need a lady tutor for your English and arithmetic." Something else crossed his mind. "Doña Maria Luisa is inviting us to come on weekends to their ranch and go horseback riding with them. She told me last week but I keep forgetting."

"**De veras**? Really?" Her pools of turquoise glowed with anticipation. "**Que precioso!** I am a happy girl! Wheee!" She was dancing the steps of a **merengue** without music while preparing roast beef sandwiches. After the sandwiches were ready, she threw oil and vinegar into a bowl of leafy salad and mixed the ingredients.

While waiting for lunch, Scottie had gone to the patio where he read the newspapers. Still, he was bothered by what Mel told him that morning. His distracted attention could not absorb the news items and he stole glances at Gabby through the kitchen's large window.

I could love that woman and be happy with her forever. Oh God! If I only could.... His morale took another nosedive.

The doorbell rang. He did not react until he remembered Carmen was not around to answer the door. "I'll answer it," he told her in a loud voice. "Must be someone from the office." *Something always happens at the office whenever the phone is not working*. Complaining silently, he opened the front door. There was no one. Venturing outside, he scanned the tree-lined road where not a soul was in sight. Turning around to go back inside, his left foot tripped over an object lying by the door. There was a weak cry. Looking down, there was a blanket-covered wicker basket. When he pull the blanket down, Scottie could not believe his eyes.

"Oh my God! A baby!" Scottie swallowed hard. Taking a closer look, he saw a wrinkled reddish face and tiny moving arms. *Must be just a couple of days old.* Overwhelmed and suddenly feeling helpless, he hollered, "Gabby! Come out quick! **Venga aqui pronto**!"

She came out holding up her blue apron and a spatula in hand. "**Que quieres conmigo**?" Speechless by then, he could only point at the basket. Her chatter got the baby excited and began cooing and moving its arms rapidly about. "**Una bebe! Que linda**! Amazed at the bonanza, she stooped down for a closer look. *The baby's eyes were nearly shut,* she observed, pulling the blanket to shade the baby's face. "The sunlight is too strong for her. She must be just a few days old."

"That's exactly what I thought." He was getting mad. "I wonder who is the irresponsible mother? Just imagine! Abandoning her!"

The baby opened its mouth and yawned.

"Oh-h-h!" Gabby smiled, captivated by the tiny tyke. "I love this baby. I wonder if it is a boy or a girl?"

"Hell! How am I supposed to know! It's just...another baby. That's all." Scottie was uneasy, nervous that someone left him with a baby. Having grown up without babies around, he was at wits end what to do next. Carrie was only two years younger than he and he did not remember her as a baby. Only maiden aunts abound when he was growing up in Laredo. Recalling his feeble attempt to help Mel deliver his baby, he wondered why he didn't panic then.

"Oh! **Que guapita**! What a cute baby!" she gushed, her mother instinct charmed by the uninvited visitor. "Somebody gave this baby to us. Let us keep her."

"Don't you say that!" He shushed her, feeling very threatened by the idea. His mind shifted into high gear planning his next move. "I must talk to people who can help me dispose of this baby."

"That is no good talk about a helpless baby," she chided him. Then, she could not resist her aroused mother instinct. "Oh, **Dios mio**! She is so cute. We should keep her."

This time he ignored her fawning over the baby and started thinking aloud. "Maybe Padre Joe should know somebody. A childless couple perhaps. Even Aurora Lebrun." The very idea of a baby in his domain made him nervous.

"Do not talk to that Lebrun woman. She never had children. Especially babies." She touched the baby's nose with a finger. "Oh-h-h! What a cute tiny nose you have. **Que chiquilla linda**."

"You don't even know if the baby is a girl."

"Let's take a look...."

"Lord no! I have enough of this!" Scottie threw his slippers aside. "I'm going now and see Padre Joe. He must know a couple who wants a baby." After putting his loafers on, he stood up. "Keep an eye on her...or him. Whatever." Gabby picked up the basket and followed him to the living room.

"Damn! Something's burning in the kitchen!" A whitish smoke was spewing out of the kitchen's swinging doors.

"**Madre de Dios**!" she screamed putting down the baby basket and charging into the kitchen. "The sandwiches! **Quemao**! Burned!" As soon as she switched off the oven, he helped her open windows and fan the smoke out to the outside with towels.

"It must be the jinks," he remarked after the house was tolerably free of the smoke. "Nothing has turned out right today."

"What do you mean '**jeenks**' ?"

"Sorry, Gabby. I don't have the time to explain." After locating his wallet and set of keys, he added: "Find out who's the saint for today. We have to attend a novena to that holy guy and plead to him to remove these jinks." She knew Scottie was not a Catholic but was only rude because he was irritated someone had dumped a baby at his door.

With tires squealing, Scottie took off for the rectory. Visions of basket upon basket of babies piling up at his front door plagued him. "I won't run an orphanage in my house. Never!" he muttered to himself as the car dashed through the narrow streets. Astonished town folks, more accustomed to the slow pace of their burros and carts, turned their heads. The padre was not home but was having a leisurely lunch with Heidi inside Cafe El Porvenir when a shaky Scottie materialized at the foyer and stopped by their table with a desperate bewildered look. Juancho, who always regarded Scottie as cool and collected, was alarmed.

"Emergencia? Accidente?" Juancho inquired. Scottie did not respond, just stared at them. The padre and Heidi, surprised by his sudden appearance and strange behavior, stopped eating.

"**Estas bien**, Scootee?" Heidi was becoming concerned. Still he was stone silent.

"**Que pasa, hombre**! Can you talk at all?" the padre asked. Unlike Heidi, he was simply getting impatient by the minute. "Sit down and compose yourself."

Scottie sat down slowly, looking blankly at them with Juancho assisting with the chair. Tight-lipped, he placed his hands together on the table.

"Here, I pour you a glass full of Santa Helena," Heidi volunteered hoping the wine would relax him.

"Good girl!" the padre praised his woman and impulsively gave her a playful slap on the rump. "You have something more in your brains than your pretty **culito,** your cute rear**, eh, chica**?"

"You embarrass me," she complained frowning, relieved that other customers did not notice the padre's indiscretion. The two empty bottles, aside from the one the padre was working on, got him shellacked and was ready to take a siesta with his **mujer**.

Scottie began sipping the red wine as he thawed from his numbed condition. "Padre...you gotta help me...." His voice was faint and halting as if his words were choking him. He blinked his eyes.

"You must explain yourself more clearly, amigo, before I can help you." Annoyed with his strange behavior, the padre was tempted to chastise him.

"Padre Joe," Scottie started again, his thoughts gnawed by the fear of having to bring up that baby. "I can't believe what happened...." Unable to continue, the dead silence which followed strained his listeners' patience. "Somebody...." he attempted to explain himself again, "somebody left a baby…**un bebe**... at my door!" Getting his problem out in the open, he emptied his glass of Santa Helena with one swig. "**Fijate**, just think, left her baby! to me...a bachelor! **Un soltero**!"

The padre and Heidi sighed with relief while Juancho's face broke into a big smile. Now that they knew what bothered him.

"That is easy to explain, amigo," the padre said. "You have become famous for hundreds of kilometers around as **'El Patron'** who is ready to help anybody. Just think how many parents of our parish school who are grateful for your donation of desks and blackboards. And the **liga de beisbol** you organized for the boys in Barrio Chino. And for the **liga de voleibol** for the **chicas**, you gave nets and **balones**. Any time of day, you are there to give support and encouragement to the less fortunate. And now, some luckless woman believes you can help her baby to a better life."

"But...but...I'm not a woman...." Scottie protested getting desperate again. "I can never be a mother...." Finishing what little was left in his glass, he stood up. "Looks like you won't be able to help me with this problem. I'm sorry I interrupted your lunch. **Lo siento**."

"**Un momento**!" the padre stood, reached and hooked his arm to Scottie's. "I was talking to Señora Lebrun a few evenings before. There is a couple, she mentioned, who are despairing for a child. I have seen that poor woman attending novenas, one after another, begging **la Santissima Virgen de los Remedios** for a baby. I can' t remember her name. How about another **copita** before you go?"

"Thanks, Padre Joe. I'd better go." Scottie got up. "I mean I must run along. 'Bye, Heidi, Juancho...."

Before they could wish him luck, he was already inside his pickup careening in great haste disappearing behind clouds of dust.

The scene was unlikely. Scottie, repelled by "that woman," was ringing the doorbell of Señora Lebrun's two-story house. He had enough of her over aggressiveness and on the other side of the coin, self-pitying character. But desperate to solve his "baby dilemma," he had no choice. Minutes trickled by and nobody answered the door despite that he could hear a radio blaring inside.

"SE-ÑO-RAH-H LE-BRU-N-N-N!" he shouted thunderously venting his impatience. His loud voice was carried through the narrow street down to the theatre below at the street's dead end and echoed back to him. The involuntary possession of a baby transformed him into a desperate loudmouth. Any delay in solving the baby problem frayed his nerves even more. He hollered once more, even louder.

"Sh-h-h!" Somebody shushed him from a slightly open window on the second floor. "Come up the side door. To your left. It's open."

Sounded like Aurora, he thought, but he could not see distinctly with the bright sun at high noon. Walking to the side door, it dawned on him siesta time had arrived. *What if Pablo comes home and sees me inside alone with his wife*? He had to think fast explaining to the violent husband what they were up to during the siesta. The questionable timing of his visit was giving him some second thoughts. But the vision of the tiny baby and the never-ending diapers hanging everywhere in his apartment hovered vividly in his mind -- he decided to take the risk.

The side door was jammed shut as he tried to open it. Getting into a fit, he pulled and pushed the door knob until the wall shook. "Damn! and dammit!" he swore. If no busybodies were peeking behind their window curtains by then, the noisy racket and loud cusses he was generating should alert them of his perceived vicarious tryst. Unexpectedly, the door hinges gave way. The strong sunlight invaded a dusty and obviously neglected stairway. Entering and closing the loose door gingerly behind him, it became dark inside. Reluctantly, he climbed up blindly one slow step at a time feeling the next step carefully with one of his shoes.

A flashlight beamed on the stairs from above. "**Suba aqui pa' arriba.** Up here," Aurora said. "Be careful. **Cuidao**. Do not fall." The stairs creaked as Scottie climbed with more confidence to the second floor. He noted the second floor was darkened too.

"How come you don't have lights here and above the stairway? Your window shutters are down."

"Nobody has used those stairs since **Abuela** Escolastica fell down and died of her injuries."

"Oh my God!" he gasped, imagining the ghastly accident. Getting over the shock, he was still unclear why Aurora had not explained he had to enter by the decrepit side door and the darkened interior. "Why didn't you let me in by your front door?" He demanded, smarting about the lost time getting in from that side door which he could have used for the unfinished chores at the office.

"Pablo took off last night, locked the front door, and kept the only key. I do not know where he is." Scottie thought that was the dumbest thing to do he had ever heard of since he bought a used jeep in Isfahan. Its ignition key also served as the front door key of the former jeep owner's house!

"Come here to the **sala**," she told him pointing the flashlight to the spacious living room facing the street.

"It's too dark here, Aurora. **Muy oscuro**. Could you possibly turn on a lamp, maybe that one on the side table? Please? **Por favor**?" He could not stand dark places. As a child, he demanded a lighted lamp in his bedroom before he was able to sleep.

She obliged and turned on the table lamp beside the couch. With light in the room, he noted she was still wearing a morning coat. "Please sit down. Would you like a beer or perhaps a sherry?"

"After what I've been through, I could use a beer if you can spare one," he replied sitting down on the couch. "I've been running a sweat all morning."

Aurora knitted her eyebrows unsure what he meant by "running a sweat." Anyway, she thought, these **norteamericanos** have a peculiar manner of talking. She poured more sherry for herself and handed him the beer. Drinking straight from the bottle, and not from the glass she provided, convinced her of his eccentricity.

"Aurora! Your eyes are bloody! **Sangrientos**!" He remarked naively seeing her face clearly for the first time. Embarrassed by him, she wished she had turned on the lamp in the dining room which was farther away.

"**Si**, Scootee, I am glad you are with me during this trying time," she confessed peering at him with her bloodshot, scheming eyes. "I was crying since last night." Starting to sob, she was out to win his sympathy. "That is why I did not hear you knock."

Determined not to waste any more time, he just wanted the name and address of the childless couple from her and then return to the office right away. "I want to apologize for shouting but I'm desperate about that ...."

"Not necessary to apologize," she intervened. "I am in worse shape since Pablo beat me up again last night after drinking fourteen bottles of **guarapo**. Then he had the nerve to accuse me of stealing money from his wallet." Raising her hands towards the heavens, she swore, "**Dios sera´ mi testigo**. I saved money from the food allowance and have the right to do what I want with that money. I can bet on horses if I want to. I have my God-given rights as a woman. God is my witness! I warned him. **Pero estaba muy borracho**. I tell you he is becoming worse, **peor**...." She rambled on with her sob story frustrating him to get a word in.

"Aurora, I have something important...."

"God is my witness! I must leave him for good. Leave this dreadful town and the dreadful people who hate me. One of these days, I shall die of fright when Pablo beats me again with that leather..."

"Aurora, I must tell you about..," he tried to interrupt her.

"...belt. I got to leave and you must help me escape before I get crazy and end up at the insane asylum in Santa Marta. Tomorrow I must...."

Disgusted beyond civility, Scottie jumped up from the couch surprising her in mid-sentence. Running down the rickety stairs, he pushed the loose door open and took off as if the dead grandma was chasing after him. He left his parked pick-up truck.

"**Espera**, Scootee, wait," she shouted from the window. "Come back, pleeze...." He was sprinting four blocks away with the trained gait of his Laredo High track days. Not for one second did he slow down until he reached the sanctuary of his office.

Mauro and the rest of the office help were surprised to see him breathing hard and sweating. *Never again,* he swore locking himself inside his office, *will I ever visit that crazy...(*a couple of more puffs) *stupid...* (more puffs) *broad....*

****

"Jooh-nee can roon," Gabby read aloud a first grade textbook pursing her lips which Scottie viewed as exaggerated mannerism due to her nervousness learning a new tongue and limited schooling. It had been two weeks since she had those last lessons from the lecherous maestro. Scottie was even more circumspect on hiring another tutor -- checking references even for a lady teacher. Señora Maria Luisa, the mayor's wife, had taken over Gabby like a surrogate aunt and was helping Scottie find a suitable tutor.

"Run," he corrected her. "Just relax, and try not to pull your mouth. Say 'run,' " he repeated.

"I was not pulling my mouth." She was indignant, disagreeable.

"Okay, let us not waste more time arguing. Say, 'run.' "

"Run," she repeated. Her enunciation was perfect this time. "But this word is spelled with a vowel, u, and should be pronounced 'rooh-n.' "

"Forget to think in Spanish. In English, it's pronounced 'run.' You pronounced it correctly. Let me hear you say it again."

"English is too hard," she grumbled. "In Spanish you pronounce words like it is written."

"You'll get used to speaking in English. Now, let's go on."

"I can roon...I mean...run.

"Good!"

"Susie can run...."

Half hour later, she was tiring of the lesson and wishing silently he would not be so pushy, **agresivo**. But she had an idea.

"We should leave this place and live in America where everybody speaks English. Then, I can speak English like Americans…."

"You got a point there. But we live in Peñalosa. I have to work here and you are learning English right here. Now, let's leave English and move on to arithmetic. Where's your math book?"

Gabby was amazed with her **patron's** patience and dedication to her education, his desire for her to become an office secretary. "**Que maravilloso!** You are so patient with me, so understanding, so kind, so different from other men." At last, her turquoise eyes were filled with admiration for her **hombre**. Those worshipful eyes betrayed her adoration for him which made him smile. He decided to move on with the lesson.

Two math lessons for tonight was his target. "We were on page twenty-three last time, I think. I have this book marker here. So, we start on page twenty-four. Hey! This is easy. We have multiplication with two sets of numbers...." He pointed at them. "You call them aloud as you write those numbers and their products on the sheet, okey-dokey?"

One hour passed, then, another half-hour. Gabby was struggling with the multiplication slowly, grudgingly.

Suddenly, they became aware that the baby was crying. "I will warm the bottle," she told him scurrying quickly to the kitchen before he could insist on continuing the lesson. Unknown to her, he was more fatigued than her, unaccustomed with tutoring.

His thoughts drifted from the lesson to the vexing "baby problem." The British-made washing machine in the apartment was too small and could not keep up with the onslaught of the dirty diapers. Within two days, he hired a washer woman. *Never in my wildest dream have I envisioned living in a South American town with a balcony whose view was marred by a sagging laundry line full of wet diapers of a baby who was not even my own! Cripes!*

After taking care of the pending business items in the office, he was back at Aurora's house. Eating his own words, he was at a loss whom to contact about his "baby problem" except the "silly, stupid broad." This time, he placed his hand boldly over her mouth without warning scaring the wits out of her. Taken aback by his brusque approach, for once she was ready to listen to him.

"I shall help you with your problem with Pablo," he began apologetically, "but for God's sake, you got to find me that couple first who wanted to adopt a baby so badly." Expressing his despair, he confessed, "I'm going out of my mind if that baby were to stay another week at my apartment. **Este asunto es muy serio para mi**!" This problem is very serious for me.

"You must have the Cerruzas in mind. Let us go and visit them."

So finally, the "baby problem" was resolved painlessly for Scottie and his excruciating discomfort melted away. The Cerruzas were overjoyed to adopt the sweetly disposed baby boy and willingly spent a small fortune for the legal procedure. Gabby, who had gotten attached to the baby, shed profuse tears when it was time to hand over the "bundle of joy" to the couple. With legal red tape surmounted, it was easy to guess who were asked to become the **madrina** and **padrino** for the baby's christening.

Aurora, after innumerable talk sessions with Scottie and some consultations with Padre Joe, was dissuaded from escaping her perennial abuser, at least for the time being. Padre Joe, full of anger and blustery threats, raked the coals over the contrite wife beater while waving a prepared excommunication edict for the bishop's signature.

To stay clear of Aurora's nagging and avoid verbal confrontation, Pablo began to spend the nights with his buddies playing Spanish cards and dominoes at the Bodegon Alegria and prowling questionable dens outside town and finally coming home during the small hours of the morning and sleeping all day long. After that excommunication threat from the padre, the domestic life of the Lebruns settled to an undeclared truce and uneasy co-existence much to everybody's relief.

Ostensibly, the "Committee of Three," as the trio of Padre Casals, Aurora, and Scottie, facetiously dubbed themselves, had been congregating at Cafe El Porvenir several evenings a week to discuss and plan the next social event for the town: the **verbena** for San Martin de Porres, a religious fiesta with a bacchanalian underlay. Beyond a palpable reason to hold their quasi-civic meetings, each committee member had a compelling need to get away from his or her domestic life.

For Aurora, planning the next fiesta always had been a compulsive craving since she got married to the abusive boring Pablo. Without a hand on organizing the fiestas, she told her friends she might just as well write her epitaph and hang herself. Ever since Heidi became chummy with Gabby, (who was provided with dressy clothes and fine lingerie by her doting **patron**), Heidi began to whine to the padre for a bigger clothes allowance and shopping trips to Bogota′ which he could ill afford on his clerical stipends. The "committee meetings" gave the beleaguered padre an excuse to get away from her nagging. Scottie was tiring of the tutoring duties with a reluctant Gabby. After he hired a lady tutor for English and arithmetic, he enjoyed some evenings away from her. Lately she was overly possessive of his companionship.

With Pablo virtually vanquished from Aurora's life, she felt liberated. Heidi did not appreciate her sugar-daddy-with-cassock to spend that much time with the hateful domineering Aurora. Neither did Gabby like her hombre to spend those committee evenings away from her.

Every night the "Committee of Three" held court at Cafe El Porvenir, chances were Heidi and Gabby usually got together at the latter's **quinta**. During one Saturday evening while these lonesome two were sipping their umpteenth glasses of sherry on the terrace, Gabby's patient waiting for Scottie to come home was nearing the flash point after half past eleven. Although the padre was the prime instigator for the nocturnal gatherings, Gabby blamed Aurora as the scheming manipulator who wanted revenge on the two by depraving them of their **hombres**.

"Scootee told me we shall be giving parties. I want the first one to start **prontisimo**!" There was something in the humid breeze which triggered Gabby to lose her patience. Instantly, her smoldering anger exploded. "I must find an excuse not to invite Aurora! That vixen! I hate her! **La odio!"** She punched an innocent pillow on the garden love seat to vent her fury. "I want my **hombre** right here. By my side."

"You have to think of something clever to exclude that **perra**, that bitch from your parties," Heidi pouted while toying with a glass of sherry.

"Well then," Gabby added up their consensus, "I will not invite her to the parties." She snapped her fingers as if that would vanish Aurora into thin air.

"You cannot get rid of that **perra** so easily. By now she has our **hombres** by their ears, especially Scootee. Listen, I got a better idea." Heidi poured more sherry into her glass. "Why not send invitation cards to couples only? Since Pablo is never around and she hates him, then she, being alone, would not be able to show up for the party. **Ya! ya! Eso es!** That's it!"

"**Perfecto! Muy bien!** That is a smart idea, Heidi." In her excitement, Gabby knocked down her glass. "**Madre de Dios**!" Suddenly, she was feeling dizzy and saw Heidi, the house and everything else turning in a rapid blurry spin. "**Pronto**, Heidi! Get my medicine! Two pink pills! Medicine cabinet! Bathroom!" Carmen, who was eavesdropping behind the door, nearly collided with Heidi in the living room as she had already the two pills and a glass of water. Together, they held up a groggy Gabby and tucked her in bed.

The following day, Gabby recovered and was her normal self again. She did not remember what happened to herself last night. Carmen, busy with her house chore, forgot to tell Scottie. That evening, Gabby decided to try some French cuisine recipes which she had been learning secretly from a chef. Carmen assisted her in the preparation and cooking of a French dinner. Besides demonstrating her ability to cook exotic dishes for the promised parties, she wanted to hint strongly to her **hombre** that her dinners were worth staying at home for. That evening, she was happy to keep her **hombre** away from another "dreadful committee meeting."

"Hey! This lobster tastes great! What do you call it?" Scottie asked relishing the unusual dish for supper.

"Howard a la Parisienne."

"I don't know if I can remember all those French names but I love this food." With slender candlesticks and a Madeira hand woven table cloth, the dinner glowed in an atmosphere contrasting in his mind with Cafe El Porvenir of its rustic noisy setting. Gabby had shooed Carmen away to her private room. "And what's this dish? I bet you have some fancy French name for it too."

"Pommes saladaise."

"I knew it! Fancy words for potato salad." It finally dawned on him that Gabby had been up to something behind his back. A few months back, he recalled that Gabby could not tell the difference between a dinner fork from a dessert fork nor a water goblet from a brandy glass. "Where did you learn how to set the table and cook these delicious dishes?"

"I can't tell you. It's my secret," she answered coyly pleased that she got her **hombre** wondering.

"Come on! You wouldn't keep a secret from me, would you?"

"Well, you have been staying away so many evenings and I have been studying…**como un estudiante con mucha diligencia**...." Smiling enigmatically, she was not about to reveal her covert cooking lessons, at least not yet, and was satisfied to get her sweet revenge for those solitary nights.

"To change the subject, the bosses in Bogota′ decided that it's time to show the Commissioner of Public Works how the highway project is coming along. And that means...we're going to throw a party, a big party in his honor."

"**Ay, que bueno**!" What Scottie just told her was music to her spirits. All these months she had been preparing for this chance to demonstrate her abilities to him. *The long hours I spent learning from Señor Ortiz has finally paid off,* she thought and recalled again what the chef kept telling her about those special dishes: "Worthy of serving to the King of France."

To Gabby's delight, planning the party kept Scottie home every night. She feigned being dumb on certain aspects of the party preparations in order to get her **hombre** concerned and come home every night foregoing his habitual stopover at the Cafe after work. Their interminable discussions about the party led to frequent hugs and kisses initiated by her. Trying hard to be kissed on her lips but not being obvious about it, she was disappointed that somehow her **hombre** would always end up giving her a peck on the forehead. She was falling madly in love with this adorable gentle fellow. There and then, she decided he shall become more than just her **patron.** *There will never be another hombre like Scootee to cross my life again.* ***If*** *he does not marry me soon, I shall seduce him and become his mistress. Have his baby. Then, he will marry me* ***para siempre****!*

The preparations for the maiden party at the **quinta** went into high gear stressing out a nervous Scottie. Telephone calls and telexes buzzed back and forth between the Bogota′ and Peñalosa offices. Temporary workers were hired to spruce up the courtyard. New trees and shrubs were planted along the inside walls. New expensive drapes, on special order from a commercial interior-decorator house in Bogota′, replaced the old ones in the dining and living rooms. Multi-colored lights were strung all over the courtyard reaching to the roof. Additional spotlights were mounted at floor level from the second-story's balcony.

For several nights, Scottie studied the overall lighting requirements and its control system until he was satisfied with the ambience he desired depending on the time of the night and the crowd's mood. Rafael, whom he considered the smartest foreman, was assigned to the lighting and music monitoring and control. Using his carefully prepared program and prearranged hand signals with Rafael, he would be able to make instant changes with the lighting and musical pieces played by the combo. Mauro, the comical handyman, gave advice and a hand with the installation of the floodlights and sound system.

While Gabby watched the preparations Scottie was supervising in the courtyard and inside the house, she concentrated on the menu and ordering of the soft drinks, beer, and wines, the table settings and flower arrangements and where the bar would be set up. Although the food was catered, Gabby insisted on deciding the menu and having the preparation of the ingredients right at the quinta. Scottie complimented her for the manner she was conducting herself. Silently, he was gratified there was no inkling of her malady despite the stress she was subjected to by the party preparations. She made several more secret trips to Señor Ortiz' house for some last-minute coaching on the menu and choice of wines.

If Scottie had not been checking up on her studies regularly, she would have devoted her total attention on the party preparations. When he suggested that she should get some help from the veteran fiesta organizer, Aurora, she used her wiles on him so she would not be obliged to contact Aurora. He was not aware that Aurora was being blackballed from the party.

When the invitation cards were sent out to the high and mighty of the Cuyapo′ Valley, the news of the grand party traveled swiftly especially in Peñalosa. Aurora, with hardly any friends left, did not hear about the party for that weekend. When she saw Padre Casals at a wine store on that Wednesday, the padre assumed Aurora had received an invitation and remarked casually that Gabby ordered several cases of his favorite Santa Helena for the party. On learning about the party, she was shocked to her wits for not having received an invitation card. Putting up a front, she lied to the padre that she also received an invitation and learned from him some of the invited guests: many of whom she considered below her social status. Coming home feeling distressed, she locked herself inside. Her self-esteem took a deep plunge while angrily speculating why Scottie did not send her an invitation.

On Friday before the party, Scottie read the guest list and discovered Aurora was not on it. Asked about this discrepancy, Gabby admitted reluctantly the invitation was sent to Aurora that morning and she had not listed her name yet. Scottie, becoming suspicious, asked more questions and learned a couples-only invitation card and a R.S.V.P. return card was sent in Pablo's name.

"If we follow your couples-only rule, then, Señor Pertierra, the guest of honor, can't be invited since he's a widower. And so with the bosses who are coming without their wives."

Chastised, Gabby had no choice but to send a regular invitation with Aurora's name by a special messenger keeping her chagrin to herself. Scottie smelled a conspiracy against Aurora but decided to let the incident pass.

On Saturday morning, Scottie was edgy due to last minute glitches like blown fuses. This time, the happy busy Gabby had a calming influence on him. Amazingly enough for him, the perceived inexperienced Gabby kept at her task until the cooks, waiters, helpers and the caterer himself, were working together with clocklike diligence. At dusk, all the necessary tasks for the party fell into place like pieces in a jigsaw puzzle and the assembled crew at the **quinta** was ready for the big evening. Even the hired waiters in their white jackets and black trousers harmonized with the meticulously set tables which had fresh flowers of vivid colors displayed in crystal vases, immaculately white smoothed-down table cloths, sparkling clear wine glasses, shining silverware, tulip-shaped napkins on the dinner plates under the glow of lighted thin scarlet candles. A combo, borrowed from Hotel Nacional was rehearsing in the court yard with musical pieces selected by Gabby. A temporary black-and-brown parquet floor was installed temporarily in the middle of the courtyard for dancing to accommodate at least fifty couples.

By seven that evening, Scottie was tired but pleased that he could affirm to himself that his place was ready for the party. Gabby was too excited to feel tired and was stirring about with what he jokingly described as her "nervous energy."

"Great work, Gabby," Scottie praised her as they viewed the transformed courtyard. "Let's keep at it."

"**Gracias**. Glad you are pleased. **Lo hago para ti**. I did it for you," she confessed. Those devoted pools of turquoise glistened from the candlelight like windows to her passionate soul. Sitting side by side on the terrace and reviewing the whole ensemble, Scottie became emotionally keyed up. A soft tender kiss was inevitable and imparted on the receptive damsel. Yet during that flitting moment, he did not give her even a hint of commitment which she had been expecting since that impassioned drive home from Piscina Tamayo. Worried about his secret, he was hurting inside. More frustrated and apprehensive about expressing his affection he knew was impossible to consummate.

A waiter approached them informing Scottie of a telephone call interrupting their magical interlude. Mauro called from Hotel Nacional and told him Señor Pertierra had just checked in with his young wife. *Young wife?* Scottie was certain he was a widower. *A mistress?* He was concerned. The press had been invited and he would not savor any scandalous gossip leaking into Bogota's newspapers tomorrow and overshadowing the highway inauguration. Scottie was biting his lips wishing the pepper-haired commissioner would not show up with his mistress at the party.

Messieurs J.J. Whitelaw, the general manager, and W. Corry Jefferson, the operations manager, of the Bogota´ office, were the first to arrive to the party. From their astounded looks, Scottie knew they were impressed with what Gabby noted and whispered to Scottie as "**ambiento magico**" of the party set-up.

"Amazing!" J.J. remarked looking around, pleased with the party setting. "Congrats, Scottie."

"If anybody deserves recognition for organizing the party, Gabby does." Scottie told the bosses after introducing her. He believed strongly in giving recognition to whoever deserved it. Moreover, he was still under the glow of their stronger bonding brought on by working side-by-side with the party preparations. W. Corry acted a bit clumsy towards her betraying his thoughts of presumed illicit relationship between the two. J.J., more worldly wise than W. Corry, cracked a few jokes which Gabby understood, coaxed her to laugh, putting her at ease.

Taking Scottie aside, J.J. hinted strongly to Scottie that pleasing Señor Pertierra, was of paramount importance since this commissioner's decisions were crucial to future government contracts. On Monday, Señor Pertierra was scheduled to inspect the new highway. Naturally, Scottie would like to make a good impression on him.

Next to arrive was Aurora Lebrun, resplendent once more in her festive trademark of the white flowing Grecian chiton and adorned with an antique Inca gold chain and a two-carat emerald pendant, her family heirloom, dangling on her ample bosom. She greeted everyone with civility including Gabby, betraying not a smidgen of rancor which Gabby had anticipated from her.

Padre Casals showed up in a sporty sky-blue safari outfit with only a cleric's collar to denote his calling. Without hesitation, he complimented Scottie and Gabby on the party decor. Minutes later, Heidi came through the kitchen's back door where Gabby had arranged to meet her. They retired to a secluded corner of the courtyard exchanging the latest town gossip. While Aurora was conversing with the mayor of Villapuente, she was watching these two gabbing women and trying to read their lips. Heidi wore an eye-catching red dress with many flounces, frills and a low decolletage. Mad but helpless about Heidi's outfit, the padre was careful not to arrive with her. The moment Heidi joined the chatting group with the padre, he began scolding her for revealing too much skin. Lately, they had been embroiled in petty domestic issues.

With more guests pouring in, Scottie checked his watch wondering what was causing Señor Pertierra's delayed arrival. His disquieting nervousness was aggravated by J.J.'s repeated eagerness reminding Scottie, "We got to please Señor Pertierra. Do everything to keep him happy. I give you a blank check." Close by, W. Corry was nodding his approval and placed his hand on Scottie's shoulder with his body language implying Scottie's own personal success depended on pleasing the commissioner.

The doorman announced the arrival of another group. Scottie did not catch the name and assumed the commissioner and his entourage had rolled in their limousines. He was wrong. Don Jose´ Luis, the mayor, stepped out of the car followed by his wife. The six town councilors and their wives trailed behind them in their cars. While greeting these guests, Scottie was apprehensive if Señor Pertierra was in some sort of trouble.

By then, Aurora was drinking compulsively one glass of sherry after another while her voice noticeably increased in reach and loudness to the consternation of other guests and especially Gabby, who was annoyed. Only when eating hors d'oeuvres did Aurora take a respite from imbibing the sherry which the solicitous waiters kept pouring into her glass. Meandering and gabbing with guests, Aurora would laugh obscenely with the least provocation while shaking hands and kissing just about everyone as if she was campaigning for a political office.

The much awaited black Mercedes-Benz limousine finally arrived. As the guests stepped out, they were readily identified by the doorman who immediately dashed in to alert Scottie. In turn, Scottie zipped outside in time to open the car door himself. Señor Pertierra, a man of dignified mien with wavy pepper-and-salt hair, stepped out, recognized and greeted Scottie (who was relieved the commissioner remembered him since their meeting two years ago in San Francisco) with a Latin **abrazo**. Then Scottie reached inside the limousine to assist his pretty companion out while noting her long luxuriant raven black hair and off-shoulder black evening dress which contrasted with her peachy white complexion. Her enormous breasts subtly encased by the bodice drew his attention as well.

"This is my daughter, Maria Consuelo," the commissioner introduced his companion to Scottie who discerned a haughty mien behind her plastic half-hearted smile. Deep-set azure eyes dominated her small almond-shaped face.

They make an impressive pair, Scottie concluded and breathed easier knowing the paramour gossip was untrue. *The newshounds can concentrate on the positive stories of the who's who attending the party.* "How was your ride from Bogota?"

"No problem," Señor Pertierra answered. "It was fine weather all the way." As they entered the foyer, J.J. and W. Corry zeroed in on the prized guests. J.J. and Señor Pertierra did the Latin **abrazo**. followed by ceremonial backslappings. W. Curry performed the same ritual but was more perfunctory than J.J.

"Nice to have you here, Joselito," J.J. effused with implied familiarity. Señor Pertierra introduced his daughter to them who displayed the same plastic smile through an insouciant exchange of civilities.

J.J. and W. Corry focused their attention exclusively on the commissioner monopolizing his attention with small talk about events in Bogota´. With Scottie's bosses practically turning their backs on him, he felt ignored, stranded with Maria Consuelo.

"Joselito," J.J. gushed, "Let's fix ourselves some glorious drinks. What's your pleasure tonight, amigo?" His hand on the commissioner's shoulder, J.J. steered him towards the bar on the terrace with W. Corry trailing a step behind them.

It looks like buttering up the commissioner has been taken off my hands, Scottie thought sarcastically. Despite his aversion of being left with a strange woman, he escorted her gallantly to the living room where she drew curious glances from the other guests.

"Who really are these jerks who shanghai'ed my father away?" she asked with eyes blazing. Scottie was startled by her sarcasm and unexpected Yankee twang.

Her sharp tongue, he concluded*, didn't harmonize with her demure appearance.* "I'm sorry," he apologized to her. "Those are my bosses from Bogota´."

"That explains it," she replied, twitching her mouth. "Their decadent intentions are so obvious." She kept firing more caustic salvos which got him concerned that such behavior might ruin the party.

I must soothe her ruffled feelings, he decided. "Your English is quite colloquial. I didn't expect that from you." He refrained from complimenting her Yankee twang not sure if she would take offense. Then, he noticed her face softened which he thought was brought on by his appreciative compliments. *It's a good omen.*

"That makes us even. Your Spanish is very Castilian," she countered, her azure blue eyes focusing benignly on him.

Was she being sarcastic? Scottie was cautious and could not recall if he spoke in Spanish at length when he greeted them at the porte cochere. Anyway, he decided to take the remark at face value. "Do I detect a Bostonian accent too?"

"Hey! You're very observant." Her attitude softened further with their friendly banter. She was beginning to like this engaging **norteamericano.** "I took courses at Barnard for three summers and stayed at my aunt's house in Cambridge. Her husband was a Fullbright exchange professor at that time." Then, she added, still doubtful, "Do you really think I have a Bostonian accent? My God! You're the first person to tell me that!"

"You certainly don't have that suh-thern drawl, ma'am, where I come from." Sensing his hokum, she laughed heartily radiating sparkles from her azure blue eyes and causing her enormous breasts to jiggle.

"Call me Concha, please. I think we shall become friends."

"Yes, why not!" he answered smiling even though he had reservations on the proffered friendship. Her earlier acerbic remarks did not sit too well with him. "How about a drink?"

"A glass of cream sherry would be nice."

"I'll be back in a jiffy," he promised and headed for the kitchen aware that the two bars did not have cream sherry. While he was searching for the cream sherry his mind was assessing Concha's personality: *She's quite a frank woman. Rare for a Latin girl. And quite independent too*. He located the cream sherry among the Perrier bottles. *Gabby is just the opposite. So dependent on me.* On the way back, he picked up a margarita from the terrace bar. J.J. and W. Corry, he noted, had completely barricaded Señor Pertierra between the terrace bar and themselves oblivious of everyone else.

Aurora crossed Scottie's path and whispered to him, "Careful with my niece. She's quite a woman." Concha was still standing where Scottie left her, talking to no one and just stood out in contrast from the other guests for her Amazonian built and colossal breasts.

"Shall we sit down and talk?" Concha suggested after accepting the sherry. Several items to check and make sure that everything was running smoothly came to his mind but he could not leave her just then. They sat down on one of the snowy velvet covered sofas in the reception room which led to the living room and farther away from the noisy combo in the courtyard.

After a few minutes of chat, he knew he must extricate himself and get on with his chores. Gabby was nowhere in sight as he scanned the courtyard speculating how she would react with Concha sitting next to him. He had noticed lately that Gabby was possessive of him and this time jealous to see him with this sexy guest. While they talked, Concha was sizing up Scottie. Although they just met, she was intrigued by this Spanish-speaking **norteamericano.** There was something about him which got her juices galloping and her tongue loosely coarse, especially after a few gulps of cream sherry.

"I can read your mind, Scottie," she said when he was quiet and was searching for an excuse to leave her. "Let's see what you're thinking now... 'What is a girl like her doing in Bogota´? Is she engaged to some guy? Is she still a virgin?' "

Scottie was dumbfounded unable to speak as she giggled and wiggled her body suggestively. Blushing from her brazen vulgarity, the dim light in the reception room did not betray his reddened face. Something intimidating about Concha kept him from leaving her sooner.

"So much for your dirty thoughts," she assumed her coarse assault would push him under her spell and this attractive fellow was ripe for her undisclosed scheme. "I have a certificate on anthropology from Javierana. During those summers at Barnard, I took courses on archeology." He blinked his eyes, befuddled by her sudden switch to benign cultural achievements. "Digging into the past has become my cardinal passion," she added, still sizing up her quarry.

"So what have you done lately to satisfy this cardinal passion of yours?" Dubious of her motives, he became sardonic.

"It may surprise you," she laughed at his provocative rejoinder, still unsure who this man really is, and decided to impress him. "I participated in several digs in Crete. The last one was three years ago. For May this year I signed up to dig in Antalya. That is in southern Turkey. Next time, I would like to be sponsored by a foundation for a dig right here in Colombia. Are you aware there's an Inca temple some three hundred forty kilometers south of Peñalosa?

He confessed his ignorance about the existence of this ruin and added, "I didn't know the Incas came this far, north of Peru. But I'm no expert on the Incas nor on pre-Colombian archeology like you." *Is she serious? Or just leading me on?*

"That's exactly what I want to prove. My hunch tells me the Incas built a road to Cuyapo´ valley. Some fifteen years ago a **campesino** from Villapuente brought several rocks with Inca-like shapes to Doctor Weiss Ramos of the Museo de Oro while he was visiting this region. Intrigued with the peculiarly hewn rocks, the doctor took this **campesino** on a trip to the ruins which, in his field sketch, were near the confluence of two rivers south of this town. If the ruins can be confirmed officially as Incan handiwork, then, it would be the farthest point north of their political center in Peru."

"How do you know for sure where these ruins are located?" *Maybe she's for real this time.* Scottie was becoming curious, totally forgetting Rafael who was waiting for him to choose the next music line-up for the evening.

"I have a copy of the map, which was sketched by the doctor, in my bags in the hotel. I want to find these ruins and start the dig soon. I want you to help me, **si**?"

"Me? To help you?" He was surprised, intrigued. "How's that?"

"With a four-wheel drive truck, we can search for the ruins. That's it." She spoke with such deliberation that he felt compelled to believe her sobriety and determination by then.

Yet how dared she make such a demand on me? he wondered, flabbergasted with the idea. *How dare she! I came here to work on road projects. My job. Not to be a tourist guide.* At a loss how to answer her, he remembered what J.J. kept repeating earlier that day: "We got to make it with Pertierra." *Maybe that includes the daughter too!*

Scottie realized he was in a pickle. Her mind was made up and like it or not, he was just appointed to be her "tour guide" to locate those ruins. "I'd better check with the bosses. My work load is heavy right now." He decided to blunt her decision to involve him by remaining noncommittal. As the evening wore on, he expected this pert woman to imbibe enough sherry that would blur her capricious idea.

The sherry should do its magic on her, he reckoned, *and that ruins-trip idea would be dissolved by the alcohol. She'd wake up with a throbbing headache in the morning and remember nothing.*

"Your bosses can stay over here in Peñalosa and hold your job while we go on this important mission," she persisted. "Look! Look at them. Their behavior at this moment tells me precisely the jobs they do in Bogota´ -- they sit on their fat **culos** all day."

*Oh brother! That retread Yankee streak comes on strong with this **mujeracha**! This gross broad!* he thought. "You can tell me that," he laughed, "but I just can't." Her continuing vulgarity was strangely turning him on. "I'll help you find the ruins if my bosses approve." He was trying to be polite and pleasant outwardly. Leaving his job during its critical phase and taking off on this wild goose chase was downright frivolous to him.

"Could you talk to your bosses tonight and get their approval?" Concha asked in a soft voice. Sparkles glistened in her eyes reverting once more to an improbable image of a sweet demure lady.

"I could try," he answered reluctantly, amazed and yet puzzled by this woman's persistence. From the corner of his eye, he spied the trio standing at the bar. *J.J. is soused up to his gills and won't make heads nor tails about this crazy trip to the ruins.*

"Oh! oh! I'm getting excited!" Concha cupped her hands over her breasts as if they were about to jump up. Suddenly she saw her dream turning into reality. "Oh! you're so nice!" She placed her arms around a much surprised Scottie and bent closer to kiss him.

"Yikes!" he shouted jumping up after an ice-cold spine tingling liquid hurried down his back. Turning, he saw Gabby behind the couch.

"O-ops! **Lo siento**! Sorry." Gabby apologized after she unloaded a watery ice bucket on him.

"What did you do that for?" Scottie was angry at her obvious prank, giving her a scolding look. By then, the cold water had reached his socks.

"I was running to tell you that dinner is almost ready. I **choque´d** into the sofa...."

"You mean you bumped into the couch."

"**Si**, then, I spilled the ice water...by accident. I...better go back to the kitchen. Sorry…Excuse me." Like a sparrow, she winged away disappearing as quickly as she had appeared.

"Who the devil is she?" Concha asked, her eyes followed Gabby's hasty retreat behind the kitchen's swinging doors.

"She is...ahem...my ward...."

"Your ward! **Espiritusanto**! That wench is not a child." She contradicted, stared at him until he looked sheepish. "Why, she is old enough to be your mistress."

"No! Nothing of the sort," he denied her charge vehemently. But she persisted with a sly, suspicious grin. "You have to excuse me. I have to change my wet clothes."

"You better," she laughed. "A man with a wet **culo** is usually not himself. And you're no exception." He grimaced and was mad of her accusation, but decided to rein in his tongue.

Making a hurried departure to his bedroom upstairs, he dressed after a quick shower. Resting on a recliner after changing into a new pair of shoes, he was perplexed by Concha's rude remark. *What does she really mean by not being myself when my ass is wet? That woman is as rough as sailors go,* he thought. *And Gabby. Why does she have to humiliate me ? I bet she was jealous of Concha sitting close to me. That's it!*

A few more guests were filling their plates when Scottie came downstairs. Some guests approached him, shook his hand, and congratulated him on the delicious food. Grateful for the compliments, he explained to them that the fresh seafood was flown directly from Cartagena and Buenaventura. Someone grasped his forearm.

"You should tell these **caballeros** that Heidi and Gabriela have worked together and organized this **fiesta estupenda**," the padre remarked in a stage whisper turning heads in the dining room. Scottie was not sure if Heidi helped that much as claimed by the padre since he had hardly seen her around during the hectic preparations. But he didn't want to discredit the padre. Hearing the padre's praise, a bashful Heidi blushed into deep pink. Scottie noted a plain-looking knitted shawl was draped over her shoulders which did not compliment her slinky red dress. Later, he learned from Gabby that the padre insisted Heidi cover her bare shoulders and decolletage. Just then, Aurora passed out while holding tightly to her sherry glass. Due to her corpulent size, four men had to carry her home.

"Where is sweet Gabriela, **ama de la casa**?" the padre boomed causing the guests to listen once more. After imbibing two bottles of Santa Helena, the padre was feeling no pain and unlikely loud with his voice. "Where is the beautiful lady of the house?" the padre shouted even louder. Scottie, as the host, was embarrassed with that implied relationship with Gabby. "We want Gabriela! We want Gabriela!" The padre fluttered with his out-stretched arms inducing the crowd to synchronize along with his chant. "We want Gabriela!" But Gabby was nowhere to be seen.

The guests, happily ensconced, eating and drinking, obligingly followed the padre's orchestrated chant, "We want Gabriela! We want Gabriela!" The chant boomed on and on.

Gabby appeared on top of the stairway hamming out a solo tableau. Smiling, posturing this way and that, placing a hand behind her nape and the other on the hip, she cocked her head slowly to a dramatic tilt. Her hairdo was done in an upswept affair cascading from a chignon.

Her pale blue satin gown with the neckline plunging nearly to her belly button made the guests freeze again and gasp. A dolled-up beauty, sexy and slinky, was about to descend on them.

Is that Gabby? Scottie looked hard unsure of the exotic beauty now descending the stairs towards him. Waving her hand like a reigning movie goddess, the crowd loved her hoity-toity showcase and applauded enthusiastically except Concha, who turned her head away and started talking again to the two ladies sitting with her on the couch.

When dinner was winding down and the guests began drifting about and gathering to talk in huddled groups, Scottie was able to lead J.J. to the rose garden away from everybody and popped Concha's request about escorting her on that trip to the presumed Inca ruins. J.J. did not answer him. He anticipated his boss was conjuring a plausible excuse which he could use to placate the commissioner's daughter of her silly ruins search and thereby letting him off the hook from that trip. J.J. began laughing irrationally to Scottie's chagrin as he waited for an answer. *Booze*, he reckoned, *has taken hold of J.J.*

Without a hint, J.J. hollered to W. Corry and Pertierra waving them to come over and join them. These tippling new buddies, still parked by the terrace bar, took a while to join J.J. and Scottie.

"My dear Joselito, your daughter has asked Scottie to help her search for some Maya ruins south of here," J.J. explained.

As a trumpeter was blaring a mariachi tune with the band, Scottie was straining to listen what J.J. was telling the commissioner and anticipating how adroitly J.J. would circumvent the daughter's request. *That would be the end of that frivolous idea.*

"Joselito, Scottie here will be at your daughter's disposal in her search for those Maya ruins."

Scottie could not believe his ears. *J.J. is toadying to the whim of the foul-mouthed dame! Disgusting!*

*"*Maya ruins?*"* Señor Pertierra was perplexed.

"Actually Incan ruins," Scottie corrected J.J.

"Okay, Inca ruins. What the hell!" J.J. waved his hands clumsily, then, holding on to W. Corry for support, too far gone with his boozing.

"I don't know noth'in'…eh…about this trip." Señor Pertierra confessed, baffled about his daughter's plan. It was obvious to Scottie that Concha had not discussed the search with him. Señor Pertierra looked around for Concha but did not see her sitting low on the high-backed couch. "Whatever you want to do with my daughter's request, **esta´ bien conmigo.** It's all right with me."

"Then, by George, we shall do it!" J.J. proclaimed as he swung his drink in a wobbly orbit spilling some on the floor. "**Caballeros**, señoras, everybody. Drink to the success for the Maya...eh...Inca ruins search! Why not! why not!" Some turned their heads but did not understand what J.J. was talking about.

Scottie, dazed by J.J.'s shabby decision, watched helplessly as his two bosses tightened their arms around Señor Pertierra with sudden bonhomie while drifting again towards the terrace bar. Left alone, he went to the kitchen and talked to the cooks when Rafael informed him the champagne and rum were running low. A cook was sent posthaste to Hotel Nacional to procure more.

Meantime Gabby was enjoying herself on the patio as men vied to dance with her. When Scottie saw these young men queued up waiting their turns to dance with her, he became jealous. As he passed by the ornate mirror hanging in the foyer, he looked at himself and noticed his graying hair. *I'll have to find some lotion to darken my hair. Then, I won't look old alongside Gabby.*

The head waiter, Scottie noticed, was talking in a loud voice with other waiters at the far corner of the terrace. Walking towards them, he passed by Concha who was still sitting with the same old ladies. He slowed his stride, hesitated, then relented about chatting with her, still sore about that frivolous ruins trip.

Concha noticed Scottie after he had passed by. Feeling sidelined for the rest of the evening, she consoled herself with her glass of sherry and the anticipation of having Scottie for herself on that ruins trip. Still, she was mystified why she was attracted to this fellow whom she hardly knew.

After giving more instructions to the waiters, Scottie saw Gabby dancing again, this time with Señor Calderon, the mayor himself. *So lovely, so desirable. No doubt, she's the princess of the party,* he was convinced. Although not an accomplished dancer, he decided he must do at least a few twirls with her before the party was over.

"The dress you're wearing. Can't remember buying it for you," he said, as they danced the basic steps of rumba which she had taught him.

"**Ahorraba plata**, you know…**moonee** from food allowance… I bought it from…salesman from Caracas…." Nervous that Scottie might get mad, nevertheless, she answered with candor.

Surprised by her own idea of saving to buy what she wanted, he wished she had asked him. *I would gladly pay for it. I've been so busy. I neglected her needs. Señora Paquita could order some dresses from Bogota´ in time for the party.*

"Do you… like it?"

"Uh...yes, it's...it's nice." The plunging neckline bothered him for he had become jealous of the guests who stared at her. "But...but I think...**demasiao desplegado**…it's too...revealing...." At last, he gathered enough courage to tell her what concerned him all evening.

"**Me siento estupenda con**...how you say it? I feel good in this dress," she defended her choice. "You want me to be…**libre y independiente, si?"**

"Okey, dokey, you win." *I have to eat my own words. I reckon.* Reluctantly, he nodded to concede.

Her intuition revealed he was jealous of the attention she was getting from other men. After a few more twists under the stars, she confessed: "I am wearing this dress so you can admire me." Bewitched by her revealing gown, his own ego was reassured. Even though that ice bucket spilling incident came to his mind, he decided not to bring it up with her.

For Gabby, it was a night to remember -- always.

CHAPTER V

Early one evening, the Cerruzas came over to the **quinta** to show off their "basket baby." It had been three weeks since the couple took responsibility for the baby. Señora Cerruza was radiating with happiness and could hardly take off her eyes from "**un ramillete del sol brillante"** or "bouquet of sunshine" as she fancied her adopted baby .

Scottie observed how much the tiny tot had grown since he almost stumbled over him on the porte cochere. After Gabby, it was his turn to look dutifully into the portable cradle and admire the baby. Those unblinking jet-black eyes looked at him so intensely as if the baby were telling him. *So, you're the guy who rejected me! Huh!* Scottie felt so guilty and was compelled to look abruptly away puzzling the señora why he behaved oddly toward the baby.

"I have forgotten the names given to the baby during the baptism. **Digame por favor?** Tell me, pleeze?" Gabby asked.

"Simon Bolivar Jose´ de San Martin Cerruza Avila," Señora Cerruza recited without batting an eye.

"Good heavens! Won't the child become confused with so many names?" Scottie was dumbfounded, unsure whether the little lady had become daffy after wishing and praying so many novenas to the Virgin Mary for a baby.

"No, no," Gabby disagreed. "When he grows up, he can choose the names he wants to use. That is the custom here."

Señora Cerruza related she had organized an adoption committee and donated their other house as a temporary home for orphans and unwanted babies. "The interior of the house will be remodeled for this purpose," she said. "The back door will always be open and an electric bell will be installed by this door. Any mother could put down her unwanted baby in an empty cradle by the sheltered back porch and leave anonymously in plenty of time before the bell starts ringing. Then, the nurse will come out and pick up the baby." Her face glowing with pride, she announced, "The orphanage shall be named '**Asilo de Ritter y Cerruza.**' "

On hearing this unsolicited honor, Scottie, red-faced, was visibly embarrassed. Her husband, Aristoteles, hardly spoke during the visit. Scottie was not a bit surprised for his wife spoke incessantly.

After the Cerruzas left, Gabby told Scottie tearfully they should have adopted the baby themselves. Since this incident with the "basket baby," she was obsessed about having a baby for herself and kept talking about the idea to Scottie, who although stone-faced, was becoming apprehensive, afraid to think what might be brewing in her mind by what means she would acquire a baby. He kept stone silent on the matter.

****

The following week was spent in feverish preparations for the Incas ruins trip and the temporary transfer of the road construction job to W. Corry. Scottie was fuming about "this unnecessary trip" to W. Corry, who in turn, was not delighted about his indefinite stay in Peñalosa. During that week of job-exchange transition, Scottie noted W. Corry's frustration with his inability to communicate with the Spanish-speaking foremen. As a practical remedy, W. Corry used Mauro as his interpreter in the office and on trips to the job site. Since Mauro was the only bilingual clerk in the Peñalosa office, the preparation of reports and transmission of telexes in English to the Bogota′ office were slowed down, and at times, postponed. Scottie made up his mind he would not worry about his job during the trip to which he referred to, sarcastically, as his "expedition of the century to nowhere."

W. Corry stayed at the Hotel Nacional where he had to contend with the cockroaches, antiquated bathroom especially getting out of the old fashioned deep bathtub with ornate legs, and the tenacious "ladies of the night" knocking on his door. He was entitled to stay at Scottie's company-leased **quinta** but politely turned it down. Grapevine news traveled fast among the expatriate employees and their families. His wife knew of that "sensuous native girl" at Scottie's house and woe to W. Corry if he ever decide to move in.

Preparations for the "expedition of the century to nowhere" were consuming Scottie's time and he was not much help to W. Corry struggling with his nearly-forgotten high-school Spanish and learning by hunch working with the rural natives of limited schooling unlike those at the Bogota′ office. A four-wheel drive Rover equipped with a winch was leased in Bogota′ and driven to Peñalosa on a rush basis. Every item for any anticipated contingency was packed into the vehicle. Two workers were snatched from the field crew to serve as helper-guides. Both spoke the Chibcha dialect of the local Indians.

During this period, Gabby was insistent on coming along. She did not trust Concha who would be alone with her **hombre** on the trip. For a couple of days, Scottie toyed with the idea of taking Gabby along although he did not tell her. With Gabby away, the **quinta** could be free for W. Corry's convenience. But later, he relented having a presentiment of animosity between the two women which could undermine the trip.

Three days before departure, he decided Gabby must stay behind and told her so. She became despondent and scarcely talked to him. It was his turn to worry that she might sink into that harmful delusion once more.

On the trip's eve, Gabby reverted to her normal self, conversing with him, even helping in the loading of the provisions into the Rover. She was somewhat subdued. Relieved with her change of attitude, he was nonetheless taking no chances. With the pretext that he was going out to buy some more canned food at the market, he used this opportunity to bring Carmen covertly to the church rectory. In Padre Casals' presence, he grilled the poor frightened maid about her responsibility for Gabby's welfare during his absence. Sweating out of fear, Carmen swore, with her hand on a missal, promising to be ever vigilant as Gabby's interim guardian.

Later in the more relaxed environment of the market place, Carmen confessed to Scottie that in her village, the parish priest was contacted solely for baptism, marriage and last rites. Since she was baptized and married once, the only sacrament she had not taken was the last rites. In a faltering voice, she said contact with any padre could speed up her death. He had to smile thinking how Christianity got mixed up with native superstitions which permeated the lives of the locals like Carmen. He reassured her not to believe it.

At the crack of dawn on the appointed day, Scottie roared off with the loaded-down Rover and his two helper-guides. Gabby had gotten up earlier to prepare breakfast. Teary-eyed, she watched her **hombre** driving away from the porte cochere where she stood with Carmen. Arriving at the Lebrun apartment, Concha was already waiting by the front door in a khaki-clad safari outfit with two bags. She spent the night with Aurora, her distant aunt, who was still fast asleep. Her father slept at the mayor's mansion and was scheduled to fly back to Bogota′ later that morning. She rode on the front seat with Scottie who, skeptical about the trip, was reticent, sparing with his words to her, except to say "**Buenos dias**."

It was a muggy morning. The sun hid behind dark clouds as they roared into the **carretera nacional**. The heavy overcast threatened to pour down any time. Less than half hour later, the rain fell in buckets. Scottie could not see more than a few meters ahead, slowing down their progress. With rolled-up windows and the humid atmosphere inside the Rover, Concha's heavy perfume permeated into the closed-up cabin which Scottie felt began to possess his body and mind. Nonetheless, he struggled to think about the sanity of the trip despite the oppressive pall of this unfamiliar fragrance. Then, she began her rather exciting monologue about the Incas and their culture, as they drove towards the ruins site. His skepticism gradually converted into a possibility that this trip could become an archeological watershed and therefore, a worthwhile endeavor for him too after all. His deep interest in what he called "old stones," had sharpened during his three-year stint in the Persian vast desert where on off-days he explored the ruins and vestiges of the conquerors who came and left and the conquered who stayed or perished in the unforgiving sandy wastelands bridging Europe and Asia through the centuries.

A couple of hours later, they left the **carretera nacional** for a dirt road guided by the sketch made by Concha's professor several years before. The jarring ride over the uneven road was punishing their backs. Vegetation had reclaimed some portions of the road forcing him to maneuver around these rutted patches. Surprisingly, the unrelenting downpour conspired with the leafy passageway to transport them into a dreamlike world. Intense behind the steering wheel, Scottie had a strange sensation of a time machine which was rolling them back to the pre-Columbian days of the Incas. The temple ruins and the ancient people who had lived in them, restored by Concha's eloquent detailed commentary, became real to him. Then, every fifty kilometers or so tallied by the Rover increased his anxiety over the approaching revelation of the temple ruins. For several hours more, they drove through the jungle's murky greenery while the dozing two guides, heads bent, were swaying with the Rover's uneven, at times, jarring, motions.

Looking into the rear-view mirror, he saw the scars on his neck reminding him of that unfortunate incident from the past when he was a frightened teenager sitting helplessly with the burly deputy sheriff inside his souped-up patrol car as they raced at breakneck speed past the blurry orange orchards toward the Mexican border away from a lawn party given by his father, a judge, in honor of the newly elected district attorney. Scottie became groggy after sipping an innocent-looking Coke. He remembered the whispered talk between his dad and that deputy sheriff who loaded him, a dazed teenager, into his patrol car.

"The Chibchas came into this territory after the Incas," Concha related distracting him back to the present, "but they left no stone monuments. In contrast, the Incas before them, set up temples of worship wherever they settled. The stones for the temples and the walls surrounding their settlements were cut and fitted snugly one on top of another without the need for mortar. Even today the ruins have survived the elements through the centuries...."

"How do you know that certain temples were built by the Incas and not by some other tribe?"

"That's easy," she said radiating confidence from her doctoral thesis. "The niches, windows, and doors of the Incan structure usually have a trapezoidal design or shape. That's the unmistakable clue to their architecture." She fell silent after being so talkative.

Then, he noted her stolen glances which made him uneasy and distracted from his cautious driving to shun gullies and other hazards of a long-neglected dirt road. *Damn! I wish she would keep talking. Her looks are giving me the heebie-jeebies. What's she thinking? Oh! oh! I'm afraid to guess.*

More than half hour passed before she spoke once more. "If the Incas are living in these ruins now, their fruit gardens would be ripening at this time of the year and they would be celebrating the harvest festival." He smiled and began to relax again. "They call the festival, Capac Raimi. After the harvest, the women gather at one spot in the field and the men at another. They strip themselves...stark naked...."

"What the hell!" He nearly ran over a fallen rock.

"The Incas are not as inhibited as we, the supposedly civilized ones. Anyway, I'll get on with the story. The men and women placed bets on who will reach first a designated hill. A signal is given and the race is on. Any man, who catches a woman on the uphill run, enjoys her...there and then...." She could not continue, sighed deeply a couple of times, apparently affected by the story's erotic undertone.

"But I thought they are competing in a race to the appointed hill?"

"**Tonto**! That is just an excuse for sexual enjoyment...." She was hyperventilating as if she had difficulty in breathing.

My God! What is she hinting? By telling me this tale? Why is she breathing so weird? His juices got primed; and sweating profusely, he wondered uneasily what she had in mind. *I must keep calm. Not betray my agitation. Geez! She must be horny.*

Past noon they reached a tiny pueblo which consisted of a few adobe houses along the badly eroded dirt road. A weathered road sign read: Barrio de la Frontera. Scottie spent a vacation in Spain and learned that towns with de-la-Frontera appendage signified the shifting boundary between Christian and Moorish medieval territories. This time he was thinking that they were leaving modern civilization behind and plunging into the ancient past which was now almost reclaimed by the jungle vegetation.

Minutes later, the road split into two, one to the southwest and the other to the southeast. A landmark near this "Barrio" was the crumbling grave of a missionary which they readily located at this dirt road. Concha could not decide which dirt road they should take since the map only showed one sketched southward. They realized the limitations of Doctor Weiss Ramos' map which was done fifteen years before. Taking a lunch break, they ordered coffee at a nearby **cantina** while their helper-guides queried the local **indios** for directions.

Concha continued her colloquy on the Incas while they sipped the bitter coffee; but Scottie was tired and her fascinating stories about this ancient people were not being absorbed well by his brain as his mind wandered back to that fast ride with the Laredo sheriff as they crossed the international bridge to Nuevo Laredo. It was the first time young Scottie saw the Mexican slums as they endured the shakes caused by the pot-holed streets. Later in life, he figured out why this seedy section of town was euphemistically called "Boys' Town" by the his high school classmates and dropouts in Laredo who were planning a wild weekend across the Rio Grande.

The deputy sheriff entered a walled compound where a watchman waved them in. Young Scottie noticed a neat white adobe roadhouse partly hidden by blooming bougainvillea bushes. The place was bursting with parked cars and trucks mostly with Texas license plates. The sheriff helped his dazed companion alight from the patrol car and held him up from the waist as they made their way into the mariachi-pulsating roadhouse. A grossly-painted waitress wearing a side-split black satin skirt and purple peek-a-boo blouse escorted them inside to a table.

Sitting quietly in his woozy condition, Scottie watched the sheriff talking, laughing, exchanging naughty slap-for-slap-on-the-butt teases with an overdressed Mexican woman at the far end of the crowded bar which was packed tight and deep with Texas cowhands in their Stetsons and dust-covered boots. There was something peculiar about that Mexican woman which monopolized his attention until the sheriff rejoined him at their table. Another waitress in a provocative red skirt served their drinks: Carta Blanca beer for the sheriff and Coke for Scottie. The mariachi combo came by their table, causing the young lad's ears to resonate to the beat. The sheriff slipped some dollars to them. Suddenly, a hussy's obscene shrieks got his attention. Her hand was between the legs of a highly-animated gringo in tight blue jeans who, in turn, was squeezing her boobs. Scottie tried to get up, thinking of leaving, but the sheriff pushed him down on his chair.

Noisy arguments arose between the helper-guides and the **indios** diverting Scottie's thoughts back to the present. He beckoned to Pancho and Paquito to join them and get them away from the **indios**.

Oh! oh! I just did a boo-boo. She's not used to sit with ***peones****. Too radical for her patrician tastes. Too late to do much about it now without making matters worse. I'll pretend I'm not aware of her uneasiness!* Scottie was chortling inside about this silly class segregation by the Latin feudalistic society. Despite his openhanded friendliness, the guides were subdued while they self-consciously drank coffee with them. He ignored the staring message from Concha's eyes to the **peones** that they should sit at another table.

"What was that shouting argument with the **indios** all about? Did you find out which dirt road to take?" He asked them.

"Señor Reeter, these **indios** do not like our idea of searching for the ruins. They say we will disturb the spirits of their ancestors who are living in the ruins," Pancho explained, who was more outspoken than

Pepito. "One of them told us to take the dirt road more to the right. I think they are attempting to lead us away from the ruins."

By then, Scottie was certain that Concha's quiet posture and disdainful eyes were enough to intimidate these **peones** to silence unless spoken to. To get them out of their reticence, he encouraged them to talk by asking questions about their families and themselves. Pancho, the older one, heavy set and alert, told them he liked his change of work. The wiry young Pepito, a rookie employee, was more reserved but later told Scottie he sensed the indios were very upset about their search for the ruins and quite sure one of them hurled a curse on them.

Meanwhile, the windows and the entrance to the **cantina** sprouted with curious **indios**, mostly very young and some nursing mothers. After the spat with the guides, the angry elders soon left. Every movement of the strangers was watched meticulously by these **indios**. Discussing their problem among themselves, they chose the dirt road leading southeastward since they suspected the **indios** of misleading them to take the other road. They rode off.

The rains did not slow down. At several places, torrential rains cut ruts across the dirt road which slowed the Rover as they drove higher and higher on the sierras. On reaching the highlands, the rains softened into dense mists and a smoky haze hung over the dark forest surrounding them. The high humidity made them uncomfortably sweaty inducing them to unbutton their shirts and roll up their sleeves except Concha. Still uneasy to be with these **peones**, Concha kept her jacket on though her blouse clung to her sweaty body.

Several hours later, the Rover hugged the mountainside precariously as it swerved and skidded on the wet muddy road. Under those conditions, Scottie kept to four-wheel drive mode to maintain as much traction. Drenched in sweat, his memories crept back to his youth. Back to the Mexican roadhouse with its pervasive intermingled smell of beer, cheap perfumes, and loud mariachis. The sheriff was laughing boisterously, flirting with the satin-dressed whores, and enjoying every minute. Intimidated by the vulgar joint, young dopey Scottie was scared stiff and continued to suck his straw in the tainted Coke for want of anything else to do. Those big brown eyes of the sheriff watched him intently. Despite his hampered mind, he then suspected the soft drink was spiked again as his vision began to blur for the worse. He stopped drinking and tried hard to keep his head up.

Two painted hussies appeared behind Scottie, grabbed him, and forcibly carried him by his arms and legs through the darkened corridor behind the bar. Surprised, woozy, overpowered, he looked on helplessly at the receding figure of the sheriff who watched him but did nothing. *I wonder now why I didn't resist those whores. I just allowed them to carry me away. Lost my guts. I hated myself!*

Opening a door to a dimly lighted room, they dumped him on a bed. These coarse women, boisterously loud-mouthed, stripped themselves naked slowly before him while anticipating his erotic reaction.

Even in their ugly nakedness, they could not stir up any excitement from the groggy lad. Paid handsomely to seduce him, they were failing miserably. Desperate and getting mad, they ripped off his clothes as he lay drugged, supine and helplessly naked. The bleached redhead played with his penis to stiffen it. But no luck. The brunette sat behind his head and locked her heels into his armpits. Bending down, she sucked his nipples alternately. Still no reaction from him. The redhead hopped on his pelvis and pushed his dormant penis inside her but failed. Angry and frustrated, she squeezed his penis until he screamed.

Jolted by the violence on him, Scottie, although woozy, mustered every ounce left of his strength. Retracting his legs, he kicked the redhead, mule-style, against the wall which shuddered. Banging his head against the brunette's bottom in quick back-and-forth motions caused her to recoil in pain and to fall sideways on the cement floor.

Uglier with smeared lips and tangled hairs, the spurned whores, now raving maniacs, clawed him wildly into his neck and chest with their long fingernails while he cowered protecting his bloodied face with hands and arms.

"Watch out! **Cuidado!"** Concha screamed as the Rover skidded close to the dirt road's edge and compelled everyone to lean instinctively toward the mountainside. Recovering his presence of mind, he turned the front wheels inward in time. The road, which had become a sticky heavy conglomerate, kept the Rover from slipping off the edge.

"I'm sorry," Scottie apologetic, said nothing more.

Minutes later, they reached the sierra's top and began moving downhill towards a valley which opened to a savannah with waist-high grass -- a monotonous mantle of green broken up by occasional clusters of chaparral thickets. They heard a growling noise which became louder as they left the valley behind but could not see what animal was causing the noise. Riding over a hillock, a swollen raging river appeared below them. There was no bridge within sight. They argued whether it would be safe to cross.

Pepito commented that river beds in this region were usually dry until the rainy season. He had become more at ease in the company of the señores and was talking more freely. They stopped to stretch their legs and walk about. Scottie threw several whitish rocks into the middle of the river and watched how they sank.

"It's too deep for the Rover to cross," he told them. "We have to camp here until the water recedes low enough for the Rover to ford across." They saw a floating tree trunk bouncing helplessly on the seething waters dramatizing the river's nasty temper.

"We should consider ourselves lucky if it doesn't rain tomorrow," Concha conceded, disappointed that they could not go any farther. She was also thinking how to bed down for the night with these men around her -- a situation she never experienced before. She missed her servant girl. Nonetheless, the prospect of Scottie sleeping close by excited her, got her randy. Now that they were by themselves, she was determined to seduce him before this trip was over, possess him despite that low-class brunette in his house and her formal engagement to that dull Rudolfo, a distant cousin picked by the families.

Scottie told the guides to set up a camp for the night. Pepito and Pancho checked the area over and picked a slightly elevated ground about 200 meters away from the river bank. Fetching machetes from the tool box, they hacked and cleared the tall grass in a radius of about fifteen meters. The Rover was driven to the clearing's center and the tents were erected on each side of the vehicle. One tent was reserved for the off-duty guide to sleep and the other to shelter the equipment and provisions which were moved out of the vehicle. Scottie and Concha decided that she would sleep in the back of the vehicle and he would lie across the front seats.

The guides cut bush branches which they piled and topped with the cut grass leaves along the perimeter of the camp. They explained to the señores that any intruder, especially wild animals, would have to pass through the surrounding barricade betraying their presence with rustling sounds. Scottie assigned Pepito for the first shift to stand guard with a shotgun and a machete.

Night crept into the camp of these weary travelers while the river receded gradually from its banks and soft-pedaled its angry noises. Dark clouds still threatened while the quarter moon peeked through. After supper, they had coffee while listening to the Chibcha folklore recounted by Pepito who related that the **indios** knew nothing of the Incas except they believed their spirits haunted the ancient ruins. From his manner of spinning the tales with vivid details and dramatic intonation at crucial points, Scottie was convinced Pepito was a lot smarter than he appeared to be.

Pepito was dishing another tale when Scottie's thoughts wandered once more to that sordid episode in Nuevo Laredo. Regaining consciousness, he was on a hospital bed back in Laredo. His father came by, expressed his concern and blamed the sheriff for what happened. However, he did not file charges against the sheriff. After Scottie recovered, he reconstructed a conspiracy: His father connived with the sheriff to corrupt his character so he would lose his innocence and religious avocation for the ministry to which Reverend Dan had influenced him. With his innocence violated, his perception of the world around him was irreversibly altered.

His day of liberation finally arrived. Shortly after his eighteenth birthday, he ran away from home riding one bus after another. While waiting at the Dallas bus station, he sat next to a soldier who got him intrigued by ripping off pages of the paperback he was reading. Tom O'Brien, the soldier, said that he tore off the pages as he read because he wanted to make sure he did not read those pages again! Scottie had a good laugh. Tom said he was going to enlist in Spokane. Scottie thought that was a neat idea and conveniently far away from Laredo. Making up his mind, he told Tom he too would enlist in Spokane -- and then vowed never to look back, never to return to Laredo.

Pepito got up and took his post at the camp's perimeter closest to the river bank with Pancho disappearing into the empty tent for some sleep. The camp fire was crackling fiercely after Pepito threw gasoline on some damp twigs and branches. Scottie told Concha earlier that the rear space of the Rover would be her sleeping space and with himself making do with the front seats. Installed curtains could be drawn between the front seats and the rear for privacy. Concha, usually assertive, became self-conscious and excitable that she was actually about to share the same cabin with Scottie. Despite the thin drawn curtains between them, she was nervous just with the idea of lying close by, a few centimeters from the man she was inordinately attracted to. Taking the prescribed nightly dosage of her three pills escaped her distracted mind.

Scottie, although dead tired and motivated simply to lie down and rest immediately, hesitated to turn in right away until he got used to the idea of sharing the same small cabin, converted to sleeping quarters, with a woman. He bummed a cigarette from Pepito who just returned from his beat around the camp's perimeter and decided to accompany him on his next beat while indulging in small talk. All this time, he kept his eyes at the dimly lighted vehicle, half-curious, half-apprehensive, expecting her to get settled and asleep before he would claim the front seats for himself. The curtains of the side and rear windows of the vehicle were drawn. Scottie watched the curtain-trapped shadows roving inside the cabin which he interpreted that Concha was still awake and restless.

Why does it take her so long? he wondered. *I probably don't understand women.* Thinking that he had to suffer this nightly awkwardness for the rest of the trip left him uneasy. He regretted not bringing another tent for himself.

Concha had never been as carnally excited in her life before. The very idea that she would be lying so close, side by side to him, kept her keyed up and awake, unable to sleep. While consciously attempting to ease her tenseness, she allowed her imagination to run wild: a dark silhouetted lover clambering over from the front seats and making passionate love to her. Consumed by her fantasy to wander unfettered, she fancied getting herself pregnant. Having a baby from someone who excited her would fulfill her dream and make up for her coming marriage to the dull, predictable Rudolfo whom both families had agreed best for her and thus keep the fortunes of both families intact.

Making another round with Pepito and more cigarettes, a nervous Scottie began to think about the ridiculous decision to which his bosses had stooped so low to please the whim of a client's daughter. *It's not related to the project at all!* The more he thought about this trip the more he perceived it as patently absurd. The challenges and little victories from his work in Peñalosa made him wish he were back.

Gabby! Remembering her struck him like a bolt of lightning and got him worried about her mental disposition. *God knew how I grilled Carmen to be ever vigilant.* Yet he was not sure if some unexpected incident or simply his absence could upset her mental equilibrium. *And poof! She would sink into the deep end.*

Much later, Scottie assumed Concha, by then, was far gone into dreamland. Drowsiness was creeping over him after that long weary day. Opening the Rover's door carefully, noiselessly, he noted the drawn curtains between the front seats and the converted cabin at the back. He stretched himself gingerly across the bucket seats, which despite the pile of several blankets, were uncomfortable to lie on. The shift stick in the vehicle's middle pressed against his stomach.

Concha was still awake, sweaty and listless in her dusty safari shirt even though she had loosened her bra. Distracted that he was lying just a few centimeters away from her head, she trembled uncontrollably with excitement.

Tossing about on her pad, she was wrestling with an urge to chat with him. Just to talk softly in their intimate surrounding, hoping that it would ease her anxiety. But she hesitated, thinking it was too bold and Scottie might misinterpret her intention. Later, she heard an unseen animal's snarls emanating from the pitch-dark outside. The snarls became louder and intense above the jungle's incessant din. Lifting a side window's curtain, she could not see anything. Checking from the other window, she saw a furry beast lapping the water at the river's edge, snarling now and then, at another unseen animal. She was not scared being inside the Rover and with three men to protect her. Lying down again on her sweaty pad, she was restless, frustrated. as the minutes slowly turned into an hour, then another hour.

The quiet which dominated for a while was pierced again by a yelping beast which she imagined was being attacked by another. Looking out once more through a side window, she saw a dark beast humping another while chewing its neck. The unexpected sight shocked her. Witnessing the brutal mating and the piercing cries got her in an agonizing yet passionate dither, infecting her with a smoldering desire.

Slowly, she raised the curtains separating her rear cabin from the front seats where Scottie was fast asleep. She glimpsed at him in repose lying so close. Her body began to tremble, then to shake as if the dreaded malaria fever had infected her. Attempting to control herself, she still quivered until she let the curtains down. But it was too tempting for her not to look at him as she raised the curtain again and sighed. ***Me atrevo poseerle de cualquier medio!*** *I want to possess him whatever it takes!* She reached out and touched his moist hair. Scottie moved but slipped back into dreamland. Clutching his arm, she became bold enough to shake it.

"Scottie! Wake up!" she yelled. "There are beasts fighting outside and making terrible noises. I'm scared."

"A-ah...wha...at? Something wrong?" Stirring from a deep slumber, he was not alert. "What's...going on?" he asked, letting out a big yawn.

"There are beasts out there. Hear them growling and fighting? It's very scary."

"Ouch! My legs hurt! I got charley horse." He massaged his thighs and calves, then stretched his legs as much as he could in the cramped space. Sitting up and yawning again, he looked outside where she was pointing. A wolf was chasing another along the river bank. "They're mating," he said wearily. "There's no threat to us. Let's go back to sleep."

"I'm afraid...," she pleaded, her juices were shooting madly inside her, "I'm afraid...to sleep by myself...."

"But I'm sleeping right here. We're safe inside. Pepito and Pancho are outside with shotguns and machetes. Don't you worry. I don't see those **lobos** now. They're gone."

"I'm still scared to sleep by myself here. Over here." She insisted pointing to her side of the cabin -- a blatant invitation for him to climb over and sleep with her.

Scottie frowned still hampered by cobwebs of drowsiness, not totally catching on to her overt hint. Becoming more accustomed to the darkness, he was startled by the stark glimpse of her enormous milk-white breasts jutting out of her open blouse, accented by the shifting shadows caused by the bonfire. "Wha-at??!!" He stuttered, staring unwittingly, unable to speak further.

The silent impasse caused Concha to simmer down and become sufficiently embarrassed. She began to button up her blouse.

"I feel calmer now," she said, feeling obliged to retreat. "I shall be all right." Compelled to end this episode, she let the curtains down again. Putting her head down and curling up, she pulled the sheet over herself despite the humid heat, as if to cover the embarrassment of her failed seduction.

Going down to rest once more, adjusting his body while covering himself with the bed sheet, he closed his eyes not uttering another word.

Much later, Concha's embarrassment dissipated. Uncomfortable with the humidity, she pulled down the bed sheet. Yet her burning desire to possess him kept her awake. The erotic spell she attempted to cast over him fizzled before it could take on fire. Her frustration was mounting inside her. Thinking of her coming wedding to "dull, useless Rudolfo" pushed her toward the emotional brink without the calming effect of the hormone pills she forgot to take.

The high humidity caused Scottie to wake up. It was still dark. Very quietly, he got out of the Rover unaware that she was awake too. Noting the camp fire, he joined the guides for coffee. With the flickering light from the fire, he discussed the trip ahead using the sketch and the printed map.

"I can't stand it any longer! **Basta!** No more!" Concha shouted throwing things within the reach of her hands inside the Rover. A side door opened and she burst out. They all turned to look at what was happening. Her face betrayed her inner stresses. All of a sudden, she charged through the protective pile of branches and cut grasses scattering them in her wake. Screaming unintelligently, she disappeared into the jungle fastness. Scottie, caught by surprise, dropped his coffee mug, and bolted over the pile chasing after her. Branches and underbrush mercilessly swatted him as he ran headlong into the dark jungle. The guides, watching the surrealistic scene they could not understand, shouted their dismay.

"Come back, Concha! Come back!" Scottie shouted as he fought his way into the dark gloom which engulfed him. Halting momentarily, he tried to listen but she did not answer his frantic calls. No rustle of footsteps on the debris-covered ground betrayed her presence. *Concha has disappeared,* he despaired, *swallowed up by this blasted darkness*. On a hunch, he turned and walked cautiously to his right. The dense thicket forced him to move sideways using his forearm to protect his face.

He shouted her name again and again -- his voice only to be drowned by the incessant discordant sounds of the jungle -- with no response however faint from her. Failing to keep track of his direction, he realized he was lost. Lost as he walked and searched by fits and starts, and after a while keeping time became a useless conjecture. Feeling defeated and tired, he sat down and cried like that fateful afternoon when he failed to save young Carrie from the speeding car. After resting briefly, he began to wander aimlessly again seeking her anxiously for then he was scared to be alone in the dark, noisy insect-infested jungle.

"C O N C H A!" he cried out at the top of his voice some hours later. Then, he added with desperation: "WHERE ARE YOU?" The jungle, indifferent to his woes, continued to play its discordant tunes, sucking his words into oblivion as he slapped his face and arms for the unseen crawling, biting insects.

As the night became a hardly indistinguishable day turned into night again under a thick canopy of commingling leafy tree branches, lianas and perturbed screaming spider monkeys which extended over him endlessly on: he persisted calling her name tirelessly, with a hoarse throat, and each time he would stop and listen patiently for a hint of her presence. His special watch, plus those extra indicators for temperature, altitude, barometric pressure and compass, was left inside the Rover. In that primitive jungle darkness, time and space for Scottie were obliterated. There was no time for him to get hungry, to become sleepy or tired. But he was determined to find Concha as a lost human being searching for another lost human being as he went forth blindly.

Yes, there's a faint but distinct voice, a cough too? Perhaps I'm going crazy. Imagining to hear a faint voice? Oh yes, that's a human cough. He argued with himself about that faint but elusive cough filtered from those spurious sounds emitted by the insects and animals. *Do I hear a sob now? A woman sobbing?* He wondered. *But where is she?*

"CONCHA! CONCHA!" he shouted, encouraged by the perceived sobs. "Answer me! **CONTESTAME**!" he shouted and listened again and again. *Did I hear my name? Does it sound like Concha's saying 'Scootee'? Or...am I getting mad and hearing what I want to hear?* Baffled, uncertain, distrustful of his ears, he walked cautiously toward the imagined source of that sound. *Perhaps a voice?* He doggedly pushed himself through the thick underbrush, getting his body scratched and clothes torn by unseen thorns and other prickly vegetation while taking more deliberate steps toward that source.

The fainting sob became more distinct. *It's a human voice. That's for sure. That sobbing... Got to be Concha.* Taking a few more careful steps around dense bushes, he stood still and listened again. *Sounds like someone's breathing heavily. Must be Concha. But where is she in this God-forsaken place? In this darkness....* Tension was building inside him. Too much for him to bear. "Damn it! I can't stand this madness much longer. This nightmare!" Finally he shouted her name in frustration. CO-O-O-N-CH-H-A-A!!

A cough! He heard it close by. Reaching out, he touched what felt to him like human hair, then, the shape of a head. *My God! A human head!* He was overwhelmed with his obscure discovery as his hands ran wild over a human shape and then…got bitten! "Ouch!" he shouted, more in surprise than in pain. The unseen shape let out a spine-tingling yell and struck him with fists. Feeling a plump breast, scratching nails were upon him as he recoiled raising his arms to shield himself.

Got to be Concha! Got to be! "CONCHA! STOP IT! It's me, Scottie. Stop it!" he reassured her while grabbing her by the wrists and pushing those vicious nails away. "**Callate!** Shut up! **Soy yo!** Scottie! Do you hear me? I'm Scottie."

"Oh! oh! oh!" she stammered, then screamed hysterically and pulled him down. From her tight embrace, he could hardly breathe as he lay uncomfortably amidst prickly brushwood surrounding them. She let out a shrill cry unnerving him. Screaming females always blanked out his presence of mind. Finally, she loosened her grip on him.

"**Tranquilate**, Concha, calm down," he said pulling her gently up and propping her against what he felt by hand to be... *a tree?* "There. **Basta ya**! Everything will be okey-dokey. Soon we must look for our camp and guides." Glad that she quieted down at last, he was not sure if she recognized him or if she fell into the deep end and gone nuts. Being with another human, he became more hopeful, more confident in himself even though the pitch darkness which surrounded them did not offer a clue how they could return to the camp.

After mumbling some incoherent words, she simmered down and slipped into a deep slumber, even snoring softly. Her strange behavior, Scottie rationalized, was caused by sheer physical exhaustion. Putting an arm behind her, he kept her from shifting sideways. But by then, his arm was hurting with cramps and he had to withdraw and massage it with the other hand. Concha began to slump forward and he had to push her back against the "tree" with his hand pressed against her shoulder.

The gloomy forest depressed him like a hostile prison from which he wanted to escape so badly but had to wait patiently for day break. When a sliver of the moon appeared, he rationalized that they were now in a region with a thinner canopy and closer to the river. Later, he could see shafts of faint light breaking through the jungle leafy roof not far from them which reassured him that they would find their way out. Utterly exhausted, he fell asleep leaning on her. Under normal circumstances, Scottie avoided too close intimacy with any woman. Not even with the live-in Gabby. In the dismal gloom of the jungle, he found himself faced with a strange paradox which he willingly ignored to be intimate with another human regardless of later consequences.

Hordes of biting mosquitoes woke him up. His human companion was still asleep. Luckily, he had a tiny spray can of insect repellent in his pocket which he hurriedly applied to his face and arms. Brushing his hand close to her face, he warded off what appeared to be mosquitoes feasting on her. Without hesitation, he sprayed the repellent on his palm and applied it to her face and arms, then, on her exposed chest. Not deliberately aware, he was getting stirred up inside after applying the repellent on her. Puzzled by what happened to him momentarily, he tried to sleep some more.

Waiting for more sunlight, he rearranged himself to sit side by side with the sleeping Concha to better endure stiffness and to hold her better around the shoulders with both arms. Then, getting hungry, his whole body was now cramped with pain and getting weary to keep her propped up. Her limp torso began to slide down gradually over his lap while pinning his then loose left arm. Pulling out his arm, he brushed against her breasts. That unintentional caress jolted him, distracted him from his anxiety to return to the camp and reminded him of Concha's exposed milk-white breasts inside the Rover.

For the first time, he was getting curious about the other half of creation which he had intentionally shunned since that atrocious encounter with those Mexican whores. Unlike Gabby whom he sublimated to a kid sister substitute for Carrie, Concha was another species of this other half, the opposite sex, who had slumped on his lap and became a challenge for his suddenly stirred-up curiosity -- a throwback from his stunted adolescence. Yet he was struggling with the ethics of exploring this well-endowed dormant woman without her consent. Those enormous breasts did make an indelible impression on him when he first saw Concha during that fiesta at his **quinta**. With mosquitoes buzzing over Concha's partly exposed breasts, he felt justified to protect her from these pests while satisfying his belated adolescent discovery of this unknown territory. He sprayed more repellent on his right palm and began massaging her right breast while admiring its beautiful domelike shape topped with a pink nipple. Then, he massaged the left breast and made the observation how symmetrical they were and similar except the left nipple had tiny blonde hairs around its base. Those nipples felt like soft textured knobs to him. At his late age, he had opened a side door to explore the opposite sex unaware that he was erotically stimulated while he perspired, doubted, hesitated in a dark hostile environment.

Then, visions of his combat wounds in the Korean War cast grave doubts about his own manhood. He abruptly stopped caressing her and withdrew his hand. Another depression entered his head as he thought of his bleak lonely future bereft of carnal pleasure, of sharing life's joys and sorrows -- with a woman he might have loved. *It would be wonderful to love and be loved by another human being,* he was wishing. *To have a special someone to share a love that is emotional and physical. Could I do it? Could I make love to a woman and enjoy a mutual climax with her?* His thoughts rummaged on this sensitive issue which was arrested during his younger years. *How could I find out and not get humiliated?* Never in his life was he so depressed and anxious as well to find out the truth about his virility. *I want...I must...find out...before it's too late.* Doubtful, even afraid, a feeling of utter futility possessed him, believing he was losing his grip on that elusive desirable life with a companion.. *I must find out. Got to do something about it.*

Concha was becoming too heavy lying over him. After failing to prop her up again, he realized she was heftier than he anticipated. Exerting harder, he grunted pulling her up this time and leaning her against the now recognized tree once more under more sunlight. As he held her from slumping again, it dawned on him their unrehearsed intimacy in the jungle might be his last chance to check out a positive proof of his virility. Determined to do a reality check on himself -- he was now ready to gloss over the morality of his intention and find out whether he was capable of having an erection.

With great care, he lowered her down and hugged her head on his chest while lying on his right side. Lifting her right arm, he placed it between his legs. Then, rocking his torso back and forth, her arm rubbed against his crotch.

When Concha grunted, he suspended the sliding motion and then started again that motion against her limp body, waiting for a definitive erotic sensation which he was eager to associate with a married life's fulfillment and even having children -- thoughts deemed unthinkable for him before. *I have the rest of the early dawn to find out if I can still do it*, he consoled himself, *despite what those whores did to me, despite how I hated women because of my father and that sheriff, despite my war wounds.*

After much trying later, his organ was still limp and he was becoming exasperated. His heightened expectation for a sexual arousal, he then realized, made him extremely nervous. Still, he kept rocking back and forth hoping for a hint of that erotic sensation. Desperate beyond his own expectations, sheer exhaustion mercifully lull him to sleep hindered from vindicating his virility. Unwittingly, the exhausted sleeping stunted-adolescent transitory explorer was still coupled with his likewise sleeping companion in a rather compromising juxtaposition but was saved in the remote jungle setting from reproach by the absent sanctimonious puritans from his maternal forebears.

CHAPTER VI

Shafts of intense morning sunlight filtered down to the jungle floor to provide a more visible world to the two lost souls. A flock of high-flying squawking gaudy macaws stirred Scottie but he was none too alert. Red howlers came swinging through the upper reaches of the tall liana-laced trees making ear-piercing yells which aroused Concha. Becoming slowly aware she was lying next to him with her arm between his legs, she jumped up bolting away from their vulgar intimacy. Her sudden disengagement startled, then rudely woke him up.

"**Que esta´pasando aqui con nosotros, eh**?" she said, surprised, ashamed with her unintended intimacy. "Eh-er, I mean, what are we doing here? Where are we?" She straightened and smoothed down her dirty pulled-out blouse.

He explained at length what happened and how he ran after her in the jungle and eventually found her.

"I don't remember last night," she declared watching him suspiciously and wondered why her arm was between his legs. Gliding her hand inconspicuously on her slacks' zipper, she reassured herself she was not violated. "Oh no! My pills! I have not taken them. The bottle is in my bag. I'm in trouble...."

"You taking pills? I didn't know that." He speculated whether her strange behavior last night was precipitated by not taking those pills. "We better find our way back to the temporary camp before darkness." Then, guilt feelings gnawed at him even though he blamed her for running into the jungle which ended up into their close intimate contact.

Hungry and tired, they moved downhill looking for the river bank which they rationalized would lead them to their temporary camp and the guides. Scottie was sending positive thoughts to Pancho and Pepito that they stay put and do not venture into the jungle searching for them. After this rather silly chase for Concha and the terrible insect-biting alfresco sleep-out, he yearned to finish this trip quickly and return to his job.

"I can hear those rippling waters. Sort of faint. Can you?" he asked her standing up to listen more intently.

"I think I do. But which direction?"

For several minutes he listened again then swung and pointed his right arm at two o'clock direction from where he was facing. However, their view was blocked by the dense vegetation.

"I'm sorry. I…I can't hear the waters now." She began to break down and cry.

"Crying won't help," he chastised her, seemingly unsympathetic. "We got to keep moving and reach the camp before sundown. At least for now, let's follow where the rippling sound is coming from. If we find the river bank, we increase our chance to locate the camp."

They had to crawl on all fours going down the slope under the branches of the interlocking underbrush which were arduous to penetrate walking straight up. Crawling wore them out even worse. After more than an hour of crawling, the vegetation became sparse and they were glad to walk upright again. This time, they could hear the rippling sounds and though tired their spirits picked up.

When they saw the river finally, Concha was nearly hysterical. After wading near the bank and throwing water over herself, she begged him that they rest for a while. Graceful lines of slender coconut trees intermingled with the spreading mangroves on the banks where they sat and took a breather. Farther down to their left, the river followed a tortuous course through an endless procession of what she imagined poetically as "green-mantled castles" which was veiled in a gauzy fog. The disparate uneven banks to their right were sloping steeply upward flanked by vertical cliffs less than a hundred meters high, gutted with shallow fissures and deep vee-shaped ravines which led to the darker impenetrable jungle they just left behind. They recalled a somewhat similar view from their camp.

Taking their chance on a hunch, they walked to the right along the bank on the narrow sandy strip. A flock of parrots descended on a cluster of coconut trees across the river and distracted their attention with a screeching tirade. On patches of the bank where the sandy strip was washed, they swung while suspended from branch to branch of overhanging mangroves or jumped from a fallen tree trunk to another while holding on to lianas.

Concha's feet skidded off a slippery trunk and fell back on her duff. Hungry and short-tempered by then, she cussed like a foul-mouthed sailor. The fungus-covered trunk started to slip into the water.

"Water snake!" she yelled. Being ahead of her, he heard her cry and turned to look back. After he pulled her with both arms, they took off running, scared, in knee-high water and never looked back. Breathless and weary for worse, they were heartened finally to see the camp clearing. They were immediately discovered by their guides who shouted and began jumping excitedly. Running, sometimes nearly stumbling, but not slowing down for a moment until they were surrounded by their jubilant guides. Concha sat on the ground panting and holding her throat. Pepito got her a glass of drinking water.

When Scottie recovered and was able to speak sensibly, he told them about the water snake. Pancho, shotgun in hand, ran along the bank searching for the despised reptile. He returned empty-handed. Meanwhile, Pepito prepared a hearty late breakfast for them with scrambled eggs, bacon strips and hot black coffee prepared over a blazing fire.

Their involuntary propinquity during the last few days affected Scottie who felt an impulsive attraction toward the wet, unkempt Concha whose clinging sweat-soaked clothes made her wild-looking and sexy. Ever since he became bewitched by his callow repugnant experimentation on her while lost in the jungle, he did not mind being close to her and neither did she. Their unexpected intimacy in the jungle, which puzzled her, had improved since their forced relationship at the beginning of the ruins trip. Now, he had become infatuated with her, more accommodating to her whims, and forgiving of her occasional dishing out of foul bilingual profanities.

For six more days, they searched the poorly defined confluence of the two rivers and creeks which revealed no clues of the Inca ruins hidden by the jungle's dense growth.

"We have searched here, here, and here," he pointed to the approximate locations of their quests on the soiled printed map while comparing those spots with those on the sketch. "Those ruins, if they exist at all, would have to be somewhere along here. This is the last logical area to search for the ruins. Besides, our food supply won't last for more than five days and the fuel jerry cans are down to four. I checked the Texaco map which shows the nearest town is over 100 kilometers. away. Shall we try for four more days?"

"It's okay with me," Concha said as he pulled the tattered sketch closer to her. Their sides touched and both felt a tingling sensation. They looked at each other but said nothing. While still wondering and baffled about her attraction to this man, she was determined to subdue her carnal passion and find the Inca ruins before they were forced to return home by the depletion of their food, required by their civilized tastes, and petrol, and then, shamefully with nothing to show for their efforts.

A helicopter suddenly buzzed over them causing them to look up. After another downward swing, the whirly bird landed on the river with its inflated pontoons. A door slid open and somebody on board threw down two anchors into the waters.

"Señor Scootee, you are ordered to report back," the pilot barked at them, using a megaphone. Riding on a rubber boat, Mauro and the pilot went ashore and explained to him that Señor W. Corry contracted hepatitis and was flown back to Bogota´.

Disappointed and angry, Concha let out a flood of Spanish profanities. To mollify her, Scottie offered to continue the trip at some future date and she could fly back with him to Peñalosa and thence, on a commercial flight to Bogota.′ Mauro and the guides could drive the Rover back. Concha, with her streak of stubbornness, turned down his offer and decided to continue the ruins search with the two guides.

Apprehensive about her decision which he considered foolhardy, Scottie could only watch futilely the shrinking figures of Concha and the guides on the river bank as the helicopter winged back to Peñalosa. There was nothing he could do even though he hated leaving her alone. On landing at the Peñalosa airport, he harbored a nagging premonition about Concha and regretted her stubborn decision to continue the search by herself. Nevertheless, Scottie ordered more supplies for her.

"Aurora died of a heart attack while Pablo was beating her." Gabby broke the sad news when Scottie came in for lunch break at the **quinta** the day after he returned. She was afraid to tell him until he had rested overnight.

"Wha-at!" Scottie slammed his cup on the saucer. The reality of Aurora's departure was not easy for him to accept and he focused his thoughts on the fragility of human life, including his own. Gauging his vehement reaction, Gabby wondered if she should have waited a few more days to tell him. He remembered a disturbing unexplained hunch while he was on the trip. "Did she die on a Thursday three weeks ago?"

"How did you know?"

"I knew something bad happened that Thursday but I couldn‘t put my finger on it." Thinking back, he felt remorseful for dissuading Aurora from leaving her husband. Those glorious fiestas and **verbenas** organized by her paraded like ghostly pageants through his mind and he became depressed. "I wonder if someone else could arrange those fiestas with the same determination like Aurora‘s. Padre Joe will be lost without her assistance. That's for sure."

"The padre will have more than those fiestas to worry about," she said. "**Mi amiga intima**, Heidi, as you know, had been very restless. I was not surprised when she ran away with Pedro, that salesman from Caracas."

"Oh no! Not another bad news!" Then, becoming aware of the padre's intense **amor propio** or personal pride, Scottie rationalized the flamboyant cleric was gravely mortified and speculated that he had probably withdrawn from the world by now. "Have you seen him?"

"No. However, I was not looking for him. Nobody I know has seen the padre. Not the **alcalde**. I mean the mayor. Not even the chief of police." She finished her cup of coffee; by lifting it way up with her head tilted back. He noticed and had forgotten already this habit of hers. "Anyway, it does not look proper for a priest to live with a **querida** especially someone like Heidi who catches every **hombre's** attention."

Scottie felt strange, spooky. *After just my short absence, Aurora is gone. And Heidi too. If I had been around I might have convinced Heidi to stick it out with Padre Joe. I won't mind buying some clothes for her. So she can be as well-dressed as the pretty clothes I buy for Gabby which Padre Joe can't afford. Why did I have to take that stupid trip? Had Heidi not abandoned Padre Joe,* he figured, *the padre might have known what was going on with Aurora and might have saved her from Pablo's violence.* Suddenly, he became aware how his own life had become closely entwined with the lives of others in an invisible but common link of personal events.

There was something about Gabby which he did not notice before. She was more assertive in the manner she talked, more poised in dealing with people. Even those girlish giggles, he observed, had muted to gentle smiles. Sadly, he surmised his ward, the unwanted waif from the belfry's edge, left alone to fend for herself while he was gone, became more independent and self-reliant. *Maria Luisa should be given credit for training her to be more ladylike and for learning table manners.* With apprehension, he expected her to demand a more permanent relationship with him. He had not resolved his personal secret problem. *Oh Lord, give me more time.* He despaired about his impending crisis with her. *I can't let her go now. We could truly love each other like normal human beings, if I'm only able to....*

"Hey, kiddo. Are you lost again in your thoughts?" She trespassed into his introspective silence using another expression she picked up from him. Smiling at her, he thought wistfully she shouldn't read his thoughts. He couldn't help but laugh at her insouciance and did his best not to betray his personal agony. **"Mas cafe´?"** she suggested and he readily agreed. Usually they did not drink that much coffee and were using the long lunch break as a palpable excuse for their delightful reunion. His infatuation with Concha was wearing off. Nevertheless, thinking about Concha brought memories of her vulgarities which caused his sexual turn-ons. Away from her, he realized their sensual relationship was transitory.

"It's nice to be home," he said becoming sentimental. Touching, then holding her hand on the table and caressing it, they looked at each other with unspoken tenderness. Their heads came closer and a soft kiss was inevitable. Feeling blissfully satisfied with him, this time Gabby was determined to keep her hombre forever and nothing would ever get in their way. Slowly in a thoughtful monologue, she told him she did a lot of thinking while he was away about their future life together.

Scottie slept soundly in his old comfortable bed that night, even better than the previous night. It was not until late morning before he woke up and got up. He was still worn from the trip and his muscles were sore. A feeling of depression dogged him since he had not resolved his sexual virility. Gabby, assuming the trip exacted its toll noting his sad face, tiredness, and limping talk, decided to pamper him. To make sure the **quinta** was absolutely quiet she sent the maid home early that day. *The house cleaning can wait*, she decided. Meanwhile, she was in the kitchen "cooking up a storm" of a dinner in celebration of Scottie's homecoming.

The pleasure of a leisurely evening was late for Scottie who had a long session with all the foremen, but especially with Mauro and the other office help, due to the backlog of paperwork which had slowed down during W. Corry's brief on-site tour of duty.

"I truly enjoyed this dinner," he complimented her as she carried plates and silverware back to the kitchen. "What do you call the main dish? You told me already but I forgot. It was tasty. **Muy sabrosa**."

"**Pabellon criollo**."

"The rice and plantains are filling. What a treat to eat at home again!" He got up and carried the rest of the dinnerware to the kitchen. "Let me clean the dishes tonight...." He reached for the soap brush under the sink. "I need to do some house work so I can really feel I'm back. That I'm scraping a dish instead of gripping that steering wheel. Jeez! I never drove that much before and worse, on broken roads."

"No! no! Not tonight!" she grabbed the soap brush from him even more uneasy with his un-Latin proclivity to help her with house chores. She was determined to spoil him like a Latin **patron**. "Tonight you relax and read the newspapers. You have, as you say, 'much catching up to do.'"

"Well, you told me non-stop everything I need to know about the tiny world we live in right here. I'm caught up with the status of the highway project and right now, pretty fed up with the damn paper pile-up connected to the job. W. Corry got the virus before he could finish the job. Poor guy."

Suddenly, he became aware that somebody else was missing. "Where's Carmen?"

"I dismissed her."

"Dismissed her!" The news hit him like a thunder bolt. In contrast, Gabby displayed an air of triumph about her. Eyeing her, he wondered silently if it would be self-defeating to scold her. Although he had no immediate concern for someone to watch over her mental condition, he was vexed about Carmen's departure.

"I don't see why you let Carmen go. I hired her to do the house-keeping so you can spend more time on your studies. Carmen was eager to please us." Gabby's relapse into that destructive malady could happen again and he wanted someone to be with her all the time, just in case.

Gabby resented being watched so zealously by Carmen, an aspect Scottie was totally blind to. After he left for the ruins trip, she found an alibi to dismiss her. “Don’t feel sorry for her,” she said while wiping a dish. “I gave her six months’ advance on her salary.”

“Wha-at! Did you say six months’ salary?” He was shocked again.

“Yes, six months. I gave her more than the law requires for dismissing **criadas**. Do you say domestic?”

“It’s better to say servants or house maids.”

“With that money, she was able to open a restaurant with her sister in Monteria. Carmen was so happy with that money. **Me abrazo´ y me dio´ besos.** Still remember your Spanish, eh? She embraced and even kissed me.”

“That’s a generous amount,” he said after making a quick mental conversion of those pesos into familiar dollars ignoring her sarcasm. *It’s no wonder she could open that restaurant.* Then, it finally dawned on him she was finagling to be indispensable by doing the cooking herself. “Where’s the new maid? What’s her name again?”

“Maria. I sent her home early this morning. I wanted the house to be perfectly quiet while you rested. She will be back tomorrow.”

At least there’ll be someone with her while I’m at the office, he thought feeling reassured.

Having taken complete control of the household, she wanted him to forget about Carmen arguing with him she could cook better. “While you were away, I asked Señor Ortiz to teach me how to cook some delightful dishes and French pastries. He was the chef at the Hotel de Alhambra in Cartagena. It is the hotel with the casino by the sea. Tomorrow I shall make some **bollos pelones.”**

His thoughts had gone past her culinary activities to the progress of the tutoring schedule. “How’s that **maestra**? I can’t remember her name. I mean the one who teaches you English and arithmetic lessons?”

“You mean Señora Sabater. She is a **gran maestra. Muy simpatica.** We are now in chapter treintainueve...eh, how you say that?”

“Thirty-nine....”

“**Gracias. Si**, I mean, yes, with the arithmetic book. But I love best the expressions she is teaching me. Like ‘Don’t give me that crap.’ -or ‘That’s a bunch of horse sh_t.’ ” The señora said she learned those neat expressions from the **perforadores** whom she is teaching Spanish at the oil company camp. They are **norteamericanos** too.”

“Don’t tell me!” Scandalized, his face was red as a beet. “I never thought she would__….”

“Something wrong? Those are neat expressions.” She giggled like a little girl, gratified she could show off her savvy of **norteamericano** slang.

*There are many irons in the fire right now and I shall just think I never heard her speak those nasty expression*s. “And how’s the typing lesson? Is Maestro Alonzo okay?”

"**Pues**, so far so good as you would say." She was not so eager to delve into this subject for she was never enamored with the typewriter.

"What do you mean by that? I want to know how many words per minute you can type."

"Eh...twenty...three...."

"Twenty-three words per minute?"

"Yes-s...." she answered, reluctant to admit.

"That's slow, isn't it? You can do better than that."

"Eh...I am doing my best, Scootee. My fingers get too tired."

I must talk to Maestro Alonzo about her typing, he decided.

She must do better than twenty-three words to get an office job. Despite her slow progress, a feeling of sadness gripped him. Sooner or later, he concluded, she would become more proficient and will get a job.. *Earning her own money will change her and affect our shared life. She must learn a trade to survive. But I hate to think what will happen between us in the future.*

Despite his gloomy brooding, he kept on reading the newspapers. A news item on the lower front page accompanied with a gory picture of lined-up corpses on a dirt road caught his attention. As he read more he became increasingly agitated. "Hey! There was a shoot-out between the police and some outlaws! Near some ruins!" Breathing heavily, he read on. "Oh my God! A woman! Killed with them! Oh my!" Fearing the worst, he was shaken nearly crumpling the pages. She dropped the silverware she was washing on the sink and rushed to his side.

"Where is...**donde esta´ la noticia**?" she asked leaning down with her nose a few inches from the papers.

"You know, I think you need some glasses," he observed. "Maybe that's the reason you can't type faster."

"**Santamaria!** Thirteen **bandidos** and one officer were killed besides that woman," she read on, unmindful of what he just said. "Could she be....."

"No! she can't be Concha! No! no!!" Scottie was in self-denial. Suddenly, she confirmed a dreadful possibility already worming into his mind which refused to accept it.

"**Donde estan sus nombres**? Your hands are trembling, Scootee. Where are the names! Oh, turn to page six...for the continuation...." She was excited, breathless as he thumbed the pages reluctantly. They devoured the rest of the news item. "No names! **Que barbaridad**!"

"If...if Concha were killed...oh my God! I'll never...never forgive myself. And oh! Pepito and Pancho…oh my God!" They looked at each other as he tried to steady his hands from shaking. "Never! never!" Struck with a grave feeling of guilt, helplessness, frustration, he threw the papers down. Then, he got up and walked slowly to the terrace. Unable to stand still, he walked back and forth mindlessly.

"Scootee, you must keep calm. **Quedate tranquilo**. The doctor said you must not get excited." She went to the terrace and forced him to sit down on one of the wrought iron chairs. He buried his face in his hands and began to cry. She sat on the armrest, put her arm over his shoulder and tried to console him.

"What a shame! Innocent lives were lost!" he felt compelled to talk. "This world has become too violent...too...too sick...."

"**Aquella mujer no es** Concha. She is not the type of person to get involved in a shoot-out. She don't know…eh… to hold the gun. Did not even bring guns for the **viaje**…trip…when we were loading the Rover? **Te acuerdas**? Remember?"

"But that woman or Concha was caught by the bandits and forced to live with them according to the news. After the police surrounded the hideout, I imagine these trigger-happy officers just shoot and shoot. I could have been shot too if I were with them. I feel terrible. Terrible!"

"Maybe that woman killed with the **bandidos** was not Concha." She reassured him once more. "They usually take their **queridas** with them. Camilo Torres, **por ejemplo**." She thought she would be sorry if that woman turned out to be Concha. But on the other hand, her intuition warned her that the bogoteña planned to snatch her hombre using the ruins trip as an excuse. She promised herself that Scottie was hers and hers alone from then on.

"These bandits are mean bastards." The possibility that Concha might be the victim of the shoot-out could not escape his mind. A smidgen of his infatuation for Concha still dwelt inside him. "Mean bastards."

"What do you mean by bastards? **Bastardos,** in Spanish, mean illegitimate children."

"I'm too mad right now to explain my usage of that word. There's just too much violence in this world, Gabby. I never want to handle another gun nor shoot at anything again. Not even a deer. Not even a quail!" He held up his right hand. "I promise and you're my witness."

"But you told me you were a **soldado** one time, **si**?" She could not imagine how a former soldier would renounce the tool of his trade. Besides she was aware that every man of high reputation in the Cuyapo′ valley had at least one pistol and every **campesino** has a hunting rifle. "You were in the **ejercito, verdad**? **Que es**…What is that word in English?"

"Army."

"Army. Army. Army...." She repeated the word tucking it into memory. "And you were a **soldado** in the country called 'Cora'?"

"Korea," he corrected her. "You remember a lot." She found Scottie's photograph in uniform inside a flannel shirt's pocket which was hanging in the bedroom closet. That photograph led her to ask all sorts of questions about that war whose incidents he would rather forget. Now, he was puzzled how that photograph survived and got into that shirt's pocket. Before leaving California, he destroyed all his pictures taken in Korea, burned his uniforms, headgears and service ribbons having decided to erase that savage war from himself, his memories.

"Tell me more about your life in that **guerra,"** she persisted, intrigued about that period in her hombre's life.

"Gabby, I don't want to talk about that war. Not even think about it. Zilch."

"But I want to know more about your whole life. So I can understand you **mejor**…eh…better. Everything about you. **Tu vida entera.** Because..," she hesitated, "because I love you...." and kissed him on the cheek. But hardly aware of her affection, his mind was riveted on that brutal war reliving an old consuming torment once more.

Scottie was wondering how they got into this topic he had shunned adamantly. *I can't dissect my agonies of that painful past*. Moreover, he was despondent over Concha's probable fate and was already grieving. Since he was not responding to her request, she did not press on him about that war rationalizing erroneously that her hombre was just being modest about his wartime bravery. At that time, she knew what he needed after that bad news possibly about Concha and the bandits. Returning from the bar, she handed him his favorite margarita and poured a glass of sherry for herself. She sat close to him.

"Thanks, Gabby. You remember my **calmante**, my tranquilizer."

"I never forget anything that you like," she answered candidly Deeply touched by her spontaneous declaration of love and loyalty, his trouble feelings eased somewhat. The salty suave drink never tasted so refreshing to him. However, his frowned look clued her that he was still distressed. "You should talk about the **guerra** because its bad parts, I believe, are still bothering you. By talking about them, you throw them out like what cough medicine does to your **flema** when you have a bad cold, **si**? After you talk, you will feel better. **Es la verdad**. It is the truth."

Her soothing words -- *common sense*, he thought -- softened the brutal news they just read. Yet, he was depressed. The specters from the Korean War haunted him again. That long suppressed past surfaced once more and vividly paraded before him: boot camp training in Spokane; that tedious cargo plane trip across the Pacific Ocean to Seoul; the dreary barracks life in Korea; convalescence from the combat wounds at the VA hospital in San Francisco.

Scottie shuddered in the chair when his last combat mission flashed through his mind. The faces of his buddies, Tex, Harry, and Marty reappeared: so alive. During that bright morning in May, they were installing demolition charges on that bridge over Chinau river when two rifle grenades exploded in their midst.

"Somebody goofed," he began to talk and felt compelled to gesture with trembling hands. "Without warning, the enemy was upon us. I saw Tex yelling as he fell off the bridge. Machinegun fire opened up spewing bullets past us. I fled toward the other end of the bridge. Harry was running behind me and stumbled. I was hit in the legs causing me to fall at the foot of the bridge. Then, a loud explosion shook me and the truss structure collapsed under me going downward to the river below and settled above the water. I was losing a lot of blood when the medics picked me up with a stretcher. We succeeded! Then, I lost consciousness.

"When I woke up, I was in a field hospital below Pusan near the peninsula's tip. The communists were pushing hard to drive us and our allies to the sea. The medic captain who examined me said my lower torso and legs were injured but didn't give details. I was running a high fever and too sick to give a damn. Sorry, I'm talking too fast. I'm excitable.

"I knew I was hurt bad and felt the pains every time the morphine shot wore out but I survived. My buddies didn't. Why was I spared while my buddies were killed?"

"You were lucky. **Tuviste la buena suerte.**" She reached out and clasped his shoulder.

"And here I am, still alive, wounded but alive...."

"Do not feel guilty," she consoled him. "Your **amigos** were summoned by **El Señor**. It was not your time yet."

"My buddies would still be alive were it not for some idiots who were sleeping at their posts...." His hands were trembling again. Slipping away, she came back with his medicine bottle and a spoon.

"You're so efficient," he complimented her, "but I must wait. I don't want to mix this medicine with the margarita." Steadying his hand, he drank the glass empty. "Why am I telling you all this...my tragic…my painful past?" He had forgotten what induced him to talk about the war in the first place.

"Because I asked you," she answered. "I want those bad parts to come out of your intestines." She leaned down, planted her cheek against his and hugged him.

"Did you say 'out of my intestines' ?" He was puzzled.

"**Si, patron.** It is a local belief. **Nada mas**. Nothing more."

Soon he was woozy, and the bugbear from his wartime past faded away while he dreamed about those happy college days at the University of Illinois at the Champaign-Urbana campus using the GI bill to earn his civil engineering degree.

In a couple of days, Scottie was going full tilt once more with his job and enjoying every minute. Despite his work load, he got misty-eyed every time he remembered Concha. A mid-day radio news confirmed the woman killed with the bandits was indeed Commissioner Pertierra's daughter. Depressed by the truth of the news, he was slow to call the commissioner and offer his condolences. But he called him three days later.

Except for the section through the Mendieta estate, the construction schedule was moving ahead. The right-of-way dispute for this **estancia** was still pending in the court. While inspecting the section North of the Mendieta estate for the first time, he saw Mel who was overjoyed to see him again. Once more, Mel warned him about the overt threats by the landowners' henchmen. And again, Scottie dismissed that warning and he was stubbornly convinced these landlords were trying to scare him off his job.

****

Peñalosa had been boringly quiet with no major social events. With Aurora's untimely demise, no one replaced her as the pushy organizer for the town fiestas. Even some of her detractors admitted it would be difficult to organize those fiestas and **verbenas** without the guiding hand of the despised and feared **"Madre Superior."**

"Somebody else is missing too from the town scene besides Aurora and Heidi. Know whom I mean?" Scottie remarked while they were sipping their drinks in the courtyard one late afternoon.

"Pablo, Aurora's husband, **el golpista**."

"What do you mean by that?"

"Pablo beats **su mujer**, his wife," she explained.

"No, I wouldn't miss that drunkard. I'm thinking about Padre Joe. I asked you already last week when I came back. Remember? Have you seen him since then?"

"To be honest, I have not. I had lunch with the padre and Heidi the day before she ran away. That was the last time."

"Well, does he say Mass at all?" He could not accept that gregarious priest could just drop out of sight.

"I have not gone to church since you left for the trip. Last Friday I saw Don Jose´ Luis in the public market. He asked me about the padre, **tambien**. "

"That's very strange. I got to find him. If it's okay with you, I would like to invite him for supper tonight." She nodded.

Uneasy about his good friend's mysterious reclusion, he drove over to the rectory to find out. He rang the bell a couple of times. The padre did not come out. After a few more tries with the bell, nobody came to the door. While deliberating what to do, he noticed the door panels were dirty even under the fading light of the late afternoon. Five minutes passed and he became convinced the padre, even if he were inside, would not come out at all. Walking to the backyard through the garden gate, he checked the kitchen door and found it unlocked. He entered.

"Padre Joe, where are you?" His voice reverberated through the ancient stone building.

"**Vente**, Scootee. Come, I am over here," the padre answered. His voice sounded as if he was inside a deep well.

Scottie, astonished, finally found the padre on the antechamber's couch taking a nap. As the padre got up to greet him, he noticed his unkempt beard, dirty green sport shirt and crumpled plaid slacks.

Geez, *my dear friend has become a hermit.* "Padre Joe, are you okay*?"* He gestured to Scottie that he was fine, nodding his head. Yet to Scottie's perception, he looked dejected and the enthusiasm was gone from his flabby body. Uncomfortable with the darkened room, Scottie walked toward the windows and pulled open the drawn curtains allowing the afternoon sunlight inside. After much coaxing from him, the padre was persuaded to shower, shave, and change to better looking sporty clothes.

It was not until the cover of darkness dominated the outside world that the padre agreed to have dinner with Scottie and Gabby. While driving to the **quinta**, the padre told him to avoid the main street in order to lessen the chance of being seen by his parishioners. Scottie wondered how such a sociable exuberant person could so quickly become a shy recluse.

Relaxing on the living room sofa and nursing a glass of cognac, the padre's spirit buoyed up somewhat after devouring his favorite dish, **Ternera a la Sevillana**, especially prepared for him by Gabby. She also served some boiled **garbanzos** or chick peas to remind him of his Iberian homeland. Heidi was not mentioned during dinner although she was silently foremost in everyone's mind. Her abrupt departure from the padre's domain deflated his flamboyant style and contagious zest for "la dulce vita" -- which had evaporated into thin air.

Despite Heidi's palpable absence that evening, the padre seemed to be enjoying a glorious evening, even telling jokes and reminiscing his secular life before he was ordained and assigned to a parish in Tarragona. Even as he was holding up that brave front, he could no longer contain his grief later that evening.

"Life is not same for me anymore," the padre confessed wistfully. "**Nada mas**," he added, holding back his tears. "I abhor returning tonight to the empty rectory. I wish I were somewhere else where nobody knows me and nobody cares for me either." His eyes saddened as if to signal that the last chapter of his life was coming to a close.

"Padre, it doesn't help to mourn over Heidi." Gabby finally mentioned the unmentionable name hiding heavily in everybody´s conscience. "You will find somebody else. **Ya veras**.´ You will see." Scottie raised his eyebrows, surprised by Gabby's frank turnabout, but did not utter a word. He remembered her abhorrence about priests consorting with women.

No emotion registered on the padre's face when Heidi's name was mentioned. Scottie, ever vigilant of Padre Joe's fickle behavior, was puzzled.

"It is humiliating just thinking about it," the padre started to talk again and helped himself with another glass of cognac from the bottle on the coffee table.

"About what, Padre Joe?" Scottie tried to draw him out.

After a silent reflection and a few more sips of cognac, the padre continued, "I want to take you two into confidence.... This is strictly between us." Scottie was getting annoyed by the padre's laid-back propensity. "I am leaving for good. I sent...my resignation...to the bishop." His voice faltered, choked with emotion. They froze at his words and looked at each other. "I am returning to my native Spain. I need a complete rest. In mind and spirit. Perhaps in Estepona where my favorite nephew lives. Not in Catalonia where my inquisitive relatives would not let me be. You know how Catalans are."

Many hours later, the padre was cozily snuggled on the sofa with his umpteenth glass of cognac discoursing every assailable topic he could think of especially the Spanish civil war and Dictator Francisco Franco. Tired of listening, Scottie decided to keep him awake and from sleeping on their couch until the roosters crowed in the morning. Gabby had gone to the kitchen cleaning the dirty dinnerware and preparing the ingredients for tomorrow's supper.

Scottie stumbled into an innocuous solution. "Padre Joe," he interrupted his rambling monologue. "How about a **paseo** in this cool evening? My paperwork has buried me for the past three days and I could use some exercise and stretch my legs. Will you join me?"

"**Con mucho gusto**, Scootee," the padre agreed, not having seen his friend in many weeks during that ruins trip, he would relish a private chat with him. "Let's not stroll down the Gran Avenida where my parishioners might recognize me."

"Sure, Padre Joe, we'll walk wherever you want to. Want to join us, Gabby?" he hollered to her as he went to his bedroom to pick up a flashlight and a light windbreaker. Once more he realized how badly the padre's self-esteem had suffered with Heidi's departure.

"No, **caballeros**, go right ahead. I have **trabajitos** to do around the house tonight. Do not forget the front door **llave**, Scootee." By intuition, she knew the padre needed to unload his problems in private with his macho friend.

The padre chose the unlighted trail behind the **quinta** for their stroll. By themselves, he opened up to Scottie on how badly his parishioners viewed him after Heidi's departure. Derelict garbage and smelly refuse crowded the littered trail forcing them to meander into the open field. Farther down the uneven field, Scottie's flashlight exposed several garbage cans apparently overturned and their unappetizing contents scattered by foraging animals. The padre said he had no choice but to leave. Scottie noted that Padre Joe kept repeating himself. With their path blocked, they turned back into another trail still deep in their conversation and unwittingly ending up on the Gran Avenida after all.

Weary over the padre's travail about Heidi's departure, Scottie deftly brought up the apocryphal debate between the Dominicans and the Jesuits on how many angels could sit on a single pinhead. The sudden interjection of that quasi-philosophical controversy jarred the padre's thinking to a screeching halt. Heidi's image was totally obliterated by Scottie's careful aim.

"**Buenas noches,** padre," an elderly man greeted him. The padre mumbled back to him, then, looking back furtively at the man, stopped and slapped his forehead. "**Santamaria!** We are on the Gran Avenida! Let us turn back to another street and hurry to the rectory."

Once they were inside the rectory, the padre turned the lamps on and once more drew close the anteroom's curtains. "As I told you, I shall leave this place very soon," he said rather sadly, and then breathed a sigh of relief. "I have to admit I was mortified after Heidi left. But now, it doesn't matter anymore. **No me importa mas**. May I offer you a drink?"

Scottie just noticed the dark bags under those sad eyes. "Tequila with ice, if you have it." He realized Heidi's dominance still prevailed over the poor padre.

"**Vamos a ver.**" The padre walked to check the pantry. "Sorry, no tequila. I have a bottle of Tio Pepe. Also, Greek cognac."

"A glass of Tio Pepe will be okey-dokey." The padre stopped in his tracks and laughed for the first time.

"You and your 'okey-dokey'! I will miss hearing that from you." Then, he continued, "Too bad, you don't drink Santa Helena. Good for the blood. I have more left after I leave." He fetched two crystal glasses from the buffet and poured from the two bottles. "Here you are. Please sit down anywhere. I have two cases of Santa Helena. Are you sure you do not want to have them?"

"No, thank you, Padre Joe. I'm just very picky about my wines due to my sensitive stomach."

"**Bueno**. I gave you the first choice. I bet Victor, my **sacristan**, you know, my faithful help, will be very happy to have those cases of Santa Helena."

The padre sat across from him on a comfortable sofa and began to reminisce about his past life. "It is hard to survive in this world without someone who cares about you from one day to another. A priest's life is a lonely one. People were always around me every day, every minute while I attend to the church activities and my own needs. Yet they were not close to me as real friends. I was really alone, **solitario**, until you arrived. **Entiendes**? Get what I mean?"

"Thank you for counting me as your friend. But Padre Joe, as a priest you took the vow to serve God exclusively during your lifetime which means living alone, doesn't it? I hope you don't mind my saying so." Despite his bitter memories surrounding Reverend Dan back in Laredo, that man of God was still his model for clerics. The desire to return to Laredo just to see Reverend Dan intruded into his mind again.

"Not at all, Scootee. I shall explain my situation. Allow me to go back to the past which started in my native Spain. It's traditional there or shall we say acceptable, to the parishioners for a priest to have a woman around, usually a relative, to look after the upkeep of his rectory and the rest of the church with the help of some parishioners but especially to cook his meals. Consequently, I'm accustomed to that life style. I don't know how to fry an egg. I would be baffled trying to wash or iron a cassock. Those are a woman's job, whether for a priest or another parishioner. Get what I mean?"

Padre Joe is another male European, chauvinistic, egocentric. Thinks housework is degrading for men and expects only women to do those chores, Scottie surmised silently. *However, I realize he was busy with church work and practically no time for house work.*

"Now, here in South America, these **campesinos** expect their priests to be machos not **maricones** or what you say, sissies. **Justo**? Yes?"

"I believe it's homosexual for a worst definition."

"**Bueno**, you are the expert in English. Anyway, if a priest is to be respected by the parishioners as a macho, he is expected to have a girlfriend. **Una mujer**. It's the accepted life style here, in this wilderness no matter what is written in the church's canon laws. And with Heidi leaving me, my **machismo** is now in doubt. My parishioners are laughing behind my back. They have lost their respect for me." Scottie was surprised to see the padre fighting back his tears.

"Padre Joe, you're carrying this macho problem a bit too far. I know lots of people in this town. who like you for what you are and appreciate what you're doing for them."

"I hope so, I hope so," the padre repeated. "**Pero no me importa**

mas. I have made my decision to leave."

"That's too bad. Many people will miss you, Padre Joe, especially Gabby and I...." His voice quivered, his throat choked as it dawned on him that Peñalosa would never be the way it was. Aurora died. Heidi ran away with Pedro, that salesman from Caracas. And now, his best friend, the padre, was leaving too. A feeling of sadness gripped him as he thought of these people. "It's late," he said after glancing at his watch. "I better be heading home." Scottie got up with a heavy heart after drinking the last drop of his Tio Pepe.

"**Espera un momento**...wait please...." The padre pushed him gently back to his chair. He was reluctant to let Scottie go just yet and refilled their glasses to the brim. "I want you to finish this bottle of Tio Pepe and nobody else," the padre insisted, and choking with emotion, added: "We may never see each other again."

"Don't say that, Padre Joe. I might decide to make a special trip to Spain. Just to see you." Becoming sentimental again, he was not about to let his last friend in Peñalosa slip through his fingers.

"I hope so. **Espero que si**...."

"I can promise that, Padre...Joe...I swear to God, I will see you again!" As if by instinct, the two men rose and hugged each other.

While drinking his refilled glass, Scottie recounted to the padre the rather awkward time they first met at Cafe El Porvenir where they were introduced by the mayor, Don Jose′ Luis. Soon events began to happen fast: the **feria**, followed by a flurry of fiestas and **verbenas**, their nocturnal "Committee of Three" meetings with their free-wheeling conversations past midnight while time passed unnoticed like sand pouring silently down an hourglass: Remembering, he was saddened, never anticipated those happy shared occasions would come to an abrupt end.

For the last time, the proud padre resisted any show of mawkishness about their friendship ending with his imminent departure. Instead he hinted to Scottie to remember him as the flamboyant person during those exciting town celebrations. There was one topic he kept forgetting to discuss with his friend until now.

"I have been thinking a lot about you, Scootee," the padre confessed. "I said to myself, 'this Scootee is a lucky man. He came to this jungle town with a good job, good American salary, and poof! like magic he met this beautiful **mujer joven** who lives for no other reason than to love and please him.' "

"Padre Joe, you better be careful what you say around here. News travel fast in these small **pueblos**," he warned him while chuckling nervously.

"I mean what I just said, It is the truth. **Es la verdad**. You are a lucky man." The padre was determined to press his opinion at this last opportunity. "While things are in place, as you say in your English, I would suggest you marry this devoted girl."

"Padre Joe, I thought you have a license only to perform weddings but none as a marriage broker."

"**Hombre**! I am serious about this matter of Gabriela," the padre answered, half-scolding, not amused with his friend's levity. "Here you have the opportunity to increase your happiness. And hers too."

Although embarrassed with this topic which Scottie considered very personal, he wanted to put matters straight with the padre. Moreover, his friend was leaving and there was no chance his revelation would circulate in town.

"What I'm about to tell you might surprise you. I'm perfectly happy just the way things are between Gabby and me. Not more, not less. You might as well know that I'm not capable of a permanent relationship with a woman. Besides I won't be able to settle down anywhere for several years. With the nature of my job, I have to keep moving." He rose up, then with his open hands, began twirling them in a quirky manner to emphasize the futility of committing himself to a woman and marriage.

Distracted from his own private grief, the padre frowned unsure whether he understood what his friend was confiding to him. Then, those intriguing explanations confessed bit by bit through the evening suddenly fused together in his mind. "Do not tell me you are running away from something? Are you, Scootee?"

"Maybe I do. Maybe I don't."

"Amigo, we cannot part like this! Scootee, I shall leave this place and you hand me an unsolved puzzle about you. I shall die without knowing what will happen to you. **Que barbaridad**!"

"I told you already, Padre Joe. I can't commit myself to any woman. Or have a permanent relationship. That's all." Unwittingly this time, he was tapping the table nervously with his empty glass to emphasize his remark.

"**Santamaria**! You confuse me, Scootee." He leaned closer across the coffee table. "I do not desire to be personal but are you not sleeping with Gabriela? **Si**?"

Scottie smiled, peeved at the padre, not sure how to answer his embarrassing question. The padre thought he was smirking at him.

"I don't blame you for thinking that way. Hell! Everybody's doing it these days. Even the birds and the bees." Angry but unwilling to show it, he was sarcastic. "To be frank, Padre Joe, I don't sleep with Gabby." He noticed the padre's bewildered face twitching. "Nevertheless, I love that girl very much. I shall take care of her welfare from wherever I might be in the future." His words stunned the padre who was tongue-tied for several minutes, thoroughly confused. Scottie was getting uneasy.

"Scootee, I have a hard time believing my ears. **Sin embargo**, I believe you. I always do. But please forgive me for intruding into your private life. Because I care for you very much too. But, please do not leave this puzzle of yours hanging over my head **para siempre**, forever. I can't imagine a macho like you not taking a piece of that virgin pastry. **No hombre**! This is hard for me to accept." Having imbibed his limit of Santa Helenas, the padre's left eye started blinking involuntarily.

"I must confess that at times our relationship is difficult for me to bear. After saving her from jumping off your belfry, I promised her I'll help her find a niche in this crazy world of ours. Until she's stable and secure, I shall continue to take care of her even though I may be far away. I told you that already."

The padre shook his head still unable to digest his friend's words. "Most extra...extraordinary!" he exclaimed, "and I am very confused still! I thought I knew everything about you. **Pero no**! **Tu eres**…You are…the most extraordinary man. An idealist. Another Don Quixote! I... I just know nothin' what to say more...."

By then, the soothing Tio Pepe further dissolved whatever inhibitions Scottie harbored and decided to share his secret with the padre aware that they might never meet again anyway.

"Padre Joe, I want to tell you something very confidential. Can I trust you not to reveal it to anybody else? No exception?"

"I swear to our dear Lord, I do. My lips are sealed. Like in the confessional," the padre reassured him.

"You are aware that there are things in life which one can't change even if he wanted to. One has to accept his fate. The truth of the matter is...that I must. I got to be this way with Gabby. I mean my relationship with her. I don't have a choice." Having confessed his case to a departing friend, Scottie felt strangely relieved. A burden was lifted from his shoulders for sharing his secret.

"Maybe I have drunk too much **vino**," the padre said, becoming even more perplexed. **"Caramba**! I am even more confused!"

"Got to be this way, Padre Joe. I have no choice," he repeated.

At past midnight, the **vino** had taken possession of the padre. Any further explanation of Scottie's platonic arrangement with Gabby was futile. One **abrazo** after another, Scottie finally bid his friend goodbye with a heavy heart. The padre, in an emotional last-minute flare-up made Scottie repeat his promise to visit him in Spain. Scottie, soaked up with Tio Pepe and filled with melodramatic overload, swore on the padre's missal he would make that Iberian journey to visit his friend whatever it took.

Staggering home on foot, Scottie lost his way at the eastern edge of town. When he passed by the sawmill on the road to Villapuente, he realized his mistake. Eventually he got home at four in the morning. Gabby was still up, worried, steadfastly waiting. Under her watchful eye, he climbed into bed, dead tired, mumbling apologies to her.

CHAPTER VII

Padre Casals sneaked out of Peñalosa the next day on Aerotal's last night flight to Bogota´. Nobody in town knew he left until the following morning. Unknown to the padre, he had considerable admirers among the parishioners who might have tried to persuade him to stay on had they known their likable man of the cloth was planning to leave town. They were disappointed and some vocally expressed their sadness to Scottie. Scottie speculated that Don Jose´ Luis, who was tight-lipped and dismissive about the padre's departure, must have driven the padre to the airport and probably helped to disguise the padre who boarded under an bogus name.

After having lived in Peñalosa a little over a year, Scottie felt strange, alone, and missed those people, like the padre, who left the local scene for voluntary or involuntary reasons. Peñalosa, reminding him of the other places he had lived and worked before on a transient basis, would never be the same again. Experiencing those nostalgic pangs once more, he became reluctant to cultivate new friends. Besides, he was aware his time was running out too.

A Franciscan missionary, with a Goyaese sad long face, counter-weighted by a scraggy full beard, arrived in town six days after Padre Casals' unceremonious departure. The new parish priest, Luigi Pellini, was a Piedmonte native whose previous assignment was a desolate Indian mission on a plateau in the Venezuelan Gran Sabana region. Except with **indios**, this padre had difficulty relating to Scottie and even to the town folks. At first, Scottie was baffled by the missionary's rather peculiar behavior. Later, he attributed Padre Pellini's oddity to his prolonged seclusion among the primitive people. Disappointed with the padre's vapidity, he shunned contact with him.

As a consequence of Padre Pellini's unexciting demeanor and absence of town festivities due to Aurora's demise, Scottie devoted his attention totally to his work routine which recently was rather uneventful. Except for the by-passed section of the Mendieta estate which had been under court litigation for more than four months then, the highway construction project was heading towards completion.

Another suspect home-made brown envelope arrived at the **quinta**. Like previous such envelopes, the enclosed threat letter ordered him to leave town. This time though, it demanded that he leave in a week or else. Instead of tearing up the letter which he had done with the previous ones, he turned it over to Colonel Perez Alvarez. The colonel agreed with Scottie that Don Jose′ Mendieta was the prime suspect. Like the previous threat letters, the colonel said there was no positive evidence to link this letter to the disgruntled landowner. After months of investigation by the police of the threat and no progress, Scottie was losing confidence on the colonel and his staff to get results on this case. Having received a handful of these threatening letters, he was becoming rather callous about its nearly repetitious message.

"I would highly recommend you hire a couple of bodyguards and buy some firearms to defend yourself. One of these should be a **carabina**. You will need them, amigo," the police chief advised him. The colonel, an enterprising but overcautious mulatto from Cali, left his lucrative investigative agency when the Cali drug cartel began to flex its muscles. He recited a list of items and told Scottie he must buy them: bulletproof vest, armor-plated limousine, work irregular hours, hire a double, move to a maximum security compound, construct a high wall around his **quinta**, and so on. Scottie was incredulous, then dismissive of the colonel, and wished he never presented his problem to him.

"**Coronel**, I appreciate your suggestions but I'm afraid I won't be able to do my job with all these pieces of equipment on me and comply with those security measures. I can't ask my company to spend such large sums of money for my security when this construction work will be over soon. And as a matter of principle, I'll never shoot at another man again."

But the colonel's span of attention was short-lived. Having said what he honestly recommended, his mind latched its attention on the crumpled paper with the jumbled pasted letters forming words of threat and ordering the gringo to leave the country once more.

"I did my share of killing in Korea," Scottie continued. "No siree. No more violence for me." But his words fell on deaf ears for the colonel who could only "hear" his own mind.

"That third sentence worries me," the colonel observed while he rubbed his goatee. "LAST PLANE LEAVES 7:15 pm SATURDAY," he repeated many times as if he was trying to decode a secret message. "Hm-m-m....No **campesino** could have composed that letter. Whoever wrote that threat must be a well-educated men. I swear. **Sin duda**! Amigo, follow my advice, buy everything I told you and follow those security measures. I have witnessed so many killings. Just horrible...."

Later that morning, the mayor came by Scottie's office and repeated the police chief's admonition and his "laundry list" of what to buy and to do practically verbatim with the colonel's. Scottie suspected the mayor and the chief got together earlier. "I'm not easily scared," he reassured Don Jose′ Luis insisting the coward had to resort to a letter and was afraid to face him.

They had lunch at the El Porvenir Cafe. By the time they were relaxing and drinking coffee, Scottie updated the mayor on Gabby's tutoring progress and remarked she should be ready and qualified soon to work in an office.

"Mi **esposa** say Señor de Montaigne is looking for **una secretaria bilingue.** His secretary now is embarrassed…**embarazada no?**…eh, you say better preg…pregnant?" the mayor informed him. "Señor de Montaigne? You met him?"

"Hm-m-m...I don't think I have met him."

"He is the **gerente** of Servicios Petroleros Andinos. **O mejor dicho, eSe, Pe y A....** Their camp is **sur de** Villapuente."

"That job sounds like it would fit Gabby like a glove."

"Fits like a glove...**guante**, eh?"

"Just an expression, Don Jose′ Luis. It means a perfect match."

"**Ojala′ que si**. I hope so. I hope so."

"I shall take a long lunch break and tell Gabby to get in touch with Doña Maria Luisa **pronto**. I'm concerned that position may not be open anymore." Coming home late that evening, Gabby was at the door to greet Scottie. Before she could talk, Scottie easily read on her face there was good news about that job with the service company. Gabby said she could start right away but was puzzled that she was hired having no previous experience in an office. Doña Maria Luisa, he concluded silently, used her influence to get Gabby hired.

Later that evening, Gabby had mixed feelings about the job for she worried that working in an office and earning a salary might jeopardize her relationship with Scottie. She would rather stay home, keep house and cook for him, and most importantly for her, she would always be at home to greet him after work.

One evening Carmen showed up unexpectedly. Her restaurant venture in Monteria was a flop, she related. Despite the unspoken displeasure written on Gabby's face, Scottie rehired Carmen on the spot. After Carmen left, he explained to Gabby that a housekeeper was now a necessity since she would be working all day.

What he did not tell Gabby was he told Carmen to keep an eye on her while he was on the job especially if he had to travel to the Bogota′ office and stay for a couple of days. He did not trust the maid whom he considered less bright than Carmen.

The following morning when Gabby was at the **edificio municipal** getting her documents which were required for the job**,** Scottie impressed on Carmen that her primary duty, like the first time, was to keep a vigilant watch over Gabby and everything else came second. She then begged him not to bring her before the new padre and swear like he required her to do before Padre Joe.

Gabby never liked having other persons in the house whenever they were having their "happy hour" by the fountain and during supper. After arriving home from her office job, she had Carmen and Maria, the maid, prepare dinner. By the time Scottie arrived home, Carmen was sent home and the maid to her quarters. After their "happy hour," she would do the finishing touches on the dining table like lighting the slender candles and turning on the record player with one of his favorite classical pieces. When it was time for after-dinner liquors, she would call Maria back to clear the table and wash everything in the servants' kitchen insuring their privacy for the rest of the evening.

Their life was sailing smoothly with Gabby virtually in charge of the household despite her full-time office job. She was much happier with her **hombre** predictably coming home regularly every night with no detour to the Café like in the past with Padre Joe and Aurora. With the **quinta** as the centerpiece of their comfortable Camelot of sorts, their shared life went on as if, like a seaworthy boat, it would sail on forever.

Several weeks passed bringing the highway construction project closer to completion. Each morning, he had to revise the termination date depending on the progress of the previous day -- and which he summarized in the telex report sent to the Bogota′ office. This daily report made him uneasy for it also signaled the end of their blissful life together. After sleepless nights and distracting introspections at work, cold logic told him time and again to stop kidding himself: He could not make love to her. Consequently, he must gracefully leave her for good and keep his personal secret and agony to himself. The mutual heart-breaking parting, he reasoned, was preferable than the humiliation of exposing his secret to her and possibly spreading the truth to his foremen and other employees and even to the bosses in Bogota′. Lately, Scottie became more reticent about the gradually winding-down activities of the project and his job as well. When Gabby pressed him about the latest completion date of the project, he was evasive. Nonetheless, by intuition, she sensed the inconspicuous changes in his work schedule. Having bonded emotionally with him, she expected him to propose marriage eventually and could never accept the possibility their life together might end with the completion of the highway project.

With each passing day, her anxiety escalated as he consistently avoided the unmentionable topic. At her office, she tended to stare blankly through the window as if mesmerized by some unseen sorcerer. Although she knew that he was not forthcoming about what might happen to their relationship, she could not get mad at him for she was deeply in love. She sensed her hombre's behavior was becoming strange lately. Only she could not figure out what was causing it. At least not yet.

One evening after supper, Gabby was struggling to finish a letter to Heidi in the living room. She could not contain her preoccupation about their future any longer.

"What are you going to do after this **carretera** is finished?" she asked him point-blank putting her pen and writing pad aside on the coffee table. Scottie was reading the newspaper on his favorite leather chair.

"I don't know yet. I have to check with the bosses in Bogota′," he answered, feeling uneasy, again equivocal on this topic.

"But you have to know," she insisted. "When this **carretera** is done, you and your men cannot sit around and play dominoes. **No es posible.** Are you staying for another project in Colombia?" This time, she was determined to know the truth.

"I'm sure I will stay for a while. There are several projects we placed bids with the government." He was afraid to tell her about his likely departure from the country.

"I do not know if you are telling me everything." She could not bring herself to accuse him of lying to her, afraid of losing her hombre for good. "I have this feeling about your job and it is no good. I have my job, as you said, so I can become independent. I am afraid to think our life together might be ending." Tears tumbled out of her eyes. She finally told him what she wanted to say without quarreling with him.

For a long time he had dreaded this conversation would come up. And now it happened. Looking back, he realized that by breaking his own rules against living close to the opposite sex, he would eventually end up into the dilemma he was now facing. *I am never capable of making love to her or any woman. My grievous mistake*. The harsh truth, which he tried to ignore and hide from her, had finally caught up with him. There was no choice for him but to tell her the truth as gently as he could.

"Gabby dearest, I'm doing everything to help you become more independent with each passing day. Now you have a good job by which you can grow on with experience. You are starting to take care of yourself." She began to sob in earnest and he was not sure if she was listening. He continued, "Some day a young man will appear, fall in love with you and ask you to...."

"No! no! no! **No me digas!** Do not tell me!" She dropped the pen on the letter she was writing and ran outside with a wild look about her as she jumped over the patio's low stone wall. Puffing hard, she was racing beyond the garbage dump.

"Gabby, wait! I will explain," he shouted after coming out of the rear gate and sprinted toward her diminishing figure. They were heading toward the cemetery grounds when she tripped and fell hard on her face.

"Are you all right? **Estas bien**?" he asked finally catching up with her. She was sobbing and did not answer. "I'm sorry, Gabby. I didn't mean to hurt you." He stroke her back gently which he had never done before trying to placate her. "Gabby...I...I love you...dearly...." He never confessed those words to her before.

She stopped crying, turned around slowly and looked straight at him. Her stare made him uncomfortable. "Then," she said, "why are you...telling me...those terrible words...telling me to go to another man...."

"I love you, Gabby but...but I'm not...able to.... I'm...too old already...."

"You tell me that you love me...then, you want to send me away...to another man! **Tonterias**! Nonsense!" She began to sob again.

"Gabby, you don't understand. I love you. I really love you...but I'm not able to.... I don't know how to explain it...." In exasperation, he raised her up with his arm around her. They stood close, wrapped together in body and spirit, both emotionally vulnerable.

"I love you too. I'll never be interested in other men. Never! I want to be with you...for the rest...of my life...."

Oh Lord, he said to himself, holding her closer. *What will I do? I love this girl and I don't want to break her heart. You know I'm incapable of loving her totally. Must I reveal my secret to her and hope she will accept me as I am? But I'll be so humiliated. Lord help me!*

Walking back to the **quinta,** arm in arm, Scottie promised once more to stay longer in the country. Still he could not reveal his secret to her for he found it excruciating. Arriving at the **quinta** with his dilemma unresolved that night, his mental anguish worsened.

Providentially, he learned another highway project was awarded to the company. The highway between Cali and Tulua´ was to be up-graded to concrete. His bosses, aware of Scottie's rapport with the local employees, asked him if he wanted to manage that project. Temporizing on accepting, he requested a fortnight to think it over.

Two days before Gabby's birthday. Scottie asked her, "Shall we throw a party for your birthday?" Still unsure what to do about their relationship and their future, he was solicitous to please her.

"Do you think we should?" She nursed doubts, and could not remember ever having a big party for any of her birthdays.

"**Bueno**, it's up to you. It's your birthday."

"If you can combine it with your business party with a secret party for my birthday -- **esta bien para mi**. **Quizas**. Maybe. But for just my **cumpleaños**, I am not really enthusiastic. Heidi, **mi amiga**, is gone. So is dear Padre Casals. Whom shall I invite? The people in my office? **Claro que no**. But I have an idea...." She looked coy out of the corner of her eye and yet stopped short of explaining.

"Well, do you have something else in mind?"

"I think you will like my idea," she hesitated, testing his curiosity. "Maybe you may not like it..."

"Come on, Gabby. Tell me! tell me!" He was getting impatient.

"You really want me to....?" **De por si**?

"Yes, of course. Don't keep me guessing. You're driving me nuts. Tell me."

"I would rather go to the island of Margarita...**en la playa**...on the beach."

"Go to an island?" He could not relate a business party with a secret birthday celebration ending up on an island. "Where is that?"

"In Venezuela, northeast of Caracas. Heidi wrote me about it in her last letter."

"So Heidi told you about it. How do you know it's a nice place to go? Why go that far when there are nice beaches in Cartagena too."

"Heidi sent me some pictures.. Margarita is very beautiful." He was slow to absorb her unusual request. "So you do not like my idea?"

"I didn't say that. It was just I was planning a birthday party for you. You never told me about those pictures from Heidi."

"Besides the pictures, Heidi wrote a letter about the nice people there who talk like they are singing, the pearl divers. Very romantic place. They spent a week."

"So Heidi is enjoying life with that salesman, whatever his name is." She was not sure if he was being sarcastic about those two lovers. Silently he was mulling over the trip to that island. *It might be good after all to get away from Peñalosa for a while. I need to go somewhere to think over whether I should accept that new project.* "You know," he spoke again, "Margarita island is far away from here. You'll need a passport. It requires more than a weekend for a trip to go there and right now I can't stay away that long."

"It was just an idea," she sighed thinking he decided they were not going anywhere after all. *It is not the right time to ask him. He is too busy preparing the inauguration of the highway.*

"I'm thinking of an alternative," he countered not wanting to disappoint her. "What about going to Cartagena for the weekend?"

"Do you realize Cartagena is my hometown? **Que va, patron**!"

"What's wrong with going there? Your hometown? I heard there are beautiful beaches as pretty as those in Venezuela."

"I have sad memories of that pueblo, Scootee. **Muy triste**. Very sad." Any mention of that town depressed her even though she left more than five years ago. Her best friend married her **novio**. She told him that before and wondered if he remembered. "What about Bogota´?" she suggested. "I have never been there."

"Well then, señorita **muy guapa**, Bogota´, here we come!" he said, smiling, feigning enthusiasm, hoping to uplift her from a depressed mood. For him, Bogota´ was just stopover for business trips.

"Oh, Scootee, I love you! I'm so happy! So happy!" She hugged him and then tried to lead him into an impromptu **cumbia** dance.

"Hey! We can't dance without music," he wisecracked. *It would be interesting to explore the Big Town for fun.* "I shall make the hotel reservations and buy the airline tickets tomorrow. It will do us good to get out of Peñalosa even just for a weekend," he added.

The much-awaited weekend arrived. That Friday evening they were strolling along the Big Town's sidewalks incognito among the bogoteños. Scottie self-deprecatingly called themselves "bush yokels" for staring too long at store windows and getting in the way of pedestrians while looking up at the old and modern buildings interspersed with neat well-kept gardens. The sights and sounds of the metropolis awed Gabby -- it was her maiden visit, and she held on to his arm. Although nervous and intimidated by the hustle and bustle at the bottom of this alluring Big Town atmosphere, her dreams and desires began to converge into the unfamiliar milieu with its refreshing air of perpetual spring. Hours later while they were enjoying their drinks and people-watching at a sidewalk cafe, she was ready to take a bold move.

"I want to live here," she said wistfully looking at her love.

Her remark hit the right note in Scottie's mind for he was mulling over that Cali-to-Tulua´ road project. *If I should accept that project, I could live in Bogota´ and commute to the work site.* He wanted to temporize about leaving the country and continue their relationship to give it more time.

"Look at the shops with those fancy lacy things **Fabulosa**! So many places to see. I could be happy here. You can be happy here too, **si**?"

Scottie did not hear her. *Perhaps I could find a solution. God! I could love this woman forever. I wish I could.* His conflicted mind deep-six'd her wishful commentaries.

It does not matter, she thought. *I could be happy with him anywhere.* She squeezed his hand hard and looked at him adoringly with those turquoise eyes. Scottie "woke up" and assumed he must have dozed off. "I love you. Do you love me? Just a bit too?" she asked, revealing her emotional dependence on him.

"Of course, I love you…the first time I saw you," he said simply letting his candid thoughts translate orally but careful not to mention the church belfry. Yet haunted by his physical incapacity, he suffered a quiet desperation.

"Oh Scootee!" she burst out overflowing with good feelings, cheerfulness. "I am so happy! **Muy feliz**! I wish everything would last forever." Then, she noticed that tinge of sadness in his eyes. "You are quiet, **mi patron**. Are you all right?"

"I'm okay. I'm...enjoying myself. Just like you," he reassured her concealing bravely the tide of sadness he could never explain to her.

Strolling to a well-manicured park lighted with Victorian-style lamp posts, she told him she was dreaming and pinching herself to make sure it was a dream come true.

"Oh, look at the falling star," she pointed excitedly at a faint luminous streak racing downward through the darkened sky until it disappeared. "I made a wish."

"What is your wish?"

"**Oye**, **sabes las reglas**. You know the rules. One is not supposed to tell anybody. **Mala suerte**. You call that bad look?" She bit her lips. Then, in a fit of playfulness, she pinched his forearm.

"Ouch! What did you do that for?"

"Because you are teasing me."

Teasing her? Her behavior puzzled him. *She's probably feisty tonight. Shame on you, Scottie,* he scolded himself. *Loosen up, you stuffed shirt! You took her to Big Town to laugh and have fun. So be enthused like her. Hang loose, sourpuss!* He forced himself to pull in his sadness and started telling her silly jokes which surprised her at first but caught on to top them with her own more **al vivo,** naughty ones. Graduating to tickling each other unmindful of the stares from the pedestrians until a cop crossing their path caused them to behave more soberly like the upper-crust bogoteños strolling in the night scene.

After a late dinner at the Tequedama Hotel's roof garden, they danced under the stars with Gabby leading him with the steps. "**Maravillosa**! Just wonderful!," she kept repeating as they danced the evening away into the wee hours.

Swallowed by the cosmopolitan tapestry surrounding them, they danced and took sips of sparkling champagne weaving among the sybaritic elite. At past four, they got inside the elevator of their hotel, still engrossed with their silly teasing, but forgot to press the button of their floor. Astounded, unbelieving, they could not understand why they ended up at the top floor and barged into a closed restaurant surprising the waiters who were clearing the tables and mopping the floor. Exuberant and giddy, Gabby was singing her heart out with a popular love song which he accompanied with humming. Waving frivolously at the waiters, they turned around and took to the stairwell still harmonizing their voices.

"**Besame, besame mucho**, as if tonight were the last time...." Gabby kept singing in her tired hoarse voice as they descended bouncingly down the stairs. Her singing rendition was unmelodious but he was feeling no pain and thought she was singing marvelously. Doctor Viola had warned him about too much alcohol could unravel her fragile composure. Tonight, that concern was farthest from his mind.

"You do not know anything about me!" she declared and pinched his forearm again.

"Ouch! You're hurting me!" The unexpected tease was worse than the pain. She was about to do it again. "Stop it, Gabby...."

"I want to tease you tonight."

"You have teased me more than enough." She continued singing while they walked down to the fourth floor where their rooms were.

" '...I am so afraid to lose you and lose you after'.... Now sing with me."

"You know by now I can't carry a tune," he protested. "Besides we might disturb the other hotel guests." By then, he felt tired and didn't feel like humming.

"**Si**, you can sing, **mi amor**. You can do anything. Anything! Okey-dokey?"

"I can't sing. Honest." But she was not listening as he unlocked his hotel door. Mixed emotions shuffled, clashed, inside him. *Nobody else cared for me as much as her. No other woman adored me like her. Such naive trusting love for me. And for me, incapable of loving her in return.... I don't want to abandon her...yet Lord...I must leave her...*

"Here is the song I should have sang earlier tonight. '**Yo podria amar solamente una vez en mi vida'**....Remember those words... 'I can love only once in my life.' and that is you! **Tu! tu!"** She poked her finger into his chest.

Abandoning her was like stabbing her in the back, he thought and felt miserable as he unlocked her door.

"**Y otro asunto**...I do not like this business of two separate rooms. I want the door between the rooms open. **Abierta**."

"As you wish, señorita," he replied, not willing to argue with her in her tipsy condition. Moreover, he could keep a vigilant ear in case she got sick. Both in their respective rooms, Scottie enjoyed a hot shower pelting his tired body after what he considered a relaxing evening. After turning off the water, he could hear Gabby still singing in her crackly voice above her shower's monotone drizzle.

Much later, he heard her frantic voice. "Scootee! Scootee!"

"What is it?"

"Scootee, you forgot to kiss me good night."

"It's morning already."

"What are you trying to be? **Un sabetodo**? A wise guy?"

It slew him every time she threw back one of his own expressions at him, especially when he least expected it.

"Besides, I want to be tucked in my bed," she demanded.

"I'm still in my shower," he shouted back. He was spooked again by remembering he had to tuck in little sister, Carrie, after their mother passed away. *She wants my attention and I'm so tired,* he complained silently. After shaving and putting on his pajamas, he noticed how quiet she was. Gabby was not singing. *I didn't even realized she stopped.* Grabbing his morning coat, he peeked into her room. Her clothes were scattered on the empty bed. The lighted bathroom's door was open but she was not there. He became alarmed. *Where's she? Her bad dream started again?* His heart pounded while his eyes searched about her room.

"There she is!" he gasped. Gabby was bent over the balcony rail, naked except for panties. Rushing to the balcony, he grasped and pulled her down and covered her with a blanket. Her eyes were transfixed, glassy like she was in a trance.

"Wake up, Gabby!" he shouted slapping her cheeks vigorously. "Lord, why does this have to happen again?" Tears rolled out unashamedly as he neared his breaking point. Her frightened face appeared to be staring at some unseen specter he could not see yet as suddenly they were sliding together into another uncharted dimension sucked in by powerful energies. Something intervened and zapped his mind. He became aware again that they were in a hotel balcony overlooking downtown Bogota´. The glaze faded from her eyes.

"Those bad people are after me!" she screamed.

"Please, Gabby. Don't shout. I'm here with you." He could not understand what he just experienced but was glad she was awake again.

"Scootee, they gonna kill me! Kill me!" She hugged him while looking back as if her tormentors were about to grab her. "Protect me!"

"There's nobody here but us," he comforted her regaining his own presence of mind. "You had a bad dream. Everything will be okey-dokey." Loosening her embrace, he turned her around and massaged her shoulders gently inducing her to relax and close her eyes. Tucking her into bed, he then slumped on a chair, kept his eyes open until she fell into a deep sleep.

After locking the sliding windows to the balcony, he hurried back to his room and then, returned with a pillow and blanket. He stationed himself in front of the windows to catch some sleep still unable to explain this mysterious relapse of Gabby's malady.

Flying to Peñalosa by noontime from that weekend in Bogota´, Scottie was relieved to have Carmen whom he instructed privately and more bluntly than before to keep a watchful eye on Gabby. Coming home for lunch, he insisted that Gabby take a bitter-tasting medicine, despite her protestations, there and then, in his presence. Until Carmen returned from her lunch break, Scottie did not leave for the office.

The Monday after that Bogota´ weekend fling, Scottie scheduled a meeting with his foremen at the crack of dawn since the lawyers from

Bogota´ were due to arrive that same morning to discuss the court case in the afternoon at two.

Three weeks later, the court case was won in favor of the federal government and Scottie immediately ordered the survey crew into the Mendieta estate with police escort. That night, the foremen and the contract survey crew wanted to celebrate and asked Scottie to come.

He declined to attend. However, he passed money to Mel, the senior foreman, who was escorted by two policemen, and told them to go to a **bodegon** in Villapuente farther away from Peñalosa for a quiet celebration and no boisterous hoopla which might rile the landowners' henchmen.

Next morning, he flew to Bogota´ to confer with the engineers of a data processing firm where the survey data were to be turned into road construction maps. Back in Peñalosa the following day, he organized the construction crews in two 12-hour shifts to work in the Mendieta estate. A platoon of soldiers were assigned by the government for security of the crews. Rumors spread around town that Don Mendieta was upset by the court decision and was cursing at everyone in sight. Even his immediate family could not tolerate him and moved to a friend's country villa for a while.

Once that road strip through the Mendieta estate is completed, the work load will diminish, Scottie surmised that evening while working late. *Mostly clean-up work of the left-over debris.* From then on, he would devote his attention to the details of the highway's inauguration. Aurora's memory kept popping up in his mind: *She would have loved to participate in this highly visible inauguration fiesta where El Presidente will cut the ribbon.* Thinking of Gabby and having to tell her he decided to turn down that Cali-to-Tulua´ road project made him uneasy. Past midnight, he was resigned to face the truth about his impotency and the futility of the relationship with Gabby. His spirits hit rock-bottom as he struggled to finish the paperwork on the desk.

"Come on in, the door is open," he called out at someone knocking at the door. A familiar face greeted him. "Mel, I didn't expect you this late." Mel looked grave. "What's up? Nothing serious, I hope?"

"Everything's fine with the job, Señor Scootee. The concrete pouring job at the Mendieta estate is on schedule. I shall give you more details tomorrow."

"So, you have something else in mind?"

"I have been hearing bad rumors, señor. The **vaqueros** of Don Mendieta, I was told, are planning trouble with our workmen."

"Is that so! Don't you think these **vaqueros** drink too much at those **bodegones** and are just bragging too loudly?"

"I am not taking chances, señor. I heard these threats in many places. So, I moved my family with relatives in town, and I carry this...,"

Mel said unzipping his jacket and revealing quickly a holstered revolver under his left arm on the sly.

"You too, eh?" A disbeliever of violence, Scottie thought he had convinced Mel and the other foremen that they were overreacting to the rumors. "We have adequate protection from the police. And now, we have soldiers too. Carrying guns would only invite trouble. Sooner or later, someone will pull the trigger: BANG! and then another...tragedy."

"But, señor**,** the policemen and soldiers are not with us twenty-four hours a day," Mel, thrusting out his lower lip, moving his hands with palms outward, was emphasizing to him the danger of ignoring the threat. "I know these **vaqueros y son vengativos**…?" Scottie nodded he understood. "Once they hate somebody, they never give up until their victim leaves town or is killed."

Scottie was annoyed with the turn of their conversation to guns and violence. Bad memories of the Korean conflict cast their shadows over him. "Problems are never solved with bullets. We must appeal to reason. Violence will be followed by more violence. **Violencia tras violencia. De por si**. That's for sure."

Mel was not swayed. In deference to his **patron** whom he regarded as a well-intentioned foreigner who has not learned the tough realities of the Colombian interior, he stopped arguing with him. "I grew up in this valley," he continued. "My father brought me here from Santa Marta when I was this high." His hand touched slightly above his knee. "In my lifetime, I witnessed people shot in front of my eyes. Or hanged from branches of trees. No, señor. I am not looking for trouble but when I smell one, I want to be ready to defend myself. I have learned to survive."

"Thanks for your advice, Mel." Scottie put a fatherly hand on Mel's shoulder as he was about to leave. "I don't expect any serious trouble from Don Mendieta while we finish the job at his estate. We have the **gobierno** on our side and there are policemen and even some soldiers to protect us."

"You are our **patron**. We shall do what you order us to do. I just want to warn you of a possible danger. Men talk in the **bodegones** and **cantinas** that the landowners consider you a target for intruding into their estates. **A su orden,** señor. We are at your service to protect you."

As a sop to Mel's apprehension, he promised to discuss the matter again with the mayor underlining his request for increased surveillance on these landowners and their henchmen. Nonetheless, having won this court case against Don Mendieta, he had an uncanny sense that he added another enemy to his list of landowners who hated him. With his relentless zeal to keep the project moving, he reckoned that might be pressing his luck too hard. Not unexpectedly, another threat letter was left at the office building's front door. The letter was enclosed in the same crudely folded envelope. The threat was composed and pasted with the same cut-out letters and words from newspapers.

After work that day, Scottie and Gabby were relaxing on the terrace outside the kitchen sipping their favorite drinks before supper. She managed to come home early that Friday in time for a longer "happy hour." Despite the restful view of the patio with its blooming flowers and the cascading waters of the fountain, the latest threat was still foremost in his mind. Those jumbled pasted words kept coming back to dance disconcertedly in front of him. Unaware of his preoccupation, she was happy, talkative, and quite her normal self to his perception.

****

Her contact with the outside world kept expanding since she started working for the service company, talking more about the people she worked with and less about Heidi. Her mental outlook was more positive and less demanding of Scottie's attention. Still her relapse in Bogota´ worried him. One drink too many triggered that breakdown, he was convinced. *I must be watchful that she doesn't go over the edge again.*

"There will be a party at my **gerente's** mansion next Saturday. Shall we go?" His tired preoccupied mind was slow taking him a long minute to react.

"Go where?" He looked at her blankly. "Where do you want to go now?"

"I already told you. **La casa grande de mi gerente.** My beeg boss."

"Oh, you mean the Montaignes?"

"**Si, si**." Her eager voice betrayed her excitement.

"Of course, Gabby. I won't miss that for anything. We shall go. I want to meet the people from your office." Although dead-tired, he agreed to go not wishing to disappoint her. Hearing his consent, she broke into a big smile.

"You will like them," she assured him, her happy face reflecting how pleased she was with her job and the people she worked with. "We are busy, **muy ocupado**. Most of the time but the office is easy-going, relaxed I would say, **amable**, in Spanish. No day passes with at least two big laughs among us girls. I am happy with my job." She remembered something she almost forgot. "O-oh!"

"Something wrong?"

"O-oh!" She covered her mouth this time. "**Que barbaridad**! I do not have anything to wear for the party."

"A woman's eternal problem! Your **aparadores** are full of dresses and not a single dress to wear for the party!" He teased her. "Go to the **centro** and see what the stores have to offer. I heard from Maria Luisa that Paquita's Boutique has a new shipment of dresses from Bogota´ and Roma."

"I have seen them already during my lunch break last Tuesday."

"Oh yeah? How did you manage to get there from your office?"

"Oh, Marinela, another girl from the office, drove her car. The dresses are not as pretty as those formerly brought in by Heidi's **hombre** from Caracas, mostly from Paris. Anyway, I shall see what I can find. **Vamos a ver**."

Goshalmighty! Gabby surely learns fast when it comes to pretty but expensive dresses. "Any dress you wear looks good on you anyhow," he flattered her, hoping she would not buy more dresses.

"Really? You mean it?" She was beaming.

"Of course. Don't you look at yourself in the mirror?" Casting a side glance, he waited for her reaction.

"Oh! Scootee! I love you! **Te adoro**!" She burst out and kissed him." I wish we could live in a place where we could be happy forever."

"What's wrong with Peñalosa? You're happy here."

"Sometimes **si**, sometimes no," she said, then remained silent for a while. "**Es cierto que no**!" she exploded with vehemence.

"That bad, eh? But why?"

"Together, we do not belong here." She shook her head. "We belong somewhere else."

"And where could that place be?" Rather amused with her late afternoon musing, he encouraged her to open up.

"That place could be anywhere we can honestly belong, put our feet down and live there forever. Peñalosa is not forever. Your project is **finito**. You get another project. You move again. **Demasiado loco**! You say **cray-zee**?" Her remark hit a sensitive nerve in Scottie.

"But this is my work, my life now. I have to go where my job is."

He defended his way of life but his voice faltered remembering what happened last time they talked about the end of this highway project. "I am convinced it is **cray-zee**," she gestured with two hands like she was chopping the thin air. "**Es una locura.**" Her eyes became aglow with a vision, her dream "I want to have a house, a garden and a family...." Her words touched him. "What is life without amigos, eh? **Verdad**? I mean true friends to last a lifetime...**para siempre**...."

"Please, Gabby, Let's not talk now about those things." Biting his lips, he desired those things too of his earlier life she had just reminded him. But after returning from the Korean War, that life with its dreams, taken for granted by other people, was not possible for him to even think about.

The sadness so obvious on his face puzzled her and she wondered why he should be so forlorn when talking about that dreamy life so important, so refreshing for her to talk about. She reached out and held on to his hands. "I am sorry that you are not happy...."

But Scottie was far away, introverted with his thoughts, hardly aware that she was showing her affection and concern by touching his hands. *There is no solution to my problem*, he realized. *Those things I desire most in life are not possible for me. With my war wounds, I can't have a family. Without a family, what's the point of having a house? I can't have friends too long lest they discover my infirmity, my secret. So, I must move on to another place for another project. And after that, another, 'til hell freezes over!* Hiding his bitterness from her, he was suffering badly inside. *Oh Lord, must I push aside my tender feelings for this woman and leave her behind?*

"Oh...I just remember...something," she said, breaking into his musings, "but before I tell you, Let me fill our glasses, first, Okey-dokey?"

"Okey-dokey1" he repeated in jest. *This lovely creature has picked up my crazy vocabulary,* he thought. *My God! I can't stand the notion that I must abandon her for good. She could be my last chance for happiness.* Realizing that he loved this woman, he felt devastated and guilty.

Coming back with their drinks, she sat close next to him. "I think I am being followed. But I could be wrong."

His silent thoughts imploded. "Being followed! Hey, that's very serious, Gabby." Emotionally taut, his perception was muddled, distracted. "And why are you not sure?"

"Each time a different person followed me. Yesterday, a woman dressed in black with dark glasses. Two days ago, a leetle hombre. Last week, a man who looks like **el Ministro de Defensa**. That is why I am not so sure if they are truly following me."

"From now on, someone at your office should drop you off after work. You shouldn't take the autobus. Even waiting at the bus stop may not be safe." He was worried that this new problem might be related to the landowners and the threat letters. *Maybe I should carry a pistol after all and hire a bodyguard for Gabby as well. The situation appears more grim with Gabby. Yes, I am in a pickle. I have to leave. Yet I think Gabby needs a bodyguard for her safety. How can she afford a bodyguard on her salary? No! I'm the problem. She'll be safe after I leave. I'm not thinking logically about the situation here.*

****

The next day it was past six-thirty already and Gabby was not home yet. Scottie called her office at half past five. She left at five o'clock, someone answered the telephone and told him so. Feeling threatened, his imagination conjured a kidnap scheme in the offing. Mad at himself for not taking security precautions right away after their conversation last night, he grew uneasy and restless, mixed his third margarita for want of something to do. After ten more minutes, he decided to call Colonel Perez Alvarez. Before he could call, his phone rang. The caller was Gabby. Her voice somewhat raspy, he imagined she was being held for ransom. Shaken, he let the handset slip from his grasp which fell and bounced on the floor.

" 'alloo...." *The kidnapper wants me to hear her voice*, he thought, becoming stunned and tongue-tied. "Is that you, Scootee?"

"Ye-es.... It's me.... Are you...all right, Gabby?"

"Sure. **Estoy bien**. I..."

"Thank God!" Unknown to her, he was overwhelmed and fell silent.

"Scootee?" No response from him. "Scootee! Answer me!"

"Yes, I...I'm...okay...now...." he replied recovering from shock.

"Can you pick me up?"

"Yes? Me...to pick you up? Where...are you?"

"I am here at Modas de Elena."

"Thank God! I thought...you were kidnapped."

"Keednah-ahp? What do you mean?"

"Never mind. Where is that Modas?" Scottie realized he had overreacted.

"On Calle Ayacucho. The dressmakers." She gave more directions.

Scottie was self-conscious inside the fitting room being the only male among the dressmakers and fitters who were assisting their lady customers in various stages of dressing and undressing. Gabby was nowhere to be seen.

"Scootee! **Estoy aqui**. Over here." Gabby shouted above the drone of the chit-chat of the women and waved her hand above the crowded room. Blushing in a worst way, he walked toward her keeping his eyes down. "**Un momento**." She disappeared inside a dressing booth. Checking his watch and counting the seconds, he was ready to bolt out of this "no-man's land" and wait for her in his truck. But it was too late -- for she came out of the booth wearing a black strapless evening gown while exaggerating her body motions and pantomiming the jerky movements of a supermodel on a fashion runway for the benefit of her hombre's amusement while flicking her eyelashes flirtatiously at him.

"Geez, Gabby! I...I...think...." He swallowed hard and could not continue. The plunging neckline and the bare back startled him. Turning her back to him, she peek coquettishly at him over her shoulder and winked with her left eye. *Goshalmighty*! *She's smashingly attractive,* he confessed.

"Do you like it?" Scottie was lost for words. Inexplicably the naive young maiden imprinted in his mind was momentarily switched to a rather mature, alluring lady he was being mysteriously drawn to. "**Oye**, Scootee! **Echame piropos**!" she asked louder, impatient for his attention. "Eh, throw me nice words!"

"You look lovely," he said simply keeping his reservations to himself. Regaining his down-to-earth frugality, he would rather have her save her salary for the future than squander on expensive gowns. *It's my fault. I spoiled her from the beginning buying her just about everything at Paquita's Boutique.*

Gabby confessed to her friend, Manuela, she preferred black for her gown which would make her look much older when accompanied by her **hombre**. Aware that her love was admiring her, she lifted her eyes to the ceiling and was hamming it up with an air of Latin **delicadeza**. *That black gown makes her look ten years older*, he thought. Strangely enough, Gabby was vindicated with her choice. At that moment, the seduction was too much to bear and he hugged her compulsively despite the women present. "Ouch!" he cried, backing away from her.

"**Los alfileres! Dios mio**! Sorry! I forgot to warn you about the peens on the dress. Does it hurt bad?"

He sucked his fingers. "I'll be okay." Once more he scrutinized the black gown while mindful of the prickly pins. "You know, I think you look better in white dresses like the one you wore during the Cerruza baptism. You look much too old wearing a black gown."

"But I want to look older," she insisted. "I don't like people to mistake me **como tu hija**, your daughter."

"Oh geez!" he exclaimed embarrassed that the other women might hear and understand their conversation. "You mustn't say that." He whispered to her. "I don't want you to look like… my grandmother either. **Como mi abuelita**!"

"**Ay! ay**!" She did not expect him to tease her. "Why you! you!" She hit him playfully on the cheeks with open hands, and kissed him.

****

Saturday night arrived which they reserved for the party of the service company. Guided by the directions given on the invitation card, Scottie drove approximately to where the party was being held for he was not familiar with this western outskirt of the town. The housing compounds were extensive and surrounded by high concrete walls. There were no name shingles nor house numbers at the compounds' gates. With prompting from Gabby, he chose a compound which was heavily encircled with parked cars and pickup trucks suggesting a party going on inside. He had reservations though due to the rundown appearance of the outside walls which had unsightly cement patches.

"You should know by now Latinos do not maintain the exteriors of their villas and **quintas** much less the protective walls," she explained to him. Still skeptical, he took a chance and rang the doorbell. A uniformed servant opened the gate and motioned them to come in. Their attention was arrested by a dilapidated mansion looming with lights in the darkness. It was larger than most mansions he had seen in town. Even then, he didn't want to get embarrassed coming in to the wrong party. *Are we walking to one of the landowners' parties like flies to the proverbial spider's parlor?* he mused, still unsure of the right place while another servant escorted them inside.

The regal interior with its high ceiling and stained-glass windows compelled them to pause and admire the elegance of the mansion. Above the windows, a row of heraldry banners and a faded Flemish tapestry hanging on the opposite wall caught their eyes.

"I have never seen any **casa** like this before," Gabby gasped, awe-stricken. Attracted by the luxurious appointments, she ran her finger tips over a nearby scarlet velvet-covered armchair. Scottie, uneasy, hoped they were at the right party. He had seen pictures of the landowners from the portfolios prepared by the law firms hired by the company. Since no one inside resembled anyone of them, he felt more reassured. Besides, he noted expatriates in attendance.

Another servant ushered them to the open-air patio where most of the guests were gathered. To their right, a combo was playing lively Latin music. Scottie noticed the Roman and Greek mythological statues, sculpted in Carrara marble, which adorned the patio behind some potted palm trees. A waiter approached them and listened to their orders for the bar. While they marveled at the exquisite setting, a man in a dark blue safari suit and white silk ascot, walked toward them. Gabby's roving eyes noticed him.

"Oh, Señor de Montaigne! I should have recognized you **pronti-to**," she greeted the gentleman, surprised at herself for not picking him out sooner. "This is Scootee Reeter, **mi patron**."

"Pleasure to meet you, Scott Ritter. I have heard a lot about you from Gabby. Great compliments, of course." They shook hands. "Please call me, Pierre, and may I address you as Scott?"

"Please do, although I'm better known as 'Scooh-teeh .' "

They both laughed heartily except Gabby who was mystified about what was so funny. She had something else in mind.

"But **Señor** Montaigne, We never address you as Pierre in the office," she objected.

"Uh, uh. That's business. Tonight we're having a fiesta. It's an occasion for informality and relaxation." Pierre winked an eye at Scottie.

Pierre impressed him as a man of the world who was capable of controlling any unexpected situation facing him.

A smiling lady with blushing pink complexion joined their company and extended her hand to them. "I'm Emilie and I belong to him," she said laughing, pointing to her husband, Pierre. "Please make yourselves at home." Then, the hosts moved on to greet more arrivals. Scottie felt overdressed with his coat and tie after noting the sport shirts and slacks worn by the other guests. Gabby pointed to a couple boogying to the mambo piece being played by the musicians.

"I hope we are not too late," Scottie whispered to Gabby after they saw some servants collecting some dirty plates. "I could have misread the time on the invitation card."

"Not at all," Emilie remarked, who was then behind them and overheard his remark. "This is a twenty-four hour party. We have invited three sets of guests. You two, shall we say, belong to the second shift? **Oui**? Hee, hee...." After a sip of her drink, she added: "This party is a short one. We gave a three-day marathon luau in Jakarta."

"How's that possible and still get the company work done by the employees?" Scottie challenged Emilie.

"That's easy. Friday was a French holiday. Then Saturday, and Sunday. We closed down the luau party at eleven PM that Sunday." Emilie, smiling, winked her eye at him. "**Naturellement**, we invited only Christians in that Muslim country and the men on duty had to go and service the rigs. Their wives were invited and could come."

Scottie was intrigued by what Emilie just said and this strange breed of people who worked in the oil business were like those he met in Iran: fun-loving, hard-working, no inhibitions. Some guests were lying on the floor with cushions and appeared very relaxed. Others were obviously asleep on the couches despite the ongoing noise of other guests and the music. A couple got up, adjusted their clothes, and nonchalantly, began dancing to the mambo. Gabby, suppressing giggles, pointed to a mustachioed fellow snoring to his heart's content while lying on assorted pillows next to a potted palm tree.

Since the waiter who took their order was nowhere to be seen, they headed for the bar stand near the combo group and helped themselves with beer. Gabby was watching the dancing couples, itching to dance. The bar stand was too close to the combo's blaring noise and Scottie wanted to move away.

"Oh Scootee, let us dance," she begged him,, "we have not danced since our trip to Bogota´. Okey-dokey?"

"Okey-dokey," he answered reluctantly and smiling at her peculiar mannerism when talking in English and grateful the combo was playing an easy rumba. Then, a samba, a **merengue**, and another samba. After those numbers, half dozen **cumbias** with which he was coached by her.

She was in blissful heaven dancing with her **hombre** as they twirled around and around. Closing her eyes, she wished this magical interlude *would never, never end….*

"Are you asleep?" he asked, joking.

"No," she replied. "Just dreaming like I have never dreamed before. Let us keep dancing...forever!"

Scottie, enjoying the company of this rather enchanting young lady to whom he was now attracted and mystified by her alluring makeover tonight. Moreover, he realized he was falling in love with her -- inevitably as if ordained by some benevolent spirits.

After more than an hour of non-stop dancing, Scottie was exhausted trying to keep up with the different steps of his nimble partner. Taking her where she could sit down, he went to the bar stand switching their drinks to tequila-on-rocks. On the walking toward Gabby through the crowd, someone slapped him on the back.

"Well, Scott, ol' boy. I didn't know you're such a good dancer. Varsity track, yes, but not ballroom dancing. You sure ain't got a license for that!"

Scottie turned around with somewhat raised eyebrows, wondering who knew his name in this oil business crowd. This guest, in a white safari suit with thinning blond hair, was nodding and smiling broadly. He did not recognize him and the impasse was embarrassing to him. "Eh-h...sorry but I don't remember...."

"It's me, Skeeter," the fellow reminded him. "That skinny prankster from Locust Street." Scottie rubbed his chin trying to recall. "I haven't changed that much. Have I?" A tide of thirsty men filtered around them blithely locking Skeeter's arms playfully with theirs and dragging him towards the bar. Shaking his head and laughing about this "unexpected undertow," he walked back to where Scottie was. By then, he remembered Skeeter was his classmate during the sophomore year at Nixon High in Laredo until his family moved to Dallas. He introduced Skeeter to Gabby.

While the classmates were reminiscing, a French bachelor, whom Gabby had seen in her office, asked her for a dance. "**Esta bien para bailar con el** ? Dance with him?" Gabby checked with Scottie.

"Why, of course," Scottie answered, glad that he did not have to dance for a while. "Enjoy yourselves," he added, hardly glancing at them as they melted into the dancing crowd. Shortly, the reunited classmates, deeply involved recalling shared memories, decided to move to the adjoining awning-sheltered terrace where they could sit, talk, and watch the patio activities farthest from the combo's ear-tingling blare.

The last time they met, Skeeter reminded him, was in Pusan during the darkest days of the Korean conflict. Skeeter was visiting a pilot buddy in a field hospital when he chanced upon Scottie after reading his name plate on the bed. Scottie confessed he was running a high fever during his convalescence and could not remember their chance meeting.

"You look sprite and young, pal," Skeeter complimented him. "Call it incredible. When I saw you on that hospital bed wrapped in bandages like King Tut, I doubted if those docs could put you on the mend again. But now, look at you! And a dancer at that! Wow!"

"I'm a survivor all right," Scottie answered tersely. His old classmate had no inkling he was suffering from severe anguish and would rather forget that period of his life and what happened to him.

"What about you? Did you marry Hazel, that star debater of our class?" He shifted their conversation as soon as he could.

"You remember a lot of things from the past, even Hazel," Skeeter observed. "Yes, we got married after our long-distance romance, me in Dallas and she in Laredo. We raised two kids, a girl, then, a boy. Hazel and I got a divorce. It was hard to live with a hard-driving federal prosecutor that she became, earning more bucks than me. I'm a free-lance bachelor now. I represent the O'Malley Supply Company in Houston for the western side of South America, Colombia included."

While Skeeter explained the product lines handled by his company in monotonous details, Scottie realized he had not seen Gabby for quite some time and stole glances at the patio scene looking for her in the sea of dancing couples. Unable to spot her, he blamed his impaired vision for not sorting her out from the dancing, shifting guests to the tequila-on-rocks he had switched to and generously being refilled by those motivated waiters. But finally to his relief, he spotted her still dancing with that Frenchman. Waving at her, she waved back and they danced toward him.

"I am having a good time," she confessed and gripped Scottie's arm snuggling her head close to his. Her eyes widened. "**Patron! Huelo tu bebida**. I smell your dreenk. Your dreenk."

"Just a bit," he struggled, belittling his woozy status. "**Un poquito solamente.**"

"Let us dance again, okey-dokey?" she begged him. "One more time, pleeze?" She was desperate to claim him again, but Scottie was slow to answer her.

"In my painless condition, I'm not sure if I can remember one single step of any dance." Skeeter laughed on hearing Scottie's remark and soon disappeared into the far right side away from the patio.

The Frenchman was pulling her back to the patio. "Don't pull me!" She scolded him. Turning to Scottie, "Pleeze, let us dance this **merengue**...just this **merengue**...just one more time...." Unfortunately, Scottie was too soaked with tequila to make any sensible decision and was deaf to her craving for his attention. The Frenchman, persistent, pulled her back to the dancing floor.

"Is that your live-in chick?" Skeeter was back, curious, even more impressed on discovering his middle-aged classmate's sex appeal.

"Nope. She's my ward." The obvious disbelief in Skeeter's face hastened Scottie to elaborate. "I have hired tutors to teach her the basics of reading and writing plus English grammar. And now that she can hold a job, I can move to my next assignment knowing she can survive. The kid had a rough life."

"Your ward, huh? That spring chicken? Don't snowball me with that crap about platonic do-good scoutmasterhood. I've been watching you from the corner of my eye, pal. Your bedroom peepers always followed wherever that chick went." With a naughty twinkle in his Irish eyes, he pinched Scottie's cheek. "You lecher, you cradle-snatcher...."

"If you don't believe me, how can I convince you?" Scottie, too boozed up, was hard put to defend himself. Skeeter snorted in disbelief, then laughed gleefully.

The night passed beyond the midnight hour with the energetic combo still playing catchy tunes to the noisier enthusiastic dancing crowd reinforced by a fresh batch of just-arrived guests. "Third shift!" Emilie clutched Scottie's arm to remind him and went on her way again. At that late hour, Scottie confessed to his old buddy he was feeling no pain and "simply floating like a white cloud."

"Just got back from Bangkok two weeks ago," Skeeter rumbled. "It's a bachelor's paradise. A good cheap place to bang the chicks...." His eyes glistened as if he was back in that sin city. "Ah, those oriental cuties," he sighed, and proceeded to describe in spicy details the ten sensuous days he spent in that contemporary "Gomorrah of the East."

Something in Scottie's mind locked out his drinking companion's sybaritic chatter and locked in on Gabby's dancing figure whose face, mysteriously a dead ringer to Carrie, seemed bigger than life and defined by her tossed-about hair. Suddenly, loneliness surged from his internal depths. A strong desire to be with her gripped him like an eagle's talons, inducing him to close his eyes until his guarded secret, his private turmoil unmercifully choked that desire to extinction. When he opened his eyes, Gabby was gone! -- lost on the patio among the bobbing, mingling, tangoing couples. With the lively music, happy people surrounding him, he was the loneliest guy .

Then, out of the dancing crowd, Gabby reappeared to him, a center-piece like a prima ballerina swaying and swirling in the Frenchman's arms. Scottie took heart. But something was terribly wrong with what he saw. *That frog is holding her much too close*, he observed and felt deeply depressed. *Hey! That frog is kissing her! Is kissing a ritual of tango?* He worried, having never learned that intricate dance.

Skeeter kept talking, laughing, and reliving the Bangkok holidays while his inattentive classmate glued his jealous eyes to Gabby's dancing figure.

Then, the Frenchman dipped her so low their bodies were nearly horizontal disturbing Scottie even worse. Soon they were swallowed up by the crowd once more. Her disappearance increased his suffering and the party was no longer pleasant for him. In silent distress, his eyes searched for her with fanatic resolve. Still dancing, she reappeared before the marble statue of Pan as her partner dipped their bodies even lower than last time, kissing her hungrily. Scottie was outraged. Something tensed inside him, snapped, then exploded.

"STOP IT! STOP IT!" His voice boomed across the patio like a thunder bolt. The floodlights seemed to dim momentarily and the music died as if the combo group got a direct hit. The crowd froze to a silent standstill as they turned their attention to a furious Scottie. Moving with determined steps, he walked straight toward the Frenchman and Gabby like a raging snorting bull. The Frenchman withdrew from her vanishing quickly into the crowd. Looking subdued but very desirable, Gabby stood alone before him, watching him. The guests were hushed as he came to a dead stop before her.

"Let's go," Scott boomed with a resolute voice. Grabbing Gabby's forearm, he turned around walking briskly out of the patio as she struggled to catch up with his wide stride, through the mansion and out the main door, opened in time by the alert servants, with nary a backward glance from him.

"**Dios mio**!" Gabby exclaimed catching her breath. "I have never seen you this angry before!" Still enveloped in his choler, Scottie drove the truck towards home. A self-satisfied relish bloomed on her face. "And I like it! **Tiene celos, patron!** You are jealous of me! You, **mi patron, mi todo-poderoso, mi amor!"**

"**Basta**! Enough! You're making fun of me," he replied not denying he was jealous and mortally in love.

"No! no! **Mi patron**. I am not. I swear." She looked at him adoringly as if she discovered a new facet of her hombre, kissed him on the cheek and nestled her head on his shoulder. "**Estoy muy feliz**, very happy," she confessed as her hombre placed a protective arm around her. Caressing his chest, she whispered, "**Te quiero**, Scootee. I love you. You are the only one...for me...."

Calm after that outburst at the party, he was a totally different person. Gone were his tormenting doubts about his virility, and that nagging repugnance for what those Mexican whores did to him. His war wounds were relegated to the past. His mating instinct surfaced and he wanted to possess her. With emotions surging, he kissed her lips with a crushing embrace.

"**Cuidao**! Careful with the driving, **mi amor**," she cautioned him.

They arrived at their **quinta** without any incident. Coming out of the truck under the porte cochere, he steadied himself from the ravages of the tequila and opened the door for her.

"Carry me," she demanded extending her hands toward him implying she wanted to brace her arms around his neck for support.

"What!" Her caprice caught him by surprise. "What now?"

"Come'un, my beeg man. Carry me," she said, leaning forward almost touching his shoulders. Weariness and the pervasive tequila conspired to slow down his thinking process: Slow to anticipate what mischief she was up to, he hesitated. Becoming impatient, she jumped toward him grabbing him around the neck and forcing him to hold her up with both arms.

"Goshalmighty! What now?" he exclaimed sagging down with the impact of her weight. Recovering, he staggered to the main door. She placed her arms tighter around him as he fumbled with one hand searching for the keyholder in his pocket. "Damn!" he cussed as he finally located the house key and unlocked the door. Upon entering inside, he kicked back shutting the door. She giggled to watch how funny and awkward he did this kicking stunt while carrying her.

"Take me upstairs," she demanded from him.

"Damn! You're carrying this game a bit too far." Nursing his tequila-muddled mind, he relented to her whim as he struggled up the steep stairs with his unlikely load.

"**Me gusta eso!** I love this!" she rejoiced and kissed him incessantly while he climbed slowly with shaky legs to the second floor. Fortuitously, they had left the lamps lighted in the hallway. Seeing the sofa chairs on the landing, he turned and walked toward them.

"No, no! Not on the chair," she commanded him. "Take me up …there." Pointing over his shoulder, he strained to turn once more, careful not to crook his back.

"I'm getting tired of this silly game. Where to?"

"There," she pointed to the veranda through the open door.

"You had plenty to drink tonight, didn't you?" he said in a scolding voice as he struggled over the last steps to the second floor.

"Not any more than you, **mi amor**," she said, as they entered the veranda. Glad that their silly game was almost over, he gently deposited her on the bed, sighed, and felt relieved of carrying her. For her, this simple deed of her hombre was proof of his love and devotion. She kept her arms around him as her emotions swelled to a dizzying peak while kissing him passionately. Embracing, jerking her hombre tighter caused him to lose balance and fall on top of her.

"Hey! Watch what you've done!" he exclaimed, surprised, not expecting her audacity.

Gabby, aroused, gripped him in a carnal embrace, pressing her lips against his lips, her body against his body, crumbling the Carrie image shell he had superimposed on her. Her passionate sweaty body began melting all his inhibitions which isolated him from women. What those Mexican whores did to him were suppressed, his war wounds were forgotten. At that moment, they were alone, entwined in body and spirit, passionate with each other. These lovers, after throwing their shoes away, bared their pressed bodies from the restrictions of their clothes and underwear.

Jealousy had gripped his tequila-muddled mind thinking of that Frenchman, that lousy frog, but now he desired her, wanted her so desperately. As her body heaved and throbbed, she emitted rapturous sighs which excited him to unleash pecks on her neck and on the hollow of her shoulders followed by rapid, intense wandering kisses along the soft skin of her belly.

Her passion surging, she grasped him scissors-like with her thin legs. Unexpectedly, her vicarious dream of a romantic life was beginning to be fulfilled. Kissing again and again, they finally gasped for breath. Their lips parted and they looked at each other discovering an overpowering unspoken love. Even their hearts seemed to beat in unison. Until that timeless moment, he never knew what it was to love another being, a woman, and be loved in reciprocated surrender.

"I hope you will love me as I always loved you from the first time you saved my life, **mi amor**," she confessed as they were entwined passionately.

"I love you, Gabby," he responded, "but...but I was too afraid before. Even now...."

"There is nothing to be afraid of.... **Este amor entre tu y yo**...is stronger than anything in the world...even beyond this life..." she whispered reassuring him while gently stroking his back.

"I love you, Gabby. I never loved anyone before." He was shedding his fears and inhibitions.

Closing her eyes in blissful ecstasy, "Tell me again...you love me... and only me...tell me...." she begged him while caressing his buttocks and guiding him to enter her.

Visions of his hospital bed, that uniformed nurse, other wounded soldiers around him in Pusan flashed before him. Those swatches of bloodied bandages were restricting him again. Suddenly flat on his back, he was suddenly helpless, immobile. His war wounds began to pain him. His entire body sweated, shuddered, weakened and became limp.

"Dammit! I can't do it," he cried in exasperation. "I was wounded in the war." Feeling devastated, he pulled himself away from their embrace. Sitting up on the bed, he reached for his shorts and hurriedly put them on.

"**No importa nada**. Nothing matters. I love you just the same, **mi amor.** I love you..." She got hold of his left arm and tried to pull him back. "Hold me, Scootee, pleeze. I want to feel your body over mine...."

Shaking loose from her, he stood up, crestfallen, shocked and mortified. Keeping his eyes downcast, he grieved: *Now she knows my secret.* Acting like a wounded tiger, he turned to face her. "You must marry a man, a whole man who can satisfy you. I can't. Oh my God, I just can't." Hastily, he put on his shirt and slacks and slipped into his shoes in a disorderly manner.

"No! no! Pleeze do not leave me. I love you!" she pleaded, crying, and attempted to pull him back into bed. But he resisted firmly as he finished tying his shoes. "Do not leave me. I shall die!"

"I'm just half a man," he declared in a trembling voice as he grabbed his coat and ran downstairs fleeing into the balmy night.

CHAPTER VIII

The pigeons still come to the cascading waters of the fountain. Yet to Scottie, the patio was empty, sad, and their afternoon "happy hour" ritual had fled the scene. Nothing replaced the void in his life left by Gabby who was staying with the mayor and his wife. Sipping his margarita alone, he was compelled to reminisce about the recent past. The **quinta**, uncannily quiet and deserted, appeared fossilized with Gabby's disappearance. Even the drink, mixed by himself, was not as tasty as the ones concocted by her. The quiet, the emptiness, felt to him like he just came back from a funeral of a dear friend. It was a bad time to be alone and no one to talk to. Scottie was hurting inside that night.

But I had to do it, he justified to himself what happened that night and why he banished Gabby from his life. *I hope to God time shall heal our heartaches and my sorrow won't last forever*.

Nonetheless, he was not happy. Much to his grief, that shameful denouement with her that night was not what he had planned: it was heart-breaking for him and he figured for her as well. Biting his lips, he jabbed his clenched fist against the trunk of a potted palm tree recalling that humiliating exposure of his impotency. *Dammit! I must get out of this place as soon as I can!* he despaired.

Feeling lonely by the fountain as the late afternoon shadows began to encroach the patio, he was miserable no matter how much he would admit what went wrong that night. Darkness finally prevailed and the patio floodlights turned on. For him, the **quinta** appeared barren like the Persian desert as if he had left behind years before without the joys, laughter, little jokes and teases of "that face with those pools of turquoise." A flamboyant aura which Gabby weaved into their lives vanished like a pleasant remembered dream; and mercifully, the margaritas he concocted himself eased his affliction somewhat and finally eased him to a much needed sleep that night.

To ease his conscience on perceived responsibilities for Gabby, he pleaded to Maria Luisa, the mayor's wife, that she accept a monthly allowance to defray Gabby's expenses while she was their house guest.

With the solitary life that Scottie was to live until his departure from this earthly existence, he made up his mind to dedicate his life to work, work, **work**. Preparations for the inauguration was the most pressing matter at hand for him. Lending importance to the inauguration would be the presence of **El Presidente** for the ribbon-cutting ceremony**.** Señor Pertierra, still mourning for his daughter, decided to send his deputy for the ceremony. Don Jose′ Luis helped with the preparations but was slow, and at times, hesitant without the domineering Aurora to lean on. Unexpectedly, his wife took the initiative and located some private accommodations for the visiting dignitaries which were preferable to the antiquated musty rooms of Hotel Nacional.

Scottie was spending longer hours with his work away from the now less desirable **quinta** but also understandably so since the deadline for the inauguration was drawing near. There were still loose ends which he had to resolve. Except for turning in to sleep, he never returned home during the day taking his meals at Cafe El Porvenir. There were occasions when he felt the spooky presence of Padre Joe and Aurora during his evening meals. Carmen and Maria, the maid, were virtually on their own in the **quinta**.

With the inauguration just five days away, coordinating the details of the ribbon-cutting ceremony and reception banquet with the mayor while supervising the finishing touches on the new highway, Scottie was mentally stressed. Mauro noticed he was slightly dragging his right foot lately in the office. Many problems had not been cleared up. Not all the out-of-town guests had been confirmed with housing accommodations. The cargo airline misplaced the red carpet between Bogota′ and Peñalosa. The local officials, including Don Jose′ Luis, insisted this item was a "must" for a presidential reception. His must-do list kept getting longer and straining him even worse. Gabby was not around to humor him out of his dark moods, ridicule his grousing into funny absurdities. Although he would not admit it to anybody's face, he missed his self-appointed "court jester."

Two days before the deadline, Scottie took personal charge of the rubble clean-up along the highway. Another roll of red carpet was rented posthaste in Bogota′, loaded in a van, and two company chauffeurs were ordered to keep driving until they reached town. Don Jose′ Luis badgered, with Maria Luisa's help, twenty or so families to host the rest of the visiting VIPs in their homes.

Even the margaritas Scottie drank could not unwind him on the eve of the inauguration. When he fell asleep on the sofa, the spooks did not spare him. The aborted love scene with Gabby was replayed in a dream. Again, he was yelling, "I can't do it! I can't!" She pleaded with him that it did not matter. Outside, the burly deputy sheriff from Laredo was patrolling the street with his souped-up Chevy and honking his horn every time he passed by the **quinta**. Falling out from the sofa, he woke up in a cold sweat. Two tragic events in his life got mixed up in the nightmare. *What does it all mean?* he asked himself.

At exactly six the following morning, loud explosions rocked the town. A flurry of excitement rippled through the community. People ran out of their houses. Some more conservative citizens assumed fanatics started the fireworks a day too early for the inauguration and went back to bed. The **indios** were not so sure that those explosions were fireworks since their fragile houses shook violently. They were fearful that a dormant volcano, El Pico del Diablo, some 150 kilometers to the east of Peñalosa, might have come back to express the anger of their ancestors who were furious and were demanding that Don Jose′ Luis request the Department of Antiquities to return the mummies of their forebears for reburials.

What they heard, according to Scottie's experienced ear for construction explosives, were successive explosions above a section of the new highway where the asphalt topping had been poured and steam-rollered two days before. Jumping into his pickup truck, Scottie rode fast to that section and verified the chunks of rocks which had rolled down the slopes -- some of which lodged on the highway while the rest plunged beyond into the ravines. He met with the workers and soldiers assigned to guard that section. Luckily no workers nor soldiers, asleep in tents, were injured. They had ample time to flee after they heard the explosions. Immediately afterwards, they spied some suspicious-looking men scurrying away from the mountain top. The soldiers gave chase and caught some of the culprits. After roughing them up at the police station, they confessed to the sergeant that they were the hired help of Don Mendieta. At the jailhouse, these ranch hands were subjected to more subtle "persuasive interrogations" like whipping the soles of their bare feet with a bullwhip which left no permanent tell-tale marks.

Changing their stories, they admitted to Colonel Perez Alvarez they were, in fact, paid and ordered by Don Pedrazas to sabotage the new highway. This news leaked out and spread like a nifty gossip among the townspeople. Late that afternoon in the cafes and **bodegones**, speculation was rife that there was plenty of evidence to implicate Don Pedrazas and his sons as well.

Scottie heard all the bad news he cared to know from his foremen and decided the chunks of rolled down rocks on the highway were unsightly and presented hazards to the road traffic. The coming tour by El Presidente on the new highway made it a foregone decision for him that these hazardous debris must be removed before tomorrow even though they had only about twelve hours of daylight left. Four bulldozers and six dump trucks were mobilized and ordered to the landslide area. He was confident the highway could be cleared before the next day's inaugural ceremony. Just for insurance, he borrowed floodlights and power generators from the electric company and set them up in readiness -- in case it would be necessary to work through the night. Notified about the sabotage, it took well over an hour by telephone to convince his bosses that he could clean up the mess in time. They wanted to postpone the inauguration ceremony but Scottie wanted to get this project over with and before the landlords could plan more mischief. Besides he planned to leave town before his secret could spread any further as he anticipated.

Don Jose′ Luis met with Scottie at Cafe El Porvenir for a late supper during that seemingly endless evening. Scottie got a spooky feeling that Padre Casals and Aurora might be listening and would even join them any moment. While they were discussing the inaugural details, those candlelight dinners with Gabby from the past kept encroaching into his mind while he resisted the temptation to inquire about her since she was staying at their mansion. After threshing out and agreeing with those details, their conversation shifted to the troublesome landlords.

"The landslide area is nowhere near Don Pedrazas' estate." Scottie was rehashing the incident with Don Jose′ Luis. "Why would he commit such a crime?" he raised the question with the mayor who remarked he had not seen the "old curmudgeon since he crashed the banquet tent on horseback during the **feria**."

"I have been receiving tons of rumors and speculative gossip," the mayor continued. "The truth of the matter is these landlords feel threatened by the increasing intrusion of squatters into their **estancias**. This new highway would make it even easier for these landless **peones** to infiltrate their lands." Don Jose′ Luis theorized the highway sabotage was a desperate act by Don Pedrazas, and he was in connivance with Don Mendieta and other absentee landlords.

In spite of these problems with the landlords, the mayor told him he was a diehard optimist envisioning Peñalosa as a future center of commerce and industry now that this national highway has linked it to the coastal seaports of the Caribbean and the Pacific Ocean. "You can help me induce the American companies to locate their future factories in the Cuyapo′ valley."

Sorry, ***Señor alcalde****. I got another plan. I'm leaving.* Scottie was chortling inside, although sad about it.

The mayor continued his Panglossian plans of "convincing these short-sighted landlords that those squatters are potential workers in future factories of which they shall be the principal investors in partnership with American companies." Scottie perceived that Don Jose′ Luis' grandiose scheme included fantasizing himself as a power broker not just for Peñalosa but the entire Cuyapo′ valley. Later, over glasses of sherry, the mayor unveiled his dreams: "I want the valley to become prosperous. I shall be the peacemaker between the landlords, **campesinos**, and **indios**. I want to see industrial progress in this district. And for that future..." he paused, "I want to be the **gobernador**!"

Even under the soft lights of the Cafe's terrace, Scottie noticed the self-satisfied glow on the mayor's face after confiding his master plan for his beloved valley. While Don Jose′ Luis wallowed in his dreams, some unpleasant ghosts from the valley's past visited his companion's mind. "I find it rather ironic, Don Jose′ Luis, that these landowners behave so insolently and ruthlessly with the **indios** when going back to what pristine history told us that all these **estancias** surveyed and claimed by the arriving Europeans belonged to the **indios** and even beyond "where the condors fly over" as the saying goes. The ancestors of these **indios** found themselves belonging life and limb to the **encomenderos** by royal decrees . What a mockery!"

"Santamaria! Do not say that!" The mayor's idyllic reverie was shattered. "Who told all those stories? Some communists agitators in Bogota′? Were it not for Europeans, mostly Spaniards, this valley would not be what it is today. **Ahora mismo**."

Oh! oh! I'm a fool to start a controversy that will never end. Scottie realized his timing was wrong. *Oh, well. Got to bite through this.*

"These **indios** would still be fighting, killing and eating each other had not the **conquistadores** brought the Faith of Christianity and the laws of the civilized world. They built the **caminos reales** all over the continent, built churches, and established the government structure. Who told you those stories that these lands belong to the **indios**?"

"Nobody told me. I have been reading some old books I borrowed from the library of our embassy in Bogota′." Scottie wished he could move away from this subject.

"Those authors must be communists or at least, socialists. Perhaps Jewish authors. The **judios** hate us because many Germans have settled in Cuyapo′ since the end of the Great War. You know the war I am talking about. **Si**?" Scottie remain silent. "Scootee, **por favor**! Do not talk to our people about the **encomiendas** and what those authors wrote about the past," the mayor sounded apprehensive, looking worried. "Nothing good will ever come out of those dangerous ideas. Feed them to the **indios** and the **campesinos** and we shall drown into a sea of assassinations, arsons, and revolution. Please keep those books and their dangerous ideas to yourself."

"Okey dokey, Don Jose′ Luis. This is your country, not mine. I shan't discuss politics with your people. I promise." Caught between the injustice of the local politics and the expediency of his position to get along with the mayor and the other power brokers in Cuyapo′ valley and in Bogota′, Scottie, felt frustrated and guilty to remain silent.

"We are fortunate to live in Cuyapo′ valley where problems such as with the landlords are nothing compared with the murders and assassinations between the political parties as well as the Maoist **guerilleros** and **bandidos** in other regions of our country. And who are most of the victims? The **indios** and the **campesinos** who have to do the dirty killings and be killed themselves for these **partidos politicos** and **bandidos. Que barbaridad!"**

Don Jose' Luis must be reading my mind, still driving his arguments to convince me, Scottie thought. While they drank more black coffee far into the night, he received more reports from his foremen on his two-way portable radio on the rubble clean-up. *Talking about the injustices, present and past, would only destabilize the status quo between the haves and the have-nots in the valley.* He rationalized that the mayor was a realist.

True to his word, the mayor busied himself cajoling his townsmen to clean up their houses and yards, remove eyesores like garbage piles, abandoned vehicles, broken-down carts, and fallen rotten tree trunks. Beggars were rounded up, some forcibly, to stay in make-shift huts in a stockade some twenty-five kilometers north of the town limits where two policemen were assigned to keep these vagrants from infiltrating back to the **centro** during the inauguration day. On Scottie's suggestions, an animal alert committee, to round up all stray dogs, donkeys, and other animals roaming the streets, and another committee, called **"Arriba el Pueblo,"** whose objective was to instill civic pride among the people by cleaning up their houses and yards but especially by wearing their Sunday best on inauguration day, were organized.

As anticipated, the business establishments closed early on the eve of the inauguration as the town was infected with a euphoria of high expectations. Everyone was buzzing with a holiday mood in the office bullpen where Gabby worked. Not much work was being done by the employees who talked excitedly about what they would wear and which parties they would attend tomorrow.

Lonely and depressed, Gabby turned a deaf ear to the noisy office chitchat. She had no plans and decided not to accompany the mayor and his wife to the ribbon-cutting ceremony convinced it was not proper to show and embarrass herself as well as Scottie who was one of the principal speakers. Her life in Peñalosa, it seemed to her, was coming to a dead-end. There was no happiness left for her and her interest in anything was nil. Only Scottie, as she recalled her entire life in that town, temporarily arrested her inevitable slide to perdition. In spite of it all, she was doing an adequate job at the office. But her enthusiasm for living, which had suddenly perked up when Scottie appeared in her life, had evaporated.

The Calderones, childless, were very accommodating, gracious and considerate to Gabby doting on her like she was their own daughter. Undetected by them, she was withdrawing bit by bit from the real world. Doña Maria Luisa discerned occasional signs of minor distress from Gabby. But there was no drastic behavior by her which would have alarmed the kindly old lady to her possible relapse. The patrician couple stayed out of the tiff between Gabby and Scottie never hinting to give advice nor to mediate. Yet in their kind hearts, they would like the quarreling lovers to come together again.

****

Early on inauguration day, Scottie cruised at a comfortable speed along the brand new highway. A warm feeling of accomplishment glowed inside him. *Despite the problems and frustrations, this project was worth the effort,* he concluded. *If Don Jose' Luis' dreams would come true, that's even better. As for me, it's time to move on to another challenge.* With his secret exposed to Gabby, he predicted that sooner or later his private shame would leak to the far corners of the valley. *My next assignment,* he was determined, *must be far away from here. As far as possible.*

Suddenly, a mercury-arc lamp post caught his eye. Then, another, third, fourth, and a fifth one. These five had wires sticking out of the base boxes. *No time to call the electrical subcontractor*, he said to himself. *El Presidente and his entourage can't notice those unruly wires from the helicopters. Never mind!*

Minutes later, he was driving through the landslide area where the workmen were tamping the gravel on the shoulders. There were several soldiers with them. *The finishing touches are about over,* he observed, *and this rock-damaged section would soon be spic and span like the rest.* The fallen rocks, which marred the new highway, were gone. He was pleased with the emergency clean-up since those unsightly rocks would have been conspicuous and easily noticed even high above from the helicopters by El Presidente and his entourage.

Just to ensure the workmen would not tarry in the area, he told them to hurry, finish the clean up, clear out in ten minutes taking the old dirt road back to town.

Standing on a bluff near the highway's edge, Scottie admired the green foliage which undulated toward the wide fertile Cuyapo′ valley ending into the Paracuriba river which eventually converges with other rivers and tributaries into Brazil. Making a mental note, he would instruct the helicopter pilots to fly the distinguished guests over this beauty spot. Unknown to him, someone high up on the mountainside was following his movement with a spyglass.

Arriving at the recently finished section through the Mendieta estate, Scottie noted the barbed-wire fences has been re-positioned and mended on both shoulders of the right-of-way. As a gesture of goodwill, he ordered the fabrication of two gates with cattle guards for this section in order to facilitate access to the estate parcel isolated by the new highway. Nevertheless, he heard from his workmen that the old man was "smoldering in anger" about the highway trespassing his property. Scottie did not receive a thank-you note for the donated new gates.

A crew was loading used pieces of construction lumber into a flat-bed truck at another site with three soldiers on duty with them. Stopping, he made it a point to shake their hands and congratulate them for a job well done. From the smiling faces of the workmen and soldiers, he knew they were appreciative of his sincere interest in them. He reminded them to clear out of the highway as soon as they finished loading. Gabby entered into his mind even while he was conversing with the workmen. Her plea kept ringing, hounding him: "**No importa**. It does not matter, **mi amor**...." He was tempted to swallow his pride and visit her at the Calderon mansion. Moments later, he relented, rationalizing that it was too late for that.

At that very moment, Gabby was feeling distressed. She was packing her suitcases, having made up her mind last night to leave town. She intended to sneak out when Doña Maria Luisa was shopping at the market with the cook. Gabby knew it was a tricky day to skip out of the house because today, the inauguration day, the lady of the house must come back quickly from the market, take a bath, and put on that formal gown in time for the reception ceremony at the airport where **El Presidente** was arriving and she and her hubby, Don Jose´ Luis, as **alcalde**, must be on time to greet **El Presidente** and his entourage in the name of the town.

Gabby knew from observing the daily routine and habits of the household help that the other maid would be taking a shower in about ten minutes as she always did daily after sweeping and dusting for two hours. Mindless of her surroundings and juggling all sorts of decisions while packing her clothes, Gabby bumped against the wardrobe in her bedroom causing the Santo Niño porcelain statue on top to wobble and fall on the floor.

"**Ay! Dios mio**!" she exclaimed covering her mouth with a hand. The fallen statue broke into fragments. "**Mala suerte**! Bad luck!" she said in disgust as she picked up the fragments and placed them on a spread-out handkerchief. Together with the statue's lacquered base, she carried them to the kitchen table where she mended the pieces with glue. "**Lo siento muchisimo,** Jesus**.** I am clumsy today. **Perdoname**. Señor**.** Do not allow anything bad to happen today."

Then, she became aware that the old Mercedes-Benz was moving out of the garage into the street. Quickly, she replaced the mended statue with its base on top of the wardrobe. Through the side door, she slipped quietly into the alley carrying her two suitcases. Walking across the plaza, she saw again the ominous belfry beckoning to her. With morbid fascination, she paused and stared at the ancient bell. *I could go up there, jump, and end my unfortunate life forever,* she thought and was deliberating as the soaring belfry persisted to tempt her. Hiding her suitcases behind the hibiscus bushes near the graveyard, she entered the church through a back door and found herself inside the vestry. In the dimness, she nearly stumbled into a baroque vintage carriage mounted with a partially dressed statue of Santiago Apostol, the town's patron saint. Getting closer to the statue, she became entranced, almost hypnotically, with its lifelike ivory carved head and hands. The blue eyes of the saint looked so real and appeared to be looking straight at her. Suddenly, she felt embarrassed as if the saint was chiding her for invading his privacy since he was not fully clothed.

"What are you doing here, señorita?" Padre Pellini asked as he walked in, surprised to see the young woman.

"Oh, oh...."She was taken aback by being discovered. "I was looking for Padre Casals," she replied. The fully bearded padre looked puzzled and slowly twisted his mouth in a peculiar manner. Before he had a chance to speak again, she raced through the chancel and then, outside through the vestry's door. Picking up her hidden suitcases by the bushes, she ran to the bus station across from the plaza after she noticed a woman in black and dark glasses who kept staring at her.

Entering a bus and sitting way in the back, she told herself to forget everything and everybody in Peñalosa including Scottie and start a new life somewhere. Padre Pellini's unexpected presence in the vestry frightened her not to climb up the belfry while the impressive kindly head of Saint Santiago Apostol gave her spiritual strength to start a new life. The bus driver called her to come forward and show her ticket. Telling the driver, she did not have a ticket and asked where the bus was headed: Bogota´. She paid and got her ticket. The driver looked back at her wondering why she boarded the bus without knowing its destination beforehand.

Scottie drove on to inspect the rest of the highway and glanced at his watch: nine fifteen. In another thirty minutes, he reckoned he should turn back and meet the bosses at the airport. Driving near the new highway's far west end which connected to another highway to Barranquilla, he was pleased with himself for a job well done. Bubbling with enthusiasm, he was then vacillating about leaving Colombia and that other road project from Cali to Tulua´ which was offered to him again. Paranoid about further exposure of his secret, he would prefer to have another team of workers from Cali if he decided to accept that road project. Scottie headed back to town and the airport.

Atop a nearby mountainside hidden behind scrub bushes, a band of eight men had been monitoring his movement on the highway below. "Ready," a man wearing a hunting cap, whispered, alerting the others while following Scottie's truck with a spyglass. When Scottie passed by a cluster of oak trees, the man flagged down his arm and barked, "**Ahora**!" "Now!"

A deafening blast was followed by a screeching-crashing sound like two colliding trains which, in turn, echoed back and forth between the mountainside and foothills across the valley. Scottie felt being lifted up as his truck disintegrated into flying scattered debris around him.

"Oh my God! They are killing me!" he shouted, while suspended in mid-air inside the heavy-gauged cabin with his hands still gripping the steering wheel. "Oh my...my...God...!"

Witnessing the dispatch of their target, the conspirators abandoned their positions after hiding the demolition equipment behind dense bushes. With haste, they mounted the waiting horses and vanished into the woods around the other side of the mountain.

The workmen and the soldiers, who had bade goodbye to Scottie just minutes before, heard the loud explosion. The ones working along the precipice saw the truck leaping into the air and coming apart. Moments later, they heard crashing sounds as some remnants of the truck fell on the highway while the rest of the pieces cartwheeled toward the bottom of the ravine. Recovering from the shock, they ran along the highway until they saw the monstrous crater gutted by the explosives. From the crater, a mixed group of workmen and soldiers traced the tell-tale sheared cables leading to the upper reaches of the mountainside. Climbing up, they discovered the hidden demolition equipment and scattered banana peelings, mango seeds and skins. But there was nobody around. Shouting obscenities and armed only with picks and shovels, the workmen proceeded to search the mountainside for the culprits. The motivated soldiers joined them.

Another group of excited workers found Scottie's bloodied body inside the pick-up truck's chassis which had lodged on top of scrub bush cluster in the ravine just below the highway. Apparently, the dense cluster cushioned the rapid fall of the wheels-shorn chassis. After recovering Scottie from the wreck, one of the workmen checked his pulse and told the others he was still alive. Quickly, they made a makeshift bed from donated shirts and undershirts on the back of a pick-up truck where they gently put him down. The driver, accompanied by two workmen, rushed him to the hospital in Peñalosa.

In a matter of minutes after Scottie's arrival at the hospital's emergency room, the whole town became aware of the murder attempt. Mel, standing on a flat-bed truck with a megaphone, was driven around town while he repeatedly broadcasted the murder attempt on Scottie and denounced the act with inflammatory words against the landlords. The townspeople reacted vigorously to the news with some running about aimlessly in the plaza. Soon self-appointed leaders rose above the crowd who were attempting to control the swarming **indios** and **campesinos** armed with machetes and hunting rifles. To others, who just came out of their houses, thought another revolution had started.

Don Jose′ Luis hurriedly mounted the brass band gazebo at the plaza's north end and announced that, on order of **El Presidente**, the inauguration of the highway was postponed indefinitely. A battalion of soldiers was flown from Barranquilla to help the local police organize a dragnet for Scottie's assassins. A curfew was imposed from dusk to dawn. The carnival atmosphere pervading the town changed abruptly that afternoon to a highly-charged situation. Some Liberal politicians, interviewed by a local radio station, accused the Conservatives for the assassination attempt. Don Mendieta denied any connection with the assassins While Don Pedrazas could not be located. Don Jose′ Luis, fearing another outbreak of fighting between the two factions, scheduled a meeting with the leaders that afternoon.

J.J. Whitelaw and W. Corry Jefferson came to town the day before expressly for the inauguration. They were waiting for Scottie and the mayor to join them at the airport where **El Presidente** was slated to arrive at ten fifteen that morning. Resigned to sit wearily at Cafe El Porvenir for a late breakfast (which Juancho, the waiter, considered already a **merienda**) which was followed by a procession of coffee cups while they indulged in interminable speculation of what really happened to Scottie and what they could do while waiting for Mauro to come back from the hospital and report the latest news.

Their vigil was becoming intolerable for J.J. who was girding himself mentally for the inevitable bad news. Mauro had promised to return in fifteen minutes. But according to W. Corry, the self-appointed timekeeper, Mauro, was more than twenty-one minutes gone already.

"It will be tough to replace our man," J.J. finally admitted as he prepared his nervous companion for what they were reluctant to talk about. "He got along so well with the locals and somehow always managed to meet the deadlines. A rare combination of dedication and talents in our business." The sorrowful tone of J.J's voice sounded like he was rehearsing a eulogy for someone defunct, whose name he was unwilling to mention. After sipping more coffee, he continued, "I was planning to discuss that Cali-to-Tulua′ project with him tonight before flying back to Bogota′."

"Scottie had the natural skills of an overseas hand," W. Corry contributed, reminiscing about the past. "We wanted to keep him another year in Frisco but no! He threatened to resign and work with Bechtel until we promised to ship him out as soon as another project manager took over that Isfahan waterworks site. For some strange reason, he wanted so badly to leave so soon. I wonder why?"

"Must be something to do with his family because he...." J.J. stopped when they noticed a solitary figure, aided by a cane, was walking slowly across the plaza towards them. Moments later, they recognized Señor Calderon, the mayor.

"Don Jose´ Luis is waddling along," J.J. whispered to his companion. "He seems to walk with a limp. Did he hurt himself?"

"I don't think so. Mauro told me the mayor is taking Scottie's misfortune badly. He's broken-hearted and blaming himself for this tragedy." They stood up and greeted the mayor while Juancho brought another chair for him.

"**Buenos dias**?" the mayor harrumphed. "What is good about it, eh? And the days which will follow? **Nada**! Nothing!" He struck his cane repeatedly on the same spot as he talked to emphasize his bitterness.

"I'm very sorry about what happened, Don Jose´ Luis. I never imagined there's much animosity between the landowners and our own employees." J.J. was attempting to smooth over an awkward postmortem situation, and to mollify a somber, irate mayor.

While sitting and making small talk, they noticed the **campesinos** were gathering in numbers on the plaza. These were not the town folks who, earlier that morning, were running aimlessly about in reaction to Scottie's mishap but **campesinos** who were organized in formations from the pueblos of Cuyapo´ valley and carrying banners and placards.

"I'm to blame for what happened to Scootee. I was distracted by what the inauguration publicity would do for Peñalosa and its people that I did not pay any attention to the worsening confrontation between your company and the landlords. **Que pena**!" the mayor talked more calmly this time. His wan appearance confirmed the hearsay passed on earlier by others to his breakfast companions: the assassination attempt had squeezed the zest from the mayor´s enthusiasm.

"Scootee **era como nuestro hermano**, like a brother and we embrace him as one of us," the mayor continued. "During the short time Scootee was among us, he left **muchas memorias y sociedades anonimas.** With Padre Casals, he organized a **feria**, many fiestas and **verbenas**; with the Cerruzas, he organized a foster home for unwanted babies; with me, La Liga de Futbol del Valle de Cuyapo´ and a credit union for the farmers; with Señora Lebrun, an orphanage for girls and a safe house for battered women. **Solamente Dios sabe** what other charitable works Scootee had set up that we are not even aware of. He hates publicity and does these good works because he loves humanity...." The mayor, emotional, was teary-eyed. "You must know his qualities more than I do." On hearing this litany of Scottie's extracurricular good deeds on top of his job, his bosses were surprised and very impressed.

"Scottie never told us about these good deeds you just told us," J.J. confessed to the mayor as their attention turned to the growing crowd gathering on the plaza. The latest group to arrive carried bouquets of flowers and placards of blown-up pictures. The women wore black dresses while their men wore white pants and shirts and black bands on their right sleeves. Juancho whispered they were from Villapuente. When six more buses arrived and unloaded its human cargo including two brass bands, W. Corry got edgy and imagined this growing crowd would end up in a long funeral procession.

"Oh my God! Is Scottie dying?" W. Corry blurted out, mindless, as he gulped his coffee nervously spilling some on the table. Juancho, quick as a sparrow, wiped the table clean.

"Shoot! Do you have to mention that?" J.J. retorted, mildly scolding, fearful of the foreboding himself.

"Just look at those...black dresses... and...black arm bands. Do they signal... something to you?" W. Corry was totally distraught, choking on his words. "If Mauro doesn't show up in another...ten minutes, I'll...I'll be heading...to the…ahem!… hospital."

The brass bands began playing a sorrowful piece from Bach stirring these visitors even more. The noon sun caused glares on the huge glossy posters held by the **campesinos**. When some **campesinos** sought the shade of an acacia tree, the two foreigners were able to see the posters clearly. They were incredulous: the posters were blown-up larger-than-life portrait of Scottie!

"Where did they obtain his pictures?" W. Corry wondered. "And so suddenly? Something weird is brewing here."

"I would like to know why they're carrying his portraits in the first place. Scottie is not even a native son," said a puzzled J.J., and he was reluctant to accept they could be witnessing a mystique enveloping Scottie towards a "native demigod" status as opined by Juancho.

"Señores, I cannot answer your questions,' the mayor spoke again. "It is premature to get the answers so soon. All I know is Scottie has become popular with our people. **Es muy simpatico**. Our hero did so much during the short time he was with us. We consider him **como nuestro hermano.** Whatever fate the good Lord decides for him, he shall remain in our hearts." His eyes were misty as he pulled out a hankie and dried his eyes unwilling to shed tears before these visitors. Then he blew his nose making an audible embarrassing noise. "**Caballeros**," he continued, "I must leave your company **muy pronto** and go to the gazebo where I must address our gathered people. **Que jodon!** How annoying!"

Despite the noon sun's unforgiving heat, the entire plaza was packed with demonstrators. The mayor confided to his visitors that he was hesitant to address the crowd about Scottie under the tragic circumstances, but he had no choice.

A commotion rippled through the gathered masses which in the last few minutes had grown over ten thousand according to Juancho's last head count before he disappeared into the kitchen. More were arriving.

Then, something triggered the crowd into a crescendo of shouting and impromptu pounding of the cobbled ground with their poster-bearing poles. The unintelligible shouts, intermixed and synchronized with the pole pounding, began to sound like an ancient battle cry of pre-historic savages unnerving the wits of the two Americans.

"I can't understand what the hue-and-cry is all about," J.J. finally spoke nervously. "Hey! Wait! They're looking up at the sky! It's getting scary!" He sheltered his eyes with the palm of his hand to look up but the sun's glare blotted out his sight. "It's too damn bright to see. What the hell is up there?"

"Maybe Scottie has flown out of the hospital's window and is about to show up and announce his resurrection," W. Corry nervously replied. But to J.J. he seemed to be cracking an ill-timed joke.

Displaying an irritated look, the mayor was not amused with W. Corry's sacrilegious dig. "You have to excuse me, **caballeros**," he told them, maintaining his dignity, got up, and ambled towards the restive crowd.

"My nerves can't stand this weird chanting and pounding any longer," W. Corry declared. "I'm going to the hospital right now and find out about Scottie. Coming J.J?" His companion nodded his assent.

Standing inside the gazebo, the mayor spoke in a mournful voice to the hushed crowd. The two American bosses, both Spanish-language illiterate except for a few words and phrases snatched here and there, left the cafe unobtrusively through an alleyway leading from the plaza to the hospital.

Meanwhile Doctor Alcuaz finished checking Scottie at an examination room, amazed with his patient's toughness, a survivor, thought dying by those workmen who brought him in.

"Call it un **milagro**, Señor Reeter. After the nurses cleaned you up of blood, ashes, and dirt, you only have a fractured bone in the left arm and minor scratches on your head and body. You have survived a **cochebomba**! You will be...how you say in English...okay? In four to six weeks, amigo."

Mauro, standing by the window, was bug-eyed on hearing the doctor's diagnosis. For hooting, hollering and jumping up and down with unbridled joy, Mauro was reprimanded by the doctor.

"But doctor," Scottie complained. "I feel woozy...**Quiero decir mareado.** What's the matter with me?"

"Nothing to worry about, the doctor reassured him, pulling down the x-ray negatives from the back-lighted glass-plate viewer and handing them to a nurse. "You were injected a dose of morphine to ease your pains. I shall prescribe a plaster cast for your broken arm and you must wear an arm sling for a while."

"Is the rest of my body, okay? **Esta bien**?" Scottie, still dubious of the diagnosis, looked for the doctor's response in earnest.

"**Si**," the doctor turned around, answered him laconically and continued to give instructions to the nurse.

"But doctor, are you sure? **De verdad**?"

"**Si, de por si,** of course, I know, I have examined you very thoroughly. You are as healthy as a **toro**." The doctor, adjusting the stethoscope around his neck, was beginning to look puzzled.

"But doctor, about my...." Scottie whispered into his ear. What he said caused the doctor's eyebrows to knit into a frown.

"Pero hombre! As I said, you as healthy as a bull. **De mejor salud**. What do you want me to prove to you? Bring here a woman and see how you can perform, eh?" the doctor huffed, frowned again and gave him a gentle slap on the cheek. "**Ay, que tio eres tu**! What a gringo!"

"I just wanted to be very sure, doctor. **Muchisimas gracias**." Although unsteady, Scottie was jubilant, managed to smile thinking of his good fortune. He felt a heavy load disappear from his mind. "Thank God! I'm okay after all! I'm okey-dokey!! Whee!"

"**Espera**, I shall check you one more time tomorrow. **Un practicante** will put that plaster cast this afternoon. Today, I want you to take it easy. **Descansete**." The doctor left, shaking his head, still confused about this crazy gringo.

"**Patron**, Señora Calderon just called the nurses' station. I was told that her maid followed Señorita Gabriela and saw her boarding an autobus bound for Bogota´." Mauro informed Scottie.

"What! Gabby took off? Mauro...ouch! My damn arm! That shot hasn't work yet. You got to help me escape out of this place**. Pronto**! Ouch!"

"**Si! si, patron. Comprendo**." Mauro stepped out of the room and surveyed the corridor. He saw no nurses in sight. After helping Scottie out of bed, he found two white uniforms in the closet which they put on. Slipping into the service elevator, they descended to the basement and sneaked out to the delivery dock at the rear area where several unattended delivery vans were parked.

About twenty minutes later, J.J. and W. Corry arrived at the hospital. Both were sweating profusely, unaccustomed to walking in the valley's humid climate. Once inside the hospital, W. Corry covered his nose and mouth with a hankie while they searched for Scottie's room.

"You don't have to do that," J.J scolded his companion. "This hospital is clean and approved as A-1 by our embassy. You might offend the staff by suggesting with your covered face that their hospital is contaminated. Then, you become another ugly gringo."

"You may be right but I'm not taking any chances by being politically correct. Not with germs. Not on my life."

"I didn't know you're that finicky about germs having grown up in El Paso. Did you ever cross to Juarez?"

"Never!" Then, W. Corry whispered to him, "I've heard some horror stories about this place from Clyde and others who preceded him in Peñalosa. Also, two hospitals in Bogota´ are off limits to us Americans. If I ever get seriously ill, I'll fly back **pronto** to the States even if I have to pay for my own ticket."

Having located Scottie's room, J.J. knocked on the door. Nobody answered. All of a sudden, the possibility that Scottie could be ghastly mangled or even dead entered his mind. He felt his knees buckle. "Are you s-s-sure...you got...the r-r-right r-r-room num-m-m-ber...? Fr-r-om the...cler-rk down s-s-stairs?"

"Well, let's take a look at this paper slip that clerk gave me...."

"Sh-h-hoot! Wrong r-r-room!" J.J. exploded after examining the slip as he inched closer to a nervous breakdown. "Dammit! This is Room 215! Scottie's at Room 275!"

"Calm down, J.J. That's not a one. These dagos put slashes across their sevens. This is it. Scottie's room: 275."

"My God! Nobody answered when I knocked. He's...oh…my God!"

Slowly, W. Corry pushed the door open and both entered the room with trepidation. Their shaky hands were about to hold each other´s waist for moral support, then withdrew them suddenly.

"Holy Mac!" J.J. exclaimed and turned around embracing the tinier W. Corry for comfort. "They took...his body...away!" The empty bed was messy with hideous blood stains on the sheets. W. Corry's sensitive nose smelled a rotten odor and he began retching and making horrible guttural sounds: "Aw-r-rgh-h-h...."

****

Inside a decrepit autobus barreling along the **carretera nacional** toward Bogota´, Gabby was having second thoughts about her chance to survive in the Big City on her own. Her impulsive decision to board this bus unwittingly was to evade a mysterious woman who was following her. As she reminisced about her first trip to the Big City with Scottie, she felt remorse, wishing she should have ended her life by jumping off the belfry. *I could have outrun that sluggish missionary to that staircase and up to the belfry.*

Getting up to fetch her carry-on bag from the overhead rack, she glanced sideways and was shaken to see the same woman with dark glasses and black dress who had followed her during her last **paseo** to the town's **centro**; and now she confirmed the same woman succeeded in boarding this autobus too. Since the autobus' departure was delayed for ten minutes, she suspected the unidentified woman had enough time to figure out which autobus she had boarded. Obsessed now why this woman was following her, Gabby was distracted from her suicidal notions.

An hour passed and nothing untoward occurred in the cruising autobus whose old engine was whining and sputtering. The driver announced the next stop was Ayacucho. Gabby regretted she did not buy a magazine to while away the long ride. All she could do was watch the monotonous scenery outside or take a siesta. By then, she concluded that that woman in black was another harmless passenger and dismissed her apprehension as another mischief of her tortured imagination. Besides, she could not spy on that woman now, seated three rows behind her, on the right side with the high backrests concealing the passengers. *I could stand up from time to time...look back. Hm-m-m... my intention becomes obvious. I would look silly to that woman and the other passengers.* ***Dejelo!*** *Forget it!*

Looking sideways across the aisle, she saw a mother with her two children, boy of two and a girl of five. That family scene reminded her of an only relative in the Big City: Manuela, a second cousin on her uncle's side, who was married to Pepe, a boorish, often tippling hypochondriac, and their children, up to six then, when she saw them last vacationing in Cartagena five years ago. She did not call them when she and Scottie were in Bogota´ afraid that her **patron** might become disgusted with Pepe and the noisy restless kids. In anticipation of job hunting in the Big City, she was not sure if they would offer her a temporary bed in their crowded apartment.

Tired of looking out at the humdrum countryside, she reclined comfortably leaning her head between the window and the backseat. Suddenly, she woke up from dozing and became aware that someone sat down next to her. *She's that woman in black and dark glasses!* Gabby, taken by surprised, nearly jumped up.

"You keep quiet," the woman warned her in a determined whisper. "See this leather bag? My right hand is inside it and holds a pistol. I will pull the trigger if you do anything foolish. A silencer at its tip will muffle the shot. You will be dead and none of the passengers will even notice." Gabby looked desperately beyond the woman and saw the mother asleep with her two kids' heads resting on her lap.

"What have I done to you?" Gabby asked. "**Y quien eres**? And who are you?"

"**Oye, no me preguntes**! No questions! Keep your mouth shut and do exactly what I tell you. Your **patron** has caused us plenty of trouble already. This time he will listen to us and leave the country -- if he is still alive."

"What do you mean 'if he is still alive?' " The woman did not answer and pressed her bag harder against Gabby's tummy. No words were necessary for her to understand the woman's threat.

Gabby was distracted and tried to figure out her delicate situation. *This woman has to be a hired gun from one of those disgruntled landowners.* ***Estoy muy seguro****. I am quite certain.*

The autobus, which had been cruising serenely for almost two hours, began to weave in and out of its right lane rather abruptly. Outside, Gabby noticed a gray van cut in front of the autobus. Reacting to his macho's ego, the bus driver accelerated his speed, and while tailgating the van, he tried to pass it. However, the van speeded up maintaining its lead forcing autobus to slow down and return to the right lane behind the van.

"**Halto**! Stop!" the van driver demanded aiming his megaphone at the bus driver. Ignoring the order, the bus driver stepped hard on the gas pedal attempting to pass the van again; but the van moved faster forcing the autobus to return on the right lane again.

By then the bus passengers were frightened, murmuring among themselves why their driver was so reckless and what that van was trying to prove. Unexpectedly, the autobus accelerated around a steep bend almost sideswiping the lighter van, and finally, it succeeded in leaving the van behind and spewing a fanlike tail of black smoke laden with foul smelling diesel on the "loser." This time some autobus passengers began clapping their hands and shouting encouragement to their driver while enjoying this seemingly macho competition between the two drivers. Gabby's attention was drawn away from the pistol-threatening woman who, herself included, watched compellingly the reckless competition going on outside.

"Bang! Bang!" Two shots were fired by the van driver shattering the autobus' rear windows but sparing the driver and passengers, some of whom screamed hysterically even though unharmed. This time, the bus driver got the message and slowed down gingerly coming to a stop on the road's right shoulder.

"Bang! Bang!" Two more shots rang out. The rear tires blew out causing the autobus to tilt backward. The bags on top and those below in the compartments gravitated toward the rear causing the autobus to look like an elephant sitting on its hunches. The van passed by and parked ahead of the autobus on the shoulder.

"Everybody out! **Afuera**! **Manos juntas sobre la cabeza**! Hands on your head!" The van driver, turned gunman with a nylon stocking drawn over his head, hollered as he stood by the bus emergency rear door, his pistols pointing their business ends at the driver and passengers, commanded them to open the side door and come out. "Bus driver first!" Gabby noticed how the stocking horribly distorted the gunman's features.

The driver, looking very worried, walked down with his hands clasped over his head.

"**Cabron**! Bloody fool!" the gunman shouted at the bus driver. "When I command you to stop, you **tu pares**! **Comprendes**?" He kicked the driver high on his back side causing him to fall hard, face down, on the road's shoulder. His nose bled. Hands on their heads, the passengers meekly stepped down from the autobus. An elderly woman, visibly shaken by the tense situation, seemed paralyzed until a young man helped her step down. They all stood single-file alongside the autobus on the gravel shoulder.

"**Oye mujeres, bajen ahora mismo**!" Gabby and the woman in black were the only ones still inside and realized they were shouted at by the gunman to disembark.

"Go down first and I shall follow you," the woman whispered to Gabby, who stepped down carefully followed by that woman with her bag pressed against Gabby's back.

"Except that lady...," the gunman pointed a pistol at Gabby, "everybody else lie down on the ground **ahora mismo**! Right now!" The passengers knelt gingerly, then sat on their hunches, and slowly lowered themselves down sideways on the hard gravel shoulder cradling their heads with their hands. An old man had difficulty to bring himself to lie down, trying in all sorts of contortions, but finally succeeded using his fragile hands and feet. The gunman chuckled then covered his mouth with one hand after replacing a pistol into its holster.

Being singled out by the gunman, Gabby, nervous and at a loss whom to obey, stood still by the bus' door as directed by the other woman in black who stood closely behind her. "This **muchacha** is under my custody," the woman in black told the gunman defiantly.

"I said, you lie down too!" the gunman ordered the woman. There was a quick exchange of gunfire. A bullet nicked the gunman's left forearm. The woman, struck by a bullet between her eyes, fell backward on the bus steps, splattering her blood. Shaking with fright, Gabby was unharmed, trembling, with her hands raised somewhat up in the air. "Do not be afraid, señorita," the gunman told Gabby with detached coolness as he pointed his pistol down keeping an eye on the dying woman in black. "Just come with me and you will not be harmed." Then, turning to the uneven row of frightened assorted passengers and the injured driver lying uneasily on the shoulder, he shouted at them: "Do not attempt to move or I shoot." To press his threat, the gunman pulled out the other pistol and fired a couple of shots closely over their heads. A child screamed.

These landowners finally caught up with me and will use me to blackmail Scootee, Gabby concluded, as the gunman assisted her into the van's rear. Locked inside the panel van's rear compartment, she sat uncomfortably on the floor, wedged between tied bundles of towels and bed sheets. She recalled reading the sign on the two rear doors of the panel van: Lavanderia La Esperanza.

Some blood stains originating from under a tarpaulin covering a lump on the floor caught a keyed-up Gabby's attention. Instinctively, she assumed the tarpaulin might be covering a corpse. Too intimidated, she was not able to scream nor move a muscle. After making a U-turn, the van was moving at a fast clip forcing her to sway helplessly while she tried to steady herself with her hands pressed on the floor. Sunlight shone through the twin rear door windows shedding more light on the tarpaulin lump. Soon the rolling motion of the speeding van finally exposed the shoes of a plausible corpse. Panic-stricken, she cried anticipating the same fate for herself too.

Surely this gunman shall dispose of me at some isolated place and dump my body with this corpse, Gabby was convinced. Resigned to die, she consoled herself that she would be spared the burden of killing herself. *There is no reason for me to live.* Everything turned desolate to her vision and the will to live began to ebb from her.

The van hit a bump on the road exposing a bandaged head. Scared out of her wits, she scooted as far away from the corpse, pushing herself against the bundles of towels and folded bed sheets after she shoved some aside for more space. Inside the darkened cabin compartment, the sunlight shone through again highlighting the bandaged head. She noted that the head was slightly moving! Not due to the motion of the van. *Could the corpse be still alive?* Gabby wondered as the compartment darkened again. *Should I pound on the partition and get the attention of the driver? No! no! He is a bad man. He does not care. If this man is alive, should I save...him?* ***No es posible.*** ***Y como podria hacerlo****? And how can I do it??* ***No es posible.***

The van turned on to the highway enabling the sun to shine through again. Despite the bandages, the shape of the head and partly exposed face looked familiar to her.

"SCOOTEE! It is...it is YOU!" she screamed at the top of her voice. "What happened? **Que pasa**?" Trying to stir and wake up, his eyes opened but closed once more. The morphine eased him back to dozing. "So the landowners captured you too. Do you know...where this bad man is...taking us?" He opened his eyes but closed them again. "Wake up! **Tenemos que huir**! We gotta go before it is too late. **Vamos pronto**!"

"That's...a long story, Gabby. The important thing is...that we are together...again...at last." Slowly sitting himself up, rather clumsily, against stacks of towels. he looked at her sheepishly while removing the tarpaulin and fighting to stay awake. "I made a big mistake...a big dumb one...during that night...when we were together. I was selfish. I was thinking only...of myself. I want to ask...your forgiveness. Your understanding...and your love...."

Hearing his conciliatory words, she cried unashamedly. Recovering her composure, her will to live began to glow again fed by his confession of love. "There is nothing to forgive," she answered with her inborn magnanimity. "I was ready to die"…. Tears rolled down her cheeks. "You saved my life and gave me shelter…and hope. I will always love you…."

Her kind words moved him deeply as he struggled to sit up straight. Grimacing, his face betrayed his pains. She came to his aid and suddenly they were physically close once more. The magic was rekindled, a gentle kiss inevitable; and with renewed intimacy, he could admire closely those lovely pools of turquoise. The rapid passing of precious time raised a red flag in her mind. "We need some understanding before we are shot by our enemies." She sniffled a bit not wishing to cry during these last moments of their lives. "As I told you that night it does not matter...if you cannot make love to me...as long as we love each other...."

With her undying devotion even in the face of execution, Scottie felt compelled to explain their perceived precarious situation.

"Gabby..., the doctor...at the hospital...said I'll be okey-dokey.... It may take some time...but I'll be okey-dokey...ouch!…I shall be...o-o-oh…I shall be able to make...."

"**Que bien**! I am glad to hear you are okey-dokey." Then, their odd situation dawned on her. "Did you say you came from the hospital?"

"Yes..., they brought me...to the hospital...after my truck hit an explosive...on the new highway…ouch!.... Doctor examine me... and said...I shall be...able to make...love...."

"Explosive on the highway? I did not know!"

"Yes, I suspect...either Don Pedrazas...or...Don Mendieta.... As you...already know...they are out...to kill me...."

"Ay! **Mi pobrecito**! **Mi amor**! I am so sorry!" she cried. "This gunman, do you know where he is taking us?"

"He's no gunman, Gabby.... He's Mauro...ouch!…you know...from the office.... I asked him...to get you…to be with me…as a favor...for me...."

"Favor for you! **Para raptarme**! Keednap me! And you to be keednapped **como una trampa**! A treek**! Cochino**! Peeg!" She slapped and punched him. "Peeg! Peeg!" He offered no resistance.

"Hit me some more.... I deserve it...," he said in pain and looking anguished. Befuddled, then remorseful for punching him, she went into a crying fit. "I had to do this...ruse, you said trick...Gabby. Had to...I was…afraid...you…will walk out...of…my life...and...and...I'll never see...you again.... I…love…you, Gabby. **Te…quiero...mucho**…"

Overwhelmed by what was happening to him, his eyes closed.

"Scootee! Scootee! Do not die on me! Do not die! **Virgen Santisima**! I do not know what to do!" Hysterical, she ran her fingers through his hair and kissed him. "Scootee, **te quiero para siempre**! I love you always! **No te mueras dejandome solita**! Do not die leaving me alone!"

Scottie recovered his senses, opening his eyes. Overjoyed, she kissed him again. Those tiny pools of turquoise encouraged him to surmount his emotional and physical setbacks. Their lips met again and a mutual love was blooming again like rosebuds greeting the first day of spring. Hugging tightly, no more words were spoken between them. They knew their renewed love would give them another chance to start a new life together away from the highlands of Cuyapo´ valley.

EPILOGUE

Scottie was reassigned to the headquarters in San Francisco. Living a happily married life together, Scottie took short business trips abroad but never to Peñalosa again. True love, verily, conquers all lovers as with Gabby and Scottie.

Carrie, still cherished and visited on her death anniversary (January 20th) every year by her brother, could now rest peacefully in her grave in Laredo, Texas. Since January 20th was also Gabby's birth date, she willingly traveled with Scottie every year to Laredo to celebrate the rather unique dual anniversaries. She now truly believed she was indeed the reincarnation of Carrie; and at the San Francisco City Hall, she changed her legal name to Gabriela Esperanza Carrie Ritter Vergel de la Reina. Still called "Gabby" by Scottie, who had a mental block to pronounce "Gabriela" properly when they first met, and to date, he still has to say slowly,..."Ga...bri...eh...lah...." Still becomes tongue-tied whenever he gazes with undiminished fascination at her eyes like "pools of turquoise" and his heart leaps with joyful love for the misty maiden who "possessed" him since that chance meeting at the belfry of the Peñalosa church.

Heidi Helmer Salas divorced Pedro, that unfaithful salesman from Caracas, and opened a bar restaurant named "Mi Sosiego" in Benidorm on the Spanish Costa Blanca. Unknown to her, Padre Jose′ Maria Casals Antonijuan or "Padre Joe" did not remain long with relatives in Estepona on the Costa del Sol but shed his Franciscan habit and joined the Benedictine monks of the Montserrat monastery perched on that mountain above Barcelona to repent his wayward past for the rest of his natural life.

Several decades later, descendants of the landowners, among whom were the Pedrazas and Mendietas, of the Cuyapo′ Valley returned home with college degrees from Ivy League schools to start their own businesses. Others took internships or jobs with corporations in America and other parts of the world. These young men and women were exposed long enough to appreciate the democratic American way of life in contrast to the still feudalistic stratified society dominating their South American society.

Forming their own American inter-college alumni association in Colombia, they always returned to their homeland for reunions. They happened to gather in Bogota′ during a grand wedding and entered into a free-wheeling discussion of what they should do different with their own personal wealth and inherited resources in the Cuyapo′ Valley. Their forebears' assassination attempt on Scott Ritter's life kept coming up in their frank conversations and the other names with whom this American (they never referred to Scott as the "gringo" or "musiu") had been associated with, like Cerruza, Lebrun, and Mayor Jose′ Luis Calderon and his wife, and those welfare institutions they organized with this unique American (or were started by him) like the foster home for unwanted babies, Liga de Futbol del Valle de Cuyapo′, a credit union for the farmers, an orphanage for girls, and a safe house for battered women.

Without explicit mention in their official communique′ of the injustices done by their ancestors on the **indios** and **campesinos**, they unanimously agreed to form a non-profit organization and donate part of their time and money as well as their special skills they had learned from the American colleges and corporations: to improve, expand and promote these still existing charitable but languishing fund-starved organizations in their ancestral and beloved Cuyapo′ valley.

Other items which they unanimously voted to do were to erect a pair of **bronze statues of Scott and Gabby** on a new park adjacent to the **plaza mayor** of **Peñalosa**, to search for all their descendants, who are Colombians, Americans and other nationalities scattered over the world, and to invite them to the historic unveiling ceremony of the statues.

Thus, a quiet selfless American, Scott Ritter, was finally vindicated for his humanitarian work and his enduring love of a despondent woman whom he called "Gabby." Nothing could define better the combined essence of altruism and true love comported by this unique human being who once lived on this earth and made a patch of it a better place and for others to emulate his life's work.

Fifty years or so later, the rather famous park surrounding the dramatic bronze statues of the two enduring lovers have become a popular open-air place for wedding ceremonies, especially for Latino couples, with its legendary reputation of time-proven unbroken vows for everlasting love and fidelity.

Did you enjoy reading "GABBY"?

Great! Tell your friends and relatives to get their own copies. Copies are available from Infinity Publishing.com (#811position), NOOK, Adobe Reader, eBook or your local bookseller can order "GABBY" for you.

At the University of Texas, Austin TX, I studied among WW II veterans, some badly wounded. Working in Columbus Ohio during the Vietnam War, I was on the local reserves list but was not called.

I was inspired to write "GABBY" thinking of these committed American heroes who never wavered to fight for their country. Some never returned alive. I had a hard time finishing my "GABBY" with a happy ending.

Every year, I contribute to the Veterans of Foreign Wars, Disabled American Veterans, Paralyzed Veterans of America. If "GABBY" is successful with readers like you, I shall contribute more to these genuine veterans' associations. God bless them.